THE LONG WALK

A Novel

Ruth Treeson

The Best is Yet To Come

Ruthe's Eries

Crystal Cove Publishing

3rd Printing
Copyright 2010 by Ruth Treeson

ISBN: 978-0615840697

Cover Design by: Shannon Ramsay
Cover Text by: Robin Rauzi

I dedicate this book in the memory of my family and all those who were lost in the Holocaust, and to my children and their children, the link between the past and the future.

Acknowledgements

I wish to acknowledge all who helped me prepare my book for publication. My special thanks go to Shannon Ramsay who designed the book cover, and Robin Rauzi who wrote the cover text. And Cybele May and Manny Treeson for their patient support, and good advice. Susan and Dick Gale who helped edit my manuscript early in the process of making this book, and Joan West my editor and publisher who has given her skill and confidence to the manuscript.

The LONG WALK

Chapter 1

May 1945

> Neither awake nor asleep,
>   Cold, hungry, we moved across ground
> A circular route over the bridge
> Across Elba River
> Back and forth
>   One foot after the other,
>   Those of us who could

Prisoners and tormentors alike, wedded in a hellish dance of attrition, we circled what remained of Hitler's ground. Artillery flashed in the night sky. Guns thundered ever nearer as the Americans advanced from the West and the Russians from the East. Each day fewer prisoners and fewer guards remained. The guards stopped wasting bullets on the dying and ran, dropping their hastily stripped uniforms in the fields.

No fat. Barely any flesh, I was little more than teenage bones enclosed in a sallow bag of skin. Between my ribs, within the hollow cave of my chest, my heart beat the way only a machine can, rhythmically, no volition, in the cadence of ceaseless action, pulse, contract.

Had I cared to listen, I would have heard it. I hardly noticed the frozen patches on the bottoms of my feet where my shoes had worn clear through. Numb after three long years of imprisonment, I had ceased listening to the rough commands of the guards, to their angry shouts and their barking dogs. I had stopped trying to understand why this was happening to us.

At end of war's day, we stopped in a field near a barn. Told that we could dig new potatoes out of the ground, we squatted where we found them and ate them raw. Then the guards herded us into a barn, and locked the door. The barn was dark. I heard a soft rustle on the floor, and felt something soft and yielding beneath my feet. Could it be fresh straw? Letting my head nestle in its softness, I escaped into dreams of home, the happier memories of childhood, and fantasy.

It was still dark when I woke up shivering with cold. Didn't know where I was or how I got there, nor did I care. Just piled more straw on and cuddled into it so it became both my pillow and blanket. The warmth and the fresh scent of hay gave me comfort. Sometime soon after, the dogs stopped barking, and I slept.

Morning brought shafts of light streaming through cracks in the barn siding. I felt the sun warm on my face, opened my eyes to see a cloud of dust motes dance in a beam of light, and heard the other women begin to stir. Straw rustled with the movement of their bodies. I listened for the dogs, but heard no barking.

One of the women got up from her makeshift straw bed on the floor, walked slowly towards the barn door, and peeked through one of the cracks.

"See anything?" another woman whispered.

"Nothing. No one," she said, turning away from the door. "I think they are gone."

She meant the guards and their dogs, I thought, appreciating the wonder of this blessed silence. After weeks of closing my ears to the ugly sounds of the guards and their dogs, I allowed myself to listen to the calm sounds of early morning, the chirps of birds, and the hush of leaves. I could smell the dew on the grass as it dried in the sun, and feel the coolness of the morning. Except for hunger and thirst, I felt almost comfortable.

After a while, one woman's courage brought her to her feet. She approached the barn door, pushed, and opened it a crack. We heard it squeak as it gave way. Everyone gasped. We were no longer confined. Was it possible at last? Still, our fear lingered on. Who knows? Maybe this was some kind of cruel game they were playing on us.

I was afraid to leave the barn. We all were, but then the first brave woman stepped over the threshold and out into the sun. We held our collective breath while we listened for the sound of bullets. None came. One by one, the other women grew bolder and began to cautiously drift towards the open door. I could hear their feet brush against the ground outside. They made no other sound. No one screamed. No one laughed. No one spoke. Each one left alone, and none returned. I sat on the straw, and watched them go.

What now? I didn't know, having forgotten how to act on my own. For three long years, the Nazi guards had controlled my every move, told me what to do, when to do it, and where to be every moment of each day.

Now I stood alone, just inside the partially opened barn door and I looked at the half frozen fields that stretched across the flat ground all the way to the horizon. I blinked against the sun's glare, felt it dispelling the chill of early morning, and without prompting or much thought, I moved slowly away from the barn. At first hesitant, my steps firmed as I walked past the farmhouse. No smoke drifted from the chimney. No sign of people. Where did they all go? At the edge of the field, where a ribbon of country road cut across the flat land, I paused. No people, no vehicles. The barrenness of this landscape echoed the emptiness I felt within me.

I wanted someone to give me a hug, needed to hear that it would be all right now. I could go home to my family. But there was no one to comfort or guide me. I felt as abandoned as the empty farm house behind me.

I was twelve when the Nazis shipped me to a concentration camp. Now at fifteen, more than anything else, I wanted to go home, back to my mother and father, back to Haniushka, my little sister. I wanted my family back; I wanted everyone I loved and missed so awfully to be there waiting for me. Home, I breathed the word, inhaled it, wishing that my fervent need would lead me there. But which way was home? There was no one to say. I was alone, and there was the road. So, picking my direction at random, I started to walk.

I walked, as I was made to walk for all those weeks of the forced march, but this time I walked on my own volition. I made

3

the decision. I picked my destination. Freedom, a concept I'd forgotten existed, was real, and it was awfully lonely. As I continued along the road, my throat became dry. I searched the barren fields for a stream or a spring, saw none, and grew thirstier still. I brushed my parched tongue against cracked lips. At last, I spotted an old, rusty water-drum sitting out in the field, and hurried towards it, only to find it empty. I plodded on.

Passing a small farmhouse by the side of the road, I stopped. Thirst propelled me up the four stone steps to the front door. Fearful but determined I knocked, but no one came, though I noticed smoke curling up from the house chimney. I knocked again, and waited. No response.

As I turned away, the door opened a crack, and a wrinkled face peered out. Eyes squinting, mouth twisting as if he'd tasted something vinegary or bitter, the old man asked, "Ya, bitte?" Looking into those suspicious, narrowed eyes of his, I saw myself as he must have seen me, one of those awful Jews they kept locked up somewhere, a walking skeleton manufactured in one of those places no one ever talked about.

I wore torn and dirty clothes, and hadn't had a chance to wash in more days than I could remember. I saw his nose wrinkle at the smell of me, and his wrinkled white knuckled, hand clutched the door. The door stayed mostly closed. His jaw worked as he ground his teeth. He didn't know me, wanted nothing to do with me. I knew that, but thirst won over my shyness. I screwed up my courage, and asked for water. "Wasser, bitte," I murmured in my best German.

He didn't respond, but neither did he close his door. He seemed to be wrestling with the decision whether to give or deny the water I asked for. For my part, I stood there facing him, hoping he'd do the right thing.

Then, his eyes widened. He opened his mouth as if to scream. At the same time, I heard heavy trucks rumbling on the road behind me, accompanied by boisterous male voices singing, "Volga, Volga," a Russian river song I knew and liked. Turning away from the old man I saw a long convoy of Russian trucks roaring past the little farmhouse. As I watched and listened, the last truck in the line slowed down, its brakes grinding, and came to a stop. At that

4

instant, the farmer's door slammed shut behind me.

One of the soldiers came up the steps, mischief in his eyes, and a big grin splitting his lips. He winked at me conspiratorially, before slamming the butt of his rifle against the farmer's door. After giving it four sharp whacks, he waited a few moments, and getting no response, resumed banging in earnest. I felt embarrassed, wanted him to stop, and I started to pull on his sleeve. He shrugged me off.

I wanted no part of this and started to turn away from the door, but just then the old farmer appeared in the open door. He was holding a tall glass of clear water, his hand stretched towards me. Wordlessly, I took the glass from him and gulped my first taste of freedom. It was better than the sweetest nectar. "Danke Shein," I thanked the old farmer, returning the empty glass.

Well satisfied with his morning's liberation routine, the Russian soldier grinned, "Harasho e harasho!" he boomed, fist punching the air. Towering over me, he gave the appearance of an overgrown boy scout, obviously pleased with his good deed of the day. And I, infected by his high spirits, threw my arms round his neck, gave him a big hug, and for good measure, kissed both his cheeks. We waved goodbye to the farmer, and started walking away.

"Are you Jewish?" he asked in Russian.

I looked at the weather-beaten skin of his face and hands, his wide and hard cheekbones, and what appeared to be a permanent squint in his eyes. I'd seen such men in summers past, seen them standing in their fields studying the skies and worrying about the rain or lack of it. He was a farmer's son, worked in the fields in all kinds of weather, and thus he looked older than his years. Probably never met a Jew till now and beyond farming and soldiering, probably knew as little as I did.

"Yes, I'm Jewish," I said in Polish. The two languages are similar enough, so each of us could understand the other.

"I'm Gregor," he beamed at me. "You, got a name?"

"Rutka," I replied.

"Listen, I want to help you. You just tell me what you need."

More than a bed for the night though I was tired, and more than bread and soup, though I was hungry, I needed my family,

5

father and mother, and little sister Haniushka, and Bubby and Zyde, and Jurek, my uncle, and Elaina, my cousin, all of them together, whole again. "I need to go home," I said.

"Where is home?" he asked.

The home of my childhood seemed like a vanished dream now. Would it even be there anymore? I wondered, thinking about my beloved courtyard with the apartment on the second floor? I recalled the rumors about an uprising in the Warsaw Ghetto. In the camps I had heard that it was destroyed, burned to the ground by the Nazis.

"We used to live in Warsaw before the war. Shortly after the war started, we moved to Krakow. That's the last place I called home." Maybe that's where I should go to look for my family. What I really wanted was to go back to Warsaw, to the first home I ever knew, the home where I spent the first nine years of my life. Living there, I was able see Bubby every day...

...I'm lucky, because my Bubby lives so close to us. I can go there right after school. Today is Friday, that makes it a special day in the whole week. That's when Bubby cooks our Shabbat feast, and I get to watch her do it, and even help a little. Right after school, I run like the wind till I reach our courtyard.

The scent of chicken soup drifts down towards me, and I take the steps two at a time, but no matter how fast I go, by the time I reach the landing, there she is standing with her arms wide open, waiting with hugs and kisses.

She is small and delicate, but she's strong. Mama says I'm just like her, full of nervous energy, skinny, and always on the move. Guess she's right, because I know neither of us can sit still for a minute.

Happy to see me even on the busiest of days, she lets me help with the making of Shabbat Challah. First, I watch her knead the dough. Next, she divides it into three equal parts, and rolls each piece into a ball. When I'm a little older, she'll let me do this myself. But for now, I can only watch her hands, so sure and swift, shaping each of the balls into a log. She arranges the three logs side by side on the wooden board. That's when I get to do my part. I know how, because Bubby showed me. Carefully, I weave the three logs of dough till it turns into a lovely braid. Meanwhile Bubby breaks an egg, and separates the white from the yolk which she reserves in a small bowl. I get to beat it up with a fork, till it turns creamy gold. Then I use a pastry brush to paint the top of the braided dough. I love to see the way the yolk glistens on top of the Challah.

"Good job!" Bubby says, and slides it into the oven. Soon the kitchen fills with the sweet scent of baking Challah.

I go to the washroom, before Bubby tells me to, and by the time I get back, there's a steamy bowl of noodles in delicious fish stock waiting for me on the kitchen table.

Bubby works and I eat and watch her whirl around her kitchen. She takes quick steps from table to stove and back again, shaping, kneading, rinsing, blanching, chopping, dicing, slicing, and all the while talking with me. She may be busy but always has time to answer my questions.

"Where do you get so many questions?" She sometimes sighs, but I think she approves. She once told me that questions are good. "The more you ask, the more you learn," she explained. I think she is very smart. When I grow up, I want to be just like her. Dad says that people can read our thoughts just by looking at our faces. It must be so, because I think her wrinkles tell a whole lot about her. The skin of her face is a pale parchment of a map that shows the smile lines round her mouth and eyes. That's because she smiles a lot, but then she also has furrows just over the bridge of her nose. Dad once told me that these are worry lines. Sometimes, when things get too wound up for her, she can get annoyed, but it never lasts, not with her. I am just like my Bubby. When I grow up, I'll worry also…

With the image of Bubby's kitchen still before me, I turned to the Russian and whispered, "Home."

"I thought you kind of went there just now," Gregor said, his bulky frame dwarfing mine as we stood at the rear of the Russian truck. "Home," he echoed with that far-away-look in his eyes. This tall, boisterous, hard-muscled fellow longed for home as I did. He reminded me of summer, crops growing and sunflowers ripening in the field. He looked like a man who made his life in the fields.

Hard and worn from work and war, but beneath his rough exterior, I thought I could see the warm and generous heart of a Russian man.

"Come, we'll give you a lift to town," he said, taking my elbow.

My feet hurt from walking all that morning, so I felt grateful. As he lifted me up onto the back of the truck, he must have heard my stomach grumble, because he poked his nearest companion as he sat down. The other responded with a comment, which produced gales of laughter from them both. The truck thundered on.

His laughter subsiding, he started to poke in his satchel.

"You must be hungry," he said.

Though hungry, I was still smarting with the shame of hearing them laugh at me, and so refused to even look in his direction.

He touched my shoulder. I shrugged him off, and turned intending to snap at him. But then I saw that good-natured grin spreading across his face, and the bread and cheese in his hands.

"Eat," he said.

I breathed in the scent of fresh bread, bit into its crust, the taste of it bathing my senses. I chewed it slowly, savoring each bite which tasted better than Mom's potato latkes, better than her honey cake, better even than Bubby's holiday Chulentz. I wanted to sing hymns of praise to the farmer who raised the grain, the miller who milled the flour, the baker who baked it, and the cheese maker who made the cheese. But my stomach wasn't used to food anymore, and after only a few bites, I stopped eating. He noticed and said, "Ah, little one. Your stomach needs to get acquainted with food again."

I placed the remainder of the bread and cheese into the pocket of my filthy camp uniform. There was a hole at the bottom of the pocket, but it was small, so I placed the cheese on top of the bread, which was bigger than the hole. I had endured the gnawing feel of hunger in the pit of my stomach for more than three years, but now it finally let up. I enjoyed the forgotten feeling of ease that comes with a full stomach, leaned against the side of the truck, and closed my eyes. Perhaps I dozed for a bit, but the chilly wind blowing across the open truck was too much for the torn shawl I had picked up along the way. It had too many holes to keep me warm, and though I tried to wrap it ever tighter, I shivered with cold. I couldn't sleep, so I sat up and rubbed my arms to ward off the worst of the chill.

The road cut through fields without end, passing the occasional farmhouse along the way. As we neared the town, more buildings appeared. The weather was nippy, yet smoke drifted from only a few chimneys.

"Where are the people?" I asked, pointing to one of the dark empty houses

"Ran like the stupid dogs they are." He laughed.

"But why?"

"They gave us hell; now it is our turn."

I saw his satisfied scowl, and recalled the way he rammed the butt of his rifle against the farmer's door.

As the truck bounced along the road, the Russian soldiers sang. Their chorus rang through the empty fields with songs that spoke of love, homeland, a yearning for the fields they had left behind, and the people who waited for them to come home. These were the songs of a victorious army glad to see the end of their dying.

It was well past noon by the time we reached the little town. The truck came to a stop in the main square. Gregor jumped down, and helped me off the truck. He pointed out a low building at one side of the square. "This is the railway station," he said. I looked beyond it, to the station platform and the railroad tracks, "Which way to Warsaw?"

"East," he said, pointing.

"I can hardly wait for tomorrow. Can you tell me when the train east is most likely to come by this town?"

"Not running yet," he said.

I bit my lower lip. "But when...," with my throat constricted I couldn't finish my question.

"Don't you worry, little bird," he handed me another loaf of bread and a hunk of cheese. "The trains will start back soon."

"How soon?"

"Who can tell?" A shrug of his considerable shoulders, "Best you stay in town. When the trains start running, you'll be going home."

Yes, he was a soldier, but nothing like those Gestapo men who never smiled, and always shouted angry commands. I was frightened of them, but not of Gregor. I was so hungry and he gave me bread. He was kind. Except for one other man, he was the only person who had been kind to me during the past three years.

This kind man, a German, was not a soldier, nor an SS man, nor a prisoner. I never knew who he was. He showed up one day in the munitions factory where I worked inspecting bullets. I saw him only twice. The first time, he stopped by my workstation, and patted my shoulder gently. When I looked up in surprise, he said that I reminded him of his own daughter. He looked so sad. Then he promised to bring a pear for me next time he came by. I looked for him to come back. Every morning I thought this could be the day when he'd bring that pear like he promised. Days, perhaps weeks went by, then one morning he did show up again. This time he smiled when he gave me the big juicy pear. As I bit into it, some of the juice escaped out the corner of my mouth, but I caught it with the tip of my tongue and licked it up; I wouldn't let one juicy drop go to waste. All the while, he watched me with his sad smile. Then he left. I hoped he'd come again, bring another pear; but he never did.

Chapter 2

Shops and boutiques lined three sides of the town square, their windows and doors were locked behind steel shutters. A few streets dotted with one-story houses led off the square. Yellow, pink, or blue, they appeared well cared for, yet abandoned. No motion, no sign of smoke drifting up from chimneys, the town appeared unreal in its silence, and hollow as the emptiness I felt within.

It seemed to me that everything and everyone was out of place. Homes without people, and here I was without a home and no place to rest. After the long days and nights of forced march across the German countryside, the ragged remains of the concentration camp uniform offered little protection against the chill. Holes in my shoes let my sore feet touch the half frozen ground. I walked down those pretty, hollow streets like an out of place ghost.

I came upon a small green island of trees, grass, and benches. Sat on the nearest one, and rubbed my sore feet to chase away the chill. The day grew colder. The trees threw long shadows on the ground as the sun dropped towards the horizon.

Hungry again, I retrieved the loaf of bread and cheese Gregor had given me at parting, tore off a piece of bread, chewed it slowly, took a bit of cheese, and would have eaten it all, but thought better of it, and tucked the remainder back in my shawl. Then mindful of its many holes, I wound it round and round, securing it under my arm.

At least I wasn't hungry now, but what to make of this strange and empty town? It seemed untouched by war, and that puzzled me. No bullet holes anywhere, no fallen bricks, not even

11

one ruined wall.

I thought about my home in the courtyard where I used to live. Was it in another lifetime? After all the years of people dying, I needed so very much for it to be there, untouched by war and not empty like this strange German town. I needed to believe it was there waiting for me, with my mom and dad, and my little sister, Haniushka, and Bubby and Zyde, and Jurek, my uncle, and all my friends, every single one of them, alive, and busy just like I remembered them.

If there were some magic words, or special prayers to make it all come back I'd say them over and over again. I'd pray again to that same God who did not listen. I'd implore the same God that did not hear my pleas, a God who did not hear the voices of so many others. Many of them perished, even as they prayed. Could there ever be words special enough to pierce the cacophony of so many, special enough to reach the ear of such a hard of hearing God? Bone chilled and weary, I lifted my sore feet off the ground, and hugging knees to chest, curled up on the narrow bench.

"Are you dead? Wake up!"

I heard the girl's impatient demand and struggled to open my eyes. "Go away," I murmured, closing them again.

"No one else in this town and you want me to go away?"

I was startled to hear the girl speak Polish.

Suddenly fully awake, I sat up, and tried to rub the sleep out of my eyes.

What I saw was another frazzled bag of bones on two skinny legs, maybe a year or two older than I. The girl's skin was stretched tight over her bones. I was looking at a pale frowning face, lips pressed against teeth. This stranger appeared to be just as lost and alone as I felt. But though they were a bit too large for her the clothes she wore were clean, and had no holes in them. By contrast, what remained of my blue and gray camp uniform had stopped being clean weeks ago and was little more than a tattered rag. I longed for a bath and some fresh clothes. It wouldn't matter if they fit or not, just so they were clean.

I looked at the girl's hair, long and black like my mother's, it was clean and brushed to a shine, nothing like my own dirty, tangled mess. Then I noticed the brush the girl held in her hand. I pointed to it and asked, "Where did you find it?"

The girl snorted. "Of all the questions you might have asked, you want to know about this brush?" She laughed bitterly and pointed to a red brick house across the park.

"You live there?"

"I don't live anywhere." She laughed, and added, "The house is empty, but there are beds in there, and sheets, and pillows, blankets too. Best of all, it's warmer inside."

"You just walked in there? Someone's house, somebody you don't even know, and you just...?"

"Why not, it's more comfortable than the hard bench you've been sleeping on. Besides, look at your clothes. We need something warmer, and there are things in there we can use."

"Things, but they don't belong to you."

She snickered. "Ah, a princess. You must live in that castle up there."

The girl's sarcasm stung. "I have been taught manners, and I'd never take what belongs to someone else."

"Yeah, and I really like looking for scraps in some stranger's house? Listen, if I had warm clothes, or if the stores were open and full of goods, and I had money in my pocket, I'd have no need to take what's not mine."

"But it's still wrong," I mumbled.

"Yeah, the war, this empty town... What's right about any of it?"

I sat up, hugging my knees to my chest. The girl sat beside me. "You've no idea how glad I am to find you here. My name is Rachel. What's yours?"

"Rutka,"

"Come," Rachel took my hand, and we walked together to the house that belonged to neither of us.

Once inside, Rachel suggested I have a look at the place while she went to wash up and start supper. She walked off down the hall, leaving me in the vestibule. I stood there for a few moments, feeling like a trespasser. But it was already getting dark, and I really didn't want to go back out into the cold, when it was

13

so nice and warm inside.

I moved from one foot to the other, taking stock of the place. Just to my right, in the dining room, chairs lay on their sides in disarray with the table overturned. I could see shards of porcelain figurines and china scattered across the floor. To my left, the handsome mahogany paneled library was also in disarray. Its shelves were nearly empty, and the books, many with pages torn out, lay strewn across the Persian carpet. A fleeting thought occurred to me. Could Rachel have done this? No, I thought, why would she want to destroy these books? Books were friends. They offered shelter from fear and pain. Books were good companions.

No books in the camps, but to escape the reality of camp life, I'd remember the favorite stories I used to read. I hid in memories of home. I'd visualize times when I felt safe, moments when cradled in my father's arms I listened to him read aloud to me from one of my books of fairytales.

There was one story I liked better than all the others. It told about a beautiful princess who had been imprisoned by a sorcerer, and kept in a room high on top of a tower in a castle on a glass mountain. This memory comforted me, because the princess had a champion, a brave knight who set out on his white stallion to set her free. But it was hard going; both knight and stallion, repeatedly loosing footing on the hard slippery glass of the mountain, fell down, and had to start over. But that brave knight never gave up. He reached the top, stormed the castle, and set the princess free. Then, of course, they lived happily ever after.

When I was little I really loved that story. Then later in the camps, it was the memory of that knight's courage and persistence that somehow gave me the will to endure. All I allowed myself to think about was my family, my home and books. I longed for them, and wished I could escape reality by hiding in the images the pages of fairytales. The memory of these stories helped me to focus away from the hunger that gnawed at my stomach, and to tune down the harsh sound of the hatefully shouted commands of camp guards.

Now, as I stood in the middle of the ruined library, I recalled a prayer book my great grandfather used to hold in the palms of his hands. Old and worn, the book appeared to be part of him, an extension of the mysterious blue veins beneath the almost transparent, paper-thin skin…

…His hands yellow like the pages of his book, wrinkled…head bowed in reverence, body moving back and forth, his half closed eyes on the brittle page, yellowed with age, like the skin of his hands. He's asleep, I think, yet his lips move, his voice a singsong murmuring mantras.

I should not disturb him, still I have to ask, "You keep such old books, why not buy new ones?"

He crinkles his eyes in a smile, and with one finger to mark his place between the pages, his other hand smoothes my hair, slides down to my cheek, "Every book must be respected," he tells me, and adds that we must treasure each one of them, for they contain mystery. He once told me that he received them from his father, and when his time comes, he'll pass them on to my Zyde…

"Who would destroy books that never hurt anyone?" I asked Rachel.

"Angry people," she said, toweling off her long hair.

I looked at her scrubbed, still rosy from the shower complexion and asked, "Would you ever get as angry as that?"

"I didn't do it, but… don't you ever want to get even?"

"What good would it do? Get even? I could no more herd people into cattle cars for slaughter, than I could climb on air to reach the moon. Get even with monsters? I'd have to become one?" I began to mumble to myself.

"What's the matter?" Rachel asked.

I bit my nails, but would not speak.

"Rutka, you've got me worried."

"I didn't mean it…."

Rachel wrapped her arms round my heaving shoulders, and listened to my stifled sobs. "Shah, shah," she repeated as she hugged me close.

"I couldn't help it."

Rachel held on, waiting for me to continue.

After a few moments, I added, "It was my fault. There was this old woman… She was shot."

"How was it your fault?"

The road was icy. An SS man shoved me from behind, and I lost my balance. I slipped and fell. There was this old woman walking just ahead me. I fell on top of her. I scrambled right up, but she wasn't quick enough. The guard shot her."

"You didn't shoot her. He did."

"I was the one who pushed her down. She lay on that ice with the SS man shouting for her to get up. She couldn't. He shouted and fired. One shot, and her whole body jerked." The horrid image still vivid in my mind, I crammed my fist into my mouth, teeth pressing against my knuckles.

"Stop this! You are not to blame," Rachel shouted.

I closed my eyes and tried to wipe the image of the dying woman from my mind. But then it was my little sister, whose face I saw, as she was being dragged away from me by an ugly SS man who held Haniushka's hand in his grasp. I remembered how Haniushka struggled in his grip, her eyes pleading with me to do something. But another SS man had both my hands pulled back, so I couldn't move. I struggled against his restraints, but all in vain. I could say or do nothing to stop it.

The image of Haniushka's sweet little trembling mouth, her big brown eyes filled with tears and confusion, would always stay with me. I was the older sister. I was supposed to protect Haniushka, and I failed. It didn't matter that I was restrained and manacled by that SS man. I could still see little Hania reaching out to me, and I couldn't move a finger to help her. I felt responsible, thought there must have been something I failed to do. Didn't quite know what it was I did wrong, but it had to be something. Why else had I been ripped away from my family? How could I otherwise explain why we were all torn from our home and from each other?

My eyes fell on the grand piano in the room, its strings hanging loose, yellowed ivory keys chipped and broken, piano bench on its side, one leg off, the pages of the sheet music scattered on the floor beside it, and I recalled our piano back home.

"Can't be fixed," I mumbled. "We had a piano just like that. Mom used to buff it until it shone like a mirror." Thinking about it now I recalled the aroma of fresh wax. I closed my eyes and could almost see my mom, her hand holding the soft polishing cloth gliding over the wood surface, back and forth...

...Each pass deepens the glow of the black ebony. Up and down, till its gloss matches Mother's black hair and gleams reflections in the wood ...

I wanted to hold on to the image, to capture in my mind's eye the roundness of Mother's chin, the soft curve of her cheek, the glow of her black hair. But all I could manage were vague outlines and shadows. How could I have so soon forgotten the features of that dear face? I felt guilt and shame.

Rachel touched my arm, "Let us see if there's something to eat."

Like an automaton, I followed her to the kitchen.

After she picked up a few chipped plates and cups, and a couple of not too badly damaged pots off the floor, Rachel declared, "Good enough, let's push the broken stuff aside for later."

I swept the stuff into a corner of the kitchen, then noticing one of the lower cabinets, I said, "Mom used to keep staples in a cupboard like this."

We bent down, opened the cabinet door and found a treasure of food stuffs: flour, potatoes, onions, a few cans of tomatoes, and a cabbage head surrounded by brown, dry leaves. Rachel struck a match to light the stove under a pot which she had filled with water, then got busy scrubbing the potatoes. As I watched, I realized that Rachel had obviously bathed. She looked clean in a blue woolen dress, while I still had my blue and gray striped camp uniform which was stiff with filth. I needed to strip it off, scratch all over, and wash myself.

"I want a bath." I said loudly.

"After we eat; food's almost ready."

"I need it right now." I felt suddenly angry. Until now it was fear that governed my feelings. I learned fear from the fearless ones. I saw what happened to those who got angry and tried to stand up for themselves in the camps. Those who refused to carry out some outrageous orders of their Nazi guards didn't live long. The brave were killed on the spot.

But I wanted to live, and learned to gag all emotion so as not to draw the attention of the watchful camp guards. But now that the guards were gone and I was free, I realized that I needed no permission to feel and express my anger.

The anger I had bottled up all these years now exploded out of all proportion to my irritation with Rachel. Here she was clean and shiny in her fresh clothes telling me to wait. Well, I wouldn't. I left the kitchen without a word, and marched purposefully to the bathroom. There was a tank with an attached gas grill for heating water. It hung suspended over the tub, just like back home, but when I started to draw my bath, the water ran cold.

"That selfish Rachel used up all the hot water," I yelled to no one in particular.

Fussing in frustration, I rummaged on the back shelf above the toilet, until I saw a box of matches. I lit the gas grill, fuming, because I knew that it would take at least half an hour to heat enough water for a good, hot bath.

Still disgruntled, but hungry, I walked back towards the kitchen. Rachel had our dinner almost ready. The aroma of potatoes, cabbage, onion, and tomatoes simmering on the stove was pleasing, and slowly I felt my annoyance dissipate. The bathwater will be hot by the time we've finished our dinner, I thought.

Without any prompting, I began to set the table with an incongruous mismatch of chipped plates, slightly bent forks and knives, and snow-white linen napkins that had escaped destruction. The loaf of bread and cheese that Gregor gave me at parting provided the final touch. The house was warm, food cooked on the stove, the table was set, but there was a stone around my heart. The prospect of the first warm meal in more weeks than I could remember did little to lift my spirits. Though I appreciated the practical, matter of fact approach and her kindness, Rachel was not my family, and this house was not my home.

With little to say, we ate quietly and sparingly. Most of the food remained in the pot. Rachel said we'd have it the next day and started to clear away the dishes. I put what remained of the bread and cheese in a clean paper bag that I found folded in one of the cabinets, and sat it next to the almost full pot of food. I swept the floor, and put the little pile of broken crockery into an empty box I found in one of the hall closets.

Ready for my bath, I complained, "I'd rather drape a clean sheet round me, than put this filthy thing back on."

Rachel found a clean nightgown in one of the bedrooms, and handing it to me said, "Here, I think this will fit." Yawning, she added, "I've put down some fresh sheets on the bed for you, that room over there." She pointed down the hall and rubbing her eyes, waved goodnight.

I slid into the tub, closed my eyes and let my head sink down into the warm water, leaving only my nose and mouth exposed to the air. Warm liquid embraced every muscle, every nerve, and I let myself float weightless, soaking every pore of my skin, so that the many layers of grime could begin to dissolve.

Arms buoyed towards the surface, my fingers drifted in the murky warm liquid, while the filth that had become part of me began to flake away. I lathered soap between the palms of my hands, and spread soap bubbles over my arms, and across my not yet budding breasts, over my neck, and into my ears and hair, till every inch of me was soapy and soft.

I wanted to scrub away the shame of each shouted insult, lathered soap over my body again and again to wash away the stench and reek of the camps, letting that blessed water cleanse and dissolve much of the grime, shame and hate.

I filled the tub once again, and sank deeper still. My rough skin softened, my fingers uncurled, relaxed, and with my short hair floating on the water I let my mind go blank. After a while, feeling almost human I willed myself out of the tub. Wrapped in a fresh towel, I put on the clean, soft nightgown Rachel had given me, and padded on bare feet across the hall to the bed with crisp, cool sheets. I had almost forgotten how lovely a bed could feel. I inhaled the clean fragrance of the sheets and was soon asleep.

Chapter 3

Getting up from my first night in a real bed with clean sheets, I felt better than I'd felt in a long time. Still half-asleep, I thought I was home, but then I remembered where I was and how I had met Rachel the day before.

After breakfast, both of us cleared the library and dining room of all the remaining crockery and glass. Saving what we could for the owners, we placed those books that had escaped the worst of the damage back on the shelves, and carted what could not be saved out to the garbage bin. By the time we finished, there were four garbage cans filled to overflowing. All the while we worked that day, we said little to one another.

I worked in the nightgown Rachel had given me the night before. Now, resourceful as ever, Rachel found some clean, warm clothes for me. Though somewhat large, the skirt, blouse, and jacket were sure to keep me warm.

"Know how to sew?" Rachel asked.

I had to admit that I didn't, so Rachel altered the skirt so it wouldn't fall off my hips. It didn't matter that both the blouse and jacket were too large for me, they were clean, and I thanked her for her kindness.

Later that evening, as we sat in the kitchen eating the reheated food left from the night before, we still found it difficult to carry on any kind of conversation. I thought it strange, considering we both shared a common experience, but I didn't want to dwell on it and, probably, Rachel didn't either. Who'd want to think about those last years in the camps? We ate in silence.

Once, Rachel stopped chewing and glanced at me with a shy

tentative expression. I got the impression she wanted to say something, yet at the same time was reluctant to do so. After a moment's hesitation, she spoke.

"Where did you live before the war?"

"Warsaw."

"My home was in Ordovician."

I had never heard of the place, "Where is it?"

Rachel chewed a potato, washed it down with some water, and said, "A small village outside Warsaw."

"Farm country, you lived there year round?" I was surprised.

"Sure, why not?"

"We used to go to the country in the summer, but I never knew any Jews who lived in the country year round. What were you, farmers?"

Rachel laughed. "What makes you think we lived on a farm?"

"What else?"

"We had a shop, the only one in the village. We sold everything, clothes, seeds, farming equipment." Rachel looked off into the distance.

At that moment I felt a special kinship towards her. "My grandfather had a toyshop, you know, and when there was no one in the store I was allowed to play with the display toys."

"Me too, we sold toys, but not many, just a few, made mostly of wood. I especially liked the marionettes. I used to pull the strings to make them dance." Rachel said.

We sat for a while, companions in silence. The clock ticked on the kitchen wall, the dishes sat stacked in the sink.

I bowed my head thinking about our home and the courtyard of my childhood days. "That was before the war," I sighed.

"What was?"

"My home in Warsaw, I can see it still. Our house, Bubbe's and Zyde's place right across the courtyard. I didn't want to ever leave that place. But Mom and Dad said we had to.

"Why?"

"The Germans had started to build walls around our neighborhood"

"You mean the Ghetto?"

21

"Yes, so Mom and Dad made plans to leave."

"Why?"

"To escape the Nazis, so we left and went to Krakow, me, Dad, Mom, and my little sister, Haniushka." I started to push the crumbs around on the table.

We sat in silence. Then I added, "They decided we'd have to change our name and pretend we were Christians, and that would make us safe."

Rachel just looked at me, expecting me to say more. But I was all talked out.

Rachel was still curious, wanted to hear more.

"There are still the dishes to do," I said closing off the subject.

"Yeah."

Rachel washed and I dried.

"That's the last of them," Rachel said, handing the last dish to me.

"I think you'd like it there," I mused

"Where?"

"Our courtyard. I'd like to show it to you someday, if it's still there." I was wistful.

"I hope you find your home. I would also like to go back to our village, see who and what is left."

I nodded. "Tomorrow if the trains start running, we'll take the first train back home, the very first train that comes by."

In bed, eyes closing, I hoped Rachel would find her home and her family. After all, she and I had survived, so why not our families? I wanted to believe we'd all be reunited, I with my family and she with hers. Once we got settled, perhaps I could invite Rachel to come visit us. More asleep then awake, I thought spring would be perfect. I wanted to show her the purple tulips that grew by the side of Bubby's house... imagined taking Rachel's hand, guiding her beneath the arched gateway...

Our Courtyard

...Here is my home. Careful, these cobblestones are old and uneven. You could trip and skin your knee.

See these carved wooden gates? We have another set at the

other end. Each morning they open to let people in and out. Walk with me a bit. Ah, here's my Zyde's toyshop, lots of toys in the window, see the pretty dolls? My sister, Hania, likes to play with them. I'm going to be ten years old next March, so I'm too old to play with dolls.

Come on in. Look at the sawdust on the floor, and all those shelves. They're filled with toys. At quiet times when there are no customers, I like to squat on the sawdust, next to the counter, and pretend I'm a General with huge armies and big strategies to plan. That's when I line up all the little soldiers, put the little drummer up front, and they become a grand army, ready to march and fight. It's fun.

Let's go on for a bit. Here's my favorite bench. It's all scratched and worn. See here, those two carved hearts pierced by one arrow? Look at the names, Rifke and Jankle. I wonder who they were.

Would you like to sit and rest a spell? There's plenty of shade beneath this old oak with its canopy of leaves. They'll be turning gold soon, now that fall has come. I often sit here and read, or talk with my friends. I can come out here by myself. It is safe, right next to our doorway. Those narrow steps lead to our home. See the windows up there on the second floor? That's where I live with my mom and my dad, and little Haniushka. And look there, across the courtyard. See the windows up there? Bubby and Zyde live up there with my uncle Jurek. Every morning, first thing, I wave and say hi to my Bubby across our courtyard. And best of all, I can go there anytime by myself. It's safe here.

School starts tomorrow, and I'll have to go there every morning. It's not far, just out the gate to the left, and down the street a couple of blocks. I like school, but I spend most of my free time right here. This is our place, these two rows of houses that face out across our courtyard.

Nothing terribly exciting ever happens here. Yet, our moments in this courtyard do vary from day to day and season to season. The flowers tell our time of year, yellow and white daffodils, purple and delicate pinks of the tulips, and the yellow buttercups speak of spring.

And after the summer, when we come back from the country,

it is fall again, time for sunflowers to grow tall and lord it over the dahlias and asters at their feet. I love the colors of autumn; love the smell of falling leaves. In a couple of weeks the air will fill with rust and gold. Then I will make music with my feet, shuffling and stirring so the fallen leaves rustle and whisper their summer tales.

In our courtyard every small event tells the time of day. First thing each morning, the milk peddler comes in, pulling his cart into the space right there, in front of this bench. I awake to the sound of his pushcart wheels rattling across the cobblestones. I listen to his song. "Milk is here, fresh eggs, butter for sale. Come ladies, see for yourselves, see how sweet my milk, how fresh my eggs, how mouth-melting my creamy butter." He sings his refrain, and I, fully awake now, run to the window to see the women gather round him with their ceramic, metal, and glass pitchers. His hand moves gracefully as he dips and pours, filling each and every container with a flourish. Sunbeams dance on the white liquid he dispenses from his metal milk can, while the white stream of milk flows into each pitcher, with not one drop spilled.

Then my Bubby opens her window across the courtyard. She waves to me, and calls out her order. "Pitcher of milk and six eggs, Ruhele will come get it."

Mom has some coins all ready, and still in my pajamas, I run down two flights of steps with the money, carrying our yellow and Bubby's blue jug. Now it is my turn to watch the milkman dip, pour, and fill till our jugs are full. The hardest part comes next, for I must carry it so no drop can spill. My morning has begun.

Right after the milkman takes his milk cart away, the baker comes in, rolling his cart. Even before I can hear his song, I smell the sweet aroma of his just-out-of-the-oven goodies.

"Bread, fresh bread, rolls, sweet and delicious cakes, Challah," he sings, looking like he enjoys his own baked goods. He is a short and round man with round pink-cheeks, wearing clothes that look like they are about to burst buttons. I guess he is as happy as he looks. After all he gets to eat those sweet cakes anytime he likes.

Mama especially likes his Challah, and we need it every Friday for our evening Shabbat meal. So every Friday, when the baker comes, it's my job to get the Challah, and because it's for

24

the Shabbat, Mama tells me to get extra goodies for dessert. Friday is a special day in our courtyard.

On Friday mornings Bubby scours and scrubs her home to make it clean for the Shabbat. By the time I come from school she's already busy in the kitchen. The house smells so fresh. Then I get to watch her cook. Would you like to come with me next Friday? Bubby likes it when I bring a friend. You can have some fish broth and noodles with me. It's my favorite after-school lunch. Just to inhale the aroma of the fish balls cooking in that rich vegetable broth will make you so hungry. I love to watch them bubble in the big pot. Nothing compares to the tang of Bubby's fish balls or the fragrance of her chicken soup.

See, we go to Bubby and Zyde every Friday night to celebrate the Shabbat and have dinner with our whole family including Mama's younger brother, Jurek, and my Great-Grandfather. He's very old, doesn't talk much, reads his old books mostly, and sings prayers. But before we start our meal, Mama and Daddy, my little sister Hania and Bubby, we all have to wait for Zyde to come back from praying at the Synagogue. I can't tell you how hungry we are by the time he finally comes home. Poor Haniushka is too little. She can't wait, so Bubby lets her have a little piece of cold fish. I'm older, so I have to be patient, like the rest of the adults. Even after we get to sit down, we still can't eat.

First Great-Grandfather has to pronounce the Shabbat blessing over the Challah. I want to tell you it's no fun to sit and listen to your stomach growl as he mumbles and mutters words I don't even understand. But that's how it has to be. It's tradition.

I don't really mind though, because afterwards we get to eat fish and Challah. My stomach stops the rude noise and I can enjoy the rest of our evening. My cheeks heat up with the hot chicken noodle soup. I taste the broth, and watch the pale green celery and the bright orange of carrot slices float over the noodles. Delicious!

We sing too, especially my Great-Grandfather. His voice is soft, and he keeps rhythm by tapping his fingers against the tabletop, while he sings songs of a refrain in words I can't understand. He sings, "Biri biri boom," over and over. Someday I'll know what the words, mean. He once told me that he learned them from his father, who learned them from his father, just as my

Zyde learned from him. Zyde explained that they come from an ancient chant. He likes to join in every once in a while, although Bubby pleads for him not to. Zyde has a strong loud voice, but know what? He can't carry a tune.

That's our Friday. Now Saturday is the second day of the Shabbat and another special day. Zyde gets to spend most of it in the Synagogue. Sometimes, before he goes there, he wraps his prayer shawl around his head and shoulders and intones his Morning Prayer right in the dining room. He stands, facing the Eastern wall with an open prayer book in his hand, bends his head and body in prayer, and tips up and down, up and down. Then he moves his body side-to-side, then back up and down. You know, when he prays like that, I hardly know him. His singsong rhythm and those strange words sound like a poem. He recites some in mumbled monotone, but for other words, he raises his voice, throws his head back, then curtsies even lower before God.

Mostly my Zyde speaks Yiddish. Though I can't speak it, I do understand it most of the time. But when he prays, I can't understand any of the words. He prays in a different language. When I ask why, he explains that "when Jews pray they do so in Hebrew, the ancient language of our forefathers."

"Doesn't God understand Yiddish?" I ask

He laughs, and I wonder if God can really hear him.

No business is allowed on Saturday, because it is Shabbat, a holy day, a day of rest. The tradesmen also rest and our courtyard is quiet on that day, but all other days in the week start with the tradesmen "song." Although the milkman and the baker come every day each with their own song, we never know when the knife sharpener will come. He shows up once in a while, but whenever he comes, it always happens right after the baker has left.

And he has his own song. "Ladies, bring your knives, bring them all, and I'll make them new again," he sings while he sets up his business. First, he sets his sharpening wheel right over there, next to the old wooden table. The size of a sunflower, his wheel is big and round, and made of gray stone. A dark brown leather strap encircles it and attaches to this wood and metal contraption that ends with a foot pedal, which is on the ground. When he pushes his foot against this pedal, it propels the leather strap, which turns the wheel.

The women gather with their dull knives. He places the edge of each knife against the spinning stone wheel till each knife is as sharp as new. I watch the sparks fly in the air. Each one lasts but a moment. Then, another takes its place and all the sparks dance to the music of the wheel. On a dark gray winter day, they light up the gray with their glint.

On other days, the pots and pans man comes in with the bang and clash of his swinging cooking utensils. The wheels of his cart roll and clatter over our cobblestones. I stand in the window, amazed to see such a slight man pushing such a huge cart. He bends to his task. His stooping shoulders shudder with the effort, and the brim of his cap goes slightly askew and slips down to cover the side of his brow.

"Pots for you, ladies, pots and pans, shiny, brand new, wonderful copper, hardly needs scrubbing to shine, Pots, Ladies, Pots for you..." He sings his song, making his own music as he strikes a metal spoon against the bottom of a copper pot.

Bubby buys most everything from the visiting tradesmen. She doesn't like the big stores. The sales people there speak Polish and she prefers Yiddish, her "mother tongue," though she does understand and speaks some Polish. I don't know how it is that I've never learned to speak Yiddish. I speak Polish to her, and she speaks Yiddish to me, and together we speak Poldish. It is, our very own language, though we don't really need words to make understanding.

So it goes each morning, except on Saturday. The tradesmen come, the milkman, the baker, the fresh fruit and vegetables man, each with his own goods, his own aromas, and his own music. Bubby gets all she needs, and that's how it goes, each day the same, each day just a bit different. My Bubby belongs in her home in our Courtyard. For her this place is like water for fish. Except the occasional trip to visit my Great-Aunt Gittle, who lives on the other side of town, and of course the synagogue, my Bubby seldom leaves our courtyard. She's comfortable here, has all she needs.

She likes to come down, when she has some time, sit here on this bench, and listen to my tall stories. That's what she calls them. I make them up, that's true. But they are not lies. They are just make-believe.

Whenever there's a holiday, a birthday, or even a wedding, we celebrate it right here, in this courtyard. Some of our holidays are somber, like The Day of Atonement, but I must be patient at such times, because that's what is expected of me. On Yom Kippur no one laughs or makes jokes.

Zyde and his friends spend most of the day at prayer in the Synagogue, but I'm not allowed sit with them because I'm only a girl. So Mother, Bubby and I sit up in the gallery, apart from the men. Seems when it comes to praying, men think women don't count. Can that mean that my Zyde who is wise with age is making a mistake? He has told me that God is good and fair, and surely loves us all equally. I'm very confused. I asked Bubby, who I think knows everything, and she explained the reason women and girls must sit upstairs while our men pray below, but what she said confused me more. I guess you have to be an adult to understand such mysteries as God and men and women and prayer. I'll just have to wait till I grow up.

On the day of Yom Kippur, adults fast, but Haniushka and I don't. We're supposed to eat, because we are children. Don't we kids count before God? Shouldn't I also consider all the good I failed to do this past year? I'm not so proud of some of the things I've done and said, either. I can be snippety, and often speak before I've had a chance to think. I ought to fast as well, I think.

So okay, but I eat very little, just enough to make my mom happy. I hope God accepts my regrets over the good I've failed to accomplish, and all the bad deeds I did commit. And, just like the adults, I also promise to try very hard to do better next year. Great Zyde says that God accepts our good intentions and He trusts us to live up to our promises. So I must not disappoint Him, and I'll have to work very hard at becoming a really good person.

I don't really like all that serious business, but after sundown we get to eat delicious sweet rolls and Bubby's chicken soup. New Year begins the very next day.

Then, five days after Yom Kippur comes the most joyous of all our holidays. Sukkoth is really special. It comes at harvest, just in time to celebrate God's bounty. This is when Zyde and his friends build a Sukkah in our courtyard. It is a little house that must be built out of things that grow in the ground, like tree branches and leaves. It must be open to the sky, because at Sukkoth, men must pray with nothing between their heads and the sky above. But what if it rains? I once asked.

"When we sit in the Sukkah, God spreads his wings over us like a mother who protects her children," Zyde says. He explains that men built the Sukkah so they can have a very special kind of a house, where we can all be with God.

They built their little house according to the law, without a roof, while the walls were made of freshly cut, loosely woven tree branches interwoven with branches of sweet smelling blackberries, along with some myrtle mixed with golden stalks of dry willow and sunflower filling our Sukkah with bright colors of autumn and sweet fragrance. It is lovely to sit inside and breathe in the aroma while I listen to the men talk and sing, and praise the Lord. What a perfect little house for God to come and visit.

We talk about the harvest and sing songs, and thank God for all we receive. The men dance, and I never want to miss one moment of it. Inside the Sukkah, I look up at the night sky, the moon and stars, and I imagine God spreading his wings to keep us safe. No roof above our heads to separate us from Him...

I awoke with a smile, but then I remembered one sunny morning in September when God withdrew his protective wings.

Chapter 4

At breakfast, the next morning, I was all business. "I must go back to Krakow," I said.

"I thought you told me you're from Warsaw."

"Yes, remember? We went to Krakow before they could lock us up in the Ghetto. So if any of them survived, that's where they'd go, the last place we called home."

"I hope you do. I suppose it's possible some of my folks survived. I want to get back to my little village. Let's start this morning. Maybe the trains are running." Rachel said.

But all we found was the deserted station, its lobby chilly, dark, and empty, the ticket windows shut. I saw a few printed notices on the bulletin board, but neither of us could speak or read German, so we didn't know what they said. I pointed to the date of the last posting, mid-March. Two months had gone by since these yellowing pieces of paper were posted. It looked like no one had been there since, and nobody was likely to show up any time soon.

We walked to the back of the train station, and looked at the empty tracks, cutting through the center of town, slipping out of sight around the bend. I stood there feeling empty and lonesome just like those tracks.

"Place feels dead," Rachel blurted out.

"I don't want to stay here."

Rachel shook her head in disgust. "So what do you propose?"

I looked up at the sun and pointed. "That way is east, so that's the direction we must take now."

"What, walk? We've got a safe place here. There's some food left in the cupboards. The way we eat, it should last us a few

30

more days, and by then maybe the trains will start running."

Rachel was making no sense. The town looked like a cemetery. Nothing was going to happen here, not for a long time. "I'm going now!" I declared.

"Rutka, don't be crazy. Where will you go? Where will you sleep? How will you eat? Stay just a couple of days more. What would it hurt?"

But I couldn't wait, not for maybe or soon. I had to start for home, and I had to do it now. I smiled gently at Rachel, said good bye, and began to walk.

"Wait, Rutele. Don't go!" Rachel yelled.

"Sorry Rachel," I said and kept going. I was afraid that if I stopped even for a moment, I would not be able to go on.

Foolhardy it may have been, but I'd made my decision, and it was the first time in my life that I was able to act under my own direction. That act of making a decision, for good or bad, it didn't matter, made me feel empowered. My resolve became even stronger.

I turned to look back, and almost bumped into her. We paused, startled by the mild collision. Suddenly, I felt very sad and alone.

"I'd like it very much if we could go on together," I said.

"Then stay with me; you'll see, the trains have got to start running soon."

"You can't leave, and I can't stay," I said, taking her hands into my own.

"But..."

I stopped her. I had heard her reasons for staying and didn't want to hear them again. "I've been hungry before, and I know how to sleep on the ground. Please understand, Rachel, I need to go home now." I gave her a last hug and planted a kiss on her cheek. Then I pulled away, and started my long walk towards the morning sun. A moment later I heard Rachel's footsteps pounding the sidewalk behind me. She caught at my sleeve.

"I thought we were friends, and we'd stay together." Breathless from running, Rachel tried to hold on, her arms tightening around my shoulders. I didn't want to leave her behind. Rachel had found me when I was alone and frightened. We shared the shelter she had found, shared what little food remained in that abandoned house and we shared our feelings giving comfort to one another. After all these long years of being crammed in with strangers and feeling all alone, I appreciated Rachel's kindness and her commonsense manner. Those last few days we had shared together felt so good. I didn't feel so alone anymore. I hesitated, was tempted to go back with Rachel and wait for the trains to start running. But the moment passed and my urge to go home won out. I just couldn't wait to see if any of my family had survived. Mom and Dad, and my little sister, Haniushka must be there, home, waiting for me. Without knowing it, I prayed to the God who never listened, prayed for him to open his ears.

In the end, Rachel accepted my resolve. We hugged again, and promised to look each other up after we got back to Poland.

"Once the trains start running, I'll be on my way too," Rachel promised, releasing me from her embrace. "God keep you," she whispered.

I walked on alone. Slow at first, my steps picked up speed gradually as my thoughts turned homeward. I imagined myself back in our courtyard, the place where I had spent the first nine years of my life. Memories flooded in, and I remembered how sad I was when we had to leave our home in Warsaw. I could not understand why, and refused to listen to my mom and dad, no matter how hard they tried to explain. We'd have to leave though none of us wanted to, they told me, but I refused to understand and pleaded with them to let me stay with Bubby. In the end, even Bubby told me to go. It was the first of many partings. I had to obey. I left my beloved Bubby, and went with my parents and sister just before the last wall went up around the Warsaw Ghetto, just before the last bit of barbed wire was put into position, and the last gate was shut.

We moved to Krakow. My parents rented a pleasant apartment on the second floor of a recently built house overlooking a small park. For a while we called it home. We all hoped it would shelter us from the Nazis and the war. But it didn't. Three years in concentration camps, and the only things that kept me going were my memories of home. I daydreamed about going back to our Warsaw courtyard to the first home I knew, the home where my family was whole. And I dreamed about the second home, the Krakow apartment which for a little while did provide shelter for us.

Now, the war had ended and the Nazis had been defeated. I'm coming, please be there, I whispered. I imagined the wonder of coming home; visualized our street, the little park across the street, the smell of lilacs. I could almost touch the velvet feel of blossoms. In my mind I was already home…

…A shaft of sunlight through narrow window lights a path across the stairs… I climb up to the second floor landing, stop in front of the familiar blue door, and press the white button. Chimes sound, and I hear Mom's high heels click across the parquet floor. The door opens and so do her arms. I step into her embrace, and feel her warm breath on my face. Her hand strokes my hair. We kiss. She takes my hand and leads me to the dining room.

Dad looks up from his paper. "Just look at her. We have to fatten her up."

My dad is alive, and I run to him. I barely have a chance to hug him, when Haniushka, her short plump arms clutching her favorite rag doll and blanket, shouts, "Ruti!" and charges into my arms. I catch her, but am too weak to hold on, and we both tumble down into the soft pillows of the daybed. We laugh and kiss and laugh…

Such wish-dreams as these fueled my determination to hurry home. I had been walking all that morning, my mind spinning wishes, prayers, and hopes. By noon, more houses appeared along the unfamiliar road. Must be nearing a larger town, I thought. I was tired and thirsty, but my spirits rose with the hope that a larger city might have a functioning train station with running trains.

Ever more houses appeared along the road, but I noticed few of them had smoke coming from their chimneys. Most seemed abandoned. What caused so many people to leave their homes unattended? As usual, when a question occurred to me, I soon managed to think of an answer.

Right there, along the deserted stretch of a German road, I decided that there was a God, after all, a God who had this huge scale for keeping balance in the world. So after things got knocked off balance, like they did when the Germans forced people from their homes, this grand universal scale would tip, and it was the Germans who had to leave their homes in turn. It took a long time for that to happen, but the scale did tip. After all, I argued, it would take a major defeat before most of the Germans would realize what they had done. I figured that now at last, they saw the enormity of evil they'd set loose upon the world and they became frightened. That is why they ran away, and left their homes behind. I thought their empty homes represented a kind of justice, an evening of scales.

Thinking these thoughts somehow reassured me, but then thirst, which I had been ignoring for quite a while, began to claim my attention. My throat seemed so dry I feared it would crack. Why hadn't I brought some water? I chastised myself, and felt desperate enough to consider approaching one of the few houses that did have smoke drifting from its chimney. Someone would surely let me have some water. But I hesitated, worried about my appearance. My toothpick legs, and my pale skin stretched over hollow cheekbones were likely to frighten any normal person. I knew I looked like a walking cadaver.

But thirst made its demands, and I decided to chance it. What's the worst they could do, slam the door in my face? I've survived worse. I noticed a pretty brick walk leading towards a large house. There would be servants, I thought. People living in such homes tend to have servants. I expected such a person would be more likely to let me have some water. I decided to walk around to the back entrance.

No servant opened the door. The man who did open it looked more like a concentration camp victim than a servant or a master of the house. He wore what looked like a dressing gown, which probably had belonged to the owner of the house. Tall and stooping, he looked haggard. His bones seemed about to pierce his pale skin. His hair was thin, long, and straggly, but clean and brushed. He smelled of soap.

"No, you need something, maybe?" He smiled, recognizing another lost soul.

Although I didn't speak Yiddish, I understood his words.

34

That's how it was with Zyde and Bubby. They spoke Yiddish and I would reply in Polish. "I could use some cold water."

"So, come in, already." He took my hand and pulled me into the warm house. "Come, come. There's some food here, a good shelter for the night."

"I'm thirsty, just want water, please."

"Nonsense! What, are you afraid of me? Don't worry, come and meet Elaina and Sam. They are in the kitchen."

I followed him to the warm kitchen. The first thing to catch my eye was a plate of bread with cheese and a teapot in the middle of a large, wooden table. I eyed these with hunger. A woman of undetermined age and an older man sitting and drinking tea looked up at me with welcoming smiles, as my host pulled out a chair saying, "Sit, sit don't be shy."

I sat down. He took a glass from the cupboard, and poured some tea. "Please, take some bread and cheese," he urged me, sliding the plate over.

He began to make introductions. "Elaina," he said pointing to the woman whose face was long and thin. Her lips, a thin line of a grimace, and yet its corners curled up in a faint smile of welcome She reminded me of my cousin, Helenka. What a coincidence, I thought, realizing the similarity of name. This woman looked not that much older than my cousin, but there the comparison ended. She didn't have the glowing skin of my beautiful cousin. It was sallow, stretched over her face like some tissue paper that might tear at any moment. Her hair had lost its gloss and she was skinny as a rail. So was everyone else in that room.

"This is Sam," my host said, pointing to the man sitting next to Elaina.

"And I'm Jacob." Ending the introductions, he sat down, but when he noticed that I had refrained from eating or drinking, he asked, "What's the matter; aren't you hungry?"

"Could I have some cold water?"

Jacob hit his forehead, "Look at me, I already forgot." He moved quickly to make amends, and got me a tall glass of water.

I drank it down, took a sip of tea, and asked if the trains

35

were running.

"No one knows when," Sam shrugged his bony, stooped shoulders. A man of small stature, he sat hunched over the table, a yarmulke on his head, his fingers restless on the table top moving tiny breadcrumbs around in circles. I was reminded of cousin Abe, a Yeshiva student. He too was shy and restless, his fingers in perpetual motion except when he held an open book in front of him. Then he was at peace, his eyes scanning the pages and his lips murmuring the words of a prayer.

Jacob patted my shoulder and told me not to worry. Then he went on to tell about a man he had met that very day, a peasant who lived in the village, and owned a couple of horses with a wagon. He stopped talking and looked at us sitting expectantly at the table. If he wanted to see our response, he wasn't disappointed.

"Does that mean he'll help us maybe?" Sam could hardly contain himself.

Elaina interrupted, "What about the trains? Does he know if they're running?"

Horses and wagon, I thought. Could it mean that we could be moving on soon?

We waited for Jacob to go on, and he didn't fail us; he said that the peasant agreed to drive us to a town some 50 kilometers distant. "Rumor has it the trains are running over there," he said.

"How did you make him agree to drive us?" Elaina asked.

"I gave him a choice. I told him he could deal either with me, or with the Russians," Jacob said, laughing.

I wasn't sure it was funny, but I was glad to be going on.

"When?" I asked Jacob.

"First thing tomorrow morning," he replied.

"Can I go with you?" I asked.

"What are you talking about? Of course, I wouldn't have it any other way." Jacob smiled at me.

I felt reassured at once, and immediately thanked him for including me in their little group.

"You're welcome," he said, his eyes crinkling with mischief. "Is it maybe too much to ask, but, you got a name maybe?" His thin lips stretched in a good natured grin.

Having forgotten to introduce myself before, I felt embarrassed. "Rutka," I whispered.

Elaina stood up and gave me a hug. "Welcome," she said. Then seeing me yawn, she smiled and suggested I should get some sleep.

I wanted a bath. As if reading my mind, Elaina asked if I'd like to wash up.

"Would it be possible to have a bath?"

Elaina nodded, stood up, and said, "Sure, but we better get going, early start tomorrow morning."

She led the way to the bathroom and immediately started running warm water into the bathtub, pointing to the soap and towels. She left me to go across the hall and came back with a flannel nightgown and a warm robe. She hung these on the door hook, and then asked me to follow her to the bedroom across the hall, "This room is empty. You can sleep here."

I watched her open a wardrobe with dresses, skirts, blouses, and warm coats hanging inside, and shoes neatly lined up on a shelf below. "Use anything that'll fit you." She said.

I looked down at the shoes, hoping to find a pair that would fit, as the shoes I was wearing were too small for my feet, and pinched my toes. Then too, I really needed something warm and sturdy enough to get me home.

"Danke," I managed to thank her in Yiddish.

"Sleep tight," Elaina said.

I remembered the way my mom used to wash my hair when I was little, recalled how the soap got into my eyes and I begged her to stop. But if she was with me now, I'd let her wash my hair, and I wouldn't cry even if the soap stung my eyes. This time, I would thank her instead.

I had bathed one day earlier, but I still enjoyed the luxurious moment of slipping into the warm water. I lathered with soap that smelled of spring flowers, and then immersed my whole body into the water, letting my head sink right up to my ears, with my hair spread out on the water. My eyes closed, I savored the luxury aware that there was no way to know when I'd have a chance to bathe again.

Elaina came to wake me in the morning. She stayed with me to make sure the clothes I chose to wear would be warm enough and fit right. She also supervised my selection of shoes. We both agreed on the wool-lined high tops which laced up over the ankles because the nights were still cool. Elaina also insisted I wear a pair of heavy socks and packed additional socks and underwear for me to take along. She placed these extra items in a paper bag. "Take them. You'll need them," she said in Yiddish, shoving the bag into my hands.

No one had fussed over me lately, but I was still a little girl at heart, so I appreciated Elaina's kindness. It gave me that warm feeling of being cared for, and I thanked her again.

We started up right after breakfast. Good to his word, the German farmer arrived with his horse and wagon, which was lined with fresh hay. As I settled myself next to Elaina, the aroma of hay reminded me of our pleasant family outings in the country, before the war.

Eager to return to his farm quickly, the farmer started the horses at a fast trot. We were happy about that, as our little group of Jews was anxious to reach the small city as quickly as possible. We all hoped to find the train station busy with bustling travelers and loud with the megaphones of the train announcers.

But that did not happen. What we found was another dark and empty train station, not much different from the one I'd seen in the last town I'd been to. We started out with hope, but found only disappointment.

Despairing of ever getting back home, I wanted to sit down on the cold, dusty floor, and beat my fists against the tiles. Our little group stood in the drafty hall looking at each other, then without a word, we all turned as one and made for the exit. But even as we ran down the steps, it was already too late. The farmer and his wagon were gone.

We stood on the steps of the defunct train station, in silence. I wanted to scream till my voice grew hoarse, till my throat gave out. Having grown accustomed to disappointments and abandonment, Elaina smiled sadly, but she reached out to me, placing her arm round my shoulders. Giving me a hug, she whispered. "You are not alone."

Jacob said, "We've been through much worse." He shrugged, casting his gaze around the street. Jacob pointed to the hotel across the street and the lettering, ROSALIN, over the door. "As good a name as any," he said.

We trooped over, and climbed the steps, stopping in front of the doors. We didn't know what to expect. Would there be any people inside? Jacob turned the knob, and we entered the dimly lit lobby. The first thing we saw was a black-rimmed wall clock that hung silent over the front desk, its hands pointing to half past twelve. But that clock had stopped. It no longer told the time. Dead plants in dry planters and a thick layer of dust covered desks, chairs, tables, and marble floors. The hotel appeared as empty and unoccupied as the railroad station.

"Let's find the kitchen," Elaina said.

Jacob stopped her. "We must stay together."

We walked soundlessly across the dust-laden floor with Jacob in the lead. Sam followed coughing, and Jacob placed his finger across his lips to shush him. We threaded our way between dark red velvet upholstered couches and chairs, looking into the gloom for someone who might be hiding. Suddenly, the clang of a heavy steel door broke the silence.

Sam pointed to the floor. "The basement," he said.

"Stay here," Jacob ordered. His steps slow, he proceeded as quietly as he could, but he couldn't silence his shoes. They clicked on the hard surface of the stone floor, as he continued towards the partially opened door and the stairwell beyond. We lost sight of him when he started down, and could only wait and listen for his receding steps, which gradually grew softer, until we could hear them no more.

We huddled in silence, imagining what or whom he might encounter down there. As Sam began to mumble prayers, the image of my grandfather and Uncle Abe came to mind. They used to pray in just the same way, facing the wall with their heads bowed, bodies moving side to side, and up and down. I could almost see them just that way, as I observed Sam beseech God to keep watch over Jacob. I wanted to add my prayers to Sam's. No one moved.

After what seemed a long time, we heard a loud voice. It may have been Jacob's. It sounded less like a conversation than an interrogation. The sound grew louder, and we could distinguish

39

the voice of Jacob speaking in Yiddish.

Soon after that, a round little man with a floor mop appeared in the open doorway. Jacob was right behind him. Addressing Jacob as Herr Ubbermaister, the janitor kept repeating something in German. I could not make it out, and so turned to Elaina to ask what he was saying.

Jacob quickly explained that the poor man was frightened. "He claims everybody is gone. He doesn't know where."

While Jacob spoke, the man watched him closely, as if trying to understand every word, which was not a surprise, considering that Jacob was speaking Yiddish, which is similar to German. When Jacob stopped speaking, the janitor raised his shoulders so his short neck all but disappeared between the folds of his chin. He offered an apologetic little smile. I figured he was a servant who wanted to please, but had nothing useful to say to them.

"How is it you don't understand German?" Jacob asked me.

"Don't like it. Sounds like a lot of coughing and spitting," I answered.

Jacob laughed and called me a little rebel. I had all but forgotten how, but it felt good to be laughing with him now.

After dismissing the janitor, Jacob led us to the hotel dining room, sat us around the table, and started our little conference. He told us that all the janitor knew was to sweep the place and stay out of everyone's way. "He can do us neither harm nor good," Jacob said.

Nothing was happening. I was impatient, wanted to move, to do something. I saw a small lake through the tall windows across the room. It looked pretty and I left the table to get a better view, but Jacob called me back. "Don't go wondering off," he told me sternly. Expecting to be obeyed, he returned to the discussion around the table.

I didn't want to sit down. Talk was boring. I needed action. I wanted out of that cavernous and gloomy room. I wanted to go out into the air and sunshine. At the same time, I respected Jacob. He seemed wise, and certainly old enough to be my father. While I wished to follow his instructions, I was also impatient like a colt waiting to run free. I couldn't sit, so I stood and fidgeted instead, my fingers playing an imaginary scale across a nonexistent piano.

This stopping in empty towns where the trains didn't run was getting me down. I had almost made up my mind to leave these people right there, and start walking east as far as I could get. At the same time, having found some sense of security among this little group of strangers, I really didn't want to be alone again. After all, we shared a common goal. Each one of us needed to get back home, to look for family, to pick up what pieces remained.

Jacob interrupted my thoughts, "Ruti, look at that lovely lake out there. Why don't we all take a few moments to enjoy it?" he suggested, leading us to the French doors. He opened them wide, and walked out onto a vast terrace paved with red bricks.

Elaina put her arm around my shoulders and we walked out together, followed by Sam. Warmed by the mid-day sun, we gazed at a vista of gently sloping hills, their lush green reflecting in the liquid surface of the lake.

As he inhaled the fresh pine-scented air, Sam's stooping shoulders seemed to straighten. The slight breeze ruffled his thin strands of hair, which protruded from beneath his Yarmulke, and a beatific smile lit up his face. "How long has it been?" he asked.

"Too long," Jacob said, inhaling the pine fragrance. He moved closer to his friend, and arm in arm, they both relished the moment.

Observing the quiet serenity and beauty of this spot, I was surprised that it existed at all. This place seemed almost holy in its harmonious blend of mountains that touched the sky, reflected in the water of the lake, the clear sharp air tinged by the encircling green. It appeared timeless, impervious to human hate and strife. Perhaps there was a God after all, I thought. How could such beauty exist without a creator? Sam believed in God. I too believed that God was good and wise. But then I was a child, one who could play even in midst of war.

At the Ursuline summer convent where we hid from war, during days of berry picking, games of hide and seek among the apple trees, when the sun was especially bright, and the laughter louder than usual, I had been able to briefly forget my worries. But then I would remember Mother. I hadn't seen her for three weeks. I worried because she'd never been away that long. Everyday I hoped she'd return to us, but she did not return. What could keep her away all these long weeks?

And if that hadn't been enough, there was Dora, my mother's friend. A few days earlier, when she had come to see Hania and me, I'd thought it was just one of her friendly visits. I knew she was concerned for our safety and I'm sure she meant well, but her words had caused me even more anguish. I listened in distress and confusion as she tried to warn me...

...*"You have to be strong. Now listen. There is a war on, and there are people who'll do anything for money. I hope no soldiers will come for you here. But, if they do, if you see those Gestapo uniforms, you must take Hania by the hand, and run, run as fast as you can..."*

Standing there by the lake, recalling Dora's words, I understood what she had been trying to tell me on that late August afternoon in 1942. But then, I could not take in her words. I should have been ready to run away from the Gestapo, ready to do all I could to save Haniushka and myself. But I didn't want to understand Dora, not then, not when I hoped that my mother would come back any day, as she always had before.

Besides, weren't we safe there? Why else would she have entrusted us to the Ursuline Sisters? Except for Dora, I had been certain that nobody knew that Hania and I were spending the summer with the Ursulines in the country.

Days passed, and still Mother hadn't returned. I was worried. Surely, I had thought, Dora didn't say these things just to frighten me. She was my mother's best friend. I knew she only wanted to help, but I hadn't known where to run for safety, hadn't known any safer place than the convent. Our mother was wise. Surely she wouldn't have left us if she thought the Sisters would not protect us. Dad used to call her his warrior. Indeed I had seldom seen her cry. She was strong. But after the Nazis took Dad away, she had become distracted, sad; I had even seen her cry one day, when she thought she was alone...

...Her face buried in her hands, she hears my steps, looks up

42

to see me standing on the veranda, and tries to smile. But she can't. Her eyes are red. Her cheeks are swollen. I run to wrap my arms round her shoulders, press my face to hers, and feel her tears on my cheek.

She's been gone so many times since Dad's arrest. She wants to find him, get him free somehow. I thing she searches every prison. That is why she's gone now. But she doesn't tell me where she goes. I never know when she'll come back. She'd spare me the worry if she could, I know, but she can't. This time she's been away so long. I hope she finds him...hope she'll come back...

Each time my mother returned from one of those trips, she had looked thinner, paler, and sadder. The time came when she hardly ever smiled, and I had seen how hard it was for her to pretend that all was well. Each time, when she left, I worried all the more. But at the same time, I hoped that all would be well once Mother succeeded in rescuing Dad.

And every time when she came back without him, our hopes faded and our fears grew stronger. I had felt Mother's distress, realized how very painful it was for her to fail so many times. Yet she refused to give up. She bribed officials, kept on asking questions, and continued to go off each time she learned of another camp where Father was imprisoned. Always she came back to us, except for that last time. That time she went, and did not return.

Those last few summer days had turned darker somehow. Nights were worse. I had been anxious, worried about both my mom and dad. Dora's warning words had kept me awake, fearing the Nazis would come one day, find us at the Convent and take us away. But no matter how I wracked my brain, I could think of no safe place to run for safety from the Nazis.

Chapter 5

The next few days, our little group of survivors stayed at the hotel on the lake. Jacob elevated the janitor's position to handyman/cook, and taught him to keep kosher, by separating the dishes used for milk products from those used for meat. Neither Jacob nor Sam needed to worry much about keeping the food strictly kosher. The larder was empty except for some potatoes, flour, and a scattering of cabbage and carrots. There was certainly no meat around, nor milk for that matter. But the fare was plentiful, and we began to lose some of our skeleton-like appearance. My cheeks filled out a bit, while the sores on my feet turned to hard callused skin.

The lake was lovely and peaceful, with a narrow path surrounding it. I liked to walk along this path every day. Each morning I'd take the same route to a spot where it was blocked by a huge granite boulder. I liked to sit on a partially submerged flat rock, my feet dangling in the water, and watch tiny colorful fish nibble my toes. It didn't hurt, just tickled a bit.

The heady aroma of pine trees mixed with a scattering of needles across the moist earth reminded me of the Carpathian Mountains and the hotel where our family spent the holidays. I recalled our walks along a path, much like this one, with Haniushka sitting on Dad's shoulders, her plump little fingers wrapped in his hair, and Mother calling, "Watch out Hania! You'll pull out the last bit of hair he has left."

"His hair is stronger than my fingers," Hania would respond.

Those few days I spent with my new friends at the hotel on the lake seemed almost idyllic. I took my lone walks and thought of my family and going home. I was impatient for Mother's arms.

44

Some part of me probably knew better, but the little girl within held on to the hope and imagined it a reality. Now, with the war over, everything would again be as it once was. Daydreams of homecoming became my solace as I walked by the lake.

That's why I preferred to go alone, but when Elaina asked to come along, I couldn't refuse, not when I thought of her kindness. Though we'd only met a few days earlier, Elaina seemed determined to take care of me. She rummaged through the closets of strangers to insure that I had clean underwear, warm clothes and dry shoes to wear, and at mealtimes she always made certain that my plate was filled.

Elaina seemed to be acting on some need to fulfill her maternal instincts. Had she been married? Could she have had children at some point? I didn't want to ask, but suspected she may have, and that her children had been taken from her. So when Elaina asked if she could come along, I stretched my hand to her and said, "Yes, of course."

We walked on a bed of spongy pine needles. The lake glistened with reflected sunlight, and when the shore trail forked, we turned right and followed the inland path along a stream towards a waterfall. Elaina marveled at the deep shade, the height of the trees, and the aroma of pinewoods. I taught her a game I'd invented. It involved looking up at the branches to see how each one twisted to form a design against the sky. Elaina was a fast learner, and took up the game quickly. A twisted branch became a snake, or an eel, while a straight one looked like a sword.

"Look, there's the head of a dog up there."

"No, that's a hungry wolf." Elaina laughed.

By the time we reached the waterfall, we were both laughing. Elaina took her shoes and socks off, and without testing the water, waded in. "Cold!" she yelled, jumping back.

For those few moments, we felt almost carefree, but then as if on a signal, we fell silent. Suddenly, there were no more shapes in the sky, only the dense wood, and the dark path.

"I want to go home." I announced.

"Where is that?" Elaina asked.

"Krakow," I answered.

"Thought you were a Warsaw girl?"

45

"Yes, but we left just before they locked the last gate of the Warsaw Ghetto. We moved to Krakow."

I had survived. I kept hoping that my mother, Hania and, please God, Daddy too had lived through the ordeal. Hope kept me going. Hope made me remember. Walking through the woods with the scent of pine triggering my memories, I'd imagine that wondrous moment of coming home, my mom's warm breath on my face, her hugs and kisses. I wanted to believe, had to imagine the day of our reunion. We'd pretend that it was all a nightmare, nothing really happened, and we were together now. I'd hug them all at once, Mom and Dad, and Haniushka. I could hardly wait for that wonderful moment. The urge to move on overwhelmed me and I resolved to tell Jacob that I'd be leaving in the morning, alone if necessary.

But even before I could begin to tell him my plans, he had an announcement of his own. Right after dinner, Jacob stood at the head of the table and told us it was all arranged. We'd be going back to Poland. A small convoy with five Russian soldiers had arrived at the hotel that morning while we were out walking in the woods. Jacob had introduced himself to Captain Slobotkin, and asked if the convoy was heading to Poland, and if so would there be enough room for us to come along. The two trucks were carrying cargo, but Captain Slobotkin told Jacob there'd be enough room for us. "It will be a bumpy ride," he added, but he agreed to let us ride in the back of the trucks.

It was still dark when we started the next morning. Elaina insisted on taking the warmest clothes, and even ran after me with the heavy wool coat she had found hanging in the closet. Then she ran back to get some woolen blankets for each of us.

We clambered aboard and tried to make ourselves as comfortable as possible. Although a stack of big square boxes filled the back of the trucks, there was sufficient room for all of us. I sat on a box next to Elaina, and we used the ones behind for backrests.

Once the "girls," as Jacob and Sam referred to us, were taken care of, the two men took their seats on similar boxes in the second truck. I wrapped my blanket around me from head to toe, and snuggled in so only my nose was exposed to air. Cold wind swept in under the flaps of the truck, but the heavy woolen coat along with the blanket kept me warm.

The two trucks followed Captain Slobotkin and his driver in the lead car as we sped past towns, villages, and farmhouses with occasional dogs barking and chasing after. I listened to the hypnotic pattern of wheels on rough pavement, and leaning on Elaina in the cocoon of the warm blanket, I fell into a deep sleep. I was tired, but Elaina's pointy shoulder poked my ear. I sought a softer spot to lean on, and finding none I slumbered on. Hours later, the trucks pulled to a stop with a loud hiss of brakes, and I woke up.

At dusk, when the light of day began to blend with the darkening of the night and the sky was streaked with red and orange, our little convoy stopped in front of an old wooden structure. A sign above the front door read, "Come Inn." I peered in through the lighted windows and saw several men talking, eating, and drinking at a large round table. Looking at them, I felt thirsty and hungry. Everything hurt, and I was glad to climb off the truck and stretch my stiff muscles.

Captain Slobotkin led us inside. Coming from the crisp chill air into the warmth of a wood fire blazing on the hearth, I felt my cheeks becoming flushed. Candlelight illuminated the bar, giving it a dreamlike quality. All conversation and laughter ceased, as the men round that table saw the broad shouldered Russian Captain, their enemy turned victor, gun holstered, but with refugees from a concentration camp in tow. The locals stopped, drinks midway between table and lip, and gaped at the hollow cheeked, skeletal figures who stared right back.

"We must look like their worst nightmares come calling," I muttered under my breath. My eyes on the bright movement of the flames on the hearth, I breathed in the fresh aroma of wood smoke, and tried to ignore the stares of the men. Jacob and Captain Slobotkin went to speak to the man behind the bar. A few moments later, they came back with several room keys. "Here's number four," Jacob told Elaina, handing her the key. "I'm told it's a double, so you two can bunk together." After a meal of potatoes and cabbage, I followed Elaina up to our room. "Who is

paying for it?" I asked, as Elaina inserted the key in the lock.
"Captain Slobotkin and Jacob organized everything." Elaina laughed.

"Organized?" I remembered what the word meant in camps. It meant to take or steal whatever could be found wherever it was found. Bread, soup, a blanket, the lower bunk, all of it was scarce and the younger more aggressive fellows took what they found and called it organizing. Noticing my discomfort at profiting from taking what was not freely offered, Elaina snapped at me. "You can always sleep outside in the truck, if you prefer."

Well, I certainly didn't prefer to spend my night, teeth chattering in a freezing truck, so I followed Elaina up the steps to the second floor. We found room number four, and Elaina inserted the key in the lock. We entered a small room, its walls covered by worn faded wallpaper. There was an ancient wardrobe, a couple of narrow beds, with a small step stool between.

Another door opened onto a smallish water closet. What luxury. We wouldn't have to visit the outhouse in the middle of the night. There was also a small sink with a single faucet in the room. The room was warm and Elaina opened the tall narrow window to let in fresh air. Then she tried to turn the water tap. Nothing at first, but after a few moments some brownish water trickled out. We watched it run and it cleared up a few moments later.

"Want to wash first?" Elaina asked.

I didn't need coaxing, washed quickly, and then with my eyes closed, my hands groped for the towel.

"You are helpless," Elaina laughed, handing it over. "We're only about twenty kilometers from the Polish border," she continued. "Have you decided where you'll go first?"

"Krakow, I hope to find at least some of my family there. Are the soldiers going to Poland? Can they take us all the way?"

Elaina nodded, "I think we'll be going first thing in the morning. Let's get some sleep."

We got ready for bed, and although I had slept for the most part of our trip, I had no trouble falling asleep almost immediately.

The soldiers remained in the bar swallowing vodka by the bottle. They had been drinking steadily since shortly after dinner.

Then around midnight they started to sing and toast one another. Even in my sleep, I could hear their loud banter. And why not; they were happy at the prospect of going home.

The bartender must have been tired from standing on his feet for more than twelve hours and probably hoped they'd give it up and go to sleep, so he could close for the night. In my sleep, I heard one soldier in a loud bellicose voice asking "Where are the women?" Hearing his bellows in my sleep, I thought I was having a nightmare.

"Room number four, where is it?" He kept repeating. "Room number four, I want the women in room number four."

He raised such a ruckus with his loud yelling and his drunken stumbling up the stairs that he woke up Elaina. She staggered from her bed, and crossed over to where I shivered, my face buried in the pillow.

"Get up, quick," she hissed, pulling at my arm.

The man's voice grew louder, closer, as Elaina tried to drag me out of bed. "Get up, get up." Elaina whispered in a voiceless hiss as she pulled at me in exasperation.

Finally, more asleep than awake, I dragged myself out of bed and stumbled to my feet. The room door shuddered with a loud bang. Startled, we both jumped at the sound. The soldier had found our room, and was banging at the door with both his fists. I was fully awake, frightened and bewildered. Elaine grabbed a blanket and threw it around my shoulders. She pulled me across the room and shoved me into the tiny water closet.

"Lock the door!" Elaina hissed.

Alone inside the small cubicle, I turned the lock as instructed. I was cold and frightened, and I wished Elaina was with me. A thin sheen of cold sweat covered my skin, and even after I wrapped the blanket around my shoulders and tucked it under me, I couldn't stop shaking. I thought our hotel room door would come off its hinges from the thunderous blows of the drunken soldier.

My mouth and lips went dry; I thought they'd break into a thousand pieces. A thin sheen of cold sweat covered my skin. I slid down to the floor in the tiny space between the wall, the door, and the toilet bowl.

Suddenly, the banging on the room door ceased. Silence. Did he get tired of banging? Had he gone away? Uncertain, and afraid to make a sound, I stayed put.

A sudden sharp crack at the door to our room, dashed my hopes. Then came a louder thud. It sounded as if the door, had been smashed from its hinges had crashed onto the floor. The soldier's heavy steps thundered through the room.

Elaina gasped. I held my breath and pressed my ear to the door. Quiet, but a moment later I heard a hush of soft slippers moving across the floor. Was Elaina trying to back away from the soldier? Why was she moving towards the window? Was she going to jump? I wanted to call for help, but there was no window in my tiny cubicle. I could do nothing but wait.

A harder, sharper sound of heavy boots followed Elaina's soft footsteps. She stopped. Was she trapped between the window and the soldier? Would she jump out the window in her need to get away? I wanted to open my door, to stop Elaina from jumping but my bare feet felt cemented to that cold stone floor. There seemed no room for me to move. I remained crouched down and terrified.

"Shouldn't you be asleep by now?" Elaina asked in her quiet soothing voice. "It's a bit late for a visit." How could she be so calm?

"Yeah, let's go to bed." The soldier rumbled with laughter. I could hear the sound of a stool being shoved., scraping across the rough floor.

"Come on sweet thing," he taunted. "I've got something for you."

Someone stumbled, fell to the floor. Was it Elaina? I stifled an involuntary cry and I pressed my hands over my ears, but I couldn't stop the sound of Elaina's groans and the soldier's lascivious whispers.

I needed to replace this sound with another, and tried to imagine violins, a full orchestra, playing the waltz from the Vienna Woods, the waltz my mother loved. I had always associated it with happy moments. Mother loved it when I played it for her. Yet, now it was wrong. Something about the sound of that music in my mind made me want to run. Terror gripped me anew.

I pulled the blanket tighter over my head, and whimpered in

confusion. All noise stopped. I hugged my knees to my chest, and rocked back and forth in my little cubicle on the floor. Perhaps I dozed for a bit, but came to attention with the thud of heavy boots pacing across the floor. The door which the soldier had smashed down to the floor earlier that night now rattled beneath his weight. I held my breath and listened to his heavy footsteps retreating down the hall.

Why did he hurt Elaina? He didn't even know her. It seemed to me that the hurt he inflicted had turned into slimy, oozing mud that now appeared to be seeping under the water closet door towards me. I imagined it creeping around me. Felt dirty and ashamed. I had failed Elaina because I was afraid to leave the relative safety of my tiny space. But then I reminded myself that it was Elaina who was hurt. She needed to be comforted, and I didn't know how to do that. I felt repulsed by what the soldier did to Elaina. Was it contamination I feared? Is that why I was so afraid to touch her?

I wanted to banish the memory of Elaina's whimpers, wanted to forget those horrid guttural groans that issued from the soldier's throat. I wanted these sounds expunged from my brain, the sounds of rape silenced in my ears. So I stayed in my cramped position till I didn't know if I could ever move again. Elaina was hurt, and here I was feeling sorry for myself. That was disgusting I thought. Enough! I decided, and forced myself to stand, and turn the key in the lock.

Elaina lay unmoving on the floor curled up into herself. I knelt beside her, and turned her face towards me. I kissed her, caressed her smeared and puffy cheeks, but she didn't respond to me. Eyes rimmed in red, she stared at the ceiling.

"I'm so sorry, Elaina." I asked, touching her arm for comfort.

Elaina made an attempt at a reassuring smile. It came off as a grimace.

"He didn't touch you, thank God," she sighed.

I leaned down to her, and tried to lift her body off the floor. "Help, Elaina. I want to get you to bed" I whispered.

She was slight and didn't weigh all that much, so I was able to help her back into bed, and tuck the blanket around her. I filled the small glass by the sink and brought her some water to drink. She drained it and I brushed Elaina's hair off her forehead, kissed her, and whispered, "Rest, sleep now."

I also tried to sleep, but one unanswered question kept me awake. How could we look at any of those soldiers again? The one who hurt Elaina would be there in the morning, all loud talk and swagger. How could we bring ourselves to face that soldier? I certainly wanted never to see any of them again.

Yet I wanted to go home, and the only available transportation was those Russian trucks. I was conflicted with a frustration that kept my body in motion. I twisted and turned, kicked away the blanket, and when chilled tried to cover myself again. I wrestled with the mess I'd made, but in the end, exhaustion won out. I decided to leave Jacob to deal with the problem. He'll know what to do, I told myself, and allowed my mind to shut down.

No sooner did I fall asleep, it seemed I was awakened again. It was morning. Sounds of imminent departure came from the hallway and the stairs. I heard men's voices. I recognized Jacob's a little way down the corridor. I looked for Elaina, but saw only her empty bed, the blankets tossed aside. Then I heard her soft voice. It was followed by a bellow from Captain Slobotkin. From the sound of it, Captain Slobotkin was angry. Surely, he couldn't be mad at Elaina. She had done nothing wrong. Then I heard Elaina talking again, but couldn't make out what she was saying. Jacob spoke next, and again I couldn't make out his words, but his voice was calm and soothing.

Shortly after that, Elaina came back into the room.

"What, still in bed? You'd better move. There's little time," she said, folding her own blanket.

"You can go. I'm staying here."

"Don't be an idiot." Elaina snapped.

"How can I go? I can't face him."

"You can't! That's rich. Listen, you don't have to face him. Captain Slobotkin put that guy in the slammer, and promised no further harm would come to either of us. He's even appointed a guard to make sure nothing bad happens again."

I felt better knowing the stupid drunk was going to get his

comeuppance, and so allowed myself to be persuaded to join the convoy for the rest of the way. I trusted both Elaina and Jacob. If they said it would be all right, then I wasn't going to argue.

The trucks rattled on, passing farms and small towns, on and on through the day, and on throughout the night. The two of us talked till there was nothing more to say. At one point, I dozed, but even as the truck took us nearer to home, I had restless dreams. I stirred in my sleep and woke shivering with fear, my hands balled into fists. Yet I couldn't remember what had frightened me. So I snuggled closer to Elaina and fell asleep again.

The Waltz from the Vienna Woods got mixed with the piercing whistle of falling bombs, and I'd wake again to the sound of buildings imploding into rubble. To still my agitation I thought about my cousin Helena and the wondrous stories she told.

Was she still alive? I didn't know. I hadn't seen or spoken to her since the start of war. Helena was so pretty. Had she become like other holocaust survivors not quite dead yet not quite alive? The few of us who remained wandered across the land, our roots severed, with no home, family, or country. Like other Holocaust survivors, I now traversed the land which had been so recently ruled by Hitler. All of us had this one thing in common; our need to reclaim some part of what was lost.

The dreams of homecoming and my hopes of finding my parents and Haniushka helped me endure those long days and nights of imprisonment. To dispel the darkness, I continued to paint images of homecoming in my head. I pictured that wonderful day, over and over again, that first moment of hugs and embraces. It had to be so. How else could I go on?

Yet the doubts I so staunchly refused to acknowledge during the day turned to nightmares that plagued me when I slept. So it had gone all those years, when I used daydreams to fight against nightmares. Perhaps it was those daydreams that allowed me to survive the years of cruelty and deprivation. The longer the war had dragged on, the more I had lost myself in daydreams; the closer to home, the more fervent had been my hope that my family was alive and waiting for me.

For now each of us, Elaina, Jacob, and Samuel, was a seeker for some piece of what remained of our earlier lives. But we each had to follow a different path. Elaina planned to return to Warsaw where she had lived before the war. I needed to look for my family in Krakow. I'm coming, I thought, dreaming of the apartment on the second floor, where the balcony over- looked the vacant lot across the street. They had to be there. They must be there waiting for me. That was the only reality I could acknowledge.

We traveled all that day and through the night. I awoke to the gray thin light of morning and recognized the small resort called Zakopanie. I was back in Poland. This little mountain town brought happy memories of family holidays. This used to be the playground where we spent many a careless day hiking, swimming, or just feasting our eyes on the surroundings before we were ripped apart.

The truck pulled to a stop in front of the train station. Krakow was not far. Maybe by this time tomorrow, I'd be home. I'd miss my travel companions. I had grown to respect Jacob, cared about Samuel and his gentle ways, and really appreciated Elaina's kind and caring nature. They sustained me and helped me to go on. Yet now I could hardly wait to leave them.

Captain Slobotkin sent his driver to inquire and we learned that the trains were running on schedule. In fact, there was one scheduled to leave for Krakow later that afternoon. I could hardly keep from jumping up and down and I kept hugging every one, even Captain Slobotkin. After all, He made it possible.

"You must be patient," Captain Slobotkin told me. "Don't expect to get there in two hours. These days train schedules are like the weather, uncertain. The train may not leave as expected, and when it does, it will have to make numerous stops. Our troop trains have priority over the passenger trains. It may take a whole night before you reach Krakow."

I thanked the Captain for his kindness, and prepared to wait as long as required. But all the same, now that I was so close to home, I couldn't help being anxious and impatient.

Captain Slobotkin told us that he too was scheduled to go home in the next few days. Then smiling broadly he gave each of us a train ticket home. I couldn't be more grateful and I thanked him again. He gave me a bear hug, wished me good journey, and I kissed him on the cheek. We were all very thankful for his kindness, and told him so over and over again. He laughed his low rumble of a laugh and wished us each a pleasant and speedy journey.

Our little group prepared to wait. I walked arm in arm with Elaina towards the train station. We planned to wait there until it was time to board. The rail station waiting room was dark and cool. We sat on some wooden benches. We had been thrown together for a little while like so much refuse, strangers who banded together in mutual need. I would always remember every one of them, though I didn't know if any of us would ever meet again.

Our thoughts followed in their separate ways towards our families, and as we waited for the train that would take us home, we were each lost in our own thoughts. Tomorrow would be my homecoming day.

Chapter 6

Less than a half a block away, there it was at last, the familiar house at the end of the street. I glanced up at the balcony to see our pale green curtains blowing in the soft breeze that came through the open French doors. At last, here it was, my moment of homecoming just as I had dreamed it all through those long years in camps. Memories. They all came rushing back, the memories of home that had helped me endure hunger and thirst, the cruelty of the SS, and my fear of them. During those terrible moments when I needed Mother's arms around me, it was the hope I'd see them all again that gave me the power to survive in the damp and the cold, behind the electrified barbed wire fence.

Daydreams of home and family made my separation from them almost bearable. I endured because I believed the war would end one day, and I'd return home to Mom, Dad, and Haniushka.

Now, glancing up at the balcony, I trembled with anticipation. Quickening my steps beneath the protective shade of the familiar old oak trees, I broke into a run passing apple trees and marigolds growing in the empty lot across the street. That lot was just as I remembered it. Nothing had changed, and I ran almost certain now they were waiting for me upstairs. Mom would open the door, and I'd fall into her arms. Then it would be my dad's turn to hug me, while little Haniushka draped herself over my leg, begging to be picked up. Only a few moments now, and I'll be giving and receiving a thousand kisses, one for each hour we had been apart. I my heart banged in my breast. My hands felt at once icy and sweaty, and by the time I reached the front door to our apartment house, I was out of breath. I paused for a moment, then entered the vestibule and mounted the stairs, two at a time.

56

At the familiar door on the second floor, I stopped. I could not bring myself to knock. I had to face it now as I asked the one question I had been avoiding for weeks: who would come to open the door at my knock?

All these years I needed to believe they were alive, but now doubts crowded my mind. I began to suspect that only my fantasies had survived. Now as I stood before that familiar door, I felt fear. It was the same fear I had experienced all along but refused to acknowledge, when only dreams could camouflage my dread and provide escape...

...His grip is like a vise that holds me to the spot, while Hania stretches out her hand to me...she's so frightened... I cannot touch her, or go near... he will not let me go...... another SS man...his face is cut of stone... grips little Hania by her arm... yanks her up into the air... makes her fly like a rag doll...while my arm twists behind my back, his grip tightens...keeps me from going to her... I hear her final whimper... the door clangs shut...

The image of Haniushka's tiny hand stretching out to me remained imprinted on my mind—a memory I could not repress. Even as I daydreamed that she was somehow rescued and taken back home, I couldn't obliterate the echo of that heavy door slamming shut, cutting Haniushka from my sight.

My dreams were nothing but air and wisps of an impossible hope. How could I have thought that Haniushka could survive?

And yet I had made this long, long journey back home, hoping and dreaming they'd all be there waiting for me. Now, as I stood before that old familiar door, I was afraid. "Please God, let it not be some stranger," I whispered. The shiny brass ring felt cold and hard in my sweating hand.

My heart drummed in my chest so loud I scarcely heard the sound of high heels clicking across the parquet floor. The door opened. A woman in a flowery print silk dress stood in the open door. I felt faint, and had to steady myself against the doorframe, my eyes riveted to the printed red roses spattered across the white fabric of the woman's dress. She wore a matching hat with flowers that looked like great stains of blood.

Startled to see me standing at her front door, the woman picked up her purse from the hall table with quick, birdlike movements that suggested she was on her way out, and in a hurry.

"What do you want?" she asked, spitting her words like bullets from her mouth.

I could not control my shivers. Words stuck in my throat.

"Well, say something, I haven't got all day."

"I, I am..." my words refused to leave my mouth.

"Yes, yes, what is it?"

"Please... I need to speak to you. I used to live here." Now my words spilled and fell over one another. I was desperate to make the woman understand.

She looked me up and down, noticed my clothes hanging loosely like rags on a scarecrow. She saw my flat and bony chest. Her eyes grazed my hollow cheeks, my fragile white skin stretched over bony hands and fingers. Her eyes slid down to the worn boots on my feet. They showed every mile of the German ground I had covered during my long walk home.

"Ah," she said. "You're a Jew."

"Yes, you see... it's my home...I live...I mean, used to... before... we lived here... hoped to find them... here, my mom and dad..." My stammer and stutter came to an abrupt stop.

The woman grimaced, as if she'd tasted something bitter. The well-applied cosmetics creased as her face distorted. She made her way across the threshold, as I stepped back to avoid her touch.

"I know nothing about your folks," she said, about to close the door.

Without pausing to think, I reached out to stop her. "Wait!" I pleaded.

The woman stopped, door still open, while in the foyer a clock began to sound the hour. The woman glanced impatiently to see the time and said, "I really must go now." Yet something stopped her from closing the door.

Each stroke of the gong reverberated against the brass. I listened to the familiar sound. I saw the clock, the gilded mirror hanging over the hall table, the old umbrella stand. each and every item in the same spot as I remembered. This was my home, and

58

though none of my family was here, I felt an urge to see it one last time.

"Could I just see inside? Please."

"I have a luncheon appointment," the woman said in a dismissing manner.

"Surely, you can spare a few moments." I pleaded.

The woman sighed and let me in. Brisk, she led the way to the kitchen. Stopping at the sink, she filled a glass with water, drank it down, then as an afterthought offered some to me. I accepted the glass, and gulped the cool clear liquid, feeling embarrassed by my thirst and the woman's obvious impatience.

I followed her quick steps to our living/dining room. The familiar white tiled stove stood in one corner of the room. I remembered sitting there on cold winter afternoons reading with my back against the warm tiles. Dad called me his kitten.

As I glanced at the table, I noticed the first unfamiliar item in the house, a gaily flowered tablecloth. It didn't belong to us, but it covered our table, which I recognized by its gracefully curving legs whose bottoms were carved in the shape of cat's paws.

I closed my eyes for moment, trying to imagine Haniushka, great pink bow in her hair, sitting at this table with her paper doll cutouts. She used to be quite the artist with those dolls, her pudgy little fingers curling around the crayons, dressing each doll in crayon colored costume. The table used to be covered by her creations. I opened my eyes, and looked at the now empty table. Reality hit me like a hard fist. I had to acknowledge that none of us would ever sit at this table again. My mom and dad and Hania, the whole family that I loved and longed to see again would never be coming home.

In a hurry to finish the tour, the woman led the way to the bedroom. I paused at the foot of the large mahogany double bed where my parents used to sleep. I saw the familiar wardrobes, the night tables, and the miniature clock. It stood in its accustomed place, on top of the nightstand next to Mom's side of the bed.

"It is fragile," Mom used to say. "But if you promise to be careful, you may hold it for a little while."

This was my favorite object in the room, less than two inches tall, with its silver casing and jeweled blue face. I liked the feel of it and the sound of its tiny silvery bell as it announced each hour of the day. I wanted to hold it now, if only for a moment, and so began to reach for it, but I paused, hand in mid air, as I heard the woman's impatient voice. "What is it you want?"

As if caught red-handed, I felt apologetic. God only knows why. I smiled a lame smile, and muttered, "Everything is in the same place, just as I remember it."

Silent, the woman maintained her stony little smile. I felt embarrassed and angry all at the same time. She made me feel like a thief, and I wanted to hide my hand in my pocket, but held back. The woman had no right to act as if I was going to steal that miniature clock. It belonged to us in the first place, and I had no way of knowing how this stranger came to own it now. All the same I wished I could take it for a keepsake.

But this was no longer my family home. I took one last look around the room where my parents used to sleep. I knew they would never again sleep in this bed. I'd never again see my mother's black hair spread upon her white pillow, never see my dad's arms open at seeing me come in to greet them each morning. There'd be no good morning kisses in this room for me, ever. This was real, and I had no way to deny it.

As the familiar door of what used to be my home shut behind me, I felt lightheaded and dazed. My throat constricted; my heart pounded and I gulped for air. The imagination that allowed me to visualize a happy family reunion was replaced by chilling reality. I had no Mother, no Father, and no Haniushka, no one to come back to. Where just a little while earlier, I was filled with joy and anticipation; now I felt stunned, oblivious to my surroundings, and lost. Like a pricked balloon with all the air gone, I now felt empty. I didn't have any tears left, not for my lost family or for me. Had I turned to stone?

Standing alone at the top of the stairs, I felt faint. Great sorrow overcame me like a shroud, and made me blind and deaf. Seeing nothing, I stumbled down the stairs and out the door. I had no place to go.

I started walking like an automaton, senseless of where I was or which way I was heading. I felt empty at first. Then rage exploded within me, undirected at first, but so strong I felt my

60

anger could blow me to pieces. I wanted to smash at something or someone, but there was no one handy to rail at, so I turned against myself.

Whose fault was it, if not mine? It was I who blinded me. Through all the years of war I clung to a fantasy, an unfounded belief that I could return home after the war and our lives would continue as if nothing had happened. I maintained this blind hope after the bombs came whistling down chimneys, after houses toppled into ruins, and Nazis marched into my family courtyard. After all that, I surely had to know that nothing could ever be the same. But then, I was only nine-years-old. If I feared the hard sound of marching boots, if I trembled at the sight of those hard angry faces of soldiers who penetrated our neighborhood and our homes, I stilled my fear and hid in the one place they could not touch me, my imagination. I daydreamed and pretended that what was happening to me was only a scary game.

Now I had no more stories to spin. I could no longer hide inside my head. Here was reality: I had no home, no family, and no place to go. But my feet kept moving, one after the other while my mind filled with memories of bombs, smashed buildings, hungry beggars in the street, and the jail where I had to urinate into a steel pail in the middle of the night, thereby waking up my cellmates, who complained that I was making too much noise,.

Six years of war, and from the first day to the last, I had been telling myself fairytales, and spinning empty wishes out of nothing but the need to believe that my family would be there for me in the end. Only an idiot child could cling to such a hope, I thought, unable to forgive myself for my own stupidity.

I should have known better, certainly if not by the time of Father's arrest, then surely the following summer when Mother also disappeared. That summer it had all come to an end. I had those three nightmares a few weeks after Mother went missing. Death dreams are what they had been, terrifying apparitions that came out of the night. I had hardly recognized them as Mother and Father. They had tried to speak to me, but I was too frightened to hear them. Even as I watched their mouths move, I struggled to get free of the dread they instilled in me by their appearance. I refused to listen and hear what they had to tell me. Each time I had that awful dream, I'd forced myself out of my nightmare and into wakefulness: Three night visits in all, two from Mother and one from Father. But I had been paralyzed with fear at each encounter, hadn't listened, and had forced myself awake.

I didn't know why or how these frightful apparitions had come to me in my sleep. Had they been trying to warn me of the coming danger? I could not say, not then, when all I could feel was terror. I had been twelve-years-old that summer, and could not imagine death when sunflowers ripened in the fields. So I had chosen fantasy instead. All those years I had made myself believe that my mom and dad were alive, and we'd all be reunited as soon as the war was over.

Now as my aimless steps covered the streets of Krakow, I was remembering the events of that summer. I shuddered remembering how the Gestapo had arrived at the convent in the night; remembering their snatching tiny Haniushka away, their interrogation chambers and the never ending questions, and all the horror that had followed. They had come while I slept and wakened me into a nightmare that lasted three long years.

I had tried to escape those years of loss and pain, years of hunger and fear, and in a sense I had. I had escaped into my imagination. But now I was done with all pretenses; I could no longer deny what should have been obvious to me all along, that before reaching the age of seven, Haniushka had become part of Hitler's "final solution," and that my parents were never going to return to me. I could no longer hide from the knowledge that there was nothing left of my family, not even their graves...

...Daddy is getting ready to leave for work. But this morning is different somehow. Standing there holding this white armband, he looks kind of sad. He's trying to wrap it round the sleeve of his suit, but his fingers can't get a good grip on the safety pin. Rising up on my tiptoes, I help him fasten it in place. I don't know why he'd choose to wear this white armband with the blue star on top. I've never seen anyone wear such a thing before.

It is the Star of David. My great-grandfather calls it Mogen David, that's Hebrew for the Shield of David. I learned about King David in school. He shot the great big giant, Goliath, and saved our people. It happened a very long time ago, but we remember him as our great hero. Zyde says King David had a lot of help from the Almighty. It was God who shielded David from harm. That's why the Jewish star is also known as the Shield of David. It came from God. My Zyde talks with God every day, and I wonder why I can't hear God the way Zyde can.

Once he tried to explain to me about the Star of David, said that it makes us know who we are, where we came from, and what it means to be a Jew. But I don't know what he's saying, especially when he mumbles in Hebrew. I asked him once what he was saying in Hebrew, and he translated, "Blessed are you God, Shield of David." I think this blessing is the way my Zyde thanks God for shielding King David from harm.

I understand the words, but I am not certain if God shields us all, or only the great kings, like King David.

Now, here is my dad wearing the blue and white Star of David. Does that mean he has God wrapped round his arm? If so, then God is his shield. But then why does he look so sad?

When I ask why he wears it, he just presses his lips tight, the way he always does when he doesn't want to answer. But whenever I hug him good-by these days, he holds me tighter than ever, as if he's afraid to let me go. This morning I feel that something is very wrong, but I don't know what it is.

Time for school, and I must hurry along. I'm almost out the door, when Mom comes running after me with a little brown parcel in one hand, a yellow patch in the other, and a safety pin between her lips.

"You forgot your lunch, again," she complains, and stuffs the brown parcel into my schoolbag. Then she pins the yellow patch on my jacket, and I see that it is also the Jewish star. Looks just like Dad's, except it is yellow. Mother seems distracted, as she bends to plant a good-bye kiss on my cheek. Nothing seems right this morning, and I will not eat lunch today. I'll just give it away to one of the beggars. There are so many...

What I could not grasp when I was nine-years-old became clear to me now that I was fifteen. The connection between the wearing of the Jewish star and the events that destroyed my family now stood out in my mind like an equation written on a blackboard.

A couple of weeks after they marched into Poland, the Nazis issued orders. Every Jewish man, woman, and child over six had to wear the Jewish Star. It had to be fastened on to our clothing at all times. It was to be worn as an armband or a patch. All of us Jews were forced to wear these armbands and patches everywhere we went. We had to wear them or go to jail. Only now did I begin to realize that with this order the Nazis signaled their intent to mark, isolate, and hunt us down.

They built the Ghetto to separate us from our non-Jewish neighbors. They used the Star of David as an emblem to mark us as the despised, the pariahs, the sub-humans not fit to live in the community of ordinary people. This emblem displayed on our clothes is what allowed the Nazis to impose cataclysmic changes on our lives...

...Dad comes home and pulls it off his sleeve, as if it is a brand that burns his arm. After he throws it on the little table by the front door, he straightens up, as if some heavy weight has been lifted off his shoulder. Only then does he give me a hug and a kiss.

Mom is less accepting. She rips the despised armband from her arm and looks as though she would throw it away if she could. She can't, so she says, "They've marked us for scorn. We're not some cattle to be branded and marked for slaughter."

Why is she so angry? I think that the Star of David is good. Zyde says it connects us to the Almighty, so how could it be a mark of scorn? It's more like a badge of honor, I think, but when I ask Daddy why he and Mom dislike it so, he gives me one of his sad smiles, and says nothing.

"Well, I wear it with pride," I insist.

Mother is not one to keep quiet. "The Nazis want us to wear it, because they mean to dishonor us, make of us objects of derision. This symbol you'd wear with pride is meant to mark you as different from all the others."

She seems so angry. I'm afraid to ask, but I do anyway, "What others?"

"Everybody who's not a Jew." She is furious.

64

That's really confusing. Most of the people I know are Jewish. So what if we are different, I think about my Bubby and Zyde. It's true, neither of them can speak Polish very well, and the long black silk coat my Old Zyde wears looks very different from clothes worn by others. So what? I love them and they love me, and I really don't care if we're different from the others. We're just fine the way we are. But things have gotten so unpleasant recently. Mom frowns all the time. Dad hardly speaks anymore, and I'm afraid to ask them any more questions.

I hear Mom saying that she wants to get away and move to another town, where no one knows us. Dad disagrees. He wants to stay here and wait.

"Wait for what?"

I'm almost asleep, when I hear Mom's voice through the wall.

These days my father is always trying to calm Mother. I can hear him say, "Shah, you'll wake the children."

"Oh, and is that the worse that can happen?"

One morning as I'm getting ready for school, Mom tells me that I don't have to go. "Why should I stay home? I'm not sick."

She gets angry, tries to explain. Finally I get it, no school for Jewish children.

Mom tells me that perhaps in a few days I may go to our teacher's house. She has invited all the children from school to come and learn in her house, but there's a problem. The Nazis have decreed that it is a crime for any teacher to teach children in her home. Disobeyers will suffer the penalty of jail or worse. So I guess I'll have to stay ignorant for the rest of my life. But I don't even have time to worry about growing up stupid, because there are new signs everywhere.

"Juden Verboten!" "No Jews!" These signs are plastered all over, huge, ugly signs that spell out rejection. "Juden Rouse!" Those signs spell "Jews keep out!"

We may no longer visit shops, theatres, movie houses, and parks. All the many places we used to go are now forbidden to us. We're not even allowed to play in the playgrounds. Signs appear everywhere. I've never seen so many ugly signs on shop doors and the walls of buildings. Most of them are scrawled in red paint that

65

looks like blood, and they appear everywhere in variations of the same rant and rage. "Jews get out!" "No Jews Allowed." Many of the Jewish shops have been broken into and looted, their windows smashed with rocks, and every day more hateful signs appear.

Our home, our courtyard, and our whole neighborhood, the place I've grown up in and love is all changing, becoming something it never was. Jewish Ghetto is what they call it now. I don't know what that means.

Mom's been fuming for weeks now and Dad has been trying to keep her calm. Nothing helps. She keeps repeating. "We've got to get away, the sooner the better."

A new decree has been issued. No Jew may have any contact with non-Jews. Dad can no longer conduct his business, and Mother complains. "There's no money coming in, and one loaf of bread costs more than a week's supply of food before the war."

Mom no longer just shops. She now hunts for bargains on the black market. But there are no bargains to be had. And now they've started to build brick walls all around us. Mom tells Dad to stay in the house. She's seen Nazis out in the streets grabbing some of our men and older boys. They are forced to build these walls, laboring long days into night, while the Nazis stand guard with pointed rifles. Mom says that she had seen some of the older men become so tired that they can hardly stand on their feet let alone lift up a brick, and still they are forced to keep piling them on, one brick upon another.

Our household has become a refuge. None of us leave it except for my mom, and she only goes out to the black market for the food we need. Each time she comes back, she's got new horrors to report. The brick walls keep getting taller rising to nine, ten and even twelve feet in some spots. They're topped by rolls of barbed wire to keep people from trying to climb over. Mom urges Dad to stay out of the way. She doesn't want him to end up like those poor men who install the sharp iron barbs. This work pierces their hands and makes them bleed.

Fear pervades our neighborhood. But that is only the beginning. In other sections of town the Nazis are driving Jewish families away from their homes. These poor folks are forced to resettle into our neighborhood which is now called the Ghetto.

Two, three, and more of these families crowd into one small apartment. Things are getting very tight around here.

One morning when I get up, I discover our house is a mess. Boxes of clothes, pots, pans, our lovely china, flower vases, books, pictures, even the little miniature clock that I love so much, all these things go into boxes. My parents are packing, and they seem in a great hurry.

"What's this?" I ask, though I'm not sure I really want to know.

"We're moving," Dad says.

Mom is impatient with me. "Go pack your things. Don't stand there like a dummy."

But I stand as if rooted to the spot. Our home, my courtyard, everything I've loved has changed. I don't want to leave.

Mom is about to blow. "Move!" she yells. "Haven't you got eyes? Do you want to live behind brick walls?

"I will not go with you," I scream at the top of my lungs.

Hands folded across her chest, Mom just gives me that look of hers. I know what it means, but I'm not about ready to give up.

I stamp my foot. "You can't make me go. I want to stay here with Bubby. She can protect me."

Dad intervenes, speaking softly. "We want to stay here too, but we must go before they finish all the walls and lock the gates." His eyes seem to plead with Mom. He wants to keep peace between us.

Mom gentles a bit, "It is not safe for us to stay," she reasons.

But I don't want to be reasoned with. I only want life to go on as before. Why can't they understand that?...

We had no choice but to cut all ties to our home and family. My parents knew that not only our freedom, but also our very lives were at stake. Being marked, isolated, and imprisoned was just the beginning of who knew what? The Nazis hated the Jews. They proclaimed their hate and derision before the entire world. Mom and Dad realized that once the walling off was done, no Jew would be allowed outside of the Ghetto walls, so they decided to leave while they still could. I now understood why we had to leave the

Ghetto, why we had to change our Jewish sounding family name. I remembered how the Nazi police took to stopping people in the streets to check identity papers. They were looking for Jews, the way a farmer searches for weeds to destroy.

My parents must have thought we would be safe if we could obtain falsified papers under a Polish name and move somewhere else. So we moved to Krakow and I became Ludka Bronek. The Bronek family, that was us, rented an apartment in a lovely section of town. And to prove our new identity, every time we left the house, each one of us, even Haniushka, had to carry our new identity papers. My parents thought that these would provide a shield against arrest and imprisonment.

My given name had to undergo a minor change. I was named Ludka because it sounded similar to Rutka, and also because Polish Catholics preferred to name their daughters after Christian saints. As I was originally named after the Ruth in the Bible, my new name was derived from Saint Lyudmila.

It took a long time before I adjusted to my new home, new school, and new name. I missed Bubby and Zyde. But we had to escape from the Warsaw Ghetto, even if it meant a painful separation from all other family members, and also from our friends. It was hard on the whole family. We missed the only home we ever had. We had to masquerade as Polish Catholics. But that was the cost of living in what my parents hoped was relative safety. Then too, both my parents got busy with their new business, and the two of us, Haniushka and I began to attend a new school, a boarding school at the Convent of the Ursulines. They were a religious order of nuns whose patron saint was Saint Ursula.

Chapter 7

My mind filled with a jumble of images and recollections from my previous life, I walked aimlessly for the better part of a day. I walked without knowing my destination. My feet hurt. I paused. I was surprised to see the gates of Ursuline Convent before me. My feet had taken me there without the intervention of my mind. I certainly had not intended to present myself at their gate, but here I was nevertheless, in front of the boarding school where Mother had thought we'd be safe.

The place was enclosed by a black iron fence, but I could see beyond it to the garden profuse with flowers their soft colors shimmering in the afternoon light. How many times had I stood in this very spot? I followed the old route Haniushka and I used to take back to the convent after visiting Mom and Dad at home. We had loved to visit home, but afterwards we always had to return to the boarding school.

Now I rang the bell and wondered who'd come at my summons. Would it be someone I knew, a familiar nun glad to see me return? It took only a few minutes before the little window in the wooden gate opened.

"Is there someone you seek here?" a voice asked.

"I need to speak to Mother Superior."

"What is your business with Mother Superior?"

"I used to be a student here."

"What name shall I say?"

"She knew me as Ludka Bronek."

The nun let me in, and I followed her across the familiar courtyard. My feet felt swollen. I must have been walking all this long day, without once stopping to rest.

69

Mother Agnes had changed very little since I last saw her, the same pale face and slim figure that seemed almost hidden in the folds of her black habit. That meant that she was still the principal here. I smiled, hoping Mother Agnes would be delighted to see me alive. But the eyes that now turned toward me were devoid of all expression. I felt as if a bucket of ice water had been splashed over my head.

Had Mother Agnes forgotten me? Had my appearance changed so drastically during the three years in the camps? Could it be the nun's sight was failing? I tried to understand her frostiness. Where was the kind, gentle, and patient woman I knew?

I found it hard to look at that forbidding face.

"Ludka," Mother Agnes acknowledged. She had not forgotten me. Surely she also remembers Haniushka, I thought, upset that she didn't even enquire if Hania had survived the war.

I stood silent not knowing what to say or how to act. Mother Superior appeared to be angry at me. I didn't know why.

"When you were first enrolled as a student here, you lied about your name. What is your name?" she asked, her fingers curled into a tight ball.

"Rutka Wasserberg." I answered softly, although I'd much prefer to have screamed out of anger and disappointment. I was certain of one thing. Nothing could induce me to make excuses for the decisions my parents had to make during the war. Nazis were killing Jews. My parents attempted to preserve our family the only way they knew, moving from our home in Warsaw, changing our name and masquerading as Christians. Was the woman dense? I wondered.

"Your parents should have told us." Mother Agnes said, pressing her lips into a tight line. "Had your mother informed me that you're Jewish, had she asked my permission to leave you here with us, maybe we could have done something. As it was…"

Was she blaming my folks for what the Nazis did? I was outraged, and before I could stifle them, words tumbled from my mouth. "Mom was desperate to save us."

"As we all were," Mother Agnes agreed, lifting her shoulders in another deep sigh.

"I don't suppose you've heard from…" I trailed off, not

knowing what exactly I expected to hear or why I was standing here before this implacable Mother Superior. At this point, I was almost certain no one had survived. But it was so very hard to give up all hope. As if in prayer, I whispered, "Mom?"

"I've had a letter from your cousin Genia. She inquired about Hania and you. I'll write to tell her you've come back."

Gentle Genia, Mother's first cousin, was alive, and she was looking for me. Someone was alive after all. I felt elated, and wondered if Marek, Genia's little boy had survived as well? I hoped he had. He was fragile, I remembered, a shy slim boy who seldom joined us kids in our games at family gatherings. "Genia is alive," I kept repeating to myself. I should have felt an overwhelming joy at hearing this news; yet just as earlier that day I had no tears for my mother or father or little Haniushka, so now I could feel no true joy, only relief that I had at least one relative left, someone who used to love me.

I wanted to ask many questions. Was she well? Did she mention her son, Marek? When did she write? But seeing the calm, distant look in Mother Agnes's eyes, I stood mute watching her rummage in her desk drawer.

Then she found what she was looking for. It was a small box and a thick envelope. "These are yours," Mother Agnes said, pushing the items across her desk towards me.

I glanced at the small box with incomprehension.

"What about my cousin? When is she coming?" I asked.

"Not so fast. She wrote she is living in Warsaw. Now I plan to inform her that you're back. Mail takes a few days, so don't expect to hear from your cousin for at least two weeks."

I sighed, and turned my attention to the little box. Bending over the desk, I lifted its cover and looked uncomprehending at the contents which looked like gold fountain pen nibs. I had no idea of what use these could be to me.

"Your mother used these as money to pay for your tuition in advance," Mother Agnes explained. "Paper money was worthless at that time, you see. They are made of gold, so you might want to barter them for something you'll need."

"But if these were meant to pay our tuition, why are you giving them back to me now?"

"Your tuition was paid up for a year in advance and included the fall semester. However the Nazis came for you and Hania before the start of the fall semester. That's why you're due a refund."

I had come to Krakow looking for my family. These little golden nibs were a poor substitute for what I needed and wanted. I closed the box, and put it aside.

"Aren't you going to see what's inside the envelope?" Mother Agnes asked.

Ah yes, the envelope; I used my thumb to slide it open. Several old photos of my family spilled out on the desk. Mom in her fashionable hat, a smart purse under her arm, with Dad standing next to her, holding what appeared to be a bakery cake box. Looking at this photo, I was reminded of the many times my parents came home with cookies, doughnuts, or some delicious confection from the bakery. Seeing them there, in a momentary flash from the past, I wanted to scream my sorrow and disappointment. My parents were gone, and this faded photo could not bring them back. The beloved images of my mom and dad, the people I had loved and lost, smiled at me from the confines of the photo. Seeing their dear smiling faces only made my loss more acute. I felt empty and scared.

Exhausted from my long trek across town, and sick of my useless search for a family that was no longer here, I felt my knees buckling under me. I rested my hand on the back of a chair to steady myself and spread the remaining photos on the desk. There was tiny Haniushka with the ever-present ribbon on the top of her head; in another photo she was trying to jump rope and not succeeding very well. I almost smiled at the memory of Haniushka trying to imitate me in everything I did.

Mother Agnes interrupted my reverie. "I suppose you can stay here with us for the time being. Go with Sister Josephine," she said and rang for the young sister who had shown me in.

Sister Josephine led me down some stairs to the kitchen. Here was a part of the building I had never seen during my years at the boarding school. Sister Josephine approached a nun who was busy dishing out platters of hot food onto large trays. She had rolled her black habit sleeves above her elbows to keep them clean. My senses flooded with the aroma of freshly cooked beef stew reminding me that I hadn't eaten since breakfast. The stew smelled awfully good, and I hoped they'd give me some.

I was told to sit and wait at a small table. After the last platter of food was placed on the tray and sent up the dumb waiter to be served to the students, it was my turn. A plate of stew was set before me, along with some salad and a glass of milk.

I thanked the nun who served me, and began to eat, feeling shame at being treated as a charity case. Sitting alone in the corner of the kitchen, I remembered the days when I was enrolled here in the boarding school. At that time my mom was paying for the food and I didn't eat alone in the kitchen, but with the other girls in the upstairs dining room.

Now I'm a charity case, I thought bitterly, remembering the time the nuns took some of us school girls to visit an orphanage maintained by the Ursuline Sisters. It was situated in the poor section of town. These orphan girls looked very different from us. They smiled and greeted us politely, but their eyes were sad, and I felt at once superior to these poor girls, and also sorry for them. But until now, I never knew how it felt to be treated as an orphan.

Mopping up the last bit of gravy with a piece of bread, I chewed the last morsel, feeling sad, and thinking about how very happy I had been earlier that morning when I first arrived in town. The excitement and anticipation of coming home was gone. Now I felt weary and sorry for myself. When the nun placed another glass of milk with a small piece of cake before me, I pushed it away.

"Don't you like cake?" Sister Josephine asked, her round face dimpled in a smile. She looked so jolly, full of milk, honey, and God. All that innocence, I thought. I would never feel innocent again. My innocence had gone the way of my family. I was alone, felt hollowed out. I couldn't think of one tiny fraction of the whole world where I could belong.

No longer hungry, I told the young nun that I couldn't eat another bite, and followed her through the service exit, and up the five narrow flights of stairs to the vast, shadowy, and mostly empty attic. A bare bulb hung suspended on a single cord above a narrow cot. It cast a small pool of light on the fresh linen, a pillow, and a gray woolen blanket, my bed for the night. Nothing had been overlooked, I thought, noticing a pair of clean and pressed pajamas on top.

I felt banished from my life. All these weeks since the war ended, I had lived for the day of homecoming. Perhaps this need had made me believe my dreams would come true. But now empty of dreams, I felt as if the Nazis left me breathing and moving, but they had taken my life away.

Although I tried to escape through sleep, I lay on the hard narrow cot, turning and twisting. It was too warm. The blanket bothered me, but when I tried to push it from me, it got tangled round my feet. I became too brain fogged to deal with it, and drifted off into a nightmare...

...I tried to run from the soldier in a black uniform, but my feet were bound, and I fell on the ground. He came nearer and stood above me with a pointed gun. Time stopped. I heard the blast, saw the bullet come out of the hole in the barrel. All in slow motion, I saw it come towards my heart. The flash of the gun exploded, its sound reverberating in my ears, and it thumped and pounded within my chest...

I forced myself awake, but was too groggy and exhausted to realize that the blanket had twisted around my feet, I continued to struggle and finally managed to untangle myself. I dozed for a bit, then awoke to the gray light of dawn. But this new day offered no consolation. The waiting, wanting, hoping were finished. The futility of my long trek across half of Germany and most of Poland had brought me to an empty place. And I didn't know where else to go.

Lying in bed, tired from a night of too much worry and not enough sleep, I listened to the clatter of dishes and utensils, and inhaled the tang of pancakes and sausage cooking in the kitchen below. I'd almost forgotten those familiar morning aromas of my student days.

Lying there in the attic, with the normal sounds and smells of life drifting up towards me, I thought about the weeks of walking on sore feet, the many stops in strange and empty towns, the encounters with other survivors who like me roamed the German countryside, the train station where trains didn't run, my entire pilgrimage that led to a home that was no longer mine. No one welcomed me back. No one celebrated because I had survived, and no daydreams would make it any different.

Entering the room, Sister Josephine said, "Come on down to breakfast, then Mother Superior wants to see you."

Alone at the little table in the kitchen, I felt like a leper as I chewed and swallowed the eggs and drank a glass of milk that had been set before me. I mumbled my thanks and wiped my mouth. Then I was reminded that Mother Agnes was waiting.

Mother Agnes smiled briefly at me and dismissed Sister Josephine. I would have liked to have been dismissed as well. I stood there nervously. Mother Agnes did not ask me to sit.

"It won't do, you know. We are not expected to stay in bed until someone comes to fetch us." Mother Agnes said, peering over her wire spectacles.

"I'm sorry, Mother Agnes."

Mother Agnes went on, but I was so upset that I missed some of what she had to say. I did however come to attention when she said, "In the meanwhile, I'm looking to find a good home for you. One of our parishioners has expressed an interest in taking you in, in case your cousin can't take on that responsibility."

My mouth went dry. Was it possible that Genia wouldn't come? Would she also abandon me? No, not Genia, not the gentle lovely woman that I remembered. She was family, and I cherished the thought that at least Genia had survived.

As usual, Mother Agnes's glasses slid down her nose, and she was obliged to peer over them again, fixing me with a hard look, "Well, have you got any questions?"

"School?"

"For you?"

"I need to finish my education."

"We taught you to read and write. You've been taught good manners."

My hands went cold and clammy. I must have swayed a bit, because Mother Agnes told me to sit down.

"Your circumstances have changed. You've missed three years of school; too late to make them up now." She stood, signaling the interview was over.

I wanted to disappear. After leaving Mother Agnes's office, I walked along the brick path towards the garden. I didn't know anything about Genia's present situation; therefore, I could not count on her. But I wanted to get away from the convent, as soon as possible. I needed to make some plans. But I had never learned, and had no experience in making plans or decisions. That task was always reserved for the grownups. I sat among the garden flowers, breathed in the aroma of lilac and freshly clipped grass, and realized that nothing in my life had prepared me for this moment. I was a fifteen year old girl with no skills, and no prospect of acquiring any. Throughout my life someone else had made plans and decisions for me. My parents made them for me when I was a child growing up at home. At the Convent I had to obey the nun's rules and routines. As for the camps, there was certainly no possibility of acting on my own. There all plans and decisions were imposed on me by uniformed guards with guns and dogs and barbed wire...

...Mid-winter gray, barefoot on the icy ground we stand in rows of gray and black. I shiver in my raggedy sweater worn over a summer dress. Selection morning, someone said. The Camp Commandant makes his choice today. The ones he picks will die.

But if he lets me live, then I must do my job, inspect the bullets, so that each one hits its mark. Each day and late into the night I roll those bullets across my palm. My practiced wrist tips up and down and makes those bullets roll. They roll all day and through the dark, they roll for days and weeks and months. My guts turn yellow like the guts inside the bullets that I roll. Their metal casings in my hands; they roll across my palm, leaking their nasty sulfur guts, through skin and bones into my core. I flick with a practiced motion of my wrist, and in and out, and up and down this sulfur yellow streaks my legs.

The guards laugh poking each other. They know I've wet myself. I did, and now these ugly yellow/orange streaks keep running down my legs.

76

They laugh at me, but they don't feel the goose bumps on their legs, They are comfy in their uniforms, warm and fat. They laugh, and I feel shame. Humiliation freezes from the inside out, and is harder to dismiss than freezing air, my empty stomach, barking dogs, and rifles at my head. The shame grows hard just like the sulfur in my gut...

The decisions had been theirs then, but I had gotten back to Kracow, hadn't I? I had made decisions all along the way and if Genia failed to come for me. I would continue to make them.

Chapter 8

Cool and sweet, the early morning air wafted in through the open attic window. The bells rang for morning prayers, and I longed to be one of the students, innocent as they were, innocent as I had been three years earlier. Back then morning prayers gave me comfort. I still believed that God would protect Haniushka, and I prayed He would help my mother to free my dad from the Nazis.

Each morning in chapel, I had sat with other students listening to the nuns chant as they walked in solemn procession. Regal in their traditional long black habits, their faces framed by white headdress, they entered in pairs, and took their seats on either side of the altar while the sweet aroma of incense filled the chapel.

As I lay in bed, I remembered the painting hanging above the main altar. It depicted Christ on his cross with Mary at his feet. Now, alone on my cot, I thought about how Christ died asking God why he had forsaken him. When I was here as a student, I wanted to believe that God was merciful. Now it bothered me to think that this all-powerful God chose not to save his own son from crucifixion. Where was his mercy then? Only now did I realize that such a God would hardly bother to save my mom and dad, and my little sister, Haniushka.

Back then, I had often heard the nuns say that God protects all little children. I had needed to believe them, so each day I fingered my rosary beads as I prayed for God's mercy. At the same time, I had worried about what the Nazis might do to our family. Fear burned in my guts even as I prayed that an all powerful, merciful God would spare them.

Now, after three years in German concentration camps, I understood that the God of the Catholics did not protect Jewish children. Little Haniushka was only six years old, yet she was murdered, as were many other innocent children. The Catholic God didn't save them, but then, I remembered, neither did the Jewish God.

My bitter thoughts were interrupted by the knowledge that Genia was alive. Does that mean that it was God who spared her? I hoped Moshe had been saved as well. I remembered that Genia always preferred to listen rather than to speak, and I recalled that Moshe was a pale and really skinny, small, mostly frail, and quiet boy, who seldom smiled. Unlike the other boys, he never pulled my braids or teased me. I liked him.

I now woke each morning hoping that this would be the day Genia would come, and bring Moshe with her. I had a lot of time, because no one asked me to help with the work, and when I offered, I was dismissed with a kind smile. The convent was just another stopping place along the journey that seemed to be leading nowhere.

I didn't belong there, and so tried to make myself invisible. I preferred to miss meals rather than sit in the kitchen while the busy nuns sent pitying looks in my direction.

Each day, I'd leave the convent to prowl the streets and parks of Krakow for hours with no special destination in mind. The city was as I remembered it. There were no burned out or bomb fragmented homes here, no shell-scarred roads or deserted neighborhoods like the ones I passed on my way from Germany to Poland. Though old, these houses were well cared for; the streets were neat and clean. The town showed no scars of war. Only a couple months had elapsed since that first morning after the war when I woke up in the barn, but it seemed to me as if many years had passed. I walked on, feeling as if I had stepped back into the past. The city appeared at once ancient and timeless.

Up on the hill stood the familiar fortress, an ancient castle where kings ruled long ago. Untouched by the many centuries and wars, it looked like something out of a fairytale, a medieval town with its forbidding walls and battlements that carried no scars. Perhaps with good reason, I remembered the recent history and how the good citizens of Krakow stood by, while their Jewish neighbors lost their homes and their lives to the Nazis.

At least Genia survived. There was one living human being

left in this world who I knew cared for me. It was a thought that gave me some comfort. I wondered about Moshe, how would he look now? Did his thin face fill out? I remembered it used to be hard to get a word out of him. Was he still as shy, or did he speak more freely now? I thought about little else. Genia was my mother's first cousin, yet they were as unlike one another as any two people could be. Where my mom was bold and always spoke her mind, Genia was reserved and seldom expressed her opinion. Where my mother stayed out in the open during the German occupation, Genia remained hidden with Moshe. She preferred to stay out of sight, saying, "Rose, if no one gives me a second look, I like it just fine."

A memory of the time Genia invited me to come with her to see the ballet popped into my mind. We had seen Sleeping Beauty. The experience transported me to a magical world of light, color, music, and dance. I loved seeing the familiar fairy tale through the movements of the dancers. I found the beauty and grandeur of the music so inviting. I wanted to enter the performance and live in it forever, and I loved Genia for taking me to see it. When I thanked her, she responded in her usual understated manner.

"I thought you'd like it," she said, her soft little smile playing on her lips.

Now, after two days of roaming the streets, I began to worry. If Genia didn't show up soon, Mother Agnes would farm me out to one of the parishioners. She had one all ready for me, a "good Christian home," where I could make myself useful, help with the housekeeping and care for the little ones.

A few more days passed with no sign of my cousin, and I began worry in earnest. I started to think that perhaps Genia couldn't afford the price of the train ticket. I remembered Warsaw was a long way from Krakow, an overnight trip. Maybe it was too expensive.

One morning Mother Agnes summoned me to her office. I wasn't sure what I had done wrong this time, and I hurried afraid she'd grow even more impatient with me. Then too, I feared Mother Agnes would be waiting to tell me that Genia wasn't coming after all. I'd have to go live in this good Christian home. I was beside myself with worry by the time I reached the black door that led to Mother Superior's study; I had to collect myself and gather up the courage to knock. My heart skipped a beat at the sight of a woman in the visitor's chair. Could it be Genia? She was facing Mother Agnes, so I could see only the back of her head. But I saw something familiar in the way the woman leaned forward to listen.

"Genia?" I whispered.

Hearing my soft voice behind her, Genia stood and I ran into her open arms. We hugged. She covered my face with kisses. I smothered her with my kisses in return, and whispered, "Moshe?"

"He is well. You will see him soon." Her fingers smoothed my hair, caressed my face, and we hugged again.

Genia finally stepped back for a better look. Not missing an inch, her eyes surveyed me from the top of my head to the tip of my toes.

She sighed deeply, expelled air, and said, "You've come through it, thank God."

I wanted to laugh and cry at the same time, wanted to ask about Marek, and if any one else had survived, but before I could even open my mouth, Genia asked, "Have you heard anything? Any one…"

Thinking about my mom and dad and Haniushka, I grew sad again, and wordlessly moved my head from side to side. Genia opened her arms. I stepped into them. The anguish I'd kept locked up all this time now suddenly broke free and wretched sounds, like those of an animal caught in a trap escaped from deep in my gut.

After looking on in silence, Mother Agnes smiled gently and said, "Lovely day for a walk in the garden."

Genia immediately thanked Mother Agnes for her kindness. She explained that she'd be taking me back with her to Warsaw that very afternoon.

"I'm ready now right this minute," I almost shouted, and had to restrain myself from jumping up and down. Genia wanted me, was taking me back to Warsaw. I'd be seeing Moshe soon, and I was not alone anymore.

We decided to skip our walk in the garden, and instead, I took Genia's hand and for the last time climbed the steps to the attic. Except for a few pieces of underwear and a spare skirt and blouse, I had little else. It took but a few moments to stuff my sparse belongings into a paper bag. We had a train to catch and little time to spare.

On the way to the train station, I asked Genia about Michael, Genia's husband. At that, lines of sorrow deepened around her eyes and mouth. It was her turn to move her head in the negative. I could find nothing to say, but I wrapped my arms around her and holding her close brushed my cheek against hers. At least Moshe was alive. I was afraid to ask her about Jurek, my uncle, only nineteen years old when I last saw him, but instead I asked about Moshe. I wanted to know where he was and when I would see him.

"He is fine, staying on a Kibbutz, in a village near Warsaw. He lives there with other young boys and girls. You'll be seeing them all tomorrow."

Later that evening, after we found a compartment on the train, Genia told me that it was a good thing Mother Agnes's letter reached her when it did, because in a few weeks she'd be leaving Poland with Moshe. I couldn't believe how close we came to missing one another.

"Guess there's nothing to keep us here anymore," I mumbled.

We huddled together on the hard bench with Genia's arm cradling me. The wheels clicked along the tracks. I felt the gentle sway of the train and listened to the mournful sound of its whistle.

"I knew something had happened when Rose stopped writing," Genia said. "At the same time, I hoped and waited to hear from her. I tried to persuade myself that she was too busy to write. But after months of waiting, I knew there'd be no more letters from her, not ever. Then I wrote to Mother Agnes to ask about you and Hania. That's when I learned what happened. She told me how the Gestapo came in the middle of the night and took you and Haniushka away." Genia hugged me more closely, as if needing the physical touch to know I was indeed alive.

"Dad was arrested a year before they came for us. Did Mother write you about that?"

"Yes, Rose wrote, told me how she tried to get him released."

"She could think of nothing else, followed every lead, every rumor to search him out. Each time she left for another camp where she thought he may be kept, she'd go with hope, promising to return soon. I never knew where it was exactly that she went. But each time she left us, I hoped for her speedy return with my dad. I thought she'd be back in a couple of weeks the last time we said good-by.

But that was it. She never returned. I never saw her again." I didn't want Genia to see my tears, so I buried my face against her shoulder. Genia just held me close to her, stroking my head.

The train stopped at a little village station to allow more people to board. A couple of men entered our compartment. Suddenly our small quiet cubicle filled with their sound and size. Their muscles bulging, they were tall and broad. They looked like peasants. Without even so much as a by your leave, they commandeered the drop leaf table by the window and commenced to lay out the contents of two heavy wicker baskets, Then assembling garlic, pork sausage, and onion, they devoted themselves to the serious business of dinner preparation on that little pop-up table. They sliced, minced and stuffed it all between thick slices of black bread, as our compartment filled with a pungent odor.

"Are you hungry?" Genia asked, as we made room for them, moving to the opposite corner of the bench.

"No," I replied, "I think I'll try to sleep now."

Genia kissed my forehead and suggested I stretch out on the bench and put my head on her lap. I did so, but though I was tired, I couldn't sleep, what with the loud chomping and the rowdy conversation. I just wished those two peasants would leave at the next station stop.

I looked over their heads through the window and watched the telegraph lines against the dark sky. As the train moved forward it made them look as if they were in motion, shimmering in the moonlight as they moved up and down crossing one another as if in a dance. The sight of these lines soothed me and I remembered the faint strains of The Waltz from the Vienna Wood, the same waltz that I used to play on the piano as a child. Mother's favorite waltz. The one I had tried unsuccessfully to use to shut out the sounds of the Russian attacking Elaina. Now the music seemed to relax me. But, as the train wheels clicked on, and I drifted with the remembered sounds of the dance. I floated on its lilting melody, my fingers moving…

…Striking the notes on the keyboard … I want to stop, but cannot. My fingers seem to have a mind of their own, and the haunting strain of the melody goes on, as if sounding an invitation

83

to the dance. I do not want to play this Waltz from the Vienna Woods, for suddenly I fear that which may come at its bidding. And yet, I go on, press the yellowed ivory keys, filling the room with music.

Each note is a step for her to walk on. Each note brings her nearer. I sense her approach, and fear it. I know that all too soon she'll enter, yet I cannot stop playing.

The doors open slowly allowing a thin wedge of darkness to squeeze through. And with the darkness, icy cold air flows into the room, while fear clamors within me. My body shakes. I'm bathed in sweat. My teeth are clenched. I want to get away...

"Wake up, you're having a nightmare," Genia whispered, shaking my shoulder.

"That dream again. I dreamed it years ago." I whispered, waking up. I rubbed my eyes, as if to purge the image from my mind.

"It's the horrible experiences of camp, no doubt." Genia murmured trying to comfort me.

I shook my head, "No, this is a nightmare I had a couple of weeks before the Gestapo came for us. It was a ghostly nightmare and it was repeated twice. I was so frightened, Genia, so very frightened."

Genia hugged and rocked me in her arms, "Your dad was in prison, or worse; your mom gone. No wonder you had nightmares, but you survived, thank God. You're here with me now.

The two peasants snored across the isle. Their relaxed deep breath seemed free of nightmares. I wondered if mine would ever end.

"After the first nightmare, I called Mom's friend, Dora," I whispered into Genia's ear.

"Why did you call her?"

I hadn't seen Mom for almost three weeks, and I was worried about her. Dora and Mom were best friends. Mother trusted her completely. That's why I called. I hoped she might have heard something."

Genia waited for me to go on, but when I remained silent, she prompted, "Well, did she?"

"What?" I was distraught. I could hardly follow the train of

84

my own thoughts. They were scattered fragments in my brain.

"Dora. Did she have a word from your mother?"

"No, she had heard nothing, and she was also very worried. But then she told me about the argument they had. It made her especially sad because that was the last time she had seen my mother alive."

"Did she tell you what they argued about?"

"Dora thought that Mother was putting us all at risk, by wandering across the country to save Father. She said I had to be a big girl and understand how it was now, with Mom gone. She told me that both Hania and I were in danger, that the Nazis might already know where we are. Her words made me even more afraid, but I didn't know what to do about it. She told me to be careful, but I didn't know how."

Chapter 9

Dora's Story

...Late afternoon paced towards evening. An old gnarled oak threw long shadows across the antique tapestry above the couch, which showed Victorian ladies at tea sitting around a flowing fountain.. The mood of this pleasant garden scene contrasted sharply with the mood of the two women sitting around a table inside the room itself.

Rose looked at Dora's hands, saw her white knuckles, bit her lip, and looked away. She glanced at the open French doors on her left, and to the balcony beyond. The street below was lined with ancient oaks whose branches reached up towards the balcony.

Knitting needles flashing in her hands, Rose snapped, "Don't try to change my mind,"

"Think of the risk," Dora implored, her hands clasped as in fervent prayer. The Grandfather clock's pendulum ticked softly in the hall. It was spring of 1942. Europe was at war, and the Germans occupied Poland.

Sprinkled by rays of the afternoon sun, the two women sat near the open balcony at a table set for tea: rose-bud studded cups and plates, white damask cloth, napkins, silver cutlery, a pot of tea, and an untouched platter of teacakes. Mouth pressed closed, hands restlessly working needles through yarn, Rose did not respond to Dora. Dora kept kneading her hands. Neither woman spoke. Were they quiet because all was well, or were they both holding back screams?

Head bent over a little blue sweater, Rose continued to knit. Dora looked at her friend with a mixture of sympathy and exasperation. Barely thirty-one years old, pretty too, Dora thought, observing the broad Slavic cheekbones, the snub nose, and the milk and rose-petals complexion. Only the lustrous dark brown hair, brushed back severely and twisted into a bun, could betray her origin. Still at a glance, she wouldn't be taken for a Jew, Dora thought.

Dora had met Rose in Krakow. The two women became good friends, sharing their concerns. Dora worried about her husband Stan, a Captain in the Polish Army. She hadn't seen him since he'd left for the front. Rose had a great deal of respect for Dora. She sympathized with her loss, and even suggested that Stan might have gone to join the Polish unit fighting with the Brits. Dora hoped that was so, but she had no confirmation, and continually wondered if he were dead or alive.

As Rose came to trust Dora, she gradually began to confide in her and depend on her good counsel. For her part, Dora proved herself a trusty friend. After Maurice's arrest, it was she who suggested that Rose place the girls at the Ursuline boarding school. Fortunately, none of the members of the family looked Jewish. Dora thought they could all pass, provided they didn't call attention to themselves.

But when his own mother became ill, Maurice had visited her in the Krakow ghetto every single day, sometimes even twice a day. Each time he went, he had to stop at the gate, show his ID, and tell the guards the purpose of his visit. He carried a second set of identity paper, in case he got caught, no one would draw any connection between himself and his wife and children. It was risky, but he thought he could get away with it. Besides, with each passing day his mother was getting more frail and worn, and he feared she was dying. A loving and caring son, he surely couldn't be faulted for being concerned over his mother's health.

It didn't take long before the guards began to notice the quiet, worried man who claimed to have daily business in the Ghetto. Soon they wanted to know what sort of business caused the man's hands to shake. He never smiled or traded jokes like the other men who came on business to trade shoddy goods in exchange for Jewish money. The guards grew ever more suspicious, until they arrested him. He was taken to the local jail for interrogation. When he failed to come home, Rose was certain that the police had detained him.

The next morning, wearing a great deal of make up and a blond wig, she presented herself at the local police station, produced her spare set of false identity documents, and requested information about an employee that had gone missing. She explained that she had sent him to the Ghetto on business. Now she was worried, as he was carrying a large sum of the firm's money with him. She offered whatever sum they required to help her find him.

By linking herself to a man the police were holding under suspicion, she was taking a big risk, and she knew it. But she hoped that her disguise and false documents would prevent any trace back to the girls.

Her ploy almost worked. The guards admitted they were holding him under suspicion, but as money was involved, they'd see what could be done. They named their sum, she agreed, and they promised to release Maurice the next day. Unfortunately, the precinct captain discovered the plan, and Maurice was shipped to a concentration camp. Rose could not give up. She felt compelled to find another way to find him and free him

Dora understood why Rose had to try, no matter the risk, wanted to tell her that it was all right, but she couldn't. She was convinced that Maurice was now beyond saving. There was nothing Rose could do to alter the inevitable. These were not normal times. Dora feared that Rose's action might risk not only her own safety but also that of her children. Rose had no right to take futile risks to accomplish the impossible. "Stay low, and save yourself and the children," Dora told her. She tried to soften her hard words with a gentle hand on Rose's shoulder. Rose paused her knitting and stretched the almost completed sweater before her.

"Nice shade of blue, is it for Hania?" Dora asked.

"For her, yes," Rose said. Just thinking about the image of her daughter's round little face, those big brown eyes, and the big pink bow in her hair brought a smile to her lips. Only five years old, she reflected, and so precocious.

Putting her knitting aside, Rose selected a photo from the small pile on the table, showed it to Dora. Dora saw three pairs of eyes gazing at her from the photograph. Rose in the middle, her cheek leaning on Hania's small head, her arms around the dimply child in a protective embrace. In her little pink taffeta dress, all ruffles and bows, pink ribbon in her short hair, mouth parted in an uncertain smile, the little girl's eyes were wistful. Her left arm around Rose's shoulder, Rutka sat by her mother's side, right hand resting on her mother's arm. She was dressed in her favorite blue silk dress, and her hair bound with silk ribbon was plaited into a single long braid that fell over her shoulder. Her eyes expressed a world of sorrow. Their dress may have looked festive, but none of them had a smile on their lips.

Looking at the photo, Dora could detect traces of tears in both girls' eyes. They miss their dad almost as much as Rose misses her husband, she thought.

"What was the occasion?" she asked.

"I wanted to cheer us up because I'd been so depressed on my last visit with them. It was hard for me to hide my feelings. I thought getting all dressed up for a formal photograph would give me something to do with them, distract us from worry. It didn't work. I can see they're beginning to sense trouble, though I've tried to hide it from them. Look there" Rose pointed to the photograph, "Look at Rutka's eyes. They look so forlorn..." Rose sighed, and replaced the photograph back in its pile. "It didn't comfort us, after all."

"Who'll protect them if something happens to you?"

"They are safe with the nuns, Hania and Rutka both," Rose snapped and resumed her knitting.

But Dora knew that Rose could never convince herself of that. Her friend was plagued by the nightmares of the Gestapo coming for her girls, coming to the convent to take them away.

"I know you too well, Rose. Not a day passes, but you worry about the girls," Dora said.

Rose stifled a cry. "Rutka is only eleven years old, so bookish and given to daydreams. What can she do if they come?

"Yet..."

"Don't, don't say it," Rose warned.

They both lapsed into silence, each with her thoughts.

Dora ached for her friend. Both ached for their husbands, but she didn't have to worry about her kids, like Rose did.

Having resumed her knitting, Rose suddenly broke the silence. "Why would anyone look for Jewish girls in a Catholic convent?" she asked.

Dora leaned towards her friend and placed her hand over the busy hands to still the knitting. "Rose, you're the bravest woman I know. Maybe the girls are safe with the nuns, but what if there is someone out there who knows you, knows where the girls are now, and who is willing to talk in exchange for a few coins."

"No one knows."

"Maurice's old friend Yaakov knows and so do the people who work for him. They've known Maurice since before the war, and don't forget, I know."

"I trust you, Dora. You have no reason to hurt my girls."

"What about his friend Yaakov? Haven't you ever wondered how it is that he, a known Jew, can conduct his business outside the Ghetto?" Dora said.

Rose chewed on her lower lip. "He wouldn't harm my girls. He couldn't."

"You're taking risks, asking too many questions, offering too much money in bribes. You can't help but raise suspicions. How long will it be before the guards come for you?"

Rose stopped knitting. "Do I have a choice? Tell me Dora, if Stanley were drowning, would you just swim away, and leave your husband to die?"

Dora placed her arms around Rose. "You can't be faulted for wanting to save your man," she whispered, feeling Rose's body tense like a steel rod. Dora kept her arms around her friend. If anything happened to the girls, Rose would never forgive herself. Dora knew that, but she also knew that her friend was up against impossible odds.

Rose's hands became motionless. Most days, she could not avoid the nagging question: Would the nuns really protect her girls? She couldn't know the answer, because she had been afraid to take the chance of telling them. What if she confided in Mother Agnes? Would the nun keep still about it? She didn't know.

And she couldn't rid herself of the disturbing sense of fore-

boding. Each night, before uneasy sleep made her oblivious, her imagination replayed the same worn strip of film. Fearful visions of her girls arrest seldom left her. She had imagined the Gestapo coming to the convent for them, until she was covered in sweat, beating her fists against her own forehead. At the same time, she thought about Maurice, imagined him somewhere behind those barbed-wired stonewalls. Those images never changed, kept on flickering across her mind. Rose feared for Maurice. His life could be taken at any moment. How could she abandon him, when he needed her?

She looked past Dora to the window; saw the branch of the tree, its leaves aglow with late afternoon light. Absently, she lifted the half empty cup to her lips, took a sip of the cold tea, and grimaced at the bitter taste.

"I wrote him a letter."

"How did you get it to him?"

"Money, the guards smuggled it in and brought me back his reply."

"What did he say?"

"Go home; take care of the girls."

"But you won't listen." Dora fisted her hands.

Rose put her thumb to her forefinger so that only a thin line of daylight showed between. "I'm this close. How can I give him up? It's all arranged. I've sent them money. Only one last try and I'll bring him home."

Dora got out of her chair and started to pace. "You're smarter than that. What's to stop them from taking your money and keeping Maurice?"

"I've had a message. They say I can come get him, tomorrow." Her mind was set. The room was still, except for the metallic clicking of knitting needles and the steady sound of the old pendulum clock.

Listen! Consider the meadow.
Yes, why not. Meadows are
Places for dreams and intimations.
On a meadow once, long ago,
Mother saw Father for the last time

91

She didn't know
He was already dead.
Saw him in her dream,
In the meadow.
She didn't know.

When Rose arrived to take Maurice home, she was told that he had been shipped to Auschwitz. The man she bribed blamed it on his superior. "Nothing I could do," he said and shrugged.

Exhausted and dispirited, she went back to her empty house, shuffled through the hall past the unwound clock, its pendulum stilled, and like a spinning top that falls over on its side when all energy is depleted, she sank into a chair, her purpose spent. Her head felt too heavy for her neck, so she leaned it on the table.

Some time after dark, the doorbell rang. It rang several times. She wished it would stop. It didn't. Stiff after the hours of sitting, she stood up, and haltingly shuffled towards the front door.

She cracked it open, but left the chain in place. The stale reek of whiskey assailed her nostrils even before she saw the two men standing before her in the dark hallway. Both in their mid-twenties, perhaps, the taller one, a sweaty cap sitting low over his forehead, said, "We've come from Mr. Zolotov, dear lady."

The second, grubby looking fellow, in a jacket that looked like something he'd slept in, just stood there nodding his bare head in confirmation.

Rose knew Yaakov Zolotov. He was Maurice's childhood friend. They had done business together right up to the day Maurice was arrested. Surprisingly, Yaakov remained free to do business from behind the Ghetto walls. Rose sometimes wondered how that was possible, but Maurice explained that Yaakov was useful to the Germans, so they left him alone. Rose wondered what manner of use they made of him.

"I don't know this man. You must be mistaken," she said.

They smirked. The grimy one moved restlessly from one foot to the other, while the second spread his hands as if offering a gift. "We can help you, dear lady. A lone woman with two little girls, we can protect you," he wheedled.

92

"What is it you want?"

"You can trust us. We come from your friend." The tall one placed his foot in the door.

"It's late. Go away,"

"We only want to be of service." He lit a cigarette, and tried to muscle in.

Rose leaned heavily against the doorway, wanting to be rid of them, but she was fearful of causing a disturbance, and drunk and determined as they were, she had no choice but to let them in.

The strong body odor mixed with stale whiskey breath repulsed Rose, but she stepped back, however reluctantly, and they walked in.

In a parody of good manners, the taller one said, *"This is my friend, Janek. I am Stanislaw."* He gave her an exaggerated bow.

"What do you want?"

"Oh, don't be like that. How's about a little drink? Janek sniveled.

"You got something to say. Say it."

"We are friends wanting to help. Give us a little drink, dear lady," Stanislaw cajoled.

"We're all living in these hard times, especially hard for the Jews." They both nodded to emphasize that point.

"We're not greedy," Stanislaw said.

"Jews are rich," Janek added, *"Wouldn't even miss the little we ask of you."*

Take hold of yourself, she commanded silently. Her knees felt weak, buckling under her, but she forced herself to take a couple of slow deep breaths, letting the silence hang between them. *"You're here for blackmail,"* she acknowledged.

"No, dear lady, you misunderstand, we're friends. Friends help each other. You help us; we keep silent. That's how it works. See?"

"Yes, I see. You want money. How much?" Rose seemed to have lost all fight.

"Fifty thousand zlotys should be easy for you. We need it by tomorrow, and please, small bills only."

"Raking fingers through her hair, Rose stalled for time. I

93

don't know how much I can free up by tomorrow."

"Dear lady, what are friends for?" The lout spread his hands innocently.

Rose closed the door behind them. Her throat was parched, and she went into the kitchen for a glass of cold water, gulped it down, leaving the faucet open with the water running. Fear for her two girls, Rutka and Hania, rose up in her throat until it felt so constricted that she could hardly get her breath. Her teeth clenched and her jaw began to hurt, while she tried to stifle her panic, breathed in and out deeply and slowly, and took a few more sips of water.

Hands clasped together, as if in supplication, she started to pace back and forth through the apartment, her thoughts on her two girls. Could those blackmailers know about the Summer Convent? Would they be able to point out the location for the Germans? Rose wanted to pummel their ugly faces, men who lied, and offered not protection, but veiled threats. These were the faces of war-coarsened monsters who only wanted money and were quite willing to make it off other people's grief.

She couldn't let them find her sweet little cherub, Hania or Rutka, her dreamy, long-legged daughter. Above all, she had to protect her girls.

By the next afternoon, Rose felt she'd done all she could to insure the safety of her girls. When the bell rang, she went to answer it. Janek and Stanislaw stood on the doorstep and she let them in.

Fifty thousand zlotys," she said, handing over the manila envelope. "Fifty thousand zlotys," she said, handing over the manila envelope. They accepted it, big smiles on their faces, "That's fine. We'll see you around," Janek said.

They accepted it, big smiles on their faces. "That's fine. We'll see you around," Janek said.

"I doubt it," Rose replied, just as two policemen walked in through the open dining room door. Each of them carried a pair of handcuffs.

After clamping the imprisoning bracelets on the wrists of the thugs, one of the policemen said, "You're both under arrest."

The stunned would-be blackmailers shouted in unison, "You

can't arrest us. You've got to arrest her. She is a filthy Jew."

The police laughed as they took them away.

Rose had known there'd never be enough money, and they would come back time after time, till she had none to pay. She reasoned that only an innocent person with nothing to fear would ask for police protection. So that's what she did, asked the police to stop the two thugs from blackmailing her. Rose knew that Polish people generally had a low opinion of Jews, and thought them cowards. No Polish policeman would ever believe a Jew would have the gumption.

Now, Rose opened the windows to let in fresh air. Then remembering that Dora was coming for tea, she went into the kitchen to put the kettle on and took out some English breakfast tea, along with orange marmalade and cinnamon biscuits. She'd been saving these for a special occasion, and now for the first time in days, Rose felt hungry...

Genia listened without interruption. "When was it Dora saw your mother that last time?"

"She told me she had seen her just a couple of hours after the police took the blackmailers away. Rose had called her all excited about how well she had managed those hoodlums. Dora never saw her again. After weeks of waiting for Mother to come back, I got really worried. That's why I called Dora. That's why she came to us, to warn us."

"I can't imagine what she expected. There was absolutely nothing you could have done, Genia said. But I agree with Dora on one point. Rose took too many chances. The police may have taken those thugs away, but I doubt they'd keep them long. As soon as they were released, I suspect they came looking for revenge. Your mother was a courageous woman. She was proud. She was smart, loving and loyal, but I'm afraid she had no common sense." "Mom did what she had to. That's who she was," I said, wanting to defend my mother. I loved and missed her awfully.

We were so engrossed in our conversation that we didn't notice when the two peasants left the train at one of the station stops. It was still dark, and I started to fidget. "How much longer,

95

before we get to Warsaw?" I asked.

"You are your mother's daughter, impatient just like she was." Genia laughed. "Go back to sleep."

"Genia, do you think those two thugs hurt her?"

Genia didn't reply, only held me closer still. "Can you sleep a little?" she asked.

"Too many questions, they keep me awake. I keep thinking about Dora's warning and what I could have done about it."

"What exactly did she say to you?"

"She warned me about those men with the skull and crossbones emblems on their hats, said they might come for us."

"And what did she suggest you do then?"

"Take Hania, and run into the woods. Hide till they go away. I was so scared I didn't even know which I was more afraid of the Nazis or being alone in the woods with Hania. That night I had another nightmare."

"Was it a repeat of the one where you're playing the Waltz?"

"Yes, that was really so strange; the second nightmare picked up exactly where the last one had stopped…"

…Imperceptibly at first, a tiny wedge of darkness squeezes through the door. I watch the dark and narrow space grow wider. No more than a white blur at first, a figure moves out of the darkness. It comes nearer. My fingers continue to strike the piano keys, the Waltz from Vienna Woods. I watch her glide towards me and I want to move, but can't.

The swollen, mutilated, blood spattered body with its bloated face, and sickly yellow complexion keeps gliding towards me. It fills me with dread. This can't be my mother. She comes closer still, and I want to shrink from her approach, get away from the overpowering urgency she carries with her. I shiver in the chill of the icy draft that escapes her mouth. She speaks, but my anxiety stifles the sound of her words. Cold sweat beads my forehead. I want to run; strain with every fiber of my being to get away, from the murdered remains of what was once my mother. I cannot move.

This I know. Somehow I know that though she fully knows

how very scared I am, she has come because she is desperate to tell me what she must say and I must know. I sense her urgency, but my fear is stronger. It silences her words. I dread what she's compelled to tell me now. Alarms ring loud within my head. I scream, "Away!" again and again. I must blot out all sound, to run, to get away, but my feet refuse to move.

"Away!" This silent scream fills my gut and mind. My very soul cries out for me to run. Away, I cannot stop shouting that word. It reverberates within. My body shakes and I must get far away from this apparition that cannot be my mother. My thoughts are incoherent. The one word, a drum repeating in my ear, "Away, away, away!"...

I'm awake, covered with sweat. Could it be that in telling Genia about that frightful dream, I had experienced it again? Genia hugged me to her, stroked my hair, and murmured, "It's over now. You're here," she said over and over, as if she needed to calm herself no less than me.

But I was too excited now, couldn't stop talking, "I just couldn't admit that she was dead. I didn't want to know the way she looked, cold and dead and still trying to talk. It was just awful."

I listened to the steady sound of train wheels clicking along the tracks. After a few moments I sat up, took a deep breath, and stretched. I tried to put on a brave face for Genia, but I couldn't do it.

"You were a child, Rutka. The sight of what may have been your mother's ghost was too much for you to handle. Come, it's almost morning. You must be exhausted from lack of sleep. Why don't you stretch out next to me on the bench? There's room. Sleep a little." Genia coaxed.

Taking Genia's advice, I once again curled my feet under me and my head in Genia's lap, but I couldn't sleep. Instead I thought about those last weeks in August...

...The cool country breeze wafts in through the window. Awake on the narrow convent cot, I tell myself that it was only a nightmare, nothing more. Yet, with my eyes wide open, I still can

97

see that bloated face. I lie unmoving on my cot, and watch the early gray turn pink. The nightmare of my sleep is gone, but the fear is not.

I haven't seen my father in a year. Our mother has been gone these past two months. Who can I trust? Who can help me, who can I confide in? My sister is much too young to share the burden of my night, too young for nightmares. At least I'll spare her these for now.

I dress and go into the field where sunflowers grow. They glow. I walk among their tall stalks, hidden within, beneath, while they tower high above me. I wish I could be just like them and warm in the sun, and unafraid of dark.

But I'm afraid, and need someone who can explain my fear. Someone who'll say it is all right, your mother will return. Then I remember the old peasant woman who lives nearby. Some say she's more than a hundred years old. She has sparse hair, and it is white. Her skin is pale, transparent, wrinkled, but her voice is strong, surprising for someone so old.

She lives alone in a little whitewashed cottage at the edge of the village. I've heard people say that she is a witch, a fortuneteller. Sometimes they even say that she's a madwoman.

Girls from the Summer Convent visit her sometimes, in early evenings, and occasionally I go with them. We always bring flowers and a pint of red raspberries, strawberries, or blueberries, whatever we find growing in the fields along the way. She accepts the gifts with a little nod and a smile, then she settles down outside, on a small stool beneath the window of her cottage wall. The ritual never changes.

Sitting on her stool, she slowly, very slowly, munches on the berries, putting them in her mouth, one by one. When she's finished with her meal, we get to listen to one of her stories. They are wondrous, full of dead apparitions who come back from the grave to issue warnings and give advice. Sitting cross-legged on the brown straw that serves as ground cover around her cottage, we listen to tales filled with enchantment, peopled by magicians, wandering souls, spirits of the dead, and shades of the night.

I can think of no one more equipped to advise me, and so decide to seek her out. I go alone, and as is the custom, carry my *gifts of blue Forget-me-nots, and red raspberries. She is in her usual spot on the stool, her head against the wall face up to the late afternoon sun. Her eyes are closed, and I worry she may be asleep, but she must hear my footsteps because she opens her eyes and smiles.*

"Hi, Granny," I offer my gifts.

"God be with you, child," she takes the berries, and says, "Go on inside, child, and put those flowers in a bit of cold water."

I do her bidding while she munches on her berries. After putting the pot of flowers in water on the windowsill, I come out to settle down on the brown straw beside her, and according to the established custom, we sit in silence for a while, but this time the silence seems to last a long time. Perhaps it only seems so, because I'm more impatient than usual. Finally, she sighs, and looks at me with more than her usual casual glance.

"Ah, then you saw her, child."

"Who?" I ask, wondering if she could actually be reading my mind.

"You know, child," she insists, "You saw her."

"My mother," I agree.

"Dead," she says.

"How can you know?"

"I know. Now, tell me, child, tell me how you saw her. What did she say?"

"I could not hear, Granny. She spoke but the words were silent. I was so frightened, Granny, of my own mother. Why was I so frightened?"

"Death, child, you were frightened of death. There's a powerful barrier between the dead and the living, a barrier not possible to breach for one as young as you."

"Do you think I saw a ghost of my mother, Granny?" I ask.

"Not a ghost, child. What you saw was your dead mother. Somehow she managed to get through, must have had a powerful reason to try so hard. She had something she needed to tell you."

"But I could not hear the words."

"The barrier is full of power. You saw her. She spoke. That's enough."

Crying now, between sobs, I ask, "Is it really true? Was she actually there, dead, but still there, in my mind?"

"Yes, child, she was there. What I wonder is why, what terrible urgency brought her forth from the place of death?"

"Something she wanted me to know. Oh, it's my fault. I just didn't listen hard enough. If I had listened, I might have heard." I bury my face in my hands.

"Don't blame yourself, child; you're young and the task was too hard for you."

"Task?" I ask.

"Why yes, the task of listening to the knowledge of the dead; such knowledge is not for the young. How old are you, child?"

"Twelve."

"So young, and are you alone?"

"I have a sister."

"Yes, a little one, how old?"

"She is six."

"Your father then, where is he?" she prods.

I feel uneasy. Not wanting to lie to her, but afraid to tell the truth, I tell the same lie I've been telling for the past year, ever since Dad was arrested. "My father was a captain in the army. He was killed back in the fall of 39." Even as I say it, I can see that she knows I'm lying. She looks at me very intently, nods her agreement.

"Yes, he's dead, but no more than a year." She remains quiet for a bit, then adds, "Life is hard and war makes liars of honest folk."

I don't ever want to lie to her again, and feel even more ashamed because she knows that I lied. Yet, I cannot take the risk of speaking the truth. I cannot tell her that my father was a Jew and the Gestapo took him away. Reluctant to speak and reluctant to go, I sit facing her in silence, while her face is turned to the setting sun. Then she stands up, and speaks.

"Child, I can tell you this, your mother came to you in hardship. She came because she loves you. She came to warn you of danger. Look out for yourself and your sister." Her eyes express a strange kind of sadness, as if seeing something yet to happen. "Look out for yourself and your sister," she says before she leaves me. I watch her enter her cottage and close the door, leaving me

100

alone.

On my way back to the convent, her words echo in my brain. "There is danger... look out... for your sister."

Where can we run? Where can we find a safe place to hide? I think about the good nuns, how they pray each day, how they talk about Christian charity and goodness, and I fear that if the Gestapo comes for us, they might turn us over to them. I can hardly believe my evil thoughts, but then, if they find out we are Jewish, who knows? I am filled with fears of the Gestapo and with hopes for the good will and true Christian piety of the nuns.

Churning with contrasting emotions, feeling like a stranger in this world that seems so benign with trees laden with fruit, fields filled with harvest. As I walk through the fields in the soft glow of the late summer afternoon, I think that I don't belong here in the warm sun, with soft breeze and not a cloud in the sky. It is late August, summer is coming to an end, and as I walk through the ripening fields, I feel a sudden chill.

During the next few days I try to push the memory of the nightmare from my mind. Each night, even as I grieve for my parents, some part of me still holds onto the hope that they are still alive. My worry about their safety alternates with my fears for me and my sister. The old women's words keep echoing in my mind. We are in danger, and I don't know what I can do about it. There are no woods of any size, only fields and crops growing low. And even as I contemplate the sunflowers as a possible hiding place they are being harvested for their seeds.

Summer harvest is here, and our days are filled with berry picking, jam making, and playing in the tall haystacks out in the fields. My problems remain, and I don't know any way to solve them. The days go by, my mind turns to the immediacy of the moment, and I allow the old woman's warning to fade into a nagging worry, which I manage to suppress during the day.

The city and the war seem far away. The experience of my twelve years of life with caring parents, happy friends, and kind teachers wins out over the warnings of my nightmares. My thoughts turn positive. Surely the war will end one of these days. Mom and Dad will return, and Haniushka and I will be waiting for them. We'll be safe with the nuns. The good Ursuline Sisters will surely protect us.

As far as I know, we are safe at the Summer Convent. Except for Dora, no one else knows our whereabouts. After Father's arrest, Mother made me promise to write to no one, and I've kept that promise. Even Dad's best friend, Jacob hasn't been told, so how could the Gestapo find us here?

During the day, the sun is bright, and the berries sweet, but with the coming of the night, dark thoughts keep me from sleep. I turn and sweat, and pull my blanket off, then pull it over me again in the growing chill. My worries revolve about my head with no conclusion, and no respite.

And then my third and final nightmare comes...

I hear the sound of horses' hoofs on cobblestones, feel the motion of the carriage as it sways from side to side, and hear the patter of rain drops on the roof of my horse drawn cab.

I'm afraid, alone in the carriage, alone in the night, alone in the rain. The rain turns to mist, and I feel the approach of a fearful presence. It seems to come out of the mist, coalesce out of the shadows. With it comes stillness. Even the carriage has ceased its motion.

"Go on!" I shout to the driver, "Don't stop, not here, not now." I fear this stopping place, this eerie misty night.

Even the rain has stopped. The silence is complete, uninterrupted by the horse's snort. I fear this void, the fearful presence that keeps coming closer. We seem to have stopped at the edge of an abyss.

I want to leave, to run but remain frozen in my place, my legs will not obey me. Forced to sit motionless, I watch it come out of the darkness. Only a slim shadow at first, but as he comes nearer, I can see his pale, gray face. He stands besides the carriage. Deep in their sockets his eyes look at me.

""No, Father! Don't come nearer." I shrink back, as every fiber of my body struggles to escape. I shiver. My throat constricts even as I open my mouth in a silent scream. The apparition stays motionless next to the carriage window, in the dark, silence, and the cold. I shiver. Could this be my father, the man who lifted me up, and held me in his arms with ease, the man who sat me high upon his shoulders?

102

Strong in life, now he seems shrunken somehow, smaller, really more shadow than man. All color is drained from him. His almost translucent face looks like a pale gray globe. His eyes are pools of profound sadness. A brooding silence marks him. There's no attempt to speak. I sense his overwhelming grief, his need to reach and touch, to warn me in some way. Yet he is silent, and only his eyes implore me to accept some knowledge that he has. I can't get past the dread and sadness in his eyes. My fear drowns out all else.

It reverberates throughout my body, is a clanging, clamoring thing that makes me shiver as I struggle to get free. Away, I scream in silence. Away, the word repeats. It fills my mind; I want to shout. Away! I hear repeating in my brain, away from apparitions, and from the paralyzing chill, away from grief and sorrow, way, away...

I wake and now the real horror begins.

Someone is standing by my bed.

"Wake up," she shakes my shoulder.

"It's all right. I am awake."

"Get up." I hear the whispered hiss.

Confused and still frightened from my dream, I ask, "Now?"

"Quickly."

I find it hard to move.

"Now," she hisses. "Get up! The soldiers cannot wait."

Suddenly, I'm fully awake, jump out of bed, and though it's August, and the night is warm, I shiver. "Must Hania come with me?"

"They want you both." Sister Teresa says.

I find Haniushka sitting in the Gestapo car, when I arrive. She's frightened, confused, rubbing her eyes still half-asleep. I sit beside her, wrap my arms around her little body and rock her gently. I must be brave, must not admit my fear. I hold on to Hania and try to stay calm.

And as we drive into the night, I hear the echo of the old woman's warning, "look out... there's danger for you both... look out for yourself and your sister."...

I must have been drifting in and out of sleep, experiencing

part memory part repetition of my old nightmares. But one thought stood out clearly in my mind. I did not heed the warning. It was a phrase that refused to stop repeating. I felt the guilt of omission. I should have found a place to hide, should have run, but I didn't.

Again I stretched and sat up, rubbing my eyes. Genia looked at me, and as if reading my mind, she said, "Not much longer now. We should be arriving in Warsaw in a couple of hours. I noticed the sky was lightening in the east. Dawn at last, but what a very long night this has been, I thought.

"I should have done something," I said as much to myself as to Genia.

"There was no place for you to hide. No one you could trust," Genia replied.

I was not so sure. "Dora warned me, and there was also an old village woman. It was like she could foresee the future. She warned me too. And I did nothing. Can you imagine? I ate berries, and played in the haystacks."

"You're much too hard on yourself," Genia interrupted. "If the sisters could not protect you, no one could."

We fell silent, each of us lost in our own thoughts. We sat side by side while the train moved on towards morning, and I sobbed quietly against Genia's shoulder.

"Can you tell me what happened when they arrested you?"

"They came out to the country and yanked Hania and me out of bed. The nuns just let them take us away. We got back to Krakow at dawn. The car pulled up in front of a big iron gate. We drove through. Then the soldiers yanked Haniushka out of the car. She was so light that she appeared to fly. They pulled me out too and we entered the Gestapo headquarters. They took me away from Haniushka into a room where they kept at me for hours, asking one question again and again. 'Where is your Mother?' That's what they wanted to know. I couldn't answer even if I wanted to. Still they kept on asking the same question again and again. My eyes kept closing from hearing their insistent repetition. I wanted to cover my ears. I wanted to lie down and sleep. And still they kept on.

Finally they stopped, took me out of that room. In the corridor outside, I saw Hania. One of the Gestapo brutes with skull and bones on his hat held her tiny hand in his grip. Pulling hard on that little arm, he was dragging her away. Twisting back, she tried to reach out to me, her silent mouth trembling. She was beseeching me to make him stop. I can still see her pleading eyes, her trembling mouth and her trembling little body..."

I sighed.

Genia rocked me in her arms. "Don't blame yourself. There was nothing you could do."

"Did I mention to you that I saw Dora after we were arrested?

"When, where?"

"After the interrogation, they were taking me somewhere. I didn't know where, and I saw her walking towards me, under guard, in the corridor at the Gestapo headquarters."

Startled by this new revelation, Genia gasped, "She turned you both in."

"I don't think so. Mother and Dora were such good friends. Besides I could see the way the Gestapo officer handled her. He was really rough as he herded her to one of the interrogation rooms. It looked to me like she was under arrest. At the time, I thought maybe it was a chance meeting, but now I wonder if they set it up on purpose."

"Why would they arrest her, and why would they want you to see her there?" Genia looked at me quizzically.

"I don't know. It happened very fast. She passed right by me, with no greeting, as if she didn't want to reveal that we were in any way connected. The way she stared straight ahead, she appeared desperate for me pass by, as if we'd never met before. There was fear in her eyes."

"You may be right to think she was not the one responsible for your arrest. She couldn't be if she didn't want them to know that she knew you."

"Someone else turned us in; I'm sure of it. But I never knew if her charade worked. Maybe they didn't believe her. Maybe the same one, who turned Hania and me in, also did the same to Dora."

"Someone did this out of spite or for money."

"That thought did occur to me."

"Seeing Dora there must have been awful for you," Genia said.

"No, see? They kept asking me about Mother and claimed they wanted me tell them where she was hiding. But when I saw Dora there, I realized that they were also questioning her for the same reason, so seeing Dora there confirmed for me that the Nazis didn't know where Mom was. To know that the Gestapo didn't get her, that was a big relief."

"But if they didn't get to her, who did?"

"I hope no one did. I still have a cinder of hope that she's alive somewhere."

"She was a lioness, never one to leave her young," Genia said. "If she had a breath left in her, she'd come for you.

The lateness of the hour finally caught up with me, and despite protestations to the contrary, I found my lids growing heavier and heavier. Genia again offered her lap as a cushion. I gratefully accepted, and put my feet up, snuggling my cheek against the soft material of her skirt. I stretched out on the hard and narrow bench, and fell asleep to dream of another, happier journey...

...We're off to visit Dad's side of the family. We seldom see them, because they live so far away. His mom, two brothers, three sisters, and all his cousins live in Krakow. So to see them we have to take a train. It is so far away. It will take us a whole night to get there, so we shall have to sleep on the train.

We did this last year, when I was seven. Hania was a tiny baby and Dad had to carry her in his arms.

There goes the train whistle. A sudden hiss of steam boils up from beneath the locomotive, and my mom tugs at my hand to get me clear. She needn't worry. I'm almost eight years old now, so I know that steam is hot and can burn.

There is our compartment. I know, because number 23 is painted on the outside. Dad mounts the steps, with Hania in his arms. I follow with Mom.

Once the train starts going, the wheels make a click-click-clack on the tracks, like music, it makes the telegraph lines dance across the sky. The sky glows red; the lines dance across the flames that fade from gold and red to purple, darker still, until they merge with night...

The train lurched and I opened my eyes. The slats of the wooden bench had managed to poke every bone in my body, and my muscles ached.

The train came to a stop with a final hiss of steam. I looked through the window at the thin slice of pink on the horizon, and thought that perhaps we had finally arrived in Warsaw. But Genia told me no, not yet. We'd get there at the next stop. I sat up, stretched out the kinks in my body, and looked through the window at the milling crowd.

Peasants with their produce and livestock hastened to board the train. They came pouring in; several of them jammed themselves into our compartment, competing for every bit of available space on the two benches.

"Genia pointed to the parcels, bags, and boxes. They'll be selling these at the market today," she said.

One woman, babushka tied around her head, squeezed in with her big basket, holding a little girl firmly by the hand. Then three more peasants entered, all of them men. The little compartment was filled with sacks full of potatoes, carrots, leeks, onions, and cabbages both purple and green. Geese and chickens squawked in their wire baskets making enough clamor to make our ears ring. Before long, the odor from the sweat of their bodies mixed with that of garlic and onions. Some of the peasants commenced to eat hard boiled eggs, smelly herring, thick slices of black bread, all the while smacking their lips and chewing with much enthusiasm.

A man across the aisle leaned against his neighbor, who refused to act as a pillow and pushed him off his shoulder. The sleepy one promptly switched sides and started to lean against his neighbor on the other side, but that didn't work out well for him either. The next thing I knew, he lurched forward and fell into my lap. The stench of drink on his breath made me want to wretch. I braced myself against the back of the bench, and using both my hands shoved him off my lap.

I snuggled close to Genia and feeling her hand held protect-tively around me, I was able to doze a bit. Less than an hour later our train pulled into the station.

Chapter 10

I had dreamed about the day of homecoming, but that home in the courtyard where I had played with my friends had been burned to the ground. Genia told me that it happened during the Warsaw uprising. Nothing remained after the Germans torched the ghetto and the last few people in it. Warsaw was no longer my hometown. It was just another stop along my way.

Genia said we'd have to take a bus before we could be reunited with Marek. He was living in Kibbutz, about an hour's drive from Warsaw. I wondered if this Kibbutz was the name of the village, but was too tired to ask.

I nodded off sitting next Genia on the bus, and when I woke the sun was high in the sky. It had to be noon, I judged. After the bus dropped us off, I just wanted to lie down, right there in the middle of the dirt road. I was tired out after the long train trip, and the bumpy bus ride with barely any sleep. The place looked desolate, empty fields and no farm house in sight.

"Where is it?"

"We're almost there," Genia said, picking up her small overnight case. She started down the road, and I, feet dragging, followed after. My curiosity winning over my exhaustion, I asked, "Kibbutz, what kind of a name is that?"

"There it is." Genia sighed, as we rounded a bend in the road.

I saw just one single-story whitewashed farm building in the middle of a field, no other structures. The door swung open even before we reached it, and a tall, youngish looking fellow with blond hair stood there stooping to avoid hitting his head on the low doorframe. It was a tight fit, but he stepped out to greet us with a big grin, hand extended, "Shalom, Moshe is on pins and needles waiting to see you. Come, he's with the others." he paused, "and who have we here?" he asked bending down towards me.

"Tzvi, this is Rutka, my first cousin's daughter." Genia beamed, then went on to tell him the whole saga about the Ursuline Convent, and how I showed up on their doorstep, and the letter Sister Agnes wrote her. Breathless, she continued "I thought she was gone, but here she is." We followed Tzvi inside.

He grinned, "Hoo-ha that will be something to see, Moshe and Rutka after all these years." His grin was so infectious I had to smile. But I couldn't remember knowing any Moshe. Who is he talking about? I wondered.

Stooping a little more, Tzvi took my hands in his, and I noticed a little dimple in the middle of his chin. He had clear pale blue eyes with tiny smile crinkles round them. Full of good cheer, he seemed really glad to see me, though he'd never met me till now.

We followed him into a small room containing a rough-hewn wooden table and a couple of wooden chairs. The place looked simple and poor, with its whitewashed walls and the single tiny window which admitted light and some fresh air.

"Don't look so worried, you'll like it here," he said, smiling a warm embracing welcome. "You're among family now."

I was confused. Family, what did he mean? I didn't know him. And Genia clearly planned to leave me there. I was not entirely sure that I'd like it any better than the Convent. At least there were flowers in the Convent garden, and they didn't use words I didn't understand. "Shalom," I said, testing the new word whose meaning I didn't know. It sounded friendly and I guessed it must be some kind of greeting.

Genia asked about Marek, but she called him Moshe. So that was his name now, Moshe. Why did he change it? "He's with the others," Tzvi nodded down the hall, where an open door led into a larger room. I heard the sound of people singing.

Genia gave me a little squeeze and over her shoulder said, "I'll see you soon," as she walked towards the sound of song, where Moshe waited for her.

I stood, feeling lost, my eyes on Tzvi. He was tall, forced to bend almost in half to get his face down to my level. "I'm so glad you're here," he said, "You can call me Tzvi."

Because he was so tall, Tzvi reminded me of Mom's brother, Uncle Joseph. He had to dip down under every doorframe to keep from hitting his head, just like Tzvi. Now I recalled that Uncle Joseph had talked about Hebrew, said it was a language spoken hundreds of years ago in the "Land of Israel." That's what he called it, "The Land of Israel," like in the Bible. I remembered thinking that it was a beautiful name, so musical that it sounded like a line in a poem. I used to beg him to tell me more. And he always obliged, because he loved to talk about the place.

"Long, long ago, it was a garden. Now it is a desert, but we will make it bloom again," he used to say. He left Poland before the war started, planning to go to here. I could still recall the longing, dreamy look in his eyes, whenever he talked about that land of long ago. Even before he went to live there, he talked about it all the time. I never understood why. How did he know he'd like it over there? Why did he seem to love a land he'd only read about? It was as if something magical propelled him to leave the doomed country of his birth and go on a journey to "The promised land."

During the war, he lived in Turkey, while we lived in Krakow. I don't know how many gifts he sent us. We received only one, but it was so very welcome. It arrived one day, a wooden crate filled with dark thick bars of chocolate, dried fruit, and numerous tins of sardines. None of these delicacies could be bought in Krakow, not even on the black market. So we relished the delicious treats for weeks till every last chocolate was gone. I could still remember the way that dark chocolate melted in my mouth. As it turned out, that gift was the last time we heard from him. The war continued, and we received no letters.

Now here was Tzvi, using the same ancient language. Was he also planning to make the desert bloom like Uncle Joseph? He liked the language, and I wondered if he also knew how to speak it. Genia trusted him with Marek, oops I mean Moshe, and so I guessed he must be a good guy. I'd have to get used to calling him by that name. Here I'd find a whole world of sounds and words I'd never heard before. Just then, I heard a chorus of joyful, exuberant voices drifting in through the open door. I could hear the faint sound of feet stamping in rhythm with a song. Were they dancing, I wondered.

"What is it they're singing?" I asked.

"It is a circle dance. We dance as we sing the Hora."

I listened to them sing, and learned another word, "Maim, Maim, Maim, Maim..."

"What does Maim mean?" I asked.

"Water," Tzvi answered, and laughed. "You must have many more questions. So sit down," he said as he pulled out a couple of chairs for us. I didn't know where to start. But he was way ahead me.

"Ever heard the name Tzvi, before?"

"No."

He smiled, "How about Henrik?"

"Sure."

"That was my Polish name, but I'm not Polish. I am a Jew, and prefer to be called by my Hebrew name, Tzvi."

I still don't understand. Why not Henrik? It's a nice name."

"Your name tells who you are. Henrik is not a proper name for a Jew.

"Why not?" I persisted.

"Our people come from a long way off, the Land of Israel. But we've been gone from there so long that most of us forgot our language. You see, language is very important. The language you speak defines who you are. Take your name, for example. You can be proud of that name, because first of all, your mom and dad gave it to you, and also because you were named after the famous Rut in the Bible."

As I listened to him, I recalled my grandfather telling me the story of Rut. I was happy then to learn that the biblical Rut was an extraordinary woman, wise and brave. In a curious way I felt proud because I carried her name. But then the Germans came. I frowned remembering how my parents changed it to save my life.

As he spoke, I began to realize that one's identity could make the difference between life and death. The Germans killed us, men, women, and children, simply because we were Jews. The very idea of it made me dizzy.

Good riddance to them. They lost the war, and we Jews no longer had to be afraid of being who we are. I no longer needed to hide my true identity. Now I could accept my heredity, not be frightened by it. We, those of us Jews who survived had foiled Hitler's plans. I thought I understood why Henrik became Tzvi. He is not afraid to be who he is. He is not afraid to say, I'm a Jew, and I have a Hebrew name as befits a Jew.

"Shalom, what does it mean?" I asked.

"Peace. We say Shalom by way of greeting, like hello or good by, and we mean, 'come in peace,' and 'go in peace.'"

"Shalom," I repeated, testing the word on my tongue. Peace is what I prayed and hoped for. I had longed for it all those hard years. Now the soft, serene sound of the word became for me at once a blessing and a prayer. Shalom, a good word, and an honorable word I thought, whispering, "Shalom, shalom, shalom." It was a gift, and I wanted to thank Tzvi for giving it to me.

"Will I be staying here with you and Moshe?" I asked.

"Yes, with all of us. Soon you'll meet the others and see how glad we are that you have come among us. We're together, and that makes us a family." He sniffed the air, taking in the aroma of roasted chicken, potatoes, and cabbage. "You must be hungry," he said. "Let's go eat."

Today I learned my first Hebrew word. Shalom had enfolded me like the arms of a friend. Now, as I walked beside Tzvi towards the aroma of roasted chicken and the sound of singing, my steps were light. I heard my first Hebrew song. It sounded happy and full of energy, and I was glad because I'd be hearing it again and again. But then I got worried, "I'll never learn Hebrew."

Tzvi laughed, "Soon, you'll be singing along with us.

The sound of shalom reminded me of my mother and her calming "Shah, shah, Ruhele…" It was a loving, soothing sound, shah, shah. It made the hurt go away. Shah, like a sigh of relief, flowed out with an exhale. Shalom just lengthened shah, and was the hope whispered on my breath, a mantra sounding deep within, a song both calming and enfolding. That day I learned Shalom, and knew it was a blessing of peace. The singing stopped as we entered the long and narrow room. All eyes turned towards me.

"Shalom, here is Rutka, Moshe's cousin." Tzvi said.

Boys and girls sat along the long benches on either side of the two wooden tables. "Shalom and welcome." With their smiles of welcome and curiosity, they looked glad to see me.

I saw a boy waving me over. Could this be Moshe? I thought I recognized his mass of short, black, curly hair and that shy smile. He had grown tall since I'd last seen him, and I noticed that he was still very thin. Impatient, he ran up to me, his smile lighting up his face. When he reached me, he stopped, apparently lost for words, and started to shuffle his feet.

"Say shalom and take her to your table already." Tzvi laughed, giving us both a little push. Moshe pulled me towards the bench, and a few kids slid over to make room. They didn't seem to mind squeezing in, and I appreciated their willingness to endure a bit of discomfort. Another tin plate, spoon, and cup appeared in front of me.

"Thank you, and sorry to interrupt your dinner," I said.

A sandy haired fellow grinned at me and said, "Always happy to make room for one of our own. Isn't that right, gang?"

A chorus of voices echoed agreement, and everybody moved just a little bit more to give me extra space at the table. As I took my seat among them, they applauded, shouting shalom, shalom, and welcome. They made me feel that I belonged. Feeling grateful, I put my hands together and clapped right along with them. The clapping and laughing didn't stop till Tzvi put his two fingers between his lips and blew a loud whistle. After we all quieted down, I used my first Hebrew word.

"Shalom to all of you, I'm glad to be here," I said, giving them one of my best smiles. Then I turned to Moshe and gave him a big hug. He hugged me right back and squeezed my hand.

Then everybody started to sing again. This time I knew the Yiddish words: "Never say that you walk your last mile." I sang along, remembering and honoring those who did indeed walk their last mile. Even now, after the Nazi death machine had ceased and the camps had emptied of prisoners and their keepers, the few who survived remained defiant. We would never forget. We'd keep on walking, keep on singing in an affirmation of life. When we sang this song in the camps, we sang out our hope and will to endure.

114

"Zog nit keynmol az du geyst dem letstn veig..." We sang out our Jewish defiance of the Nazis. Our song became a resistance hymn. Many of us had never met him, but we all knew the man called Hirsh Glik. He wrote it. That song was even adopted by all Eastern European partisans. I'd learned it in the camps, and now I added my voice to the chorus as we sang in Yiddish about courage and our resolve to "Never say that you tread your final path."

Wedged between Moshe and another girl, I blended my voice with theirs, and our voices rang out in one chorus, one body of sound, and one resolve. We had endured even though the Nazis had vowed to murder every Jew. We lived, and the fact of our being alive defied Hitler and denied him the "final solution." We continued to sing while several boys and girls came in carrying bowls full of potatoes and cabbage. The room quickly filled with the steaming aroma of food, and I remembered that I was very hungry. I wanted to pounce on the food, but restrained myself, and waited for the serving platters to reach me. Laughter, conversation, and the clinking of utensils bounced off the hard surfaces of the room. We ate. Most of us spoke Polish, though some preferred to speak Yiddish.

Moshe introduced me to a girl named Zehava. Another Hebrew name, I thought and asked, "What did they call you when you were born?"

"I was named Genia, but if I'm going to Israel, I'll need a Hebrew name," Zehava answered in Polish.

Moshe added, "We have no home in Poland anymore."

"Yeah, but you're still speaking Polish." I replied. Moshe looked at me as if I was a fool, "Well, we don't know all the words yet, but as soon as we learn to speak Hebrew, we'll never speak Polish again."

"I don't think we have a home anywhere," I retorted.

"We will, in Israel," Moshe insisted.

"Moshe, how can we just go somewhere we've never been to, and say that's where we belong?" I wanted to know

"That's where we came from, and that's where we belong," Zehava argued.

We would have continued our discussion, but for Tzvi, who

stood to announce work assignments. "There is the list," he said, pointing to a blackboard at the end of the room.

Exhausted from my long night's journey and little sleep, I wanted nothing to do with chores, but then I noticed there were no servants around. We shared food, and we had to share all the chores as well.

"What will I have to do?" I asked Moshe.

Both Zehava and Moshe stood up, "Let's go see." The three of us marched over to the blackboard. But my name wasn't listed. Since I could hardly keep my eyes open for lack of sleep, I was glad at first. But I had to ask why.

"Your first day here, and you're already raring to go," Tzvi smiled, and then spoke to a girl standing nearby, "Halinka, find her a bed." Turning to me, he added, "Tomorrow is soon enough for chores."

A special meeting had been scheduled for the next morning. All the chores were reduced to a fast clean up after breakfast. Then we rearranged the tables and chairs in the dining room so it could be used for an assembly. After we were seated in rows facing the front of the room, Tzvi stood up to announce that this was to be a very special assembly. A Sabra soldier was expected to address us shortly.

I turned to Moshe, "What is a Sabra?"

"Sabra is a Jew who was born in Israel."

I wanted to ask him more, but Tzvi stood and called for order and quiet. Next he introduced Joseph, a tall, skinny guy who could speak both Polish and Hebrew. Joseph looked to be in his early twenties. He paced back and forth across the little stage, blinking his right eye repeatedly. I wished he'd stop fidgeting, and I wondered what made him so nervous. Once he stopped his prowling across the little stage, he faced us and started to speak. He mentioned that word, Sabra, again. Here was another new word, and it sounded hard. As a collector of new words, I preferred the soft, mellifluous ones.

"Meet Haim," Joseph introduced us to Haim, a Sabra and an Israeli soldier. Now that was a big surprise. Never before had I met a Jewish soldier, didn't even know there was such a thing. The only soldiers I ever saw were the SS men, Gestapo, and SS guards, hard and angry men who hurt woman, men, and even small children. Soldiers were killers. I didn't think that Jews could also be soldiers. The Jewish men I knew were soft spoken, quiet, and gentle people. They studied and prayed. I'd never seen one hurt anybody on purpose. But here was this Sabra, this soldier who looked and acted unlike any Jew I'd ever met before. Sun-bronzed, tall, and muscular, he walked up to front of the room, wearing short pants and a short sleeved shirt. I had never seen a grown man in short pants before. He clasped Joseph's arm so hard, I thought he'd crush it. Joseph gritted his teeth, and tried to smile despite his pain. Joseph was there to translate everything Haim had to tell us, the Sabra soldier could only speak Hebrew.

"He came to lead us back to Israel," Joseph began.

Like Moses to the Promised Land? I wisecracked silently.

We quieted down, as Haim began to speak in Hebrew. Even his words sounded strong and muscular, almost aggressive, not at all like the soft gentle speech of a Jewish man. With Joseph translating, we learned that along with other Israelis, Haim was training the older boys and girls to be group leaders who could guide us on our journey to the land of Israel.

"We're ready to welcome you home," Haim said "Come Israel,"

More than anything, I and everyone else in that room yearned to go home. We had all lost ours and I still couldn't understand how we could go back to a country that once, long ago, was our home. That country no longer existed. After all these many years could it still be our homeland?

Haim explained that some Jews had never left Israel. They continued to live there for centuries and knew no other place they could call home. Many other Jews never left the general area. They scattered throughout the middle-east, he told us, then quickly got down to the business at hand, telling us about the long journey. First we'd have to cross the border from Poland to Germany, and that would not be easy. Crossing borders without proper documents was illegal and dangerous. It was important for us to know and understand that Polish border guards would be patrolling this side of the border. They would be on the lookout for anyone trying to cross without permission. And even after we got past them safely, the German border guards would be on the lookout to prevent us from crossing into Germany.

"To keep from getting caught, you'll have to cross at night," Haim said, and Joseph translated every word gravely. Then he told us that since he had already gone through the training, he'd be our group leader along with Tzvi.

Tzvi then told us that we would be spending the next few weeks training for the journey. We'd have to practice walking in the woods at night without making any noise, and we'd have to accomplish this without the benefit of even the smallest of flashlights, because a light would be certain to attract the attention of the border guards. "Even the sound of someone stepping on a twig could bring them running," Tzvi said.

I took one look at Joseph's nervous eye tick; saw his clenched hands and white knuckles. He's afraid, I thought, has no confidence in his own abilities. Then I breathed a prayer of thanks, realizing that it was Tzvi who would be leading us, with Joseph helping out. I believed that if anyone could guide us safely, Tzvi was the one.

Tzvi finished talking, and I watched Haim clap his big hand on Joseph's shoulder. The poor fellow looked like he'd fall on his face. In contrast to Joseph, Haim looked strong, confident, and brave; it was hard to imagine him afraid of anything. He didn't look like someone who'd ever been jammed into a cattle car for shipment to the crematorium. He was a Sabra, born and brought up away from Europe, the Yiddish shtetles, and the Nazis.

The experience of Diaspora did not apply to Haim. He was a Sabra. Israel was the only home he knew. He had never been dispossessed, sick, hungry, and afraid. Would he be so brave, if he weren't a Sabra? But it didn't matter. It wouldn't be Haim leading us across the border. It would be Tzvi with Joseph helping him— Joseph a boy with a nervous eye tick. It would be a daunting journey, but I refused to fear. I had survived worse calamities enduring long days and nights in the camps. Crossing the border at night should be easy by comparison. Joseph may look skinny, weak, and frightened, I thought, but he is also a survivor. I decided to trust him. I determined to make myself ready during the coming weeks of training. I would study Hebrew during day, and practice walking in the silence and darkness of the forest at night.

After breakfast the next morning, it was time to learn about Jewish history. The dining room became our classroom. We learned the story of our own people. It took no more than a couple of hours before my mind turned to a jumble. I was mesmerized by the story of Abraham and Sarah, and Isaac their son. But before I could begin to absorb the story of the sacrifice of Isaac, we were already going to Moses and story of the journey to freedom, the way he led our people through the vast desert. I would have loved to have stopped and thought about the events one at a time, but no, we had to cram, absorb hundreds of years of history in as short time as possible. After all, we were going to the Promised Land, and we had to know our ancestors and where we came from.

I listened to stories about "The Land of our Forefathers, the Land of Israel," and I tried to picture it in my mind. I imagined sand dunes stretching in all directions, and camel caravans moving slowly across that monochromatic landscape, but those images came only through the barely remembered old picture books I had seen as a child.

How could I absorb such a kaleidoscope of history when it was condensed into just a few hours of study?

But our studies, composed as they were of tiny slices of time, nevertheless showed me that I belonged in this story, was a part of it, part of the continuing tradition passed on from one generation to another for years without end. I learned a new word, Diaspora, and what it meant to belong to a group of people who were not welcome in any one land. I was one of those people. The last six years of war was the culmination of Diaspora, a story of a rejected people, banned from their homes, their land, and their place in the world, people who were forced to wonder the earth from one country to another, and never be at home. And I began to think that it was a curse to be a Jew. But I wanted to know who had cursed us and why. Was it God?

For the next several days, I sat in that study room among the other boys and girls, learning who we were and where we came from. We learned that history is not some dead bunch of other lives now gone and buried. The past lives on through the living, through now and long into the future and those yet to be born. I learned that what had gone before affects what happens now, and that every life and every event carries consequences.

Tzvi ended each lesson with the words, "Never again," a phrase that rang out through the room like a battle cry. "NEVER AGAIN," he'd say, his fist striking the air, while we chanted our response making the room resound with those words, "NEVER AGAIN." It had become a mantra that expressed our communal determination to never again be subjected to the cruelty of tyrants because we had no home of our own. Now I began to understand why we had to endure the tyranny and the indifference of citizens whose land we had to inhabit throughout the years of our Diaspora.

But now we were determined to go home again. The idea of going home, of reclaiming what had been lost hundreds of years earlier, kindled my spirit so that I could almost believe there was a better future for us finally, a future in a home of our own, a place where we belonged. Yet that home seemed far removed from everything I had experienced in my life. Israel was very far away, and our journey long and hazardous.

Joseph translated while Haim continued to talk. His clear voice resounded with determination and enthusiasm. "There is much more to accomplish," he said. "Right now the British rule in Israel. They refuse to allow anymore Jews to enter the country. "But we're determined." Haim's fist struck high into the air, as Joseph translated, "We will not be stopped from reclaiming our homeland. If they prohibit legal entry, then we'll enter illegally. The British capture our ships as they attempt to enter the port of Haifa. Still some of our ships get through. The British soldiers board the ships they catch and force them to sail to Cypress, an island where they've established camps for holding Jews imprisoned behind barbed wire." He paced the little stage like a caged tiger. Joseph translated.

Haim continued, "We have a long and hard struggle ahead and you're all a part of the great effort. Remember, nothing good or worthwhile can be won without a struggle."

I wanted none of it, not the trouble nor the struggle. Here's another dead end, I thought, wanting to leave the room.

"Why should anyone object, if we want to return to Israel?"

one of the boys asked.

"What is this place Cypress?" a girl wanted to know. Many hands were raised, and Tzvi clapped his hands for silence to prevent pandemonium.

"Cypress is a Mediterranean island controlled by the British," he said.

"So, we could end up in a concentration camp, if they catch us?" a skinny little fellow yelped.

"The Brits don't kill Jews, but yes, you could become a prisoner again," Haim said.

That was scary, to be imprisoned behind a barbed wire fence, to stand helpless on the wrong side of a barbed wire fence, NO! I wanted to scream my terror. "NEVER AGAIN!" the words rang echoes in my brain as I bolted for the door.

"You must understand the dangers, before you agree to come with us. " I heard Tzvi speak, even as I stood in the open door ready to leave. Was he speaking to me? Hand still resting on the doorknob, I paused to listen.

"How many of you came back here hoping to find your family?"

A chorus of voices and raised hands gave him the answer.

"And how many of you found even one member of your family?"

Most hands went down.

"Can you make a new home here? Do you want to have your children here?"

One voice, a resounding, "NO!" clamored through the room.

I stood by the door, thinking that I also wanted a home and a family, but I knew it could not happen here, not in Poland. At the same time, I worried about the possibility of becoming a prisoner again.

"What are you willing to risk?"

Ah, there it was, a question for which I had no answer, and I returned to my seat.

Many more questions followed. "What if we're caught at the border? Will they shoot us on the spot?" someone asked.

Tzvi laughed, "Not likely. If you're stopped on the Polish side, they'll just ship you right back. That's the danger. The

Germans are done with killing the Jews, so they'll look the other way. Remember, the worst that could happen is that the British catch you and keep you for a while on Cypress."

Like some sun God, bronzed, tall, and strong, Haim stood next to Tzvi, his fist in the air, the deep resonance of his voice reassuring. "You better believe this, and know it well. We will regain our land, we will win our independence, and we will bring you home." Haim bared his white teeth in a huge smile, and made it all seem less frightening somehow. He was brave enough for all of us, I thought. Some of his strength and determination seeped into me. My curiosity replaced my fear, and the prospect of crossing the border started to look more like an adventure. What will it really be like? I wondered. The mystery of it opened before me like a great arching doorway.

With the prospect of our journey ever nearer, I tried to work up some serious courage, reminding myself that only a couple of months earlier; I had crossed the border without a permit. I didn't know at that time that my home was not in Poland, my long walk from Germany to Poland was only the beginning of the long journey I'd have to take. I hoped that when I crossed back again from Poland to Germany, I would really be on the way home. It would be just a walk in the woods at night, I tried to persuade myself. Hadn't I lived in fear long enough? I'd not be afraid now. Nothing could be worse than the camps.

Haim's strength of purpose inspired courage. He put himself at risk for us, came here all that way from Israel just to help us, and I trusted him to deliver on his promise. He was unlike any man I'd met before, broad and tall, strong and smiling, a Jewish soldier. I couldn't help but like and admire him. Truth be told, I was a tiny bit attracted to him. Lost in my trance over Haim, I missed a bit of Joseph's translation.

"How long will it take to cross the border?" one of the braver boys piped up.

"Depends, we follow a different route each night."

Someone wanted to know how much baggage they'd be allowed to carry.

"How much have you got?" he asked.

"The clothes on my back, and I'm lucky to have that."

122

The whole room resounded with laughter.

"What about Genia?" I whispered to Moshe.

"I hope she'll be coming with us," he looked unsure. "I'm not going without her," he added.

"So go ask him," I suggested. Moshe looked uncertain, but he followed me when I marched off to talk to Tzvi, whose tall frame towered above the kids who stood around him. I pushed my way up front and got his attention. "What about Moshe's mom, Genia Pashtan, will she be going with us?" I looked at Genia who sat quietly at the table and went on, "As you know she lives in Warsaw. Surely you can appreciate that she cannot be separated from her son. Can she come along with us?"

Tzvi chuckled, "Such a speech you make. We don't break up families. That's not our way." After checking his list of names, he smiled, "Genia Pashtan is listed in the group with Moshe Pashtan, and Rutka you're on this list as well."

We studied history each morning from 9 to 12. The afternoons were devoted to the study of Hebrew. It was a peculiar language made only of consonants, no vowels. And to make it even more difficult, it was written in a script that ran across the page from right to left. And to add to my confusions the letters of this script were unlike any symbols I had ever seen. So I knew that it would be really hard to learn these strange little lines and dots written backwards across the page. Fact is, learning this language was going to be impossible. First of all, how do you learn a language with no vowels? I was told that the vowel sound was hidden in the context or the meaning of the word, but that was no help at all. How was I going to tackle a process that involved the application of unspecified vowels to specific consonants, when I didn't know the meaning of the words in the first place?

Still I persevered with all the earnest determination I could muster. After all, it was the language of my people, the language of a lost land. I had to master the one before I could help to regain the other.

History was much easier; it was just a matter of following the story of my people way back before the First Temple and after the destruction of the Second Temple. I learned about the ancient land of Judea, (land of the Jews). Even back then, the stronger, bigger neighbors preferred to ignore the borders, and crossed the land of Judea without so much as a by your leave. They crossed in peace and war. In time of peace they crossed to trade, and when they quarreled, they cut across to murder one another and as many Jews as got in the way. They used the land of Judea as their warpath. That wasn't good for the Jews to be stuck always in the middle. I didn't understand how they got in such a fix.

I learned about the Diaspora, listened to the ancient stories, and remembered our home at Passover time, and the one phrase repeated after evening meal, "next year in Jerusalem." Every year it was the same. The men would end their prayer with this phrase, "next year in Jerusalem." It was the fervent prayer of a people who never forgot their homeland throughout the hundreds of years of the Diaspora.

I learned about the dispersion of Jews throughout the world, and how it came to be that Jews became homeless, wanderers forced to live in other people's lands. It was my history, and I was a part of it, a history of generations one after another, who wandered the world, preserving their identity, their books, their history, a people who attempted to live without hurting others. Yet they endured persecution and exploitation.

I learned another phrase, "the people of the book." That's when I remembered Great-Grandfather Zyde and the ever present book in his wrinkled hands. I was too young then to know that it was the Bible. I remembered that both Grandfather and Great-Grandfather prayed each morning. I was mystified to see them with their black and white striped prayer shawls wrapped around their shoulders and over their heads. I was especially puzzled by the black leather boxes which were bound to their foreheads with leather straps that wrapped around their arm. Zyde told me that the little leather box contained the teachings of the Torah, the foundation of all Jewish life. He spoke of the Torah with reverence, for it taught how to conduct life with grace and justice. The shawl, leather box and leather straps were the symbols of God's commandments and His presence in every living moment. Zyde explained to me that the Torah teaches each of us how to be a good human being, a mench.

Now that I was much older, I understood that my Zyde fastened his little leather box to his forehead and entwined the leather strap around his left hand because that was a traditional binding of prayer, history and tradition. All the pieces started to come together for me now, my family's adherence to the tradition of study, the bible, and the law. All of it was part of the tradition that bound us through centuries and made us who we are, Jews, a homeless nation carrying our portable religion and way of being wherever we went.

The history of pogroms, inquisitions, and worst of all, the holocaust, all the pieces of the tale came together, as I began to understand who I was and where I came from. I felt no longer rootless. I felt that I belonged, was a part of the history of the Jewish people, the people of the book, the dispersed people who had wandered this earth hoping each year at Passover to return home. "Next year in Jerusalem," these were words to remind us that we longed for our home.

I learned that the word Hebrew also can be translated to mean wanderer, and I also learned another word, "Zionism."

The holocaust could only happen to people who had no land of their own. I knew that now, and I began to share the need of the dispersed to come together and become whole again.

I was not brave, and would normally prefer to shy away from unhappiness and ugliness, preferring to read a fairy tale, than to study the often-tragic facts of Jewish history. But I realized that it was time for me to grow up, and I applied myself to my studies. History in the morning, Hebrew in the afternoon, I practiced each newly learned word with the others even during meals. I was not alone. We all struggled to formulate the simplest of requests in Hebrew. When I couldn't think of a word, or a phrase, someone always came to my rescue. What with all the pointing and gesturing, our Hebrew conversations sounded comical, but we learned, even as we laughed.

One cool September morning with the leaves turning red and gold, crunching beneath our feet, we left the farmhouse for the last time to walk to the railroad station and begin the first phase of our Journey home. The train would take us to a little town in the Carpathian Mountains, near the border.

Chapter 11

A sudden shout rang in the stillness of the dark forest. "Halt!" The moment it sounded the thick rope tightened in my hand. Each one of us paused like a frightened deer, unmoving for several moments, hardly breathing for fear of making a sound.

"HALT!" we heard again, but this time we recognized the sound. It was only the hoot of an owl somewhere in a nearby tree. Except for that owl and the barely perceptible whisper of falling leaves all else was silence. The sky was dark, no moon, and no stars. Another moment passed and I felt a sharp tug of the rope, a signal that it was safe to move on. Tethered to the heavy rope, we walked single file, ten boys and girls between the ages of 15 and 18; we barely appeared as shadows in the forest, all wearing dark pants, jackets, and caps. Even our faces were dark, camouflaged with dull brown paint. I moved silently, my right hand moist with sweat, but holding fast. The heavy rope chafed my skin, and though it made my palm raw, I struggled to keep it from slipping in my hand. "Don't let go, no matter what." I told myself over and over again.

Like a mantra that phrase drummed in my head, repeating, "Don't let go…"

That's what Joseph told us everyday during our training sessions in preparation for this night. We were ready, I thought, but I was covered in sweat as we walked on, hardly making a sound in the forest.

Tzvi was in the lead. I followed the person ahead just as I'd been trained to do, matching each step in unison with the others. We were spaced roughly four feet apart; each person had to hold on to the rope tightly, so as not to allow any slack. In this manner, forming a straight line, making sure we did not veer off to either side, we walked along the path made safe by our guide.

We tried to avoid the many pebbles, stones, and roots of trees that covered the forest floor. One misstep, a single cough, or a sudden gasp could reveal our presence. Each one felt responsible for the safety of all. My position was at about mid-point between Tzvi in front, and the person who brought up the rear. Like the others, I took one step at a time, in one rhythm. Our little group formed itself into a single unit, breathing as one.

I held the rope and it held me up and helped me to keep from losing my balance. I knew that should I trip, I was supposed to signal a stop by giving three sharp tugs on the rope and hold it at all costs until I regained my balance. Then I could give the all clear by slackening up on the rope just a bit, followed immediately by two sharp tugs, so we could resume our slow, methodical progress.

In this way, each one hung on to the rope, and all of us hung together. We moved as one, with one single purpose, to cross the border without getting caught. I thought it a miracle that no one had slipped so far. Each time I stumbled, I wanted to shout, "Ouch," but I didn't. We moved through the darkness and fog in silence.

It had been raining for two days and had stopped only a little while earlier, so the ground was still spongy and slippery. Each of us knew that a single splash in a puddle, one slip of a foot on a wet stone could bring the border guards. My mouth was dry, but I couldn't stop even for one sip, although I had water in my canteen. I didn't want to hold them up, so I kept moving to the cadence of step, balance, step, in the silence, in the dark.

After hours of walking, I felt the rope slackening in my hand, and I even caught myself nodding off. That's when I stubbed my toe. I felt the sharp pain, and had to stifle my cry, and grasp the rope more firmly, to signal a stop. I gave it three sharp tugs. Alert now I balanced myself against the rope and lifted my left foot. But then my toe scraped against the side of the stone, so I had to lift my foot higher still, feeling for the stone. When my toe found it and gently touched its surface, I slid my foot over the top of the stone, all the while trying to keep my balance. That's a large stone

127

I thought, leaning forward, letting my foot slip carefully down over the front of the stone until I could feel the solid ground beneath my foot. But I was only half way done. I brushed my right foot along the ground attempting to clear the right side of the rock. Luckily I discovered that I'd already got through most of the obstacle with my left.

If I wasn't so scared, I may have been proud of my achievement of getting through the ordeal without a major mishap. My entire body was bathed in cold sweat, and I shivered in the chilly breeze. The knuckles and palms of my hands hurt from squeezing the rope so tightly. But I forced myself to stay alert, took a deep breath, and gave the signal to move on.

A short time later, we heard another sound in the distance. We couldn't quite tell at first what made this sound. But then, I heard it again, only now it was coming closer. Long mournful and longing, a sound an animal might make.

The rope tightened in my hand, and it was followed by five sharp tugs in succession. That was the signal to begin winding the circle. I had hoped never to experience such a signal on this trip, as it was to be used only in case of extreme danger. This signal told us we'd have to defend ourselves. We began the winding of the circle.

The last person in line began to turn first, spiraling back. I knew that I must be patient. Must not move while the winding continued, until it reached me, then it would be my turn to spiral back and become enfolded within the circle. I was scared beyond imagining. My teeth took on a life of their own, and all I could do was to keep them from chattering too loud. But the noise of my chattering teeth was nothing to the chorus of barks and growls as they came closer and louder. Hardest of all was having to stand still and wait, while what sounded like wild dogs approached. We'd been cautioned about those dogs. Many domesticated dogs had lost their homes during the war, and now ran in packs, hunting prey, especially in the forests.

The clamor grew ever louder. I shook in fear. They'll be upon us, pounce within moments. Every instinct screamed, RUN! Yet I knew that I must hold my ground, hold the rope, and wait. I held my breath, willed myself to patience. Of one thing I was certain. The circle had to close before the wild dogs were upon us.

Separated from the others by four feet of rope, front of the line and back, I felt alone and exposed. If the dogs got to me before I was enfolded within the circle, they'd tear me apart. Every fiber in my body screamed, drop the rope! RUN! Yet I stood, a mantra repeating in my mind, "mustn't panic, mustn't run, mustn't..."

And when I thought that I could no longer stand and wait, I felt the touch of the person next in line, and it was time for me to turn and spiral back, continuing to wind our circle till I felt the touch of the person next in line, who followed in her turn, while those behind each boy and girl continued, one by one to spiral back. Thus we continued enfolding each of us in turn, until the last person closed the circle with his own body becoming a shield. The tallest, strongest, oldest boys, stood next to Tzvi. They formed a protective shield around us. They were our defense line, each one pointing the sharp end of his stick at the oncoming howling dogs.

I recalled someone saying that wild dogs don't attack anything bigger than themselves. Our circle was big, bigger than any individual dog in the pack. But what if they were hungry, starved? Would they attack and was I somewhat safer inside the circle?

My heart thumped fast and loud, I clamped my teeth to keep them still against the ever-louder howls. Suddenly, my feet and ankles felt their moist hot breath. And then the pack split around us and passed us, while we stood still and listened to their receding barks and howls.

Tzvi, first in line started to unwind, then each of us followed in turn reversing our spiral, unwinding till all of us, boys and girls, stood four feet apart in a straight line as before. My legs felt soft and rubbery. I didn't know if they would hold me up. But then I felt the rope tighten in my hand, and I had to move forward. Step, pause, step, we moved in unison towards I knew not what.

Chapter 12

I sat cross-legged on the grass and gazed at the shallow stream covered by small, colorful pebbles, their reflections sparkling in the sun. The water ran clear, bidding me to come feel its cool liquid welcome. I gazed into that dazzling river. It looked so clear and clean. I wanted to wade in and cleanse off the filth of the camps. I felt it clinging to my body still, although I had showered earlier in the day. How much water would it take to rid me of that filth? Would it ever rinse away?

The hills clad in foliage glowed red, gold, and rust. Yet their beauty could not blot out the ugly images of the camps. The stink of death was in my nostrils still, despite the clean crisp air I breathed now.

Golden yellows of the fall echoed the war time color of my skin. It had turned yellow in the camps, yellow from rolling bullets cross my palm, back and forth. Yellow, like the color of my shame, yellow from the sulfur in those bullets that I rolled, hours, days, nights across my palm, ceaselessly...

...Their yellow guts pollute my skin, every inch. I cannot wash it off, and I feel shame each time I place a perfect bullet in a box, and go on rolling, rolling in my hand, while sulfur, like some brimstone straight from hell, leaks yellow poison through my skin...

No amount of soap, not even this clear, clean water could ever remove that stain of brimstone yellow. I'd have liked to let it go, forget it, but I couldn't, and so sitting there in the waning light I went on cataloguing memories of hell. Even the aroma of freshly

130

fallen leaves could not blot the stench of those camps where we had been crowded, pallid bags of bones resembling corpses more than living human beings. And so this stench of death clung now to me as did my memories.

Here was the cool soft grass, the fleecy clouds, the river flowing clear as it had done for generations. I admired the butterflies, gold mixed with red, and thought about the metamorphosis of butterflies. Could I transform myself as well? Could I fly free?

I recalled a little village, a mountain resort called Zakopane. In summers past, we used to visit there. Had it been only a few years ago? It seemed to me now like a dream that never was.

The slope of land, the way the river glistened in the sun, the sound it made splashing over the colored pebbles, the kuku bird, its call from a nearby maple tree, all of it now brought memories of my family, and our walks by the riverbank. Haniushka was so little then, she'd walk for a bit, and then she'd ask my dad to lift her up, place her on his shoulders, and he always obliged…

… *"Just for a little bit, honey; you're a big girl now, getting too heavy to carry. Yes, I know, it's hard to keep up with Rutechka and those long legs of hers."*

Hania sits up on his shoulders like a five-year old queen. She puts her pudgy arms around his head, fingers playing through his hair, and says, "I'm just a little tired now Daddy; I will walk soon."…

A lovely image from another life, and I recalled it now. Why? Perhaps it was this place, so bright and clean, perhaps it was the new, clean clothes that I wore now. Was it just two nights earlier when we walked through the forest in the night? The wild dogs, and the constant fear of border guards, even the rope that was my lifeline then, seemed like a dream. That rope supported me, kept me from falling, made me feel less afraid, and less alone. As I held it, I felt bound to them, the boys and girls who walked a single line in the dark along with me.

When we arrived in this place, just two days ago, each one of us was so tired that we were hardly able to keep our eyes open.

131

Now, as I looked at my white blouse and blue skirt, I smoothed the clean, new material against my skin. I felt renewed, glad to discard the used clothes that I wore before. Tzvi distributed these fresh new garments to everyone in our group before he told us to bathe and grab a couple hours of sleep. But I was much too tired from all that walking through the night. I skipped the bath, and fell into the bed, dirty and sweaty as I was, more than half-asleep even before my body touched my bed.

The clanging of the bell woke me a few hours later, and I saw the sun was well passed its zenith. I had slept that day away, I thought, seeing the sun touching the horizon.

I got up, showered, dressed and, looking in the mirror, marveled at the transformation. There was my clean face, clean clothes, and yet the stain of Auschwitz hid within, I thought, even if no one else could see it. This stain was burning in my gut. Why couldn't I forget those awful days? Why did I have to carry memories like these, as if they were some dreadful souvenir that had been thrust upon me? I didn't want it.

Everyone showered, and then we assembled in the dining hall for dinner, the girls in their new white blouses and blue skirts, the boys in white shirts and blue pants. I wondered if they too felt the hidden stain of camps under those fresh clean faces. Each of them felt it, as I did, I was sure, but no one would admit it. We all wanted to forget, leave it behind.

After dinner, Tzvi told us a little about this temporary place where he expected we'd be for a time. He didn't say how long. "They call this place the sanatorium because during the war it was used for Hitler's wounded soldiers to rest and heal. Originally it was the home of a wealthy family." Then Tzvi told us about UNRA, an agency that works to aid displaced persons. He said that after the war, UNRA decided to use the villa as a temporary refuge for people like us.

Displaced person, I cringed at this designation, didn't like the sound of it. Yet wasn't it true? Haven't I been displaced from my home, my place in life? Six years of my childhood had gone missing, and I could never get it back. Never again could I see my mother and father. I'd never see my little sister, Hania. Where once my family was now there was vast emptiness. I also thought about the uncles and the cousins whom I cared about and could never see again.

Still there were some good people left in the world, people who thought of our plight, and who provided this quiet restful place for us to rest and heal. We were no less than Hitler's soldiers deserving of such a place. We didn't fight the war, but suffered from it all the same. I wished that I could thank whoever those kind people were who gave us this refuge for a while.

We slept another night and when I awoke this morning, I was glad to see that this place of refuge that we've come to was still real and not a dream. I'd gone down to the river after our breakfast and sat by the stream for hours, so it seemed. Now with most of the morning gone, I hoped with the time I'd spend right here, this could be my healing place. It's where I'd rest, and lick my wounds, remember and then hopefully, forget.

The sound of singing drifted down towards me from the villa. Lunchtime I thought, but still I couldn't leave this quiet spot. Alone here by the stream, I felt the balm of solitude; perhaps I'd find some peace here in this quiet oasis. The quiet hours here by the flowing stream would let me heal, or so I hoped. I would come back here often, I was sure.

Lunch time and I was hungry. I'd have to leave this place, start walking up across the broad expanse of grass towards the big white house that stood on top of the hill. I climbed the broad steps up to the terrace framed by a row of pillars fronting the handsome house. As I approached, I heard the singing through the open doors. Climbing the last few steps, I hastened inside to see Moshe wave and shout from across the room, "Saved you a seat." He pointed to an empty chair across from him.

"Where did you go this morning?" Moshe asked.

"River."

"Alone?" he sounded quite amazed.

"Sometimes I like to be alone."

Moshe nodded. I think he understood, and then he smiled and made the introductions. "This is Marissa," he said, pointing to the girl sitting next to him. Curly blond hair, blue eyes, a heart shaped, face, she smiled, producing dimples in her cheeks.

"I'm Halinka," a girl sitting next to Marissa said. I admired her hair and wished mine was as thick, and long, and shiny black. My hair was mousy brown and thin, so wispy it just refused to stay in place.

Her hair has character, I thought. It stays quietly where she's put it, hangs long and thick down to her shoulders. How did she grow it this long in less than a year? I wondered, remembering those shaved heads we all had at the end of war. The Nazis had shaved our heads because of lice.

Halinka had large brown, smoky eyes. Some call them bedroom eyes. Her cheeks were pale, flat, and wide, her head held high, nose in the air.

"Halinka, what a lovely name," I said. The girl smiled sadly in response.

What's her problem? Is she shy or stuck up? I wanted to like her. I imagined she wanted to be liked as well. Yet there seemed to be a barrier between us. I felt that sad little smile of hers was almost like a shroud that kept her from the living. Her sadness appeared to swallow her up. Nothing could dispel it, or so it seemed to me, not this lovely house, not the good food, and not the clean new clothes that caressed her skin.

By contrast Marissa was livelier. She responded with interest when I mentioned the river where I had spent the afternoon.

"Is it far?" she asked. "You make it sound so lovely."

There was something almost dramatic about the way Marissa spoke. Halinka said nothing, and our conversation lagged. I looked around. The scale of the room, the elegance of the place, made me sit up straight, take my elbows off the table, and eat like the lady I'd been taught to be. I chewed slowly, putting small morsels of warm bread, or baked potato, into my mouth, one at a time, and spoke only after I swallowed. Mom and Dad insisted on proper table manners, and so did the Ursuline Sisters at the Convent. Focusing on my redeemed table manners, I wondered how long it would be before I'd get used to my new, or rather my old self.

Was I playacting? What's with the table manners? Did the camp years vanish? Had humiliation and hunger never happened? Had I not been forced to exist like a pig in a sty, starving most of

134

the days, grabbing what food came my way with mud-smeared hands?

Sitting in the handsome dining hall, at a table laden with fresh bread and sweet butter, food such as I had not seen in years, I began to feel a bit more like the person I used to be. Even the sound of utensils and conversation began to sound rhythmic and melodious to me. And I let the normalcy of the place seep slowly into my soul. It's all right, I told myself. I can enjoy the food. It is permissible to smile, maybe even laugh. All the time, a censor within chided me less I forget. Yes, I was alive, but how could I think of enjoying this meal, when I remembered Haniushka? That sweet little girl would never eat again, never enjoy a piece of fruit, a glass of chocolate milk. No candy, no meat, not even one plain boiled potato would ever pass her lips. Suddenly I was no longer hungry.

Chapter 13

Our daily routine fell into a rhythm of morning chores, followed by two hours of lessons, and one hour of free time before lunch, then more chores and free time in the afternoon. Drawn into this measured rhythm of structure and predictability, I started to unwind. I liked doing the chores. They made me feel part of the group. Also participating in what needed to be done, I felt useful. We all took our turn at preparing food, setting up before, or cleaning up after meals. Yet there was still plenty of free time during the day and in the evening to do or not, as we chose.

Once a week, after dinner clean-up, we had to prepare the room for our weekly gathering. We pushed the tables back against the walls and arranged the chairs in rows. Sometimes we'd have a guest speaker who'd tell us about immigrating to Israel. Many other times we'd watch a movie, usually one made in America or England, and although I didn't know the language, the simple story line allowed me to follow the plot, which usually revolved around two beautiful people falling in love. It almost always took place among mountains, or palm trees, or along the endless ribbons of sand washed by the foam of breaking waves. The men were all handsome, the women all beautiful.

Their reflected images moved among the many mirrored, shiny surfaces of the interior sets. It didn't matter about the strange language. I invented my own dialogue to fit the simple plot. All in all, I found that attending movies proved more fun than daydreaming.

We settled into the placid days of summer. Genia, now called Zahava, found a small apartment in Munich. Moshe went to see her there, and each time he returned he told me about the many

136

wonders he had seen in that ancient German town.

But best of all, after a few days, I made friends with the two girls I'd met the first night, Marissa and Halinka, a sad girl whom I soon realized had a club foot. There was an extra bed in their room, and they invited me to share with them. I gladly accepted. Our friendship grew slowly from that day on, and soon the three of us were best of friends. We sat together at mealtimes, volunteered for the same chores, and spent all our free time together. I showed them the stream I had discovered and it became our favorite spot.

Walking along the bank of the stream one day, Halinka found a spot where the water was deep enough to swim. We used to go there often, especially in good weather. The three of us liked to stretch our towels by the side of that stream. We'd sunbathe and talk, while the narrow river ran on murmuring in the background. Every so often, the heat of the sun forced us into the cool stream. We'd swim, splash one another, and laugh. We lost ourselves in such moments, and even Halinka shed some of her sadness.

As the days cooled, we started to explore the woods. Marissa knew all about mushrooms. She showed us the ones to pick. Halinka and I were not totally convinced. How could she really tell which were safe to eat? we wondered. But on the first day after the rain, when the mushrooms were especially plentiful, the three of us went into the woods. Marissa pointed out the little brown things growing in the soft moist ground beneath the trees. She also showed us the ones to avoid. We picked bucketfuls that afternoon, enough for everybody. After the head housekeeper was consulted and declared the mushrooms safe, all of us enjoyed the special mushroom addition to our meal.

Our placid days were occasionally interspersed by an outing. With Tzvi as our guide, we'd board a train, and go to visit an old ruin, or a famous castle. Tzvi had an old worn tourist book that he always took along. No one knew where he got it.

I moved through those days in a dreamy kind of way, taking each day without any expectation. I knew that we'd have to leave one day. I didn't know when, so I lived in the moment, letting it flow around and through me like a balm. With few demands, and much quiet time for rest and reflection, each day brought with it a sense of letting go. Life at the villa was an interval of quietude.

Without trying to, I was able to isolate my painful memories in an unused corner of my mind. I began to heal.

From the first sound of the wake up bell, my senses opened to the wonder of each new day. I lived one moment at a time, while the sun browned my skin to a healthy glow. A swim in the stream, the coolness of the water, the soft cool grass beneath my feet when I came out to dry, all those moments were my treasure house of healing remedies. I relished the quiet talk with friends at the end of the day, their sudden laughter about nothing at all. Some evenings, we'd go out arm in arm to walk by the stream. The air was warm; the water caught the reflection of the stars that filled the sky. Other evenings we'd join everyone else in the dining hall, with chairs and tables pushed against the walls, to make it a dance hall.

I loved to whirl within the circle of the dance, to feel one with all. We were one circle of feet pounding the rhythm of the Hora, one pulse beating, one voice singing, "Maim, Maim, Maim," water, yes, yes, yes, life, and the wooden floor vibrating with the beat, and my breath running short with exertion, and later, full of song and dance, stumbling away to sleep, but not to dream, till the morning bell awakened me to another day.

Moshe continued to visit his mother in Munich, and when he came back he was full of stories. He could hardly stop talking about the Bathhouse. He told us it was most impressive. After coming back from his latest visit, he said, "Now don't forget to see the Bathhouse," as he handed me a crumpled note.

What was he talking about? I wondered, but then I understood. Moshe must have told Zahava about my two friends. The note was from his mother, an invitation to visit and bring along Halinka and Marissa. We would be going two weeks hence. He knew this would be a real treat for all three of us. He kept telling us not to miss that Bathhouse. I promised him we wouldn't, though I couldn't figure why he had a bathhouse fixation.

The three of us had never been to Munich, so we were all filled with anticipation and could hardly talk about anything else for the next two weeks.

Tzvi knew how patiently we had been waiting for this trip; so on the day before we were scheduled to go, he cancelled all but one of our chores. This one entailed a horse and wagon, and several miles of bumpy ride across a dirt road to at a nearby farm. Every week a small crew was sent out to fetch our weekly supply of bread. We had done it once or twice before, and I was looking forward to the ride, especially if I could be the one to drive. Halinka didn't seem to care. She was quiet, as usual. She never spoke much as she was very self-conscious about her clubfoot, and didn't want to attract attention to herself, but Marissa always ended up in the driver's seat.

Not today, I vowed. I excused myself from the table before the end of lunch. Then, picking up my warm sweater, hat, and gloves, I ran down across the lawn to the barn, harnessed the horse to the wagon, and by the time Halinka and Marissa came down, I was already up there, in the driver's seat, whip in hand, when Halinka and Marissa approached.

"Let me drive," Marissa demanded.

"I got here first, so I drive," I replied, and waved Halinka up next to the driver's seat.

"You can sit in the back," I said, turning to Marissa.

I was getting tired of Marissa acting like being in charge was her due. So what if she was four years older? That didn't make her special. Besides, who had a cousin in Munich? I figured this time I was entitled. Let her sulk.

I gave the horse a little touch of reins and we were off. The horse's hoofs beat on the dry and dusty road, and I figured that Marissa was still in a huff; otherwise, we'd be hearing her prattle about the beauty of the day. Sitting up front reins in hand, I proudly guided the horse. His chestnut brown body glimmered while his black mane swayed with each step. He was a frisky young horse, and knew the way. The narrow road led directly to the farm, so we wouldn't be likely to get lost anyway.

Halinka buttoned her sweater all the way up to her throat. "Getting chilly," she said.

"Should have taken the jacket, like I told you," Marissa yelled from the back.

"We're almost there, and on the way back, you can ride in the back with the warm loaves. That should keep you warm," I said

139

"I'll drive, then. I am warm in my jacket, so it'll be better that way," Marissa piped in.

"Yeah, I'm getting a bit chilly also," I agreed. Besides, I was getting tired of fencing with Marissa. If it was this important to her to be in driver's seat, let her.

The farmer's wife saw us and hollered out her window, "Hedrick! The girls are here for the bread."

The aroma of the just-out of-the-oven-bread greeted us, even before we rounded the back of the house. We saw Hedrick with a wheelbarrow full of warm loaves approach the wagon as I pulled up on the reins. The horse stopped, and I jumped down to the ground, with Halinka and Marissa close behind.

All four began to load loaves of bread into the wagon. When there were none left, Hedrick rolled the empty wheelbarrow back to fetch another load. I stood by the wagon waiting and breathing in the scent of fresh bread. The aroma brought memories of grandmother's kitchen with the whiff of her freshly baked Challah. On Fridays Grandma baked Challah for the Shabbat. Unbidden tears suddenly filled my eyes. I tried to blink them away.

When Hedrick returned with the second load, I got busy loading the wagon along with the others. The brown loaves felt warm and springy in my hands as I stacked them carefully one upon the other.

When we were done, Halinka climbed in the back of the wagon with me, while Marissa, now in the driver's seat, took up the reins. The wind picked up, and to keep warm, Halinka and I snuggled on either side of the warm stacks of bread.

Marissa can have the driver's seat, I thought. I'd rather watch the sunset. Obligingly, the fleecy clouds began to glow across the sky with streaks of gold, purple, and red. But when the sun dipped beyond the hill, and the wind picked up, not even the warm bread could keep the cool air from creeping in beneath my sweater. "Marissa was right," I whispered in Halinka's ear. "We should have brought warmer jackets."

"I heard that." Marissa laughed from her driver's seat up front.

We joined in her laughter; my eyes began to tear; I blamed it on the cold, and we just couldn't stop laughing.

The next morning, before we started for the train station, Moshe reminded me once again that Genia now preferred to be called by her Hebrew name, Zahava. "And don't forget to go to the Public Baths," he reminded me again. All three of us girls had to promise him that we would.

Our friend, Henrietta, drove us to the train station. She was older than all of us, even older than Marissa, but we liked her anyway, even if she wasn't pretty. She had this short squat body, practically no neck with a large square head. Her face was marred by pockmarks. But she was smart, kind, and helpful. She had family in America so that's where she would be going, instead of going to Israel with us.

The train station was so small; it didn't even have a ticket office. There was only this narrow platform and a couple of benches fronting the tracks. Moshe had suggested it would be best to buy tickets from the conductor on the train.

It was really cold, felt like a winter morning and when a sudden gust of wind stabbed through my wool sweater, I shivered, and hurried to cross the tracks just before the train rounded the corner.

"Don't shiver so, friends. This train is not a transport to Auschwitz," Marissa gave us a crooked smile. Some joke.

"It's the wind, and I don't need reminders," I snapped back, but my bravado wasn't working that day. The memory of another train intruded…

…"*Macht Schnell!*" *I hear the rasping voice of the SS… One of them pokes my ribs with the butt of his rifle … I feel a hard push from behind, and I stumble into the cattle car…*

"Get up here," Marissa yelled. I almost tripped on the step, but Marissa reached out her hand. "Hurry!" she yelled. I let myself be pulled aboard like a sleepwalker.

"Not easy to forget, hey?" Halinka said, putting her arm around my shoulders.

I tried to shrug it off. Halinka looked hurt, and I wanted to kick myself. After all, hadn't we shared the same fate? We were both haunted by the same ghost images from hell. I didn't want to hurt Halinka. For once, Marissa was silent.

Sitting across from my two friends, I had to remind myself that we were bound for Munich, but my mind couldn't shake off images of another time, another train, other people...

...Bodies of strangers pressing against one another...hard to breathe ...stench of unwashed bodies...the sweet/sour nauseating stink of fear...

I struggled to erase that dreadful night ride from my memory, the horror of the barely living bodies squeezed into the cattle car. I had to leave those nagging images behind, and tried to focus on the here and now. I listened to the train wheels click-clack on the rails, looked at our village moving past the window, saw the one church and one tavern, and a cluster of small houses, and as the tiny village moved out of sight. It was replaced by maples and oaks, red, gold, and crinkly, their brown leaves peppering the air as they floated to the ground. It's the here and now I told my brain. This particular train is bound for Munich...

... Standing room only, in this cattle car...must not lose my footing. If I do, someone will step on my head, grind a heel into my eye--crush every bone in my body...

Stop it! I almost shouted. Marissa and Halinka looked up, startled at my sudden movement.

"You okay?" Halinka asked.

"Sit down, Ruti. We've got a way to go," Marissa's voice was calm, soothing.

Next to Marissa sat an old woman with a basket in her lap. I thought it might contain eggs for the market, but it turned out to be a basketful of little chicks. The tiny creatures lifted first one then the other of the two covers and uttered weak little squeaks, all the while turning their scrawny heads to and fro.

Marissa rolled her eyes heavenward. She'd prefer another traveling companion.

I stared out the window. With the sound of wheels on rails continuing, I began to nod off... falling...slipping...

...Must not slip, the words reverberate in my head in cadence with the click-clack-click of wheels on steel. Strangers push me this way and that, but I keep my legs beneath me...keep them straight and tight... ...must not slip... must not fall...so dark...hard to breathe...my knees lock... will not buckle...must not slip...must not fall...Oh, but the moans...stop...stop...stop...

The train stopped with a sudden lurch. Startled I glanced across the isle, to where Marissa and Halinka slept leaning against one another. The train started up again, and I took Zehava's letter from my pocket to once again look at her directions. Simple enough, but then Munich is a large city, I thought, hoping we'd find the way to her apartment.

As we approached the outskirts of Munich, the train tracks appeared to multiply, covering a wide swatch of the ground ahead like so much spaghetti. My eyes riveted to the rails that appeared to take on a gliding motion, crossing one another as they merged and separated beneath the movement of the train.

The train entered a tunnel and plunged into darkness, barreling onward as it rocked back and forth. The speed and motion of the train seemed almost violent, and I feared it might derail. The wheels rolled through the murk down the tracks, steel on steel with a grating sound, which seemed to grow louder... louder...

... The solitary track stops abruptly...black iron gates open like massive jaws... above them...a sign..."Arbeit Machts Frei," writ in black iron scrawl...

Even before the train entered Munich station, most of the passengers began to gather up their duffle bags, cases, and baskets. Halinka and Marissa stood buttoning their coats. I stood up also, and tried to shake free of my memories.

As if pursued by them, I rushed for the exit. Marissa followed close behind, but Halinka found it difficult to keep up. In my rush to get away, I had forgotten that Halinka had a clubfoot. I stopped and waited for her.

After Halinka caught up, all three of us started again, this time at a slower pace. We walked among the businessmen with briefcases, mothers with too many bundles, pulling little children by their hands, elegant ladies, and women in worn old coats wearing scarves around their heads. So many people, all hurrying along, so much noise. It echoed beneath the huge glass topped rotunda.

Above it all the sound of the German language, the language I knew only as a language of hate, harassment, commands, and insults. Above the general noise of people talking, shouting, and shuffling their feet, I could hear the clicking of boots...

...The heels of Gestapo boots on hard concrete...

I wasn't hearing the amplified voice of the station announcer. Instead I remembered the...

...Guttural voices bark..."*Achtung, Achtung...*" *skull and cross bones insignia everywhere...*

I covered my ears to stop the grating voices.

Halinka pulled at my sleeve, trying to get me away from my nightmare. We stopped and she shoved Zahava's directions in front of my nose. I read the instructions. "Exit by the East Gate." Then I looked around.

We all did, but where was that gate? We looked in vain, till Marissa took matters into her hands. She could speak several languages, German included. So when she spotted a good-looking fellow walking by, she stepped right up, "I need to find the East Gate," she said, letting him enjoy her coquettish smile. Her head tilted up to him, she pleaded through pale blue eyes, her long dark lashes blinking slowly to underscore her need for assistance.

The young fellow plunged into a long explanation with many hand motions to indicate direction. Making the most of it, Marissa added more questions and kept nodding, till neither of them could stretch it any longer. Now she embarked on the extended business of thanking him. Watching her performance, I wanted to laugh out loud, but I stifled the impulse.

Due to Marissa, we were able to find the exit gate. She led

144

us into the street and to the bus stop. We were really pleased and proud of her.

Zahava lived in the tiniest apartment that looked a bit like a dollhouse. Everything in it was old, small, but well cared for. There was one small bedroom, a sitting room with wine-colored velvet loveseat, and a small round table with room enough for only three chairs. No china closet, only a narrow couple of shelves on the wall to store the few cups, saucers, plates, and utensils. She welcomed us with a lovingly prepared tea, which she served with thin slices of lemon.

Zahava had small cucumber and cream cheese sandwiches laid out on a plate along with several sweet puff pastries. The chocolate and strawberry with cream filling melted in my mouth. I knew that Zahava had little money, and those pastries had to be expensive, but then I remembered that Zahava was gracious and generous no matter what. She would never dream of entertaining guests without serving proper tea. At that point, I didn't know whether to enjoy her hospitality, or feel guilty for the extravagant expense occasioned by my visit.

For her part, Zahava was animated and full of questions. First, she asked about Moshe. Despite the fact that she had only seen him a couple of weeks earlier, she wanted to know how he was getting on, and when would he be able to visit again. Zahava obviously missed him very much, so I plunged into a long description of Moshe's life at the Villa, telling her about his new buddy, Bennie, the same age as Moshe. The two had grown inseparable and studied Hebrew together. I added that Moshe was making great progress, and could even hold simple conversations with the teacher. Zahava couldn't be more pleased. My glowing report brightened her up, and now she started asking questions of Halinka and Marissa. Did they like living at the Villa? What did they think about going to Israel? That question became the focus of lively conversation. Halinka confided that Israel seemed remote to her.

"We know so little about it" Marissa chimed in.

"We've been told it's mostly desert, but none of us have ever seen such place," I added.

Zahava told us she'd received several letters from my uncle

in Israel. "Your Uncle Joseph is a prolific writer, and he provides a good description of Israel. His letters are so graphic I can almost imagine the place" she said.

As I listened to Zahava, I recalled my uncle and how he told the tales of camels crossing a landscape filled with sun-bleached sand that undulated like the waves on the sea.

"Remember Ali Baba and the Forty Thieves?" I asked.

Halinka did, "It was a story in a big picture book."

"Tales from 1001 Nights, that's the one. I had it at home." I said. The book contained thick glossy pages with pictures that showed the color and texture of the sand, its golden grains spread over a vast landscape. That was the desert I imagined now, an arid land where no grass or flowers grew.

"How can anyone live in a place where you can't grow vegetables, or wheat?" Marissa sneered.

"There are some olive groves and orange groves as well, Zahava said, as she began to clear the dishes from the table. Once, centuries ago, the land was fruitful and beautiful. But poor husbandry, overuse, and land exploitation stripped the nutrients away. Erosion did the rest, and the land baked under the sun without water. It could hardly support much of a population. That's why many of the people in this area have to lead a nomadic existence."

"Nomadic? What does that mean?" Halinka asked.

Zahava explained that because little could be grown on much of the land, the people have to move from one place to another in search of sustenance. "It's a hard existence, at best," she said.

We listened as Zahava continued telling us how the land had suffered from lack of water. Besides, what good land remained was held by rich absentee owners who took too much away and gave too little back. Listening to all that information, I figured Uncle Joseph must have written an awful lot of letters.

"Do they still travel on camels in caravans?" I asked.

Zahava laughed, "Who, the Jewish kibutzniks? They work hard all day every day to reclaim the desert and make it fertile." She took Joseph's letter out of her pocket and pushed it across the table to me. "Read it; it's all in there."

146

Uncle Joseph's words ran neat and small across each page and told of life in Israel. He was clearly at home there. As I read his words aloud to Marissa and Halinka. I sensed my uncle's dedication to the land. He wrote about the need for irrigation.

"The ground can't support too many people, because there's not enough water to make it fertile. But there is water far below the surface of the desert, and though hard to find and difficult to reach, deep wells are being drilled every day. It will take many new émigrés to accomplish the job."

His words made me feel optimistic. "Uncle Joseph says that they've already found some water, built irrigation systems, and fed the dry sand with nutrients and moisture. You'll see, by the time we get there, more desert will be turned into fertile ground." I tried to reassure my companions.

"The eternal optimist," Marissa scoffed.

"It must be hard. Imagine having to start with just a few implements." Halinka looked worried.

"Says here that the Americans are sending them seed money, so they can buy the needed tools," I pointed out.

"Yeah, barren land, no shelter, how do they live in the meanwhile?" Marissa sneered.

"I guess they live in tents and purchase the food they need until the land starts to produce." I said.

Later that night, we cast suspicious glances at the sofa that was to serve as our bed for the night. The little sofa was barely wide enough for one person. After removing the throw pillows, we gained perhaps five inches of width. Zahava brought sheets, blankets, and pillows, as I wondered if an extra blanket on the floor would be more comfortable than this sofa? But that brought an image of another floor unbidden to my mind…

...So sleepy... bullets roll in the palm of my hand, back and forth, rolling...rolling... my eyes close...must not sleep... go on roll...roll those bullets, or I'll get hit again...I must look for perfect ones, shiny not squashed...no, not this one... not perfect... put in spoiled box...

My head is so heavy...I can't hold it up...let me put it down only for a minute...lower...lower till I feel the bullets hard beneath

my cheek...cold rolling pillow of bullets... roll round my head...
rolling in my head, in my hand, roll...rolling...roll...

...A woman bends down...helps me stand...walks me to
where I can hide and sleep...

...the bathroom floor is hard beneath my bones...I lie on the
cold squares of black and white... bullets and grime beneath my
head...my cheek rests on the slimy tiles... I close my eyes ...

I glanced at the miniscule bed that was to serve the three of us this night, and I smile. "Hey, it's nice and small, soft and clean. Just look at this palatial bed." All three of us began to laugh.

"We'll sleep like a log,." Marissa agreed.

Enough of this chit-chat, we were all tired out. We washed and brushed our teeth, each one in turn, for there was no way we could all crowd into the little washroom at one time. Then we tried to figure out how to we could sleep without falling off this miniscule couch. We couldn't stretch out fully as it was a bit too short. Finally we had a plan. Each of us would curl up, one around another, in the same direction. This configuration allowed the three of us to form one fat person. We thought the plan could work, as each of us was slim.

We started with Marissa first, facing the back of the sofa, Halinka in the middle right behind Marissa, and I brought up the rear. Sometime in the middle of the night, I found myself slipping off, and signaled Halinka, who tapped Marissa's shoulder, and we all turned in unison. Now my knees rested on the air, but I considered it an improvement.

The strong aroma of cocoa woke me up, bringing with it memory of home. Cocoa was the hot, sweet drink Mom made us on cold winter mornings. It was the family tradition, and I was glad to see that it lived on with Zahava. When she came carrying three mugs of steaming cocoa, we were delighted. Zahava refused all our help, and by herself set the little table with sweet rolls, butter, and jam. After we took our bedding off the sofa, she sat down on it, and told us to enjoy our breakfast.

"Aren't you eating?" Halinka asked softly. She felt uncomfortable seeing Zahava serving us while she took nothing for herself.

Zahava assured us that she'd been up for hours, and had already eaten. She had been busy making plans, and hoped we were ready for a full day of sightseeing.

After helping Zahava with breakfast clean up, the four of us walked down to the corner to catch a streetcar that would take us to the first destination. The morning felt fresh. The skies were clear and the sun was shining. We boarded the streetcar, and as it moved slowly past well-kept houses, we couldn't stop ourselves from gaping at the sight of stone angels blasting on their stone trumpets; it looked like every building was adorned with these stone carvings.

Observing the handsome town, I couldn't help but think of those communities that couldn't get away from the ravages of war. But Munich remained one of the few to escape the fate of other European cities. Except for an occasional bomb crater here and there, this ancient Bavarian town stood as it had for centuries, trees still shading its broad avenues, handsome buildings and gardens, the late fall flowers still in bloom, and all undamaged. The town looked untouched by the recent bloodshed and bombings, with its plazas, parks and statues of heroes, with pigeons crowning their heads, and the children playing on the grass.

The streetcar passed several fat men standing outside a tavern in their short pants and Tyrolean hats. Marissa whispered, "Now, that's gemuetlichkeit."

"Charming," I agreed, watching them hoist their great Bavarian mugs of beer.

The irony of it didn't escape me. Here was the city of Munich, the beer capital of the world, and Hitler's former stomping ground. It was the birthing place where first he hatched his notions of The Third Reich. Yet this city remained unblemished, as if Hitler had never released his storm troopers with their swastika armbands, and skull and bones insignia to march against other nations. This city stood washed clean in the mid-morning sun, as if none of the Nazis had ever gone forth to murder my family and shatter my world. Munich appeared as timeless as a fairytale town. It was indeed an old town, its roots dating back to the twelfth century.

Marissa tugged at my arm. We had arrived, and I followed

her, stepping off the streetcar. We crossed the street, and walked up the wide steps that led into the rotunda of the bathhouse. Looking at its façade, I had to agree with Moshe. The structure was indeed impressive. It looked more like a museum than a bathhouse.

We walked into the great atrium, its shafts of light streaming down from the high vaulted glass and illuminating the white marble walls, floors, and curving staircase. The atrium was a rotunda hung with many paintings of bathers in various stages of undress.

Zahava paid the entrance fee, and we followed a plump lady in a white uniform, with a white scarf over her head. Our footsteps echoed, as we walked.

We followed as she led each one towards a separate bathroom. As I entered mine, I noticed the faint aroma of disinfectant beneath the stronger perfume of Lilac. Here too all was marble, even the tub. Light shimmered on every surface reflecting off the white walls, white bathtub, white ceiling, the white doors. Even the attendant wore white right down to her stockings.

Pointing to an open door and the dressing room beyond, the attendant told me to disrobe and leave my clothes in there...

...We must shed our things. One by one we stop at each pile in turn. Clothes, great big piles... on the floor, arranged according to type, and use: hats, ladies purses, scarves, blouses, skirts, dresses, panties, bras, stockings, socks, boots, ladies dress shoes, tiny baby shoes, old shoes, new shoes, in huge separate piles, all on the floor.

One item at a time, we discard each one of our possessions, moving forward along the many rows of piles. We must obey the orders of the women in SS uniforms. They are all stocky like sausages stuffed tightly into their uniforms. Each one of them issues orders... They sound like the barking of dogs... they use whips. I'm naked... stand in line... wait my turn...the barber's chair...the floor all covered with hair. I need to keep...don't, please don't take away my hair... No one hears my plea. My turn... I sit and watch my hair, the hair I've brushed each night to make it gleam... shaved clean... It falls to mingle with the mass already on the floor.

*   ... Our naked bodies fill the vast, cold space...waiting...beneath the showerheads, women, children..., bare feet on moist tiles... the room revolves around me... No grace here, only the damp tile walls. I feel exposed ... tremble with cold or fear, cannot tell which ...my feet are glued to slimy tiles...over my head, a showerhead...menaces...hear it hiss, as something turns...releasing... God, please...let it be water...*

I found a white terry robe draped over a chair in the dressing room. There were also several hooks for my clothes. I undressed, put on the robe, fluffed my hair. It had grown some five inches since the spring. By the time I came into the room, the woman attendant was filling the tub with warm water. I watched her sprinkle some bath salts on top, and leave.

I stepped into the fragrant water, and immersed myself head to foot, leaving only my eyes, nose, and mouth free to breathe as I had done that first day out of the camp in the deserted house with Rachel. The lilac scented warm liquid felt like a caress on my body. I let my hair float free on the water. It was bliss.

I was almost asleep, when the church bells rang out the hour. Moments later a knock at the door reminded me that time was up. This piece of paradise has been lent me for three-quarters of an hour only. I had to relinquish my warm bath, and step under the cool spray to rinse off. I did not wish to hurry as I wrapped my pink and scented body in a fluffy soft white towel.

By the time I emerged, my three companions were already there. Arm in arm the four of us walked down the steps. Where next? I wondered.

Genia gave the answer. "We can stop for a snack, and still have enough time to make the matinee performance," she said, leading us to a nearby café.

After we took seats at our table, she produced a little envelope and waved it before us with an impish smile. "Tickets for the opera," she said with pride.

An opera, I'd never seen an opera, and was excited to learn I'd be seeing it this very afternoon. At the same time I felt guilty, thinking that Zahava was giving us this precious gift at too high a cost. Her resources were meager.

"Oh, Zahava, that's much too expensive."

But Zahava laughed, "These tickets, expensive? Bread is expensive, but these are about the cheapest things you can get in this city."

I was surprised to hear that. I thought going to the Opera was a gala affair. I remembered how Mom would put on her best evening dress, and how handsome Dad looked in his black evening suit. I always thought that tickets to the opera would be costly. But Zahava said they were not.

Fearing that she was spending too much on us, I couldn't stop worrying as we sat in the little café. So I said that I was too excited to eat, and only wanted a cup of tea and some toast with jam. Halinka and Marissa followed suit, and I loved them for being so thoughtful, and because they too didn't want to impose on Zahava's meager circumstances, though I suspected each one of them could have eaten a horse.

Sipping our tea and munching our toast and jam, we listened as Zahava spoke about the Bavarian State Opera house. She told us that it was famous all over the world. I recalled how much I wanted to go along to the opera, whenever Mom and Dad were getting ready to go. But I was too young to go before the war, so I never had a chance to see the inside of an opera house; neither had Marissa or Halinka. Now the three of us could hardly wait.

As the first chords of the overture sounded I remembered my father. He loved music, and would listen to it on the radio, when he couldn't attend the live performance. At those times our house would fill with the rich sound of string, brass, and human voices. Dad would often hum or whistle along, while I sat on his lap. I knew the names of all the operas, loved every one, Madame Butterfly, La Boheme, La Traviata, or Tosca. I may not have understood the words, but I could hear and feel the beauty and the sadness of the songs.

Now, as I sat in the orchestra of the Bavarian State Opera House, I gave myself over to the sound, and mourned with Cio-Cio San as she clasped her baby son to her breast for the last time. I didn't have to understand the words to know what this young mother was feeling. I knew that her last song told of her tragedy. She was saying goodbye to her son, and to her life. Her sorrow echoed mine.

My parents never had a chance to say goodbye to me and Haniushka. I was never allowed to say goodbye to them.

The beauty and sadness of the song washed over me, resonating within. It took Cio-Cio San's death song to release my own need to grieve, a need I had tried to hold back all these years since our parting. When the curtain came down, my eyes were swollen, and my cheeks were wet. Seeing my face, Zahava hugged me. I hung on tight.

Marissa prattled on, about the beauty of the music, the singers and the scenery. Halinka remained silent, sadness like a cloak wrapped around her...

...One foot, another, painful, slow, Halinka walks... Her frail and starved body can not support its own weight...yet she holds her mother up with strength she does not have...she must, to keep her mom from falling down... bent and, wrinkled beyond her years...her mom grows heavier leans more... with each step...

Halinka's arms grow weaker still, her legs can barely move..."hold on, Mom please, keep on..." Halinka prays.

...She and her mother, two prisoners among the many...forced to their march of death... across the German land... many have fallen... some were shot...Halinka stumbles, yet keeps on...her clubfoot—hurts, she limps, but will not stop...arm barely holds the heavy weight...but cannot let it go...Mom slips... she tries to hold her up... but Mom is down... the ground is hard ...Halinka on her knees... hears her mom whisper, "Go on...they'll shoot...must live...go on..."'

I knew about that march of death, for I was there and saw the daughters struggle and fail to hold their mothers up, as one by one, the older women, their strength gone, fell to the ground.

Halinka told me how she watched her mother die, there on that road. She had to go to save herself and left the body lying on frozen ground. The war was almost done. She lost her mother just before the end.

153

I glanced at Halinka. She stood still as stone. Mere words could hardly help, I knew but still embraced Halinka, whispered in her ear, "You held her, and she saw you're alive. You had a chance to say good-by."

Cio-Cio's grief recalled our own. It sounded echoes in my ears. My eyes were swollen. I had a running nose, and I embraced my friend who couldn't be consoled. Something so sad and full of pain could yet be beautiful, I thought, Cio-Cio's song an echo releasing my own grief.

Marissa tried to break our somber mood. "Why cry over make believe? We've lived through real tragedy, and we survived. If you ask me, Cio-Cio San was a whimp. She should have kept her child. I wouldn't give it up, and I sure wouldn't kill myself over that cold piece of fish, that Captain Pinkerton."

"The music, the lights, the costumes, the beauty of the song, her grief was true." I said.

Halinka chimed in, "Put up the front, Marissa. I know you were touched as much as we. Don't be a fool. Admit it now."

"He had a wife at home. He lied! He'd never marry Cio-Cio San, only pretended that he would. She was a geisha to him, very pretty and exotic, what with those slanted eyes and yellow skin. But she was a plaything that he tossed away." Marissa judged him hard.

Halinka stood her ground, lifted her chin. "She trusted him, thought that he loved her very much. That's not stupid. Aren't Americans better than that Pinkerton fellow?"

Considering her aunt and uncle in America, Halinka was shaken by the thought that Americans could be as thoughtless and cruel as that Lieutenant Pinkerton in Madame Butterfly. "I don't suppose they're all like that," she said softly.

But Marissa didn't seem to hear her. "He was a shit, and Cio-Cio-San trusted him. She took her own life because of him. That's stupidity, not tragedy. Stop your bawling already. It's just a stage-show. An opera is meant to make you cry."

"I've known guys like Captain Pinkerton," Halinka said.

I was ready to end this particular debate. "OK, enough. What's the use of crying over make-believe?"

"That's right." Marissa had to put her last word in. "Besides,

I'm sure that all American men are nothing like this Captain Pinkerton." Marissa spit his name as if it were a piece of day old fish. I noticed that her brows knitted together, while the corners of her mouth turned down.

I struggled with the notion that sometimes even good folks can be cruel, and then reminded myself about the food we eat, the clothes we wear, the lovely place where we get to live. All of it comes from the Americans. They're helping us, making sure we're taken care of until we can find our new home. I told Halinka so to reassure her. But all the same it troubled me to think that men who love their wives and children, and are considered good neighbors can still be cruel. Pinkerton was a Navy man, a soldier trained to kill. Was it possible such training would transform men into beasts? Is that what happened in the war with soldiers who followed brutal orders, like they'd been told to do.

The line between reality and illusion can be very thin, and for me Cio-Cio San seemed more than make-believe. Her song of grief reminded me of Mother's grief. I couldn't even think what she had felt, losing my father, worried about Haniushka and me and now they're gone. There are no graves, no stones to mark their passing, and no one place where I can go to mourn for them.

I felt a special sadness at the thought that Mom and Dad would never know that I survived. They lost their freedom before they lost their lives. They wanted to protect us. Knowing this must have been most painful.

I had to remind myself that we three were survivors. We had to go on and make the most of the lives we had been spared.

Chapter 14

I awoke to a world of white snow. The hills were covered with the stuff, tree branches quivered in the wind, dipping beneath it. Somewhere a loose board knocked against the side of a building. The world was white. My bed was warm and cozy, and I didn't want to leave it yet. But it was my turn in the kitchen this morning, and I had to hurry. I really didn't want Halinka, Marissa, Henrietta, and Rachel to get there before me. Well, I found them already there, setting up a racket, with banter and laughter, moving from counter to stove, while banging every pot and pan that came their way.

Looking up from the huge bowlful of eggs she'd been beating, Marissa gave me one of her ironic smiles. "At last, I see you've made it just in time to eat. Set the table," she ordered.

"And a fine good morning to you, boss lady," I retorted, starting to assemble stacks of plates, cups, and cutlery on a large tray.

"Did you hear, Henrietta is leaving next week," Rachel said.

"For sure?" Halinka almost dropped a plate.

Though usually calm, Henrietta could hardly contain her excitement. "Yes. Next week, I'm off to Bremen to board the ship for New York. Imagine, I'm actually going; I really can't believe it."

Was it envy, or sorrow, I couldn't tell, but I suddenly felt very alone. My friends would be leaving for America. It seemed everyone I knew had a family in America. Even Henrietta, the unlovable, plain looking Henrietta, with her bad skin and short neck, even she'd get a chance to start a new life with her aunt and uncle in America.

156

Halinka appeared lost in thought. Her mouth was pinched, and there was a deep frown between her brows. What did she have to worry about? I wondered. She'd get her letter any day now, and like Henrietta, she'd be leaving to join her aunt and uncle in America. But then I saw my friend bite her lower lip. She had that far away look in her eyes, and I realized that Halinka didn't know for sure, wouldn't know till she was notified that her papers were in order that she too could join her family in New York.

I nudged her, "How about a little help here?" I said, picking up my tray heavy with dishes and cutlery. Halinka picked up another full tray, and followed me to the dining hall. We hurried to set the tables before the hungry troops descended for their breakfast.

Our unspoken concerns hung dense in the silence while we worked. Halinka had no letter as Henrietta did. Why not? Could there be something wrong with her documents? Was it possible she would not be going to America after all? Whenever Halinka was worried, she'd just stand up a little straighter and hold her head up a little higher. Now seeing her chin lift up, I wished there was something I could say, something to make her feel less worried. But there was nothing I could think of. We continued to work in silence, finishing just as the early arrivals began to file in.

I wrapped my arms around Halinka's shoulders and steered her out to the terrace. "Look at all the snow. How about having a go at skiing today?"

"What? Oh...yes... snow..." Halinka looked, but didn't really see what she was looking at.

I stroked her hair and cheek saying, "There are many ships. You may be scheduled for the next ship, and if not, then surely the one after." Halinka just looked at me. I tried to cheer her up. "Are you really so much in a hurry to leave us?"

"It isn't that, I just feel homeless, that's what, and I don't like it. I just want to go home to my family."

"Did you ever meet them?"

"Mom used to talk to me about them. That's all."

"And yet you feel this far-off place and people that you've never met before could be your family and home?"

"There is none other. After I get to know them, I will love

157

them, I hope." Halinka looked thoughtful. "Then too, I'm glad they want me, even if we've never met before."

"If Henrietta got her notification, then surely yours will arrive any day now. Don't worry. You're going. It just takes time."

Nothing more than nerves, I thought. I'm no different from my friend. I longed for home, and just as she, I too was tired of communal living. I wanted to stop tumbling like a weed across the world, to know one place where I belong with people who love me. I wanted to find home. Yet this temporary place, this villa, was a lovely place. Here I had found friends. Not knowing what I'd find, I wasn't sure I'd want to leave this place.

"Henrietta is on her way next week. I just wish to know when I'll be going too." Halinka expelled her breath, and it went whoosh, like the air from a deflated balloon.

"I'm actually a little afraid to leave this place, Halinka. Aren't you?"

Halinka lifted her chin a little higher, said nothing.

I didn't have a place to go. Halinka did. What was she going on about? Even if the sanatorium could never be her home, it was a place to heal and rest, a stopping place along the way... to what? I couldn't say. One thing for sure, what lay ahead for me was just another journey to an uncertain future. Just thinking about going where I had never been before unsettled me. I thought about the things I'd have to learn and do.

There'd be a new language to learn, and I would meet new people, learn their strange new ways. What would they think of me? They had not experienced what I had. I mused, thinking about the place called Israel. The Sabra's life was different from mine. What could we have in common? And would they like me? I worried about making new friends. Now with Henrietta leaving next week, and Halinka probably soon after, only Marissa and Rachel remained.

"Perhaps you could come with me," Halinka ventured, sensing my sadness.

"I have no family there."

"What about your great uncle? Didn't you say he immigrated to America before the war?"

"Yes, but he was very old then; he could be dead by now. I

158

wouldn't even know how to find him."

Halinka lowered her head remembering that it was her aunt and uncle who had looked for her, and not the other way around. They were the ones to arrange for her to come to America.

Halinka squeezed my hand. "But you've got family right here, Zahava and Moshe."

"Yes, they are the only family I have, and they are going to Israel. So that's where I'll go," I said, with little enthusiasm. I was hardly looking forward to it. Moshe was two years younger, and a boy, besides. As for Zahava, before the war I'd seen her once or twice a year, and then the hiatus of the war years. How well did I really know her? Except for the few recent days in Munich, we had hardly spent enough time together to forge strong family bonds. True, I respected and liked Zahava very much. More than that, I was grateful to her that she cared enough to seek me out at the Convent of the Ursulines. She did her best to help, brought me to a place where I was welcomed.

I was almost ashamed to admit even to myself that I felt closer to my friends here at the sanatorium. In the last few months, Halinka and Marissa, and I had grown to know and care for one another.

Now, once again I was about to lose someone I cared about. Maybe Marissa would leave soon too. I shook my head to vanquish these sad and fearful thoughts. I gazed out at the snow and put on a lighthearted air. "We should go skiing. Marissa wants to; why don't you come?"

No sooner did I say it than I saw Halinka look down at her clubfoot, and I felt stupid. No way could Halinka ski on that foot. Then I remembered seeing some old sleds in the barn, and made a quick recovery. "Will you just look at these hills? They look gentle and long, perfect for sledding."

"But aren't you going to ski with Marissa?"

"We'll go sledding instead. Now let's go in and have some breakfast."

Soon after eating, we bundled up in heavy sweaters, and cheeks burning red with the cold wind, made for the barn…

159

...Haniushka is bundled in a thick woolen sweater and coat. She's got a big woolen scarf wound around her head. Only her big round eyes are visible. Her neck and even her mouth is sheathed in the soft pink wool, so that she looks like a round pink ball with a pair of shiny brown eyes. While I pull our sled up the hill she climbs beside me, till we stop to catch our breath. We take a moment to look down the hill to see how far we've come. Haniushka claps her hands. "Look, the sun is in the river." She's delighted with the sight. The river appears like a sinuous dancer bedecked in diamonds. Our cheeks glow red with the wind, but the woolens keep us cozy...

As usual, Marissa took the lead, said she had to sit up front to steer the sled. I sat behind her, in the middle, with Halinka bringing up the rear. We pushed off and making fresh tracks in the snow glided down the hill, with Marissa telling us when to lean to the left, or the right. In this way we helped her to steer a safe course.

The wind in my face, and the sheer velocity of the sled made for a mixture of exhilaration and fear. What if Marissa loses control of the sled? What if we were to plunge right down into the freezing river? Marissa shouted the last instruction, "Hard right, now!" We all leaned to the right and stopped short on the bank, safely just above the river. Then we jumped off and started up the hill for yet another run. As we tramped up the hill again, I remembered...

...At the top of the hill, we arrange ourselves on the sled. Haniushka holds on tight, her short arms wrapping themselves around my waist. We push off, and glide through the snow down towards the river, down, down... almost there, and I shove my foot hard against the steering bar. Our sled turns sideways, and stops on the flat little embankment just above the river. Haniushka claps her hands and laughs. "More, let's go more," she shouts, between gales of laughter...

The sun hung low, almost touching the top of the hill, by the time we decided to quit. My every bone hurt. Halinka complained

160

of being sore all over.

"Yeah, but it was such fun. Let's go again tomorrow." Marissa rubbed her hands.

"I'm too tired to move," Halinka said.

Arm in arm with Halinka, Marissa in the lead, we walked back to the house. Marissa was still enthusiastic. "We'll feel better in the morning, and as long as there's snow, we should go again," she said.

After dinner, there'd be a movie featuring Charles Boyer. Although tired, I didn't want to miss it, neither did Marissa and Halinka, so we went to see the movie. There was the face of Charles Boyer, the romantic French film star, filling the whole screen, and as I sat with Halinka on one side of me, I felt an arm wrap itself around my waist from the other side. Heniek, the pest, I thought, must be his arm. He was a big ruddy guy, who was always hanging around me these last few days. He looked like a farmer, and though he was good-natured, I couldn't see him as a romantic man. I'd prefer someone more debonair, with cultured voice, wearing exquisite clothes, well, someone like Charles Boyer. The idea of having a romantic affair with Heniek was preposterous, as it would surely involve naked bodies and lots of sweat. I pushed him away. But he pulled me towards him once again. "Come on, give us a kiss," he whispered, lips close to my ear.

I felt his hot breath on my neck, his lips on my cheek. Right there, with the scene of Charles Boyer kneeling by the bedside of his dying wife, I shrugged Heniek off my arm, freed myself of his advances, and stood up. Muttering excuses while tripping over feet, I managed to exit the row and, as the last scenes of the movie flickered across the screen, I walked out of the room.

Halinka followed right behind. "What's the matter?" she asked.

"Heniek tried to kiss me."

"And I thought something was really wrong."

"He wouldn't stop even after I pushed him away." I was indignant.

"He likes you. That bothers you?"

"Yeah, I don't like it when he tries to paw me."…

...We're alone in his cubicle. What he holds in his hand is not a stethoscope. It is a riding crop. I watch him raise it, inch by inch. Not quite touching yet, he moves it up my midriff, and pauses by the missing button on my blouse, insinuates it between the folds, parting my blouse. His forehead beads with sweat, eyes on my budding breasts; he puts his hand inside my blouse, touches my nipple, and licks his lips.

"So small," he grunts.

"No," I take a step back; try to get away from him.

He moves in closer. Hand fondling my breast, hot breath hoarse in my ear, he whispers, "I'd like to take care of you, get you more food, good food. You'd like that eh?" My teeth will not stop chattering...

"You're shaking. What's wrong?" Halinka frowned.

I shrugged. "Heniek upset me."

"I'll deal with him," Halinka said brusquely.

The next morning the snow was still fluffy and white, but Halinka was too tired to go sledding. So Marissa and I decided to go skiing, though neither of us had ever been on skis before. We'd have to wait till after lunch, because it was our turn to clean up after breakfast. But as soon as we finished eating, we headed for the barn. Back in the corner behind some farm equipment, we found old wooden skis and boots. The wide, long, and heavy skis would be awkward to carry, but we were undaunted. First we tried the boots on. They fit, sort of. Mine were a bit too roomy, while Marissa's were too tight. But they'd do. We put them on, hefted our skis over our shoulders, and bending beneath the load commenced to trek up the hill.

Once at the top we gratefully dropped our load. Then without loosing one moment, Marissa went about getting her boots into her ski bindings. It wasn't easy. She had to stand on one foot managing to merge boot to ski without falling. Her chest puffed out proudly, she attacked the task and actually managed to get her first boot into the binding. "It's easy, see?" she said, proudly.

I watched in amazement, as she stepped into the second binding. After she completed what looked to me a complicated and dangerous task, I had to follow suit. Then I stood, ski poles in either hand, ready but reluctant to move.

"Are you going to stand here all day gawking at me, or do you plan to ski?"

"I'll watch for a while. Maybe I can learn something," I said.

"Rutka, you're afraid?" Marissa laughed.

"Just cautious," I told Marissa. "You go ahead."

While I felt apprehensive, Marissa seemed heedless. She gave me one of her pitying looks, and pushed off. But her feet appeared to be in an even greater hurry than Marissa was. Those skis slid out from under her so fast that she lost her balance, wobbled sideways in an attempt to regain it, but failed, and promptly fell on her fanny.

"Did you break something, stupid?" I inquired sweetly, and pushed off, intending to show I could do it better. It took only a moment, and I too felt one of my skis slide out ahead. The rest of my body followed, but not fast enough. No less disgraced than Marissa, I found myself on my fanny. We looked at each other, fell back into the snow, and wallowing in its cold, white, embrace, laughed till we cried.

"So it's not like in the movies," Marissa observed. "That's right; you thought we could take off just like the actors in 'Sunrise Serenade?'" I didn't want to admit that I also imagined myself swooping down the slope, taking each curve gracefully, smooth as butter.

When I tried to stand up again, the skis got in my way, and only after much yanking and tugging of butt, hips, and knees was I able to get to my feet. Dusting myself off, I grinned. "Look at me, the very picture of grace."

It took the better part of that day, and many more spills and laughter, before we discovered how to move without falling. But once we mastered the trick of leaning forward over the skis, keeping them under us, we began to enjoy it in earnest.

I got all puffed up with my accomplishment, became overconfident, and tried to jump over a small hump in the snow. Not smart. I lost my balance. To get it back, I started to wave my ski poles about till I pitched forward and landed on top of one of the poles, my feet and skis akimbo. I got the air knocked out of me, gasped for air and getting none, started to make strange groaning sounds.

Seeing me in trouble, Marissa pushed off the top of the hill and came barreling down, ski poles under her arms, like a seasoned skier. She executed a perfect stop next to where I lay like a beached whale, making strangling sounds.

After taking her skis off, Marissa knelt beside me. "Ease it down," she whispered. "Take a breath." Her hand gently massaged my chest. The gentle motion of Marissa's hand helped to ease my panic, and after a few more gasps I was able to resume breathing. For the first time since I'd known her, I realized Marissa was indeed my friend. I took great gulps of air into my lungs, and wondered about this unanticipated side of her. A vein of tenderness and love ran beneath that cynical exterior, after all. Looking at the concern on her face, I realized that Marissa's usual banter was only a screen behind which she chose to hide a generous and loving nature.

That's when Marissa exclaimed, "You should have sat down on your fanny, stupid!"

"I owe you my life," I said laughing, and planted a kiss on my friend's cheek.

Chapter 15

One day after lunch, Tzvi told us to expect two visitors. "We will have a special meeting this evening." Tzvi said and added that our visitors carried important news that could affect the rest of our lives.

Several of us were detailed to build a stage. We got it done in no time with a thick sheet of plywood placed over six cinder blocks. Once dinner was over, we all helped push tables against the walls, and line the chairs up in rows. Our dining hall turned into an auditorium.

Tzvi stepped onto the stage to introduce a tall, slim, small boned, youngish man who was to function as our translator. "Here is Jankle." He stood before us slightly bent over, as if his skinny frame couldn't support his height. Prematurely gray, he appeared shy with that half-smile playing on his lips.

Tzvi turned back to his audience. "We are privileged to have such a hero among us."

I couldn't make up my mind whether he looked like a hero, or a nebbish. But when I heard that this mild looking fellow fought in the Warsaw Ghetto uprising, I was amazed at the strength of his will and resolve. The men who had only handguns, rags, gasoline, and bottles to fight armored tanks and automatic weapons had to be brave. He had to be both brave and stubborn to fight against such odds, knowing he could not win, risking his life rather than let them go on murdering with impunity. I had heard many stories about the ghetto uprising. Those tales spoke of sacrifice and rescue. I couldn't see Jankle's spirit, but I knew that it was strong and unwavering.

Tzvi went on to say that Jankle could speak four languages:

Polish, Jewish, Hebrew, and English. That information made him grow another ten feet in my mind. Jankle was not only a good guy, he was also a great Zionist, Tzvi told us, and he assured us that as group leader he would be unfailing as he guided us safely in Israel. Tzvi sat down, and it was Jankle's turn to speak. He coughed, and began in a surprisingly powerful voice.

"The British don't want to let us enter Israel," his first few words exploded into the room like a bombshell, and everyone started talking at once.

"Shah, Quiet!" Tzvi clapped his hands. "First you listen, questions later."

Jankle began again, "British soldiers are stopping us at the port of Haifa. Last week, they boarded two of our ships just as our people were about to enter the port. They were celebrating the land they now saw for the first time, when the British boarded both ships and escorted them to Cyprus."

I imagined myself on the deck of one of these big ships, admiring that thin edge of land as it touched the sea, the land of our forefathers, our Promised Land. A picture formed in my mind. I imagined people cramming the ship's rails, breathing in the aroma of strange cooking odors, observing the tumult of those milling below. How would I feel after coming all that long hard way only to be told, I cannot enter here? I don't belong on this land. It isn't our home. Lost in my fantasy, I almost missed the rest of Jankle's speech.

"Our sisters and brothers are kept behind barbed wire fences," Jankle said. The British hold them on an island called Cyprus. They're keeping us there and won't let us go."

Pandemonium! Everyone was shouting at once. For several minutes Tzvi couldn't get us to quiet down. Finally he went into the kitchen. He came back with a copper pot and metal ladle. After banging the ladle against the bottom of the pot, the place quieted down so Jankle could resume.

"Who told you it would be easy? Calm down. This is not the time to lose all hope. True, the British stop some of the ships, but they can't stop them all. Many get through."

One of the older boys raised his hand. "Why do the British want to keep us out?"

Nothing Jankle could say mattered to me at this point. One thought above all filled my mind and spirit. I would not go to Israel, or anywhere else, if it meant imprisonment behind barbed wire fences, again. If the British didn't want me in Israel, then I didn't want to go there. The Poles didn't want me; neither did the Germans. I felt like a reject. Was I that ugly, that stupid, and that horrid? Was it because of that no one in the entire world wanted me?

Once long ago, my mom and dad did want me. Little Haniushka loved me. Remembering my family, I tried to blink away the tears. I thought about Uncle Strawberry, the one who went to America. Even back then he was very old and wrinkled. Would he be alive by now? He visited Warsaw a few months before the Nazis started their bombing raids. I was little then, and so could recall only a few snatches of conversations. My mom and dad listened to what he had to say. He told them it was time to leave. Time was short. He was going to America, and our family should as well. He told us we had only a little time left.

I found it very puzzling. The only thing I knew about America, I'd learned from seeing the movie, "Snow White." Based on what I had seen, I thought that everyone in America was a cartoon character. I wondered if that was what would happen to Uncle Strawberry. Would he also turn into one of those characters after he got to America? His red nose was so large, it looked like a strawberry. That's why I called him Uncle Strawberry. With that nose he looked a little like one of the seven dwarfs.

Shortly after his visit, bombs descended on Warsaw. The Nazis came rolling in. Their black motorcycles and trucks filled the streets with roar and stench. They shouted "Hail Hitler," just like barking dogs, and they made trouble wherever they went. By the time the Nazis arrived, it was too late to go to America. After that, we never heard from Uncle Strawberry again.

My attention turned back to the stage, and I saw Tzvi introducing a lanky, blond, young man. Garry was his name. He was an American who couldn't speak Polish or Yiddish. After Gary spoke a few words that no one could understand, Jankle translated what he said. I was amazed to learn that someone wanted us after all, that American Jews cared about us. He further

167

told us that they care especially about boys and girls who'd lost both parents in the war.

"America is a great big country, and it has a great big heart," Gary opened his arms to illustrate his point. "We want you in America."

He said much more that I could hardly follow, but I understood the gist. A number of Jewish agencies had organized a program to bring us to America. I missed some of the information, and tried to fill in the gaps. The word, immigration, kept coming up. And Jankle kept telling us that those of us whose parents were gone could be granted entrance to America.

How could I believe that? I had no family in America. How could I go there, when only those with family in America were allowed in? I'd heard America does not take people who have no sponsor. Who'd volunteer to sponsor me? Why?

Halinka and Henrietta had family, aunts and uncles who had made the effort, searched to see if they survived the war. Learning that they did, they sponsored them. That means they'd be responsible for those family members they'd invited to come to America. I had no family there. Nobody invited me.

Simon was the first to raise his hand, "I don't have any family there. Can I also go to America?" His thick eyeglasses kept slipping down his nose, and he kept pushing them back up. Simon of all people, the boy who hardly ever spoke, was showing enough presence of mind and the gumption to ask just the right question.

"As a rule only those with families in America are issued visas, but there is one exception." A big grin split Gary's face. "Each one of you can come." He plunged into an explanation of American immigration rules, and the need to have a sponsor. Usually that would be an American family member who was willing to sponsor his relative survivor. But fortunately, a number of Jewish agencies agreed to act on our behalf, and become our sponsors.

Could it be so? I was amazed that somewhere in this world someone cared. Somewhere there was a place for me. I hoped that Gary spoke the truth. Now I wouldn't have to separate from Halinka. I could also go to America.

After the meeting, we could not sleep, and we talked late

into the night. Henrietta was scheduled to board the ship for America next week. Halinka would surely follow soon after. Now there was a chance we could all reunite in America. Marissa planned to see Gary the very next day. I was ambiguous. What about Zahava and Moshe, how could I leave my only family?

"But you should come and talk to him," Marissa said. "Halinka, you, and me, we have a bond. I for one don't want to break it."

I was torn, but then agreed to speak to Gary.

"What can it hurt?" Marissa said, clinching the deal.

I wasn't sure, and if I were to go, America is so big, I thought, who could tell if I'd ever be reunited with my friends.

"Can we all meet in America, and if so, where?" I asked.

"The two of us could try to go together," Marissa suggested.

Halinka added, "I'll be going to Brooklyn. That's where my aunt and uncle live. Could you maybe ask Gary if that could be arranged?

"Brooklyn is in New York," Henrietta added.

"How could one town be in another one?" I didn't understand.

Halinka ran across the hall to her room to rummage in the box she kept under her bed. She retrieved the envelope which held the latest letter from her aunt and came back carrying it. She read the address aloud: "Irene Greenberg, 348 Atlantic Ave., Brooklyn, New York. That's my aunt's place."

I still couldn't understand it. How could a person live in two cities at once? Henrietta hastened to get her family's address as well. It turned out her family lived in Detroit, Michigan.

Rachel wrote down the two addresses on three slips of paper, and handed one to me, another to Marissa, then folded the third and put it away. I folded mine carefully and put it in my shirt pocket. I'd be sure to deposit it in my special box, where I kept the important stuff.

It was quite late by the time we broke up, but I was too excited to sleep, thinking about Zahava and Moshe. I wished they could also go to America. But they had no sponsor, and while America may have made a special exception for children without parents, Moshe had his mother, and Zahava was an adult. So they would be bound for Israel.

Here I had been making plans to meet my friends in America, and I had not considered my own family. I felt ashamed, and no matter how I turned the problem, I just couldn't come up with a satisfactory answer to my troubling questions. Was I really willing to go where my own family couldn't follow? I slept little that night, and when morning came was still undecided.

By the time I finished my chores after breakfast, a long line of boys and girls stood waiting to see Gary. An almost fully booked appointment sheet lay on the desk beside him, but I saw one slot still open, and I quickly wrote my name down. Ahead of me lay long hours of waiting, but that was good, because I'd need that time to sort out my dilemma between my obligation to my family of going with them to Israel, and my desire to follow my friends to America.

I went down to the river and walked along its bank for what seemed like hours. First I thought about the place called America. The little I knew about it came from one single source of information, the movies with their flickering images depicting rich interiors with shiny mirrors, highly polished floors, ladies in designer clothes and jewels; in short, beautiful people in beautiful homes, who when they ventured out of doors wrapped themselves in furs, and were driven in long, shiny limousines to other beautiful and glorious places. These images corresponded to the European notion of America as the land where streets were paved in gold. European Jews called it the "golden medina."

The picture forming in my mind could be a fable, but then again, who knows? Everybody yearned for America. We all thought that life there was beautiful and oh, so easy. I was in a dilemma.

By the time I made my way back to see Gary late in the day, I was still unresolved. I was surprised to see Marissa there, fifth in line, still waiting and, as I approached, Gary looked at his watch, and grimaced. "Almost time for dinner," he noted. By his side, Jankle, dutifully translated. "Why don't I finish up with Josie, here, and the rest of you go on and eat. We can finish afterwards."

Walking away together, Marissa and I almost collided with Halinka, as she ran towards us, waving a sheet of paper in the air.

"I'm going! Isn't it wonderful?"

"When," we asked simultaneously.

"Next week, same ship as Henrietta's. Isn't it just wonderful?" The usually undemonstrative Halinka was brimming with energy. Even her body seemed more bouncy and light than usual. If she could have done summersaults, she would have done them right then and there, I thought, feeling happy for her. Then I felt sad realizing that she wouldn't be here to celebrate my birthday. Only Marissa would be left to hoist a glass of apple juice to my meager accumulation of years on this earth. I started to feel sorry for myself, but then I scolded myself for thinking about my birthday when I had such an important decision to make.

Though a nice enough fellow, Moshe was still a boy, and hung out with other boys. We had little in common. I liked Zahava, felt very grateful to her for taking me from the nuns. I knew that it was due to her efforts that I now had the opportunity to go to America. Zahava was kind and good. It would be difficult to repay all she had done, and I felt a deep sense of obligation to her, but gratitude was not enough. It was not the same as wanting to stay close. In the end, I realized that no matter how I wiggled and turned, it all came down to the same thing. I'd either have to separate from my family, or from my friends. We couldn't all stay together.

After dinner, by the time I finally took my seat at Gary's desk, I had bitten my fingernails to the skin, and I still hadn't made up my mind.

He took one look at me and said, "What's the matter, are you afraid?"

Could he actually see my fear? I was indeed afraid, scared to make a decision, fearful of having to part from Zahava and Moshe and even more frightened of the British who didn't want me in Israel and threatened to put me behind a barbed wire fence if I attempted to go there.

Gary pulled out what looked like a formal looking document.

"What is that?" I asked.

"This is an Application for Immigration."

The breath I'd been holding for hours now whooshed out of

171

me. "America," I whispered, and watched as Gary picked up his pen, "Your name?"

Our feet, one drumbeat on the wooden floor; I was locked within the circle of the dance. My arms intertwined, each hand rested on my neighbor's shoulder. Lighter with each succeeding step, my feet barely touching the floor, carried me within the circle of their energy, adding mine to theirs so it multiplied till I felt airborne.

Our voices, one voice, insistent, determined, repeating, "Maim, Maim, Maim, Maim," the Hebrew refrain translated as water, the staff of life. Our song was the promise to reclaim the dry ground, to bring water to the Promised Land, water for the desert, water for new growth, and new life.

Our hearts beat in one rhythm as we sang, "Maim, Maim, Maim, Maim," determination matching the beat of our feet. We circled the room dancing, stamping our hope into the ground, singing our promise of "Maim, Maim, Maim," a promise of water for dry land. I danced the Hora drunk with the motion of our circle-dance; in unison with those beside me, I moved to the cadence of our collective heart.

Vowing a resolve born in the crucible of pain and loss, we sang, "Never again..." It was our promise to us and to the world. Our survival was our defiance of Hitler. No one could deter us now, neither the English, nor the Arabs. We would return to the Promised Land. Our song became both our promise and our resolve, and echoed with the drumbeat of our feet.

I felt myself caught up in the spirit of the dance, one with all, merging, becoming one organism, within the circle of entwining arms; I was one with the Hora. It was the promise of turning desert into fruitful earth that called to me now, a dream of a good place on this earth; a dream of a nation where all who worked together could share in the bounty thus created. The Hora lived around me and within, and I soared in its embrace, until out of breath, I broke the circle of the dance, and came away.

I sat down beside our visitor, the Sabra who had spoken to us earlier that evening.

His fingers brushed mine, "You dance beautifully, and will you dance on our land?"

172

How could I tell him, "No," when just a moment past I wished to keep the promise of that dance? Now the dance was done, and I knew that I could not keep that promise. I had chosen the easier life. Shame flamed my cheeks.

"So, tell me, will you come with us?"

I shook my head from side to side.

"Ah, little bird. You're feeling bad." He took my fingers in his hand, put them to his lips. His lips were soft. I trembled wishing to pull away.

"But you will come," he held on to my hand. "You'll come when our desert blooms; at harvest you'll come to partake with us.

"What about the Arabs?" I asked, wanting to understand their role on this land. "They live there now. Will there be room for all?"

He nodded, squeezed my hand, and said, "That's a fair question, and it deserves a true answer." He paused, gathering his thoughts. "We want to reclaim this ancient land and built a strong community where everyone can live in comfort and good health, and work not only for the good of some, but for the good of all. Some of us have studied soil reclamation. There is a way to do it, a way to reclaim the parched desert, turn sand into soil, and grow more vegetables and fruit. Israel can become a good home for Arab and Jew alike."

"How do they feel about us?"

"Some are good neighbors. Others want us out and preach hate and war. The neighboring nations are no friends of ours. They spread rumors, saying we'll kill all Arabs, and take their homes and land away. Many of our Arab neighbors believe these lies. They leave their homes, thinking to return after their war is won. Even as we speak, neighboring Arab nations prepare to attack us. They want to make us leave the land. But they'll not succeed. If they attack, we'll defend ourselves, like it or not."

"Surely, with good will, can't you avoid the war?" I asked.

"Good will, ah, that's pretty scarce right now." His eyes were brown, so big, and so very desolate.

I wished I could help, wished I could go with him, and yet I said, "No, I can't. You see, I can't go back to war."

"Too many corpses in your life, I understand." He kissed my

brow and gave my hand a little squeeze. Then he stood up, squared his shoulders, stiffened his back, and walked away.

I missed him even as I watched him go. He never looked back. Somehow I had a feeling that fight was not his favorite dish. But he would fight to keep his dream and make it true.

Running away from war, running to America and a peaceful life, I thought about the ones who chose another way. They also lost their families in the war. Their history was just like mine. I felt that I belonged with them. None of us wanted war. But it would come, would be imposed on us, and some would die. I could not walk with them.

Chapter 16

I heard the clamor of shouting, banging of doors, and feet running outside my cabin. The ship is sinking, I thought, or everyone's gone suddenly mad while I slept. As I came more fully awake, I felt the ship move ever slower, almost at a standstill now. Then I remembered. It was today. We have arrived. Our ship was about to enter New York harbor. That's what the shouting was about, to be the first off the boat, first to step foot on the American soil.

Hurrying into my panties and my skirt, I hastily slipped on my blouse, and rushed out of my cabin and climbed to the top deck. I was stopped by a wall of humanity pushing to get through the narrow stairs to the upper deck. I merged with the massive surge, pushing and shoving like them. We behaved like children eager to enter the circus. When it became too difficult to squeeze my way onto the narrow stairs, I stepped back, and listened to the voices from above calling. "Hurry, come see."

The crowd thinned somewhat. Propelled more by imagination than reality, I merged with the human river flowing towards our first sight of New York, the land of plenty. Once topside, I squeezed my way to the rail just in time to see the famous Statue of Liberty. As our ship moved slowly past her to the pier, the entire vessel seemed to rise on a wave of shouting. "Look how she stands there, torch in hand!"

I gasped, amazed at the sheer size of the statue. Holding her torch high above her crowned head, the stately woman looked regal, and I figured her torch was there to light the way for all who passed into the harbor. I didn't know the torch she held symbolized liberty, and so I failed to understand what all that

175

excitement was about.

Liberty was what I had felt in my bones, my sinews, and in the very center of my being that first day after war's end. That was the day I became free of imprisonment. Freedom that day meant more to me than any abstract symbol. Freedom was as real to me that day, as was the open sky, that empty field outside the barn. There were no walls and no barbed wire fences to keep me in. That day, as I stood alone, free of the guards and their barking dogs, their rifles, and their curses, I knew liberty. Liberty and freedom were awesome realities at that moment.

The Lady in the Harbor was indeed lovely. She was a welcoming figure, a great lady who greeted all newcomers who sailed into the harbor. But that aside, the statue appeared no more significant to me than any other statue I had seen. Europe was filled with them. A statue of some past warrior, or a king, or maybe even a poet with a pigeon atop his head could always been found in a plaza or a square.

The statue of this Lady, no matter how tall and imposing impressed me far less than the tall skyscrapers that formed the skyline of New York. Those tall buildings seemed to defy gravity, and I couldn't help but wonder if they might topple over and fall to earth from their height. I marveled over the mystery of their miraculous structures, and thought it quite a feat that such huge structures could be built at all. What sort of people were these Americans that could accomplish this miracle?

The two dimensional black and white images I'd seen in the American movies couldn't begin to match the vibrant colors, sounds, and smells of the real thing. Less than a hundred feet from the pier, a ribbon of elevated highway seemed suspended above the street. Many cars and trucks whizzed along the highway. I didn't know where to look first.

People crowded the rail looking for relatives on the pier below. Shouts and cries greeted each new wave of recognition, as the passengers crowded down the ramp to the pier. I turned away. No one was waiting for me. I looked for Marissa but was unable to spot her in the crowd. Suddenly I felt lost and very lonely. I had no map, no list of instructions, and didn't know what would happen next, so I just stood there hanging onto the rail.

Looking down at the crowd on the pier, I noticed a tall woman walking briskly towards the ship. She wore a gray business suit and black pumps and didn't look like anybody's relative to me. The woman stopped at the bottom of the ship's ramp. She pulled a couple of photographs from her briefcase, studied them, and then gazed around searching the faces of the few remaining people who remained leaning over the rails. When she spotted me, she quickly walked up the ramp towards me.

"Welcome to America," she said, grasping my hand.

I understood one of the three words, "America," and smiled at the well-dressed lady. It was clear that communication wasn't going to be easy. I didn't think the woman could speak Polish, and I had two English words, "America okay."

We smiled at one another, and then, as if by magic, Marissa appeared at my elbow. Amid shaking of hands and smiles all around, the lady began speaking to us in Yiddish. I understood some of what she said, as did Marissa. Her name, she told us, was Ms. Rosen.

We followed Ms. Rosen down the ramp and into the immigration hall. Good thing she was there to shepherd us. The dim hall was crowded with long lines of people waiting to talk to uniformed clerks who stood behind counters, checking documents, asking questions, and stamping papers.

No lines for Ms. Rosen. Pulling us along, she walked right past the waiting people to the back of the hall and into a private office. She pulled documents out of her briefcase and presented them to the uniformed gray-haired man behind the desk. They appeared to know one another, and exchanged what seemed to be pleasantries. They conversed for a moment or two. He glanced at the papers she handed him, applied the official stamps and certifications, smiled briefly, and handed them back. We were out of there and in her car in less than five minutes.

This was the first time in a long time that I hadn't had to wait in line. It seemed to me that miracles do happen in America. Ms. Rosen surely knew how to get around a line, and

I suddenly felt privileged.

The car plunged into the middle of New York traffic with its profusion of blaring horns and screeching wheels. Marissa and I couldn't stop looking at the passing streets, crowds of shoppers, store windows filled with goods. In front of the green grocer shop, boxes of vegetables and fruit were piled in tilted up boxes in an artful display of apples, oranges, grapes, pears, mangoes, fruits in profusion such as I had never seen before. From the open doors of restaurants, delicious aromas wafted on the air: meat frying, chicken sizzling, onions and cabbage simmering. Here was life in three dimensions, a pulsing, living organism, and a city the likes of which I couldn't have imagined. I wanted to get out of the car and dive right in. Suddenly I was in a great big hurry to learn the language, get work, get paid, and buy some of the stuff that filled every bit of space in the shop windows along the streets, no steel bars on windows here. Instead there were pyramids of apples, oranges, potatoes, cabbages, carrots, all out there for any passerby to touch, smell, take, and sample. How was it possible? Didn't people steal here? Perhaps not, why would they? There was so much of everything. A veritable horn of plenty everywhere I looked. Shop windows displayed breads, coffee cakes, wedding cakes, and pastry with fruit, with cheese, with nuts, round cakes, square cakes. I didn't blink once during the short ride from New York Harbor to 124th street.

But this neighborhood appeared anything but elegant. I couldn't remember a neighborhood like it in any of the movies I'd seen. West 124th street was no Park Avenue, and there was no uniformed doorman to greet us here. Instead, the street was lined with tenements. Behind the buildings, small back yards were crisscrossed with wash lines. Most definitely not elegant, this was a neighborhood of people who had little money and no luxuries. They had no time for dancing and jewels. I had to admit to myself that I didn't expect my first address to fall this short of Park Avenue, but after a moment's thought, it didn't really matter. Nobody walked in lockstep here. That's what I liked best of all.

Ms. Rosen pulled the car to the curb and parked. The three of us stood in front of the building where Marissa and I were to spend our first night in America. Stale odors of garlic and onion greeted us in the dark, narrow hallway. I looked at Marissa expecting her to make one of her famous cracks, and I was not disappointed.

"My lady, welcome to your sumptuous digs."

I curtsied. "Happy to be here."

A woman who couldn't speak Polish, but made up for it with some Yiddish and much gesturing of hands, showed us to our room. An old man stood up to greet us as we entered the room. He must be close to a hundred, I thought.

"Rutele," his voice quivered, and his face creased in a broad smile. I moved towards him, puzzled. He gave me a bagful of oranges. The paper bag was wrinkled and torn.

I said, "Danke," and took the fruit from him, placing it on a night table. I thanked him in German, I don't know why; would he understand? He nodded, smiled his welcome.

"Uncle Strawberry?" I whispered, His happy-to see-you smile, along with the prominent red nose brought back a flood of remembrance…

…He holds a red apple in his hand, and picks up a paring knife. The knife glides over the apple, and I watch the thin sliver of skin curl away in one unbroken continuous spiral. I had never seen anyone perform such a feat. All in one unbroken piece, the peel slides onto the plate. Uncle cuts the apple into eight even sections, and pops one of them right into my mouth, picks up another and pops it into his own, dispatches it in two bites, wipes his mouth, and smiles with satisfaction. I pick up a section and pop it into his mouth. He smiles and offers the next piece to me. We continue till no more sections remain, only the single strand of apple skin, a red spiral, on the white china plate…

I was eight when I met him. And here he was now, my Bubby's brother, Uncle Strawberry who used to live in Germany. Shortly before the war he came to visit us in Warsaw to warn us and to urge our whole family to leave Poland…

…"All the adults of the family are gathered at our table, Mom and Dad, Cousin Genia, Cousin Elaina, my Grandmother and Grandfather, and even my Great Auntie Golda, all at our dining room table. I can see and hear them through the open door. They think I am busy with my dolls, so they pay me no attention,

179

but the door is open, and I can hear some of what they say, but I can't understand most of it. Uncle Strawberry speaks to them. I think they're scared of what he has to say.

"It's not safe here," he tells them.

Mother has stopped knitting. Her needles stopped clicking. I can see how she bites on her lower lip, a bad sign.

What's wrong? Why are they so serious? No one is joking, no one is laughing. They just keep listening as my uncle speaks.

"It isn't safe,"he repeats. "I've made plans. We have our tickets...going to America."

His words are a puzzle. What isn't safe? Why is he taking his family to America? He wants us to come too. That could be fun. Snow White comes from America. I love that movie. But they are not talking about Snow White.

"CRISTAL NIGHT... SIGNS... NOT ALLOWED...JUDEN VERBOTTEN... EVERYWHERE... ON THE SIDE OF BUILDINGS...JUDEN ROUSE... paint sprayed on windowpanes of JEWISH STORES. READ THE SIGNS. I have." He is almost shouting now.

Uncle Strawberry sighs as if out of breath. He stops talking, and Mother's knitting needles have taken on a life of their own. Their incessant clicking fills the silence between words. The air stands still, like before a storm. Dad puts both of his hands over Mom's, and the needles click no more.

Ever the peacemaker, Daddy starts to speak, "How bad can it get? You folks over there are not used to it," he says. "University doors used to be open to Jewish children; now they're closed. Here it's been that way for a long time.

"It can't get much worse"

"Nobody likes the Jews... That's no news..." Their voices overlap one another.

"Maybe you're too hasty... People can get used to anything.... Look at us."

"How can we leave? Can't speak the language...we have a good life here...ignore the bastards... need stability... security...but... maybe...who knows?"

Zyde stands up. "We'll wait and see," he says...

None of my family could believe my uncle's warnings. My grandfather, grandmother, and uncle Yurek, none of them wanted to leave the comfort of their homes, and so they stayed in Warsaw till time ran out, and it was too late for them to escape. In the end the Nazis forced them from their homes and shipped them out, every one of them. I would never know which of the death camps became their final stop.

My mind flooded with memories, regrets, sorrow. I looked at Uncle Strawberry and thought; at least I do have family here. He seemed shrunken, smaller, and much older than I remembered. His skin was paper-thin now, wrinkled, and pale. His hand seemed no more than bones enclosed in parchment. I looked at the bag of oranges on the nightstand, remembering the apple, and the way he peeled its skin, a sweet apple that we shared before all sweetness vanished from my life. What followed was the war with bombs and ghettos, and the transports, cattle cars that ferried folks to death camps and to their unmarked graves.

He took me in with sunken eyes and wrinkled face. His little sad smile told me that he grieved and at the same rejoiced that I was still alive. All those years back, he had urged us to abandon our home in Poland, leave to save ourselves.

Now here he was again, his second visit in my life. How did he know that I arrived today? Who told him? I had so many questions that I didn't know how to start. Marissa left the room, and he sat down on the only chair. I perched on the bed. He took my hands and held them in his veined and wrinkled ones.

"How did you find me?" I asked, mixing some German with Yiddish, none of it good.

Then he began to speak, words spilled from him so fast that I could not follow and only got the gist, the saga of his quest. At first he didn't know if anyone of the family had survived. To find out, he went to every social agency he could find. He traipsed all over the city, asking them to check for our names in their list of survivors. He kept it up until someone said they had found a match, Rutka Wasserberg was listed. He told me that he wasn't sure it would be I, but when he learned that I'd be arriving on a ship from Bremen Harbor that April, he had no doubt. He would be there to greet me, and he knew where to go, where I'd be staying in New York. Old and fragile as he was, he succeeded in finding out the date of my arrival. No matter how, he made that effort and he came to make me welcome. Now he couldn't stop holding my hands. We hugged again and again.

All these efforts at his age must have been especially difficult. He didn't look rich, wore an old-fashioned black suit, a frayed tie, and the bag of oranges he brought might have been more than he could afford. I accepted one orange, peeled it, sectioned it, and we shared it together slowly, enjoying the moment of our reunion. Sitting there in that little room, we seemed like two stranded survivors after the destruction of our family.

I hardly knew his family, had met him only that one time he visited before the war. After a few moments, I asked about his life and his family since then.

He spoke about his life since coming to America, about his wife and daughters settling in New York. The daughters left for school, got married, and moved away to Chicago. Then his wife passed on. He stayed on alone in the old apartment that was once filled with talking and laughter, a place the family had lived together all these years.

I wondered why he chose to stay when his daughters had moved on. As if he knew what was on my mind, Uncle Strawberry explained that New York was a familiar place to him. He knew his way around, had some friends, and didn't want to move. Fact was he chose to live alone, rather than lose independence.

A lonely existence, I thought, and wished that I could help to make him feel less alone, but he assured me he was fine. I had to go on, learn the language, go to school, and then meet a young man, marry him and start a family. That is what he wanted for me, thinking of my welfare, even though he was too old to care for his own needs. It took a great effort for him to search me out, but he had come to welcome me to my new life in my new land, a new beginning. I thought it miraculous for us to meet after all those years.

He seemed a mysterious figure, appearing as he had at two important moments in my life. If his first visit augured war and the destruction of our family, his second visit brought the promise of renewal and rebirth.

We sat facing each other across the desk, smiling. Mrs. Goldstein spoke English. I didn't. Ms. Goldstein didn't speak Polish. I did. Ms. Goldstein tried a little Yiddish, and we had some form of communication going.

"There are Jewish families all over America who would like you to come and live with them," she said.

I gulped. Could it really be so? So many people want me in their homes? Hard to believe, perhaps I didn't understand. My Yiddish is a little weak, to say the least. I smiled politely, waiting for her to continue.

"America is a big place, and you can choose where you'd prefer to make yourself at home. You've got a choice. Where would you like to go?" Mrs. Goldstein asked. I understood the question, but didn't know how to reply, since I knew none of the families who were kind enough to open up their homes to me, none of the many cities where I could chose to go. But that didn't matter, because after years of being treated as an outcast, years of being despised, unwanted, and unwelcome in all of Europe, here I found a welcome from people I had never met. All this was puzzling and unreal to me, and yet it made me feel happy.

I asked if I could stay here, in New York, live with my uncle or be near, and go to school. I also wanted to end up near my friends. Halinka was here, in Brooklyn.

Ms. Goldstein gave it some thought, shook her head, and said, "We have too many requests for this location, and your uncle is much too old to care for you."

Then I recalled that Marissa had her interview with Mrs. Goldstein just before mine, so I asked, "Where does Marissa want to go?"

Ms. Goldstein looked at her notes and said, "Marissa is going to Detroit. It seems one of your friends has settled there."

"Henrietta?" I asked.

One glance at her notes, and then she replied, "Yes, Henrietta, that is her name. She lives there with her family."

It took me just a moment to decide. "I'll go there also." The way I figured it, the three of us could stay together in one town.

"And why Detroit?" Ms. Goldstein raised her brows.

"I want to stay near my friends."

"Do you know anything about that city?"

"Yeah, they make cars and trucks over there. In Europe, it's mostly horses and wagons," I laughed.

"Very well, I'll make the necessary arrangements."

I sat next to Marissa on the bus, and breathed the tempo of the city, smelled its sweat, felt its pulse. I was amazed at the speed of things. People rushed to and fro, while an endless stream of cars whizzed by. There was hardly any space along the sidewalks or the road. But most of all I marveled at the cornucopia of all those goods in all those shops. I hardly blinked for fear of missing any of the stuff. I marveled at the pyramids built with potatoes, carrots, apples, grapes, all kinds of fruit. That wasn't all. I saw couches, chairs, tables, refrigerators, dresses for ladies and for little girls and so much more, all displayed so shoppers passing by could look and like, and buy. The speeding trucks were full of goods, hauling products who knew where? Energy and speed defined the place and I wanted to dive in, merge with the crowd, and become one with the rest. This was America, my new home, and surely a land of plenty, I thought seeing the trucks that carried the things, so all the people had all they needed. I thought it wondrous to see so many drive their cars, for they were free to come and go at will. And I was going to Detroit, the town that would make such freedom possible for me. I would be proud to live in such a town.

Chapter 17

Naomi Silverstein lived in Detroit with her husband, Irving, and her son Seymour. One year before they took me in, the family had suffered a great loss. While on vacation in Mexico, their seventeen-year-old daughter died tragically in a car accident. Naomi wished her own life was over too. Her home seemed empty, useless, but after one year of mourning, it was time to pick up the frayed remainder of her life. Time could not relieve the pain Naomi felt at her daughter's loss, but she wished her home could be of use again. There was talk around town and in the Temple about an exciting new project. The whole Jewish community was gearing up to take in some of the young survivors of the war. Naomi thought it would be right and good to help a child, to care for an orphan's needs. This task, she hoped, could ease her own grief.

The family was still in mourning on the day of my arrival. Naomi welcomed me warmly; so did Irving, a city cop. Irving Silverstein was a big, benign, and silent man. Kind of beefy with a double chin and a rather prominent belly, he carried a leather-holstered police gun on his hip. The belt sagged slightly beneath his stomach. The first time I saw Irving, the thought of Haim popped into my mind. Haim was strong, tall and lean, a Sabra soldier, trained to defend and protect, though I never saw him with a gun. Irving was also Jewish and he carried a big gun, reminiscent of the guns the Nazis carried all the time. But Irving's broad, moon-shaped face belied his vocation. His mouth curved in a perpetual smile; no tension showed in his face or his slow moving, lumbering body. In all the time I lived with his family, I never heard him raise his voice. Indeed, he seldom spoke at all.

When he did, his words were few, monosyllabic. Sometimes he'd nod when he agreed with what he heard.

During the two years I spent in Naomi's home, I never once heard Irving involve himself in a long conversation, not with Naomi, not with his son, Seymour, or with me, and most decidedly not with Naomi's sister, who lived with them.

Still Irving exuded warmth and good feelings, and I responded with a silent smile, a nod of my head, and gave off a general sense of amiability. In our silence, we were comfortable together. He appeared to approach all with kindness, gentleness, and equanimity.

Naomi explained that I would share a bedroom with her unmarried sister, Moira. I soon learned that she was a quiet woman, even more so than Irving. She rarely spoke, going to work each morning and going early to bed each night. Sometimes, she would mutter something, but I could never understand what she was saying.

Seymour was a year younger than I. Unlike the rest of the household, Seymour was deeply religious. He wore a Yarmulke on his head, and offered his prayers to God each morning and evening. When I saw him pray, I'd recall the way Grandfather worshipped. Each of them wore a similar white and black striped prayer shawl over the head. They both faced the eastern wall, and both prayed aloud. But Seymour was sixteen years old and looked nothing like my grandfather, who had seemed ancient even when I was a little girl.

Seymour was a tall and skinny boy, with a long bony face and huge dark eyes framed by long dark eyelashes, and he had a full head of black wavy hair. He was handsome, but his hands were moist all the time, which put me off.

The two of us enjoyed long and pointless arguments, even before I learned enough English to speak fluently. That was all right. When I found words missing, I used my hands, and made him guess what it was I wanted to say. I learned some English while he attempted to persuade me that there was a God. I, on the other hand, struggled to convince him that it really didn't matter. The God I knew allowed cruelty and destruction in His world.

"If there is a God who made us, then he should protect us," I told Seymour. The fact is I could do without such a God.

"We must not question God's will." he replied.

"Was it indeed His will to let the Nazis kill so many of our people, to kill the little children? Isn't that a sin?"

"He is all powerful," Seymour insisted.

"So why didn't He rise up to smite Hitler and his goons?"

"He is all knowing."

"Yeah? Then he's either blind and stupid, or evil."

"Shah! It's a sin to blaspheme against the Almighty." Seymour's face went pale. He faced the wall and started to pray, asking God to forgive me.

I wanted to tell him what I thought of God and his forgiveness. I would have laughed at Seymour, but he was earnest and decent; I didn't want to hurt him. At the same time, I could not agree with his powerful beliefs, and thought of them as just plain silliness.

From the first, it was Naomi who became my companion. We talked with each other in Yiddish, though neither of us spoke it easily. Each day, Naomi would patiently introduce me to a few words of English. I strived to absorb as many of these words as I could.

We would practice English after dinner. Most summer evenings, we had an established routine; we walked around the block twice following a well-defined path. On the first round, we'd stop at the corner drugstore. Here Naomi would take a small black leather change purse from her dress pocket and, extracting some coins, she'd pay for two one-scoop-ice-cream cones. After a while, Jerry, the soda man knew what we'd order and would start packing ice cream into cones the moment we entered the store. Chocolate was my favorite, while Naomi preferred vanilla.

We'd leave the sweet shop and licking the cones continue slowly around the block. The cool, sweet taste of ice cream on our tongues lubricated our conversation. Completing the first turn, we then dropped in for our second one-scoop-ice-cream-cone, chocolate for me, and vanilla for Naomi. That's what we did every summer evening after dinner. We'd take our stroll twice around the block eating ice-cream-cones, one scoop at a time.

As we walked, we talked, licked our cones, and learned

about each other. Ariel, Naomi's daughter came up often in our conversation. Naomi couldn't stop herself from talking about her. She told me Ariel had been very pretty and extremely bright. Naomi blamed herself for Ariel's death. The trip to Mexico was a gift from Irving and Naomi, and it was meant to celebrate Ariel's graduation from high school. Instead it took her life in a tragic car accident. Ariel was sitting next to the driver when another car swerved and hit them head on. In that moment, her life was cut. No more Ariel. Naomi could never accept that loss. She mourned all the long and happy years of life that Ariel would never have. She had been so young, and smart, and pretty, and she was dead.

From all Naomi told me of Ariel, I could almost imagine the girl. I saw many pictures that showed her growing up and becoming a lovely young woman. She had been an excellent student, planning to be an English teacher. "She was very bright, just like you," Naomi kept repeating. And I felt so very sorry for her loss. I would have liked to have met Ariel. I think we could have been friends.

As she recounted the many incidents from her daughter's short life, Naomi liked to hold my hand. Sometimes she'd squeeze it so hard it hurt. Sometimes she wept. I understood and sympathized with her great loss. I shared memories of my own; told her about Hania, how much I wished that she was still alive. I told Naomi about my mom and dad, how strong and determined she had been, how much he had loved music. And I would never see Haniushka laugh and talk and grow to be a woman. I would never get her back. I felt guilty because I was alive and she was gone. As Naomi missed her daughter, I missed the years Hania should have been alive and I missed my mom and dad.

I spoke about them all, wanting to keep their memory intact. And yet some part of me wanted to stop feeling sad. I would have liked somehow to put it all behind me, forget it even, if I could, but while each new person that I met, each new word I learned helped me to forget, Naomi kept me remembering.

It was difficult, Marissa could make me laugh, but she had little time to spend with me. Four years older than I, she was now considered an adult. She had to go to work in order to support herself but she had some help. The Jewish Agency for

Resettlement found a room for her and helped her find a job, so she could earn money and pay for her needs.

Marissa started to work as a stock clerk at a five- and-ten-cent store shortly after we arrived in Detroit. Her nights were taken up with school, learning English. We only managed to see one another occasionally on the weekends. I missed her even though my days were full.

I was attending a special summer class for non-English speaking students. In those early days in Detroit, I knew maybe ten words of English. Dazed by unfamiliar sounds, I had great difficulty catching the drift of what the teacher said. To add to my troubles, the few words I did understand, I couldn't spell.

For example, my ice cream cone tasted so delicious that I quickly learned how to ask for it in English. One day, when our teacher asked me to write a word I knew on the blackboard, I picked up the chalk and proudly wrote the word, "aiskrim," but instead of applause, I got vague stares. Didn't they know what ice cream is or what it tastes like? Surely what I had written on the board had to be correct. I spelled it out just the way I heard it. Polish is spelled phonetically. I simply applied what I knew. But Ms. Plum, our teacher, failed to recognize the particular group of letters I had written as an English word. I was puzzled, and tried to explain. I pointed to the group of letters I'd previously written on the board, and sounded each letter separately, A I S K R I M, I pronounced what in English would sound like ice cream. I turned to Ms. Plum, "Yes?" I said, expecting approval.

No," Ms. Plum replied, picking up the chalk. She wrote two other words next to mine. "ICE CREAM" She underlined each word, and said, "ice cream" expecting me to get it. Same pronunciation, but how could that be? I stood next to my teacher, examining the two groups of letters purporting to be words. Both sounded the same, but one of them had to be wrong.

Ms. Plum pointed to my AISKRIM, said, "No," and crossed it out. Next she pointed to her own group of words and said, "ice cream," smiled at me and said, "Yes!"

Now I began to see the problem. The sound was the same, but the spelling was different. I'd have to learn a language whose sound didn't match its written form. I could maybe learn to speak it. Perhaps I could learn to write it, but sure as hell I could never learn to do both. Floating on the sea of words I didn't understand, and whose spelling didn't match the sound, I decided to forget the whole thing, before I went mad.

Fortunately I discovered a miraculous place that saved my sanity. It was a library I had found in the Polish neighborhood of the city. Here were shelves full of books, all of them written in Polish. I found it through Bernard, a Wayne University student whose family had come from Poland. He took me there once, and I got a library card. After that I took out books by the dozen. I was hungry for the printed word, one that I could actually read and understand. After years of having nothing to read, it was a wonder, a joy to read a book. I didn't need to spell and read a language so mixed up when there were plenty of Polish books that I could read.

"I don't need English. It's a crazy tongue which I'll never learn to spell."

Naomi disagreed. "Most of us speak, read, and write English. You must learn it too." Reading Polish books would keep me from learning the language of my adopted country she said. From that point on, during our evening walks around the block, she would only speak English to me and insisted I do the same.

It was hard going at first; still I relented if not for my sake then for Naomi's. The poor woman had lost a brilliant and beautiful daughter. It wasn't right for her to be stuck with a poor substitute. I wanted to make amends for Naomi's sake. I agreed to cut down my time for Polish books, allowed myself one hour a day, while devoting the rest of the time to the study of English.

I purchased a Polish/English dictionary, and devising my own course of study, applied myself to the task. Using the Polish/English dictionary and children's picture books, I began looking up every word I didn't understand and translating it into Polish. That's when I discovered another, more puzzling problem. The word order in an English sentence differed from the way a Polish sentence was put together. With no apparent means to reconcile the differences, I had the additional problem of having to learn not only new words, but also the topography of an English sentence. It wasn't enough to understand and translate word for word; I had to learn which comes first.

In school one morning I mustered enough courage to raise my hand and in my halting English inquire, "How put words in correct order?"

"What?" Ms. Plum looked at me quizzically.

"Words I know, but how put together? Example: English word, 'tree.' Next, English word, 'beautiful;' put together, get 'tree beautiful,' but this no good."

Ms. Plum beamed at me, "How clever. You've just discovered syntax."

"The what?"

Ms. Plum lunged into a discussion on the subject of the English parts of speech. She identified verbs, adjectives, nouns, pronouns, and explained their arrangements, the order of which comes first, and which follows. I tried to grasp the business of how the English language is engineered. Of course, I couldn't take it in all at once, but one thing became clear to me, I was dealing with the reversal of the adjective/noun. In the Polish language an adjective may follow the noun, but in English it is always the noun that follows the adjective. I discovered that the thing itself, the word which is called a noun, always comes after the descriptive word, which is called an adjective. Once I grasped that idea, I could begin to say "beautiful tree," in place of "tree beautiful."

But many long hours of hard work lay ahead before I could truly savor my first success in school. Though I'd have preferred to escape the grind by turning to the more enjoyable reading of Polish novels, I redoubled my effort in the study of English. I tried to pay close attention to every word the teacher said. But the flood of words went right by me, and I understood less than I heard. I kept on trying, one sentence at a time, remembering to keep subject, verb, and adjective in their proper sequence. To make certain I was getting it right, I'd often check with Naomi at home and with the teacher in school. I was obsessed, gave up reading for pleasure, and devoted hours to the study of English.

By becoming so engaged, I rescued myself from a summer of total incoherence. I learned that by using adjectives sparsely, I was able to cut the job down to its essentials. I began to avoid the use of adverbs all together once I realized they are not essential to the core and meaning of the sentence. As I became more

191

proficient, my store of English words multiplied, and my ear accustomed itself to the sound of English. In time, what used to sound strange, became familiar to me. I began to understand the puzzling, slurred contractions of everyday speech and: "whasamaer?" became, "What's the matter?" "werugoin?" translated to "Where're you going?" And "hoyufiln?" meant "How are you feeling?" By the time summer neared fall, I no longer puzzled over every hurried, sloppily pronounced phrase I heard. I was eager to learn, and I did, but couldn't seem to lose my heavy accent, and I hated to hear people refer to it as "cute."

Chapter 18

By early fall, I started to attend high school with other kids my age. At least, they were chronologically, but I felt about two hundred years older than any of them. By mid-October, I hated the short, plaid and pleated skirts, the bobby sox and saddle-back shoes I had to wear, just like the other girls. I thought the skirts that ended just above my knees made me look like a little girl, and that I was too old to wear such things. Though actually I was very immature, I considered myself an adult, one with my own sense of style. Besides everybody wore the same clothes, which looked too much like a uniform to me. I hated to wear anything even remotely resembling a uniform. It reminded me of the camps where I had been forced to wear the same clothes other prisoners wore, a uniform that felt rough to the skin, and rough to my spirit.

Besides, I didn't like these short pleated skirts because they left me exposed to the chill of October mornings. I didn't particularly enjoy feeling goose pumps on my legs as I walked to school. Then too, I felt isolated from the other girls in school; I was different, not lightheaded. Perhaps I envied them their ability to giggle and preen.

My friends, Halinka and Marissa would never giggle just because a fellow gave them an inviting look. If anything, I didn't like boys very much. I didn't like the way they sweated, the way they wanted to grab at me every chance they got. I saw nothing funny about boys. Boys were scary, and I didn't understand what the girls were giggling about.

Marissa and Halinka knew how to handle them, but I had never learned, and was grateful to Halinka for rescuing me from their unsolicited advances.

The problem with my life in America was that I often felt like a square peg in a round hole. While Halinka and Marissa liked to flirt with boys, I wanted to run the other way. At school, the other girls laughed a lot. I seldom did. Nothing was funny about the way my life had gone and I felt the enormous gulf between them and me. Even if I wanted to, I wouldn't have known how to breach that gulf of difference. My years of growing up were nothing like theirs. Still deep down, I wanted to be liked, wanted to be accepted, wanted to belong, and so I went along, and wore the same clothes they wore. I looked the same on the outside, but on the inside, well, that was another thing all together. I despaired of ever fitting in.

The Agency for Resettlement provided Naomi with money to purchase clothes, books, and the like for me. And because Naomi and Irving had meager means, that money provided for the things I needed. During one afternoon of shopping, Naomi tried to help me select a small wardrobe she deemed appropriate to my age. But when Naomi suggested the white and brown saddle-shoes so popular with most girls, I chose the plain brown oxfords instead.

"Don't you want to look nice, like the other girls?" Naomi asked.

No, I didn't. What little fashion sense I had came from the movies and I preferred the more sophisticate style of clothing I'd seen beautiful ladies wear. So there was a bit of tug and pull between us over what was appropriate for me. In the end, Naomi agreed to most of my selections, but trouble developed when I noticed a little black hat with a veil such as I'd seen on British ladies riding to the hounds in the movies. I wanted that hat.

Naomi mounted an objection. "Little old ladies wear such hats. You're a pretty young girl."

But I had fallen in love with that hat, and looked at it so longingly that Naomi gave it a nod against her better judgment.

"You can wear it next month to the unveiling,"

"Unveiling? What does that mean?"

"It's been ten months since my daughter died," she said. "Our religion and our tradition require us to place a carved stone on her grave within one year of her death."

194

"But why, what is the purpose of this stone?"

"It is a marker or monument to identify the place of burial, so that relatives can find it when they visit the cemetery to honor the memory of the deceased. Ariel's name and the dates of when she was born and when she died will be engraved on her stone." Naomi took out her handkerchief and blew her nose.

I wanted her to stop talking about this unveiling, for it was obviously causing her pain. But after a deep sigh she went on. "Then it is placed by the graveside and covered with a cloth until the time of the unveiling. That's when family and friends gather at the graveside to mourn and pray and to observe the ceremony of unveiling. That's when family and friends gather at the grave-side to mourn and pray."

I hadn't known about this custom. Before the war I had been too young to learn. Talk of death and graves was not a part of my life, not then. Later, during the war, death became an everyday reality, death and the fear of dying. But I never saw graves or grave stones. People were shot, gassed, or burned, and they were buried where they died together, hundreds of them at one time, buried in the ground and forgotten. I was accustomed to death, but had no knowledge of graves, gravestones, or unveilings. I had never seen the inside of a cemetery. No graves or stones existed for Mother, Father, or Hania. Their killers dumped everyone into mass graves, dishonoring those whom they killed. I could only guess at how and where their lives had ceased.

I was curious about the custom of marking the grave with a stone and wanted to know more. Naomi told me this ancient ceremony had started in Biblical times. She went on to talk about Rachel, the wife of Jacob, and how after Rachel died, "Jacob erected a monument on Rachel's grave." These exact words appear in the book of Genesis, she explained.

My hurt was too raw to endure, and I forbade myself to feel it, hid away from it like a turtle retreating into its thick carapace, while every fiber of my being longed to have my family back. I thought the hurt of missing them had grown into a scab. It formed into a hardened crust I used to separate me from my sorrow. I had grown numb.

Now at the unveiling, I didn't know what was expected of

me. The little veil on that ridiculous riding-to-the-hounds hat fluttered against my face. Its fine mesh made me see the mourners as if through a fog. They pressed handkerchiefs to their eyes. Their sobs and the display of emotions distressed me.

I looked away from them and gazed at row upon row of gray carved stones dotting the green grass. I wanted to run from grief, escape the dead and buried. The keening of the mourners brought it back. I struggled to shut it out, become immune to anguished sighs. And yet I felt myself being sucked down into the ground, down to where the dead lay. I fought against it but the overwhelming sadness came upon me like a flood. I saw the faces of the dead. How very young they were... my mother and my dad... Hania, only five...

...Haniushka toddles beside me, bundled up in a thick wool sweater...the red wool scarf round her neck is wound right up over her nose...only her eyes shine and crinkle...she smiles seeing the snow...

My cheeks felt moist. I blinked, swiped at them with the back of my hand. But I could not wipe that sweet image of Haniushka from my mind. She was such a round and happy child. Unbidden tears leaked from my eyes, moistened my cheeks, and made me taste salt on my lips. Sweet Hania was only four when she first tasted snow, and when she was five, she no longer could

"Yis-ga-dal v'yis-ka-dash," the rabbi begins to intone Kaddish for Naomi's daughter...

..."Yis-ga-dal v'yis-ka-dash, sh'may..." Grandfather chants. I sit with legs just short of the floor, looking at him in his white shawl... looks like the prophet...picture of holy man in a book...

Standing next to Naomi, I listen to the words of Kaddish, the sobs of the mourners, and recall...

...His voice raises and falls... like music...He chants... Kaddish...mystery of words...

196

The Rabbi continued chanting the prayer for the dead, Kaddish for Ariel. Naomi sobbed. I looked at the Rabbi and remembered my grandfather bending before God speaking the words of Kaddish in memory of his father.

Naomi, Seymour, and Irving mourned Ariel, the way she used to be, eager for life, eager to make the world a better place, eager for joy, struck down by a drunken driver.

And I thought. Only I am left to say Kaddish for my mother, and Father, Hania, and Bubby and Zyde, and Uncle Jurek, and Cousin Helena. Only I remained to honor the memory of each.

As I stood among those mourners who grieved Ariel's passing, I listened to the Rabbi's words through haze of memory, as I used hear my Zyde chanting Kaddish...

"...Yis-ga-dal...v'yis-ka dash...sh'may...ra'bbo..."

Grandfather invokes the names of all who came before, his father and mother who gave him life and all who went before to shape the way we live. He sings his song remembering those he loved... he chants the ancient words, mysterious words, Kaddish for the dead...

...White shawl atop his head, it frames his bearded face, he chants his prayer for the dead... Sings out the cycle of our lives...sings out the name of the people we have loved

"This small black box here holds our treasure," Zyde says. I look at it and how he's affixed it on his forehead with the leather straps.

"Please tell me more," I plead, but Bubby has her finger across her lips. "Shush, Zyde is saying Kaddish."...

I felt no longer numb. My crusted scab of pain turned brittle, fell apart, and I uttered Kaddish for the first time, but not with sacred words. I didn't know them. There beside Ariel's graveside, I broke down, cried for my sister, wept for Haniushka who had no grave, and no carved stone, for my little Hania, perhaps left forsaken in a shallow ditch, or maybe turned to ash to mingle with the ashes of so many other dead.

I wept for her, grieved for her, and in my mind replayed that last moment, when the Nazis tore her from my hands. Once again I saw the growing dread in Hania's pleading eyes, felt her small hand in my own, even as the SS man pulled it hard, yanked those little fingers out of my grasp, and hauled her up and out of sight. The door slammed shut.

I became one with the mourners. I tried to evoke the image of everyone I loved that now was dead. At first I thought the Kaddish in my own way, without words, letting my sorrow speak, so only God could hear. I prayed for God to listen to my plea. I implored Him to place them together in some heavenly courtyard like the one we had before the Nazis came.

The rabbi spoke the words my Zyde spoke so long before, and as I listened, his chant became familiar to me, and I began to chant those sacred words of Kaddish, begging the God I wasn't sure was there to let them have some peace, I whispered, "Yis-ga-dal v'yis-ka-dash, sh'may ra'bbo, b'olmo...Oseh shalom..." speaking the words in memory of the dead.

After the Kaddish, Naomi's arms closed around me. I pressed my face to hers, and so we stood together locked in our mutual sorrow. Naomi thanked me for the sympathy I'd shown the family at this sad time. I didn't know how to respond at first, but soon recovered sufficiently to murmur, "I understand your loss. It is something we both know about."

One day after school I found a closet full of clothes on my bed. Blouses and skirts, some still on hangers, most in the style worn by my schoolmates. There were plaid and pleated skirts, white and pale blue cotton blouses, some in lavender and yellow, with ruffles down the front, and high ruffled collars. I even noticed one pink silky, slinky thing, lying next to the long and full skirts in black and also navy. I guessed they belonged to Naomi's daughter. I went looking for Naomi.

Normally, Naomi greeted me each afternoon after school, but that day she didn't. There was the customary glass of milk and a plate of cookies on the kitchen table, but no Naomi. I drank some milk, chewed a cookie, and wondered what had happened to Naomi.

The house was quiet. Was she napping? Then I wondered if

she might be ill. I tiptoed down the hall, and peeked into her bedroom. There was Naomi sitting on the side of her bed, her face buried in her hands.

I froze. I would have gone over to give her a hug, but thought better of it not wanting to intrude on her grief. As silently as I opened it, I closed the door. Naomi had given me those clothes, even as she mourned her daughter. How could she bare to see me wearing them? They didn't belong to me. I'd ask her to take them away, give them to someone she'll never see, someone who can use them.

Irving seemed to avoid us all. I had not seen him since the funeral. He grieved alone and in silence. I wanted to speak to him, tell him how sorry I was for his loss. But days had passed. I didn't know how I could. He was a good man, yet he kept a gun. I knew Irving to be a kind and peaceful man, couldn't picture him using such a hateful object, even in the line of duty. I understood the job of a policeman required him to have a gun. In his hand it was a tool for enforcing the law and keeping peace. Irving kept his spare one in the top drawer of the breakfront in the dining room. And sometimes when no one else was home, I'd open the drawer and peek in. A dark brown metal object, it was big and ugly, heavy too, as I discovered when one day I mustered sufficient courage to pick it up. I almost dropped it, for the weight. The metal felt cold to the touch, so smooth that it seemed almost slimy in my hand. It brought back memories I'd prefer to forget. I put it back, and closed the drawer. Yet I could not leave it be. I even told Marissa about it. When she asked to see it, I made the mistake of opening the drawer so she'd believe me.

We saw one another seldom, as Marissa worked all week, and only had Saturdays free. That's when she usually came over for a visit, and mostly complained about her job, and about how dull it was. When she wasn't talking about the hateful job, she talked about Detroit. She didn't like it. It was boring and ugly, and she didn't like the people, pretty much for the same reason that she hated the town and the job. On top of all that, she couldn't stop talking about Jerry, the love of her life. She longed for him and missed him. The two of them met aboard ship and, as Marissa told it, fell in love at first sight. Unfortunately, his family lived in New York.

She couldn't stop talking about him, wondering what he was doing, and worrying that he may have met someone else to love. The fact is Marissa wasn't much fun anymore. I figured she wasn't having much fun either. All this sighing for her beloved Jerry and her dissatisfaction with her job and her life in Detroit, made me feel somewhat bored with Marissa.

Then one Saturday, Marissa bounced into the house with a tall, slim, dark, and unemployed actor in tow. Harold, I was informed, loved Marissa. For her part, she found him attractive as well, but that little fact didn't interfere with her ongoing pining for Jerry.

Harold had a handsome face. Besides his intelligent looking glasses, he had a slick head of black shiny well-brushed hair, and a square jaw. He liked to indulge in his favorite pastime and recite passages from Hamlet, which he did ponderously. Presenting himself as a serious and somber guy, he affected the manner of someone lost in deep thought.

I became somewhat infatuated with him as well, and had to compete with Marissa for his attention. He must be a great artist, I thought. I loved the dramatic air he carried about him. However yearning for him didn't last long. I soon realized that most of his posturing was nothing but a deep and abiding absorption in himself. In this he had much in common with Marissa, who was equally wrapped up in her own concerns and feelings. Together they made a dramatic couple, leaving me feeling like the audience they both craved. At the same time, I saw myself as a mirror wherein they could admire reflections of their own beautiful, dramatic selves.

After a few weeks Harold took his person away from my presence, disappeared from the little performance stage he had shared with Marissa. She was too absorbed in her abiding love for Jerry to miss Harold. She went back to sighing for her Jerry, with me serving as the consoling friend. I attempted to distract Marissa, by inviting her to picnics in the park along with some other people I'd met. But since none of the young men I knew wore intelligent glasses, like Harold, Marissa had had no use for them. Of course, the funny thing was that Jerry wore no glasses, intelligent or otherwise. In fact, I thought him to be coarse and rather dull and could not understand what it was Marissa found so enthralling about him. But she did, and her moaning and longing began to wear on my nerves.

On one particular overcast afternoon, with nothing to do but listen to Marissa's moans, I said, "You know what? You bore me. Jerry bores me. I don't know what you see in him. He is neither smart, nor good looking, wears no glasses, and I wish you'd either get over it, or go to him, and be done with it."

Whereupon, Marissa crossed over to the sideboard, opened the drawer, picked up the gun, and waved it dangerously in the air. When she pointed it dramatically at her temple, I shrieked, "Stop, it's loaded!"

Very calmly, deliberately, she began to squeeze the trigger. I lunged, shoving the gun away from her temple towards the ceiling. The gun went off. Naomi ran in from the kitchen.

Marissa lay on the floor, her face drained of color, the gun beside her. I stood frozen, hands over my mouth. "Is she dead?" I asked.

Naomi bent down to examine for wounds and injuries. She found none, and soon Marissa's eyes flickered open and gazed upon the hole in the ceiling. Naomi's eyes followed hers to the dark and gaping hole in the smooth whiteness.

"What's wrong with you?" Naomi demanded.

"Marissa wanted to kill herself," I stammered.

"Nonsense," Naomi grunted. "Get up!" she said, "No one is interested in your dramatics."

I felt mortified, just thinking about the hole in the ceiling, and all that money Naomi and Irving would have to spend in order to fix it. "I'm sorry," I whispered.

"It isn't you who should be feeling sorry. It's her," Naomi fumed, looking at Marissa.

Never having seen her so angry, I felt awful.

"Sorry. I'll never do this again." Marissa stood, and dusted herself off.

"See that you don't. Now go home." Naomi gave her a little push towards the door.

A few weeks later, Marissa left for New York.

Days grew hot with summer, schools closed for vacation, and I spent most of my time reading, and fanning my face.

Naomi nagged, "Why don't you go to the lake with the other kids?"

"I like to read." I wished she'd leave me be, but Naomi was persistent. An hour later, I would be lost in the pages of the book, and Naomi would burst in on me again, demanding I change my activity.

I just couldn't get her to accept that I preferred to read than go to some silly swimming pool or lake. Finally tired of the constant nagging, I took myself off to a small park behind the library. Here I found a bench under a big oak tree whose spreading branches provided shade and cooling breeze. This garden nook became my reading room. Best of all, no one asked me to stop reading Polish books and go out to play with friends that I didn't have anyway. I could lose myself in the fictional characters with all their motivations, responses and ideas, as I easily followed the plot of books written in my native language. I thought that I was becoming more fluent in English too, but I still couldn't understand the meaning of many idioms.

Irving liked to start his conversations with "What do you know?"

I didn't know how to answer. Thinking he meant to ask what I'd learned from reading all that day, my first impulse was to shrug and say, "Not much." I expected him to laugh. But he didn't.

Big, silent, Irving didn't know what to make of me, and he was hurt thinking that I had cut him off when he was trying to make a conversation. After that he seemed even quieter than usual around me. I was puzzled about that at first. But a few days later, I noticed that Irving used this phrase often and I also began to realize that everybody peppered his or her conversation with phrases similar to his. People were just "shooting the breeze," another phrase which caused me a hard time.

"Shoot the breeze, with what? I wondered.

Then it dawned on me, ah, I'm beginning to use these well-worn phrases too; I guess that makes me American just like everybody else. It dawned on me that his, "What do you know?"

query didn't require me to respond with a full litany of the knowledge I'd acquired during my entire life. It was simply one of the many common phrases that shouldn't be taken literally.

I saw that my ignorance of English idiom had hurt Irving inadvertently. That's when I vowed to stop wasting my time reading Polish novels. From now on, I'd make an earnest effort to learn not only the language but its common phraseology as well. I wanted to converse with others without making a fool of myself or making others feel like fools.

A few weeks later, as Irving came up the steps after work I smiled and greeted him with, "Hot isn't it?"

He beamed, "Hot enough for you?"

"Hey, that's funny," I smiled. "Yeah, hot like the devil's neighborhood."

Irving puzzled over that one, but we were friends again.

I needed more practice speaking English if I were to become an American. To that end, I agreed to join some of my schoolmates at the lake. Naomi was pleased, and made me try on my brand-new bathing-suit. I pulled it on and looked in the mirror. I didn't like what I saw, too skinny, and way too pale.

Naomi clapped her hands in admiration. "You look real nice, cute figure."

She couldn't mean it, I thought. I hated the way I looked, and rummaged for something to cover my nearly naked, bony frame. I found a pretty pale blue cotton blouse to throw over the bathing suit, and I pulled on a pair of shorts, hoping they'd hide my bony thighs. The blouse and shorts would stay over the bathing-suit I decided. I didn't know how to swim anyway.

That afternoon, while others splashed in the lake, I sat under a tree observing the droplets of water land on the naked shoulders and smiling faces of my classmates.

Someone I had never met sat down next to me. "Call me Ricky," he said.

I gave him a sidelong glance, but was too shy to respond. But then curious to see what he looked like, I turned toward him. There he was sitting beside me, bronzed, sun burnished skin, broad chest, shoulders sprinkled with sweat or water, and those sinewy arms, even browner then the rest of his body. His blond wavy hair was ruffled by the breeze; he was handsome, but the air of ease he carried about him was even more appealing. Not cocky and not smug, he simply looked as if he walked through life in an unhurried way. Perhaps his self-assurance came with age. He did seem a bit older than the other kids. Looking at him sitting there, I could not imagine anything could ever bother him. I fell in love.

"You got a name?" he asked.

"Rutka," I said.

"Here in America you should be known as Ruth."

"It is the same name, I understand.'"

"Your namesake was quite a woman. Did you know that?"

"She lived in the Bible."

He put his hand lightly on my shoulder. His touch penetrated beneath my blouse, under the mid-thigh shorts and beneath my bathing suit. I shivered, wanted him to take his hand away, wanted him to keep it there. I felt my cheeks glow red, and wanted to hide, burrow into the ground, and vanish from his sight. I felt ugly, awkward, and scrawny, but his eyes refused to let me go.

A moment or two later, he stood, smiled, and whispered, "Later." Then, he ambled towards the water's edge. I watched him stand there observing the crowd. A few minutes later, he stepped up onto the diving board, walked its length, bounced up and down a couple of times, jumped up hands extended over his head, arched over, and sliced into the water with hardly a splash.

My eyes riveted on the long strokes, his arms reaching overhead, his rhythmic, strong pull, each stroke equal in power to the next, as he cut through the water with ease, swimming towards the middle of the lake. I thought he'd turn around, swim back, but no. He continued on like a well-maintained machine; pulling his body across the water towards the other shore, growing smaller as he went.

Chapter 19

I got my first job in a nearby bakery with its aroma of deliciously sweet, melt in your mouth, drowned in chocolate frosting, cream puffs, chocolate truffles, and chocolate drenched éclairs. I sold many and tasted quite a few, and didn't mind the low pay as long as dark and rich chocolate was a part of the deal.

But after just a few days on the job, ugly red pimples began to appear on my forehead. At first, I didn't connect those pimples to the rich chocolate pastry I'd been cramming into my mouth. A few days passed, and I grew tired of sweets; couldn't stand looking at my face in the mirror. Then too, each time I washed my face, I felt the roughness of those disgusting pimples with my fingertips. Before long, I began to question my stupid career choice. What was I thinking? I had no desire to spend the rest of my life selling pastry across a counter. I grew bored, and whenever the shop emptied of customers, I'd pull out the book I kept under the counter and read.

Mr. Gross, the baker and owner caught me with an open book in my lap. For some ridiculous reason, he did not approve. "Young lady," he addressed me. "This is not a public library." He accused me of shirking my duty, and said that he wasn't paying me to read books. There were glass surfaces to be cleaned, glass counter tops and display cases to be wiped. "They must be kept sparkling clean at all times," he insisted.

All the time, that would be very difficult, I thought. My tiny customers always pressed their noses against the glass the better to examine the goodies inside. New smudges invariably appeared right after I'd wiped them off, and I complained to Naomi about those smudges on the glass surfaces. It is a thankless and a particularly unpleasant chore, I told her. No one in the household was surprised when my career as pastry dispenser and glass polisher came to an abrupt end.

To add to my troubles, Marissa was gone, and I felt lonely. It wouldn't be so bad if I had made new friends, but I just couldn't. I did not fit in with my contemporaries who all looked the same with their long hair, their short pleated skirts, and those bobby sox and saddleback shoes they liked to wear. Yes, I wanted them to like me. I wanted to like them, but we didn't know one another. We had little in common…

…The sky looks gray, and I hope the sun will rise a little later this morning, bring back the colors. I don't like it when it is so gray. The windowpanes are streaked with rain, and I feel sad; I don't think the sun will come out. I'll be stuck in the house with nothing to do.

I wish I could read. Mama says I'm still too little. But I'll learn after the summer, when I go to school. Even now I can read some words, mostly signs over the stores, like "Hot Bagels." That sign hangs right inside the bakery window, and there is another sign that hangs above it. I can read that to, "Bakery." I like to read it out loud. Mama says, "Shush," and tells me that it is not polite to yell in the street. But I do it anyway, especially when we go by the shoemaker's store. Then I sing out, "Shoes for the ladies." I really like those big gold letters, and the shoes in the window, the ones with high heels especially.

When I grow up I'll wear high heels, just like Cousin Helen. She lives far away, but whenever she comes to visit, she always wears these lovely high heel shoes. Sometimes they're brown, and sometimes deep, deep blue, like the sky at night. They shine like jewels on her feet, and she looks very pretty in them, and I can hardly wait to grow tall as she, so I too can wear such shoes.

The house is quiet. Everyone's asleep; it must be very early. Is the sun sleeping too?

Should I risk waking her up? She must be tired. It was very late when she came back from the theatre. Cousin Helen is sleeping in my Grandma's kitchen. She has come for a visit and is sleeping on a cot that Grandpa set up for her last night. It's wonderful when she comes, but I don't want to disturb her. She must be tired.

But maybe she's awake. I hope so; I want to hear all about her night in the theatre. The way she paints with words, she makes it so real, as she reveals the stage, summons the actors and speaks their lines. She takes me to a place I've never seen, a place I hope to visit when I grow up.

OK, I'll be quiet as a mouse, I decide, and leave my bed, put my soft slippers on, and instead of shuffling across the floor I make sure to pick up my feet with each step. That way she will not hear me when I peek in on her in the kitchen. I sneak along the hallway on my tiptoes. Oh good, the kitchen door is open, and there's my Cousin Helen. She is awake and smiles at me. I run to her, and she throws back the blanket and invites me in. We snuggle in the warm bed as I listen to her tell me about the world of grown ups...

Yes, I wanted friends desperately, but it sometimes seemed to me that we were from different planets. There was one girl who seemed friendly. But her conversation seemed lame. Her questions, well, there was no way I could answer so she could understand.

What could I say when Frieda asked, "How was it there in the concentration camp? Could you meet boys, and go on dates?"

"There were no boys," I snapped.

"What happened to them?"

"They were kept somewhere else."

"You missed them, I bet."

"I missed my Mom and Dad. I missed my sister," I said and walked away shaking my head in disgust.

A few minutes later, I saw the same girl gossiping with the others. They giggled, as they looked in my direction. None of them had ever lost all that they loved and cared about. They thought it funny that I'd prefer to spend time with my parents and sister rather than go out on dates with boys. For my part I thought they were brainless. Each time I experienced the insurmountable difference between us, I felt much older than they even though we were the same age in years. Just to watch them walk with books clutched to their chests made me wince. Why couldn't they carry them in book bags over their shoulders?

Coming from a different world, I cared nothing for the things they considered crucial to their lives. They loved the music I thought boring. Their conversations were peppered with such phrases as, "he's so cute..." or, "I hope he asks me for a date." They said things like, "I just love your blouse..."

Love, how can you love a thing you wear? Love is powerful and rare. I was irritated to hear the girls use words so carelessly. What interested them appeared silly and unimportant to me. Yet, I realized that those girls had never experienced life in a concentration camp. I shouldn't expect them to understand why I saw the world with different eyes than theirs.

I moved through interminable days, waiting for I knew not what. Both Halinka and Marissa were now in New York. I felt lonely and wanted to go there as well. But I couldn't go, not right away. I had to wait till I turned eighteen, another whole year.

I felt depressed. It seemed hardly worth my effort to get up in the morning. The only pleasure in my life was the odd quiet hour of reading that I managed to squeeze out of each day. As for the rest, I floated with no point of reference in a culture I didn't understand.

But I did keep up with school and even got myself another boring job, this time at the Five & Ten Cent store. It was a small, poor business, with only an occasional customer who blundered in by mistake. I worked alone. With no one to talk to, my use of language dwindled to two phrases: "Will that be all, Madam?" and "Thank you, please come again."

The store was stocked with commonplace merchandise, none of it pretty. It was my job to keep all the cheap trinkets, cosmetics, pins, threads, buttons, pens, pencils, and hundred of other small and plain items neatly arranged. I had to rearrange the merchandise each time the customers messed it up. No sooner did I straighten it up than the next customer came through the door. I felt like poor Sisyphus who kept on rolling that heavy rock up a hill, only to see it go tumbling down again.

One afternoon I watched while a woman customer rummaged through a number of cheap plastic combs...

...Mom looks beautiful, her smooth, black, hair is pulled back... the translucent comb with flecks of brown and yellow, holds her French twist in place... Dad is handsome in his black suit. He bends down for a hug, and I can smell a whiff of his favorite tobacco. Mom gives me a goodnight kiss...I inhale perfume, orange and sweet lemons...the door swings shut...and I'm left alone.

Wish I could go...see the Magic Flute...never been to the opera. Magic Flute, it sounds enchanting, like something from a fairy tale. But they say I'm too young now and promise I can come next year, when I'm ten...

After the customer left without buying anything, I straightened the combs, and wished there was an opera house in Detroit. There were lots of movie houses and a major baseball park. The sound of baseball was ever present during summer. It came from open windows and front porches and flowed into the street. The voice of the radio announcer with his blow-by-blow account of every pitch, hit, and miss, and the ever-present sound of the spectators' roar was a familiar sound most summer afternoons and evenings. Walking along the neighborhood streets, I often puzzled over the degree of interest and excitement this game engendered. I learned that it's considered the "national pastime" and important to Americans. I wanted to understand, but I didn't much care for sports, would rather play checkers or chess. Best of all I liked a good spirited exchange of ideas. In my view, a stimulating conversation rivaled the game of baseball. A conversation was like a game of words, with participants tossing ideas back and forth much as they might a ball. The goal of this game was to gain the last word. But it was the participation in the game that made it so much fun. Why would anyone prefer the passive role of a spectator? Where's the fun in that? I didn't know.

Towards the end of summer, America held its collective breath waiting to see which team would win the pennant. It seemed that everybody either listened to the radio, or went to the stadium, but I could not share the excitement that affected so many people. I felt like a transplant unable to sink its roots into the unfamiliar culture of this American working town.

As far as I knew, no one had ever heard of baseball in Europe. The hoopla over there centered on soccer. But I didn't much care for that either with all that sweating, crowding, and shouting. Although my friends had asked me to go with them, I seldom wanted to watch guys compete against one another just to see which one of them could kick a ball into the goal. Sometimes the boys used their heads instead of their feet, and I feared they'd mash their brains doing it. Baseball was a complete mystery to me. But it was a mystery I wasn't particularly interested in unraveling. I doubted it involved brain power, so I had no interest in it.

Mainly I missed my own family and my birth home, but I liked the Silverstein family, all of them, including Naomi's sister who kept me up at night with her snoring. Naomi and Irving were very kind and caring. They opened their home to me, and though I appreciated all they did for me, I felt very much alone.

Seymour, Naomi's son, spent his days in the Yeshiva, and seldom came home until just before dinner. I enjoyed our time together on those rare occasions when he came home by mid-afternoon. We'd spend hours arguing about God.

I didn't understand what made Seymour so devoted to God. His parents followed the Jewish tradition, observed holidays, ate customary food, but they were not religious. He was deeply religious, but I didn't understand how he could believe in a merciful God in heaven, after his sister was killed in a car accident. Ariel was just as dead as Haniushka.

"It's an empty place up there," I used to argue. "What use is God, even if he does exist? How can you say He is merciful, when He allows horrible things to happen to little children?"

Faith, that was his answer, and he would repeat it again and again. No matter how many questions I posed, he always had the same answer. "God is good; God is merciful; God loves us, and everything that happens is God's will. Everything is according to His plan."

I was too young then to know that faith is not a subject for disputation I figured he'd go on studying the Torah all his life, praise God every morning and night, marry and eventually grow to become like one of those patriarchs of old with many sons and daughters, and a nation of grandchildren.

I liked Seymour. He was dependable, had built his life within the religious frame. He belonged to God, as God belonged to him. Everything he did, everything he loved, everything he wanted to know sprang from his belief in a merciful, wise and good God. I wished that I too could believe as he did.

Though he was one year younger than I, Seymour reminded me of my Zyde. Like Zyde he prayed each morning and each evening, facing the Eastern wall. Like Zyde he wore a white shawl with black stripes, and the little black leather box of sacred prayers affixed with a leather strap around his arm and fastened atop his head. He rocked back and forth on his heels, bowing before God just as my Zyde did. In every other way he was different from my Zyde, but they both observed the ritual of prayer in the same way just as it had been observed by Jews the world over for many generations. In this way, Seymour was a link to my home, my only link to the courtyard of my childhood. In some strange and miraculous way, I liked him even as I disapproved of the God he shared with my Zyde.

Every so often, I'd think of Ricky, the handsome fellow who sat beside me that summer day at the lake. I didn't know where he was keeping himself, what he did for living or if he attended the university. I wondered if I'd ever see him again. Ricky seemed comfortable in his skin, and carried himself with a cool, confident air. I remembered that he understood my shyness, sensed my unease at his speaking to me as if we'd known each other all along. He didn't push, didn't insist. Instead he jumped into the lake and went for a swim.

Ricky was nothing like another guy I'd met at a party. That guy had seemed nice at first. Seeing that I was alone, he even offered to take me home, and I accepted, thinking his offer a friendly gesture. I didn't realize that friendly was the farthest thing from his mind. I knew I had made a mistake soon after he started the car. One hand on the wheel, his other hand squeezed my knee, and moved up my thigh.

"Stop the car," I yelled,

He laughed and stopped the car. I went for the door, but he pulled me roughly towards him, mashing his body against mine. His hand between my legs, his mouth on mine, he wouldn't let me go till I bit his lip and drew blood. He released with a gasp of pain. I flung open the door and ran, tasting his sticky, salty blood on my lips. I ran, and didn't stop running when he started his car engine. Fearful he'd come after me, I ran all the faster. His car gathered speed, but he didn't stop as I feared he would when he came abreast. He passed me by, his middle finger up in the air. That obscene gesture was his parting shot to me.

After he disappeared from sight, I stopped, took a deep breath, and looked around. Nothing but a dark deserted street, a few lights; I saw nothing familiar. I kept walking and after a few blocks I came to a busy street, saw a sign for the bus stop on the corner, and waited till it came I had to transfer twice. It was quite late. The third bus brought me to my street.

After that episode I was fearful of going out, and except for school and chores, I stayed mostly at home, remembering Rick, and our brief encounter at the lake. I was haunted by the image of his graceful dive into the lake, his long lean body, the way his arms sliced through the water in measured stroke. I didn't think it possible that he'd be as disgusting as that other guy.

I spent July and most of August working, and reading in my spare time. Then late one afternoon, coming home from the Five-And-Ten-Cent store, I saw Ricky reading a magazine, leaning against the lamppost by my bus stop. My cheeks grew hot and turned the color of cleanly washed beets as my bus came to a stop.

"Hi, there," he smiled, and steadied me with his hand as I came stumbling off the steps. My legs had turned to rubber. I almost fell, but his outstretched arm helped me to regain my balance.

"Wasn't easy to find you," he said, taking me by the elbow. I let him lead me towards Main Street, and away from home.

"Are you hungry?" he asked.

Naomi's waiting dinner, I remembered. "I should go home," I said.

"Why not call, say you met a friend?

Heart knocking in my chest like it could break my ribs, and burst through skin, I tried to take slow breaths, and concentrate on placing one foot in front of the other. My mind a jumble of partially formed questions, I wanted to ask if he'd been waiting just for me, or was it a chance encounter. I hoped he hadn't forgotten me, that he wanted to see me. But how would he know where to find me? It really didn't matter why or how we met. What mattered was he was here, walking beside me, and I was ecstatic. I struggled to keep from jumping, skipping, or breaking into a dance. To think that after that short encounter at the lake, he'd want to see me again.

When we entered a small restaurant, Rick didn't wait for the hostess to seat us. He brushed right by walking straight towards a booth in the rear where a man stood up to greet us. I noticed the color of his cheeks, because it matched mine.

Rick slapped his back and said, "Boychik, meet Rutka." The man offered me his cold moist hand, and turned an even deeper red. He must be very shy, I thought.

We slipped into the booth, and Rick without preamble started to talk with Boychik, as if I wasn't there. It looked like they had forgotten me. I didn't like it. Besides, I didn't know what they were talking about. It sounded to me like a heated argument about somebody named President Truman.

Could they be talking about the President of the United States?

As their conversation became more heated, Rick raised his voice, "What does it matter if he used to sell haberdashery, the man knows what he's doing."

I was bewildered. First Rick made me feel I was important to him. The next minute he forgot that I sitting right beside him. I didn't like being ignored, and I decided to go back to Naomi's for dinner. I stood up suddenly, almost spilling Rick's beer. The two men gave me startled looks, and our waitress approached at that moment with a loaded tray. I didn't know whether to sit down or go away in a huff, and I stood there feeling awkward, knowing I was making a scene. I had to remind myself that the world does not revolve around me, and decided to stay for a while to see what would happen.

"Be right back," I whispered, and breezed off towards the powder room.

When I returned Boychik smiled at me, "W-h-what d-do you th-think?" he asked.

213

"Think about what?"

"Which is b-b-better: S'socialism or C-c-communism?"

"Which do you prefer?" I dodged.

Boychik got serious. "It's not a m-matter of p-preference. It's a matter of l-logic."

"Nonsense," Rick exploded. "Eugene V. Debts was a socialist, and he was the most logical thinker around. You said so yourself, Boychik."

What did it matter, I wondered. "You guys must really like to argue." I joked.

They both laughed, and I could see there was a bond between them. The banter, their debate, was simply an entertaining game of words and logic. They were friends, comfortable with each other. They were good buddies, and I was glad that they included me in this almost nonchalant way. I wished I knew what they were going on about. I vowed to learn more, so I could participate in their debate. For now, I'd listen, and perhaps learn something.

Several days passed. No Rick. Then one dark, rainy Sunday afternoon, I looked up from my book and saw him mounting the steps to our front porch. I reached the door, even before he knocked.

"Get your coat and hat, and bring your gloves. It's raw out there," he said. "I'll wait on the porch; my shoes are wet."

It never occurred to me to play hard to get; I wanted to follow wherever he led so I hurried into my coat, tied a rain scarf under my chin, and rushed out without a word to Naomi.

On the way, Rick explained we were going to Wayne University to hear a lecture by a visiting Harvard professor. Apparently Rick was impressed by the man's books, and now wanted to take the opportunity to hear the talk.

I wondered why he thought I'd want to go, but didn't voice the question. Instead I asked, "Are you a student at the university?"

"No, but I'm interested in politics and philosophy. Professor Greely is a radical like me. That's why I want to meet him," Rick said.

I had heard of philosophy and even of politics, but radical?

I'd never heard of it, didn't know what it meant, and didn't want to reveal my ignorance. But pleased that Rick assumed I knew enough to be interested in this talk, I kept quiet, promising myself to learn the meaning of "radical" first chance I got.

On the drive over, he rested his arm on my shoulder, a friendly gesture, though not close enough for an embrace. I felt uneasy, almost as if an electric current passed between his hand and my shoulder. It was probably only my imagination, I thought.

A few weeks later, I gave up my job at the Five and Ten, and started baby-sitting instead. The pay was about the same, but I liked it much better. Little Lola, my charge, was a sweet and placid two year old. I liked reading to her, and having her point to the pictures and babble the words that described them. Her speech wasn't yet well formed, so I wasn't sure if she was making approximate sounds to match those pictures, or if she really knew the words. Sometimes, we'd play baby records on the phonograph, both of us singing along, "When the red, red Robin goes pop, pop poppin' along..."

I loved hearing her sing in that baby voice of hers. It reminded me of Haniushka. That was the hard part. After tucking Lola into her crib for the night, I'd think about my own baby sister until I could become distracted by reading my book. In this way, the hours passed pleasantly until Lola's parents returned.

Winter had set in. Soon it would be time for Hanukkah.

My thoughts turned to Rick, my peek-a-boo boyfriend.

Ours was such an on again off again relationship, I never knew when he'd show up. He never used the telephone, never let me know his plans. He'd simply pop up, and I never knew when. Perhaps that's what I found so intriguing about him. And although I really preferred Rick, it was Bernard, who became my steady companion. Unlike Rick, he was sweet, attentive, and it was he who became my honest-to-god real boyfriend. Tall, blond, thoughtful, gentle, he was attending his first year at Wayne University.

Whenever I had an evening baby-sitting job, Bernard always kept me company. He introduced me to John Donne, Blake, Shakespeare, and Keats as he read their love poems to me. "Shall I compare thee to a summer's day?"

His words of love woven into music caused me to think I loved him madly. And though his kisses sent no tremors through my body, and I really didn't like the touch of his moist trembling hands on my breasts, I thought I loved him for his words, his sighs, and declarations of love, but most of all I loved him because he loved me.

The first time he brought me home to meet his mom and dad, they seemed to welcome me. Yet something unidentifiable troubled me; maybe it was their questions. They wanted to know where I'd come from, what town, and when I told them, they looked at each other. They told me that they had come from a little village near Warsaw, where they had struggled to keep a roof over their heads, and had to work hard just to wrestle some vegetables out of the ground, and keep a few milk cows in the barn. They sounded bitter and said that they knew about people like my folks. "Your people used to drive a hard bargain with poor country folks like us. The city folks don't care that farmers are poor."

Although neither of them ever met my family, Bernard's parents didn't try to disguise their rude disrespect. Obviously they objected to their son bringing a Jewish girl home for them to meet. It wasn't city folks they objected to, it was the Jews.

How was it possible for these peasants to have sired such a son as Bernard? He was the gentlest, most considerate human being I had ever met. He wanted to marry me, but I couldn't say yes to him. I told him we were too young. Bernard told me he understood how I felt. He pleaded with me to say yes. He would leave his family if only I would agree to marry him.

But I couldn't bear the thought of his leaving his mother and father, "No, you mustn't do such a thing," I told him. How could he even consider doing such an awful thing? It was not right for me to be the cause of breaking up his family. I calmed him down, told him we could be friends, but Bernard didn't like to hear this. All the same he continued to be attentive and caring. I liked him and respected him.

He continued to visit while I baby-sat. We'd listen to records, sometimes we would even dance, while Lola slept. And yet I knew that sooner or later I'd have to stop seeing him. I didn't want to give him false hope. Bernard would do anything I asked, but I knew I had no love to give him. He must have known it too, and yet he hoped I'd change my mind.

One evening, as we sat on the sofa in Naomi's living room, he brushed a wisp of hair from my forehead and whispered, "Our children will have your looks and smarts, and my perseverance. They'll be wonderful."

"I can't have children, and I want none," I screamed, because the remembered vision of little Hania reaching out for me was too fresh in my mind, and too painful. No way would I allow myself to bring a child into this world. I told him so. I used his wanting me to be the mother of his children as an excuse to break off with him once and for all.

I had to admit that I preferred Rick, although he never showed any great love for me. Always so unconcerned and nonchalant, he spoke little about himself, but once told me he'd been married and divorced. He even showed me a picture of his ex-wife. All of it in that cool, "nothing matters" way of his.

Then one evening, quite by chance, I met his ex-wife. Joy happened to walk by our booth at the Quick Bite while Rick and I were having dinner. When Rick stood and introduced me to the woman, I saw she was everything that I was not. Tall, slim, and elegant, she had a pale narrow face softened by short-cropped blond hair. She was beautiful. Rick didn't seem to care. Before he introduced us, judging from the offhand, cool way he greeted her, I had thought she was just an unimportant acquaintance. I knew that his and Joy's marriage had lasted only a little over a year, but I would have thought he would show a stronger reaction at seeing her so unexpectedly. On the contrary, he showed no regrets and no apologies.

For her part, Joy shook hands firmly, gave me a genuine smile, giving every indication that if Rick had meant something to her once, he no longer mattered. Seeing them like that I remembered that Rick had said neither of them had been ready for marriage. They had parted without regrets, nice while it lasted, and that was that. I didn't know about Joy, but it was clear to me that Rick, my peek-a-boo boyfriend, didn't have what it took to make a marriage work.

After that chance encounter, I didn't care to see him again. I

217

didn't need him. In spite of what I had said to Bernard and of my grief over the loss of Haniuska, I wanted family, a home of my own, and Rick sure wasn't going to oblige, and even if he did, he'd make me miserable. Marriage with Rick was not what I'd wish on anyone, least of all me. I wanted to quit school, give up my baby-sitting job, and quit Detroit altogether.

Naomi was stunned at my announcement. "You can't quit school!" she exclaimed, "At least finish high school."

"What for? I've seen what the other girls do after they graduate. They work in the bakery, a hamburger joint, or the Five-&-Ten. I've done that. Don't want to do it anymore."

Naomi shook her head in bewilderment. "Why is a smart girl like you being so stupid?"

"I'm almost grown up. I'm going to New York." I had made up my mind.

Naomi shook her head in despair. "I only want what's best for you. Trust me a little. You've got to finish school."

She wrapped me in her arms, and I knew that she cared for me, and more to please her than myself, I changed my mind. I'd stick it out for another year, although I felt much older than those giggling boy chasers with whom I went to school.

I went to see my half-forgotten friend, Henrietta. Because she was several years older than I, our paths had diverged during this last year, but loneliness urged me to seek her out. I thought that now I was grown up we'd have more to talk about. Recently married, she was expecting a baby. The first time I visited her in her new apartment, I imagined myself in a similar position. She invited me to go shopping for a crib and baby carriage with her. Looking at the store filled with baby things, I tried to imagine what it would be like to really be married with a husband, apartment, and even a baby on the way; just thinking about it scared me beyond thought. I was afraid of becoming a mother, afraid of losing my child in the same way my mother lost me and Haniushka.

Henie was different from me, less inclined to think about the past. Where I was imaginative and dreamy, she was practical and confident. She obviously had no fear of having a baby. She had no fear that history would repeat itself, and her baby would be taken from her. On the contrary, she was busy preparing herself and her house for the coming of that baby; she talked about baby names and which she'd choose if it were a boy or a girl. One day, she even placed my hand on her belly so I could feel it move. It felt so strange to feel the new life stirring in her undulating belly. Henrietta could barely think of anything but the coming of the baby although she made a great effort to act like a proper hostess. She asked about my school work, while she proffered cookies she had baked.

That done she returned to her favorite subject, and revealed drawers full of baby clothes, tiny little shirts and blankets in pale pastels, the color of new grass and fresh meadow. No pink or blue as she didn't know whether to expect a girl or a boy. She even had the baby room all prepared with a tiny little crib and a strange looking contraption that she said was a dressing table for the baby. She showed me the glass jars filled with cotton swabs and cotton balls, and I dutifully examined tubes of cream intended for her baby's bottom. "This one is best for diaper rash," Henrietta said.

I responded with appropriate noises of appreciation, and forced as many smiles as I could manage, although my interest in babies remained nonexistent. For my part, I had no wish to bring another human soul into this world, and couldn't understand why Henrietta was so elated by the prospect. Hadn't she seen enough to warn her off?

Despite my disinterest in school, I dutifully attended each day, paid attention in class, and spent at least two additional hours after school on homework. And while my language skills were making steady progress, I continued to make good use of my Polish/English dictionary to look up every English word I didn't understand.

Evenings after dinner it was Fibber McGee and Molly, and Jack Benny radio time at the Silverstein household. I sat with Naomi and Irving in the living room and watched them laugh. I didn't because, although I knew most of the words, I couldn't get the jokes. Clearly, something was missing in my education, something that prevented me from responding with laughter. All the same I kept on listening, thinking this radio banter was in some way an important part of my American education. Maybe if I'd listen long enough, I would also begin to see the funny side which appeared so obvious to Americans.

Naomi would sometimes cock her head to the side and inquire, "What's wrong?" She didn't know that I wasn't sad, but only failed to understand the joke.

To make her think that I shared in their enjoyment, I started to laugh every time I heard canned laughter on the radio. Naomi continued to give me her quizzical worried looks, as if my laughter wasn't genuine enough.

"Young girls like you should be going out on dates," she'd say at such times.

It was no use explaining to her that I didn't like the boys in school, and had no desire to go out with any of them, not even if one had asked. Besides, that wasn't likely to happen. I was as different to them as they were to me.

Occasionally I still thought about Rick and I thought about Bernard and hoped he'd found a girl who could love him better than I ever could. Despite these thoughts, I had no desire to see either of them.

One day Naomi announced that Irving knew a fellow who wanted to take me out.

"He is a bit older, but he's a good man," she said. I didn't know what to make of this announcement. Naomi said that he had his own car, apparently a thing worthy of note, and he planned to take me to the Sheraton for dinner.

"It's the finest hotel in town," Naomi said, adding that its restaurant had a fine reputation. I was intrigued by the prospect of seeing it, but had major reservations about doing so with a strange guy of Irving's acquaintance, someone Irving knew from work, perhaps a fellow detective. But what would such a man want with me? I had just turned seventeen, and thought myself too young for such a fellow.

To insure that I looked presentable, Naomi made me wear stockings and a garter belt, which brought to mind girls from a house of ill repute. I felt uncomfortable with my skin exposed between the end of the garter belt and the stockings. Thankfully the long flared black skirt came down to my ankles, so it covered up that portion of my bare skin. Naomi lent me a string of pearls and I had to admit the necklace looked good lining my scooped neckline; the white pearls underlined the pale mauve of my silk blouse.

Naomi spread a white towel over my shoulders and started to apply makeup. After the base cream, Naomi dabbed a touch of rouge and rubbed it high over my cheeks; then she added a puff of scented powder for that fresh peach finish. Finally, using a fresh new lipstick brush, she carefully applied some lipstick. I watched with amazement as Naomi skillfully used special brushes to apply eye shadow and mascara around my eyes, urging me to keep them open and not to blink. When it was done, Naomi stood back to admire her artistry.

Gazing at my reflection in the mirror, I couldn't believe the face staring back at me. Surely that was some other girl, not I. That girl in the mirror was as much a stranger to me as the fellow who was coming to take me out to dinner. Rather than a participant, I felt like an observer about to watch two strangers having a date.

"Stop dreaming and put your shoes on." Naomi brought me out of my reverie.

I bent over to put on my first pair of high heels, shiny, black leather pumps. But no sooner had I tried to stand, than I started to teeter back and forth. These shoes would demand some kind of balancing act, and it was going to be embarrassing. I took my first step with trepidation, wobbled and had to brace myself to keep from falling. "I can't wear these!" I shouted.

"You'll learn," Naomi laughed, placing a book on her head, and assuming the pose of a model. "Watch me," she instructed, assuming the pose, shoulders down, stomach sucked in, back straight, she walked with the book on her head held high. "Like so, now put that book on top of your head and try to keep it there," she ordered, handing the book over.

I assumed what I thought was the pose, placed the book on my head, took one step, and felt the book slip off.

"Don't look down, and for heaven's sake, smile."

Grim but determined, I started over, book on my head, one

221

step and I almost fell on my face. The book slipped off my head, fell, and hit the floor with a bang.

"Again," Naomi said.

I tried and failed again, and again, but kept on, not bothering to count the many times that book fell off. Those spiky, high heels began to inflict pain, pinching my toes. I wanted to give the whole thing up, but Naomi wouldn't let me.

"Why do women wear these stupid things?" I shouted in exasperation.

"It makes them feel pretty and accomplished."

"They sure as hell don't make me feel that way," I retorted.

"Learn to balance, and you'll feel better. Now try again, and remember to smile."

I gave her a god-awful grin, but redoubled my efforts. This time I managed a few steps without dropping the book. I was that determined to master those stupid shoes. A few more tries, and I almost had it.

"You'll be fine," Naomi said, glancing at her watch. The blind date would arrive any minute now. Naomi took the book away, and told me to sit down and relax. I'd hardly had a moment to catch my breath, when the doorbell sounded. My heart did a little gallop. Before Naomi went to answer the door, she advised me to slow down and take a deep breath. "It's only a date," she said.

I got more nervous hearing her greet the fellow in the living room. Then she came back to fetch me. My cheeks were on fire, and I had to cool them off. Dabbing a bit of cold water on my face, I was careful not to disturb the mascara. As we moved towards the living room, I held Naomi's arm to steady myself. I walked on wooden legs, with my head held high, and I prayed the pesky high heels wouldn't make me fall.

"Slip your arm through his. It will steady you as you walk," Naomi whispered in my ear. It was time for me to cross the room to greet him. He waited patiently, a short man with a pudgy face who appeared to be almost as scared as I. He was not tall, dark, or handsome. Standing there, hat in hand, he looked more like a petitioner than a date, and I wondered how I was going to get through the evening in those shoes with this man.

Naomi made the introductions; he mumbled something about being so glad... I wasn't listening. We both felt awkward.

"Well, off you go, you two." Naomi almost pushed us out the door.

He steered me down the three steps with his hand on my elbow. I wondered if he could feel how shaky I felt on those spiked heels. But then, I thought he was probably too busy trying not to trip and fall as well. He opened the passenger door, helped me in, and inquired if I were comfortable. I'd never met anyone so polite.

"Nice weather," he offered, and put the radio on.

Good. We wouldn't have to struggle with conversation. The second movement of Mozart's Concerto No. 40 replaced the silence. What a surprise. I hadn't heard Mozart played on the radio in America. The glorious sound filled every corner of the car.

"If you don't like it, I can switch the station," he said.

"It's my favorite type of music," I assured him.

The restaurant exuded an air of romance just like in the movies, soft candlelight, white tablecloth, unobtrusive music in the background. I should have enjoyed it, but I couldn't. I felt like a mannequin in one of the slick fashion magazines.

Albert Kroennenberg, my date for the evening, appeared just as stiff as I felt, but kept forging on. After studying the menu, he ordered a lavish six-course meal. The first course was shrimp cocktail; the cold, pink morsels looked naked and fragile on the bed of ice. They glimmered with the candlelight reflected in the crystal bowl. I watched as Albert attacked his first pink morsel, dipped it in red sauce, and carried it dripping red to his mouth. I watched him masticate, and all but smack his lips. What little appetite I may have had waned.

After cleaning off his plate, Albert looked at my untouched bowl of shrimp swimming now atop the melting ice. "Ah, you don't like shrimp," he said.

But he was not discouraged, and asked me to dance. We commenced to move about the floor, in little box-like, mechanical steps that ignored the rhythm of the foxtrot.

I suffered our awkward passage round the floor in silence, and uttered silent thanks when the musicians stopped playing.

Later, when they began to play again Albert asked if I would care to dance. I told him my feet hurt, as I wasn't used to wearing high heels; thus I was spared from another stodgy romp round the dance floor.

Course after course, hot soup, cold salad, rare roast beef with juices running in rivulets into the baked potato stuffed with butter and sour cream with chives and a bit of parsley. I could hardly manage a bite of the bloody roast beef, but did shove some of the stuffed potato into my mouth. Eating his own food with relish, Albert glanced at my almost full plate and asked, "Why don't you eat something? Is it too rare for you? We can send it back, order something else."

I explained that I was not used to eating this much. The soup and salad were quite filling. He gave me a pitying look, and though he said nothing, I felt he was seeing me as one of those starving skin and bones survivors with sunken eyes, and a stomach shrunk by famine. Kind as he was, I wanted to hit him. Mercifully, the evening came to an end. Later that evening at the front door of the Silverstein household, Albert asked if he could call on me, perhaps sometime next week.

"How nice," I replied, "but no, I'm leaving on Monday, going to Chicago to visit family."

"I didn't know you had family in Chicago."

"Yeah, had a letter from them a couple of weeks ago. They sent a ticket, and asked me to come." I told him and following Naomi's instructions, I thanked him for a lovely time, said good evening, and went into the house.

Chapter 20

My excuse to Albert was not a lie. I had received a surprising letter from my distant cousins in Chicago, and figured it came because Uncle Strawberry must have asked them to invite me. So now I was on a train to Chicago. After a night of little sleep and much nervous anticipation, I woke to the amplified voice of the conductor, "Chicago next stop - fifteen minutes."

I'd spent the night in various uncomfortable positions, alternating lying down with feet folded under to fit the small space on the bench, and when my feet cramped, sitting up feeling groggy. My head hurt and my body ached, but I pulled myself together.

When the train pulled into the station, I stood in front of the window, looking for the dear, wrinkled face of my Uncle among those who waited on the platform. I searched the face of each old, shabbily dressed man in black. There were but few, and only a couple with yarmulkes on their heads. Uncle Strawberry was not among them. Then I noticed a young woman on the platform with a photo in her hand. Her gaze passed over me at first, but the second time she glanced at the photograph, and then up to the train. As our eyes met, a smile of recognition turned up the corners of her mouth. The woman looked elegant in a smart little beige suit, a pillbox hat and soft leather gloves, all earth-color coordinated.

As soon as I stepped off the train, I found myself wrapped in lilac-scented arms. I allowed myself to be hugged by this unfamiliar woman and saw myself through her eyes, a poor refugee relative to whom one must be kind. Perhaps it was my imagination, or the Sunday best suit that Naomi had bought for me

225

to wear on this occasion, a suit she had pulled off a clearance rack at Hudson's. "You'll look so cute in it," she had said.

The look on my elegant cousin's face told me otherwise. Standing together on the crowded platform, the two of us made for quite a contrast. What my American cousin wore wasn't cute and never would be found on a clearance rack. The well-cut lines of her suit and every fiber of its fine material spelled money. I wanted to turn right around and climb back on that train.

All business now, my cousin reached for my small overnight bag, and took me in tow. "I'm Irene, your cousin," she said, shepherding me through the crowd.

As we emerged into the crisp fall air, Irene steered me to the long, sleek, black car parked in the "No Parking" zone. Irene grimaced at the annoying ticket on her front windshield. She snapped it off, crumpled it, and carelessly shoved it into her bag.

"Mom's home waiting for us," Irene said, opening the passenger door. In one motion, she tossed the overnight bag into the rear seat, and as I got into my seat, I felt as insignificant as the bag Irene had tossed in over my shoulder.

After turning the key in the ignition and without bothering to check for other vehicles, Irene pressed her foot to the accelerator, and we plunged into the stop-and-go traffic of the street. I was uncomfortable because she was obviously in a hurry, and perhaps late on my account.

"I had hoped Uncle Strawberry would be here."

"Who?" Puzzled at first, Irene made a quick recovery, and "I suppose you mean Grandfather. No, he's much too old to travel." Fingers drumming on the steering wheel, Irene sought an opening in the traffic so she could squeeze her car forward.

"Is he waiting with your mother?"

"Oh dear, no; he lives in New York, wouldn't have it any other way."

I thought about the frail old man who had made such an effort to welcome me on my first day in New York. Now I began to wonder why he'd chosen to live so far away from his only daughter and her family. Having them close would have surely provided some comfort in his old age.

Irene waved in the general direction of the passing scene.

226

"How do you like it so far?"

A half-remembered line from a poem popped into my mind. "...Hog butcher to the world..." and I wondered what made me think of this particular line. Probably because the poem was about Chicago, I thought, and tried to remember if it were Sandburg or Whitman who had written it. I didn't see any stockyards, only glass and steel buildings that punched holes into the sky. As I craned this way and that, I figured I must look like a country bumpkin to my sophisticated cousin.

"Ever been in such a big city?" Irene inquired, as if on cue.

"New York." I paused. "Where are the stockyards?" I asked.

Irene laughed, glanced at her wristwatch, and pulled up to the curb.

"Let's go," she said, tossing her car keys to the doorman.

We entered a vast atrium with a half-globe glass roof soaring high above. Streaming through the glass ceiling, long shafts of light made shimmering designs across the marble walls. I stopped to admire the effect, and then had to run to catch up with Irene at the elevator. We went up quickly, and I was surprised to see the elevator doors open into the apartment foyer. A small plump woman was waiting for us. When she saw us, her mouth split in a happy grin. She opened her arms in greeting, hugged me, and then stepped back for a look. The first thing she said was, "You must be hungry." A mop of short, gray, curly hair framed her round porcelain smooth face. Was she really seeing me, or was she remembering the starving skeletons she had seen in the newsreels? I thought it must be the latter.

"This is my mother, Glenda," Irene said with an indulgent smile.

Glenda took my hand, and pulled me towards the dining room, as if feeding me at once was the most urgent task she had to perform. I wanted to stop and look at the many oil paintings that lined the walls. But Glenda would have none of it. We entered the huge dining room, large enough to accommodate twelve.

"Sit, sit," Glenda urged, practically pushing me into the chair. The table was spread with a veritable cornucopia: sliced tomatoes, red onions, platters of smoked sturgeon and white fish, shiny pink slices of smoked salmon covered one enormous platter, a bowl of greens, and a medium-size mountain of sweet rolls, bagels, and black bread, the kind I hadn't seen since I was a little girl in Poland. Does she think that I'm famished, I wondered. It's been two years since the end of the war. I have eaten sufficiently since then.

I didn't share my thoughts, but looked instead at the feast of oil paintings that appeared to match the table motif, gilt-framed still lives of apples, pears, bunches of grapes and bananas painted in velvety deep reds, purples, and greens all artfully arranged in sparkling bowls on top of various tables. There were also pictures of vases overflowing with roses, snapdragons, and lilies, all very elegant. But nothing that hung on those walls could begin to compare with the spectacular vista of the lake, which I could see through the floor to ceiling glass walls. I wanted to stand there and drink in the view, but Glenda had taken her place at the head of the table and motioned to Irene and me to sit on either side. Between chewing and sipping, Irene and Glenda talked about people and places I knew nothing about.

Glenda listened with great interest as Irene talked about her daughter, Octavia. Irene passed around recent photographs of the child. Glenda admired each one, before passing it on to me, while I made all the appropriate sounds of appreciation. One photograph showed the little girl building a tall tower using a child's wooden blocks. Lips parted, and eyes riveted in concentration, her small chubby hands reached high to place the last block on top of the tower. The next shot showed her clapping her hands in delight, eyes dancing with laughter at the tall tower standing before her.

Irene was clearly proud of her daughter. "The great architect," she said. "But wait, here, see?" Irene showed another snapshot. This time Octavia was full of glee looking down at a pile of blocks, the wreckage of what she had so painstakingly built. She who builds earns the right to knock it down, I thought remembering Haniushka, who loved to engage in similar antics. But, unlike Haniushka, Octavia was fortunate to be alive in another time, and in another country.

I sat there wondering if I too should show the couple of photographs of Hania I'd brought with me, but decided against it.

"Does she like kindergarten any better now?" Glenda asked.

As Irene plunged into her next topic, my eyes began to glaze over. I had to muster some interest, "Octavia is a beautiful name, so unusual. Does she like music?"

I wanted to make the connection between the girl's name and music, but they looked at me quizzically, and I wanted to disappear. Obviously none of Naomi's helpful hints on how to get on with Americans had done me any good. I fell silent, while the two women returned to their favorite topic: Octavia, daughter and granddaughter.

I listened politely for a while, but talk of this fortunate child reminded me of my little sister. When her life ended, Haniushka was about the same age as Octavia. During the short span of her life, Hania experienced that which little Octavia would mercifully never have to experience…

…Hania knows the circling planes when they clamor in the sky. When she hears the siren's scream she'll urge us to come and hide. Picking up her little blanket, taking up her little doll, she will clutch both to her chest, while she bids us come and hide.

Then she leads us to the basement. Oh, she knows just where to hide from the terror of the bombs, from their shrieking, whistling dives. With her body all a-tremble, she waits for the noise to cease, waits for the all-clear siren, holds her breath and waits to live. Listens to the whistling bombs as they fall on our homes, as they fall to take our lives…

Suddenly aware of silence, I looked up to see Glenda and Irene looking at me expectantly; they apparently had asked a question, and waited for me to answer. I nodded, yes, hoping it was the right response.

Sure enough, Irene followed with, "What was her name?"

"Hania." I wondered if Irene had been reading my mind.

"Yes, Hania, I remember Father told me her name," Glenda agreed.

"How old was she when…?" the unspoken word got stuck in Irene's throat.

"How old is Octavia?"

Irene was clearly uncomfortable with these questions.

229

"Five."

"Same age," I said. Why was I so cruel? Unusually anxious to please most of the time, I didn't care this time, and was not in the least sorry because I had made my cousins uncomfortable.

"I don't suppose you have any pictures of her," Glenda said.

Suddenly I didn't want Glenda to look at Hania's photo. I was afraid she'd only see a little girl with a big bow in her hair, nothing more. It was different showing the photos to Uncle Strawberry. He had met Haniushka. "Her eyes are so very sad," he had remarked, holding the photo up close in his thin, wrinkled and trembling hands, his eyes cloudy with age and tears.

"These were taken shortly after Father was arrested. None of us felt happy then," I had told him.

The old man had taken a white handkerchief from his pocket, dabbed at his eyes, and blown his nose. It was plain to see how much he loved and missed the family: his sisters, their children and grandchildren, all lost. Yet even as he grieved, he had whispered, "Thank God you're alive," and his fragile arms had closed in around me.

I had no pictures of Hania, I told Glenda.

"Do you know that in 1938 when Dad visited your folks, I almost met you."

"But you didn't come," I said.

"I was attending school in Paris at the time. There was some talk of my joining Dad for a few days, but Mom said I didn't need to go."

I laughed, "I couldn't speak German, and you didn't speak Polish."

"Yeah, you're right, but my dad told me all about Helen. She sure sounded like someone I would have liked to meet."

I realized that Glenda and our cousin Helen would have been about the same age at the time. "She was beautiful, kind and generous. Yes, I think you would have liked her a lot." I agreed.

I remembered that dear face. So popular with young men, she used to go out on dates often, and sometimes she'd talk to me about the films and plays she'd seen. She was such a good storyteller. I had listened spellbound while Helen related the tales of castles and kings. At that time my hair was always braided, but

Helen's was long and silky like a shimmering curtain. It reached down to her waist. I came out of my reverie just after Glenda asked another question, this time about my great uncle's visit to Warsaw.

"Seems like a lifetime ago. I was only a couple of years older than Octavia, but I can still recall the way he peeled an apple, spiraled the peel off so that it came down all in one piece onto the plate. It made such a pretty picture," I said.

"I thought only Octavia would notice such minute detail," Irene noted.

"His red nose reminded me of a ripe strawberry. That's why I called him Uncle Strawberry. Still call him by that name; it brings a smile to his face."

Both women laughed, and I joined in, trying to conjugate my exact relationship to Glenda and Irene. We're cousins but are we once removed, twice removed? I didn't know. In any case the vital feeling of bonding, the sense of family ties just wasn't there for them, I sensed, nor for me. Something vital was missing. Must be that what was missing were all those years of knowing each other, years of sharing our lives and experiences in the same place and at the same time.

The bonds that connected Glenda, Irene, and Octavia did not exist for me. The links between these three, mother, daughter, and granddaughter, had never been interrupted. I felt a deep void between myself and my cousins. They loved a little girl I had yet to meet.

They were my cousins, as Helen had been, but the similarity ended there. I loved Helen, cherished my memories of her...

...She was out late last night, but she promised to tell me all about the play this morning. Hamlet, she said. That's the name of the play, a fairy tale about a Danish prince and his father's ghost... I wonder if Helen's up yet... I peek in through the door to my Bubby's kitchen, and yes, she's awake. Pulls back her blanket, and I nestle near. She tells me about a great tale of enchantment, of love and of heroes, of ghosts and of kings.

My grandmother's kitchen becomes Helen's stage, while she

spins the tales of wonder she'd seen, so that I can see the palpable stage, the foreboding ramparts, and the fearful guards...

Chapter 21

Shopping with Glenda was nothing like shopping with Naomi. In the rarified atmosphere of Marshall Fields no one had the poor taste to grab a dress from under the nose of another person. With Glenda to even consider yelling, "I saw it first," was unthinkable. It would be considered rude. Where Glenda led was in no way similar to the bargain basement shopping to which I had become accustomed with Naomi. Glenda took me to a salon furnished in original antiques. She was determined to remake my bargain basement exterior into the stylish young sophisticate she could find acceptable.

An elaborately coifed lady, her silver hair glinting with highlights from the crystal chandeliers, offered refreshments and the comfort of armchairs upholstered in pink velvet.

We settled in, Glenda sipping her coffee black, while I balanced my tall, frosty glass of soda, fearful it would spill on me and that fancy chair I was sitting in. Soon tall, thin to the point of emaciation, models began to parade before us in a private fashion show. I was overwhelmed by the profusion of dresses, blouses, skirts, hats, and gloves in their rainbow of colors. Awed by the display of glamour, I quietly watched as Glenda picked out a soft gray wool dress with a tight bodice and shiny little buttons that ran from the neck down to the waist. It was the precise dress I'd wanted. Glenda sent me off to try it on and when I saw myself reflected in the mirror in the dress whose skirt flared out in a lovely spiral, I looked at Glenda with pleading eyes. Glenda nodded with satisfaction, and then we continued buying more dresses and skirts, sweaters and blouses, an array of lingerie, including stockings, and oh yes, bobby socks too. Before we left, the lovely silver-haired woman who attended our shopping spree promised to have the loot delivered later that afternoon.

Thankful to Glenda for her generosity, I nevertheless felt uneasy. Perhaps it was the atmosphere of the elegant surroundings that troubled me. With Glenda it was a stiff, serious affair, whereas shopping with Naomi was fun.

Once we laughed when a woman tried to snatch up a bargain we wanted. Naomi said, "You really don't want it, dear. Look, see the rust?"

I immediately relinquished the skirt, barely containing my merriment I watched the other woman squinting in an effort to locate the offending rust stain—the rust stain that wasn't there. Later the incident caused us more laughter at home when we both recalled how the woman dropped the dress in disgust, even though she had not found a stain in the weave.

Glenda could not be faulted for lack of generosity, but Glenda was decidedly no fun. When she placed her hand on my shoulder, it seemed to me her gesture was brought on more by pity than by genuine care. I resented the pity, despite wanting to feel gratitude. Perhaps I was unfair to Glenda, but I really didn't want to be patted, as if I were a lap dog.

Glenda snoozed in the car on the way back while I tried to sort it all out. The beautiful new wardrobe, the elegance of Glenda's huge apartment, its splendid view of Lake Michigan, the guest room with its brass bed, it all seemed at once appealing and discomfiting.

Before leaving the apartment that morning, Glenda had shown me the guest room and the bed that looked like a white and pastel pink cloud. I imagined myself nesting between its satiny white sheets, under the soft, candy-colored coverlet. I admired the handsome headboard made of gleaming brass, which provided a startling contrast to the deep red of the walls.

"Hope that bright color doesn't keep you awake," Glenda had remarked.

I recognized something patronizing in Glenda's attitude towards me, and I was annoyed as much at myself as at Glenda because I allowed it to bother me.

Neither Glenda nor Irene asked me any questions about life

in Europe during the war. Probably, they understood that I'd prefer not to talk about it or it could have been the discomfort some people feel at discussing others tragedies. Sometimes, people asked stupid questions, like, "How did you lose your family, honey?"

Not through carelessness, I wanted to say. But usually I didn't bother to answer. Such questions seemed idle curiosity more than genuine concern. So I should have found Glenda's lack of questioning refreshing, and it was. But it also troubled me. It wasn't her lack of curiosity that bothered me; it was the apparent lack of empathy.

Glenda's husband came home just as the delivery guy from Marshall Fields was leaving.

"Here she is," Glenda gushed showing me off. "Wait till she slips into one of those dresses I bought for her today. She is really quite pretty."

"Glad to meet you, Sir," I all but curtsied before the thin, tall, man, who appeared bent as if hardly able to bear his own weight. His skin pallor matched the color of the soft gray suit he wore.

"This is your Uncle. You can call him Jake, if you like."

The way he sighed when he put his briefcase on the hall table, I knew the man was tired. Yet he mustered enough of his energy to take my hands in his warm, smooth ones. He applied just the right amount of pressure to make me feel welcome. "Glad you could come," he said. I liked him at once and felt sorry to see him looking so worn, even as a genuine smile lit up his face, I felt the poor man needed to sit down and take his shoes off but Glenda would not allow it.

"You've got fifteen minutes," she said, urging him to get ready, as we had a seven o'clock reservation for dinner. She reminded him that both Irene and Bob are punctual.

With a wan smile for me, Jake took his bent-over self down the hall. I watched him go, remembering how I'd greet my dad when he came home after work. When I was nine years old, I loved those evenings of his coming home …

…A click at our front door, I run to meet him, jump into his

235

open arms...he lifts me up, gives me a big squeeze...all with one hand. The other holds a big bouquet of flowers...under his arm a pretty box wrapped in white shiny paper with gold ribbon all around. I guess it holds chocolate covered almonds, my favorite, Mom's too.

"Don't you eat these before dinner..." he hands them over, smiles...and says, "They'll spoil your appetite."

"What appetite?" Mom chimes in, joining us in the hallway. "I have to practically force feed her." She ruffles my hair.

Dad hands her the flowers, gives her a kiss, and takes off his hat and coat.

"Rutele, put these in some water." My mom knows that I love to arrange flowers in a vase...help Mom set the table with white tablecloth...white china...white and yellow daisies and blue forget-me-nots.

We're having my favorite, potato and leek soup. I carry bread and butter to the table. Cut from a very large wheel, the bread is dark, the way the farmers bake. It has a slightly sour taste, goes well with the sweet butter...Here comes the potato soup fragrant with cream, onion, and herbs...

At the restaurant, when the attendant opened our car doors, I noticed that Jake left his keys in the ignition. Wasn't he afraid somebody might steal that beautiful shiny car? Then when the attendant drove the car out of sight and into the building, I was even more surprised. "Where is he taking the car?" I asked.

Jake smiled, "He's parking it for us in the garage beneath this building." Seeing the worried expression in my face, he assured me that after dinner, when we were ready to go home, he'd bring it back to us.

By the time we arrived, little Octavia was sitting at the table between her parents. She looked nothing like Hania. Sitting there like a proper young lady, she looked more like a miniature adult, wearing a dark blue dress with a scooped neckline. It was a pretty dress, but I thought that it looked too severe for this small person. A little strand of white pearls at her throat softened her appearance. There was definitely no big ribbon in her hair.

Glenda greeted her granddaughter with a big hug, and introduced me, "Here is your cousin from Poland."

"Where is Poland?" Octavia wanted to know.

"Far, far away, and long ago," I smiled.

"Like in a fairytale?"

"Exactly, like that." Instantly I felt a kinship towards the little girl.

When the waiter arrived with the menus, Glenda took over the management of our dinner. "Bob, you'll want the steak, of course."

"I think no...." Bob started to say, but Glenda interrupted, "bring him the T-bone, well trimmed, mind you..." Bob coughed politely, but said nothing more. Glenda went on to order for each of them. I was happy to let her, as the menu selections were printed in French.

Only little Octavia balked at the halibut in white sauce that her Bubby ordered. She pulled on the waiter's sleeve to catch his attention, "I want the T-bone steak just like Daddy's," she told him.

Glenda fixed her with a look, but little Octavia wouldn't buckle. "That's what I want," she said, gracing her Bubby with a charming grin. Nodding her approval to the waiter, Glenda gave the little girl one of her indulgent smiles.

When our orders arrived, I admired the artistry of food arrangement on the plate before me. A white concoction of whipped potatoes, red salmon, and dark green spinach formed a three-color ribbon that undulated in the middle of the plate. That's when I discovered that at this elegant restaurant, food is arranged by artists and appears suitable for display at any art museum.

Not easily satisfied, Glenda cast a critical eye at each plate, finding fault first with the soup, which she claimed wasn't hot enough, then with the fillet mignon, which by turns was either too well done, too rare, or too tough. She made onerous demands forcing the waiter to rush between kitchen and table, in a vain attempt to meet all of Glenda's instructions.

"I don't know how you can let Octavia struggle with this steak," she complained.

"I like it, Bubby," Octavia said circling her plate with both arms to protect the offending piece of meat.

"What's the matter with Bob?" Glenda worried seeing him move food around the plate. "Just trying to lose weight; I'm not all that hungry." Bob cut a small piece of steak, put it in his mouth, and chewed it slowly.

"Mom, he works out everyday at the gym, just to keep it down," Irene testified.

The dinner progressed silently, though only little Octavia had a reason not to speak. She was too busy enjoying her steak. Wishing someone would come up with something to break the silence, I searched for a phrase that could prime the pump of conversation round the table, but could think of nothing.

The waiter took the main course away. I watched him use a flat implement to clear crumbs off the tablecloth. The orchestra played "Begin the Beguine," but even its lilting sound could not soften or release the palpable tension around our table.

The silence was finally broken when a plate of dessert appeared in front of Glenda. Irene took one look at the mountain of chocolate cheesecake swimming in hot fudge sauce and said, "Looks scrumptious, I want one too."

Before the unfortunate waiter had a chance to go get it, Glenda intervened. "What are you thinking, Irene? Look at your hips." Turning to the waiter, she ordered, "Bring her some nice fresh berries, no cream, and mind you, very light on the sugar." Satisfied, she returned to her own dessert and, her mouth filled with chocolate sauce, gave credit where due. "This is why I come here. They can't cook steak, but the cheesecake is to die for." She all but licked her plate clean.

I had to keep myself in check to avoid a burst of laughter. That wasn't so easy considering I'd had two full glasses of wine with dinner. It was the first time in my life I'd drunk so much wine. I didn't know I'd have to pay for it the next morning.

My head felt like a ripe melon ready to split, and I was convinced that my skull had shrunk over night, either that, or my brains had doubled in size. I promised myself never to drink more than a half a glass of wine at a time. Then I again took my aching head under the shower. I stood there letting the hot water spill over my head, until it provided a little relief, then I shuffled along the hallway in my robe to find Glenda.

She was not there, but I found a note on the kitchen table telling me that Glenda had gone to visit her dressmaker, and would be back after lunch. There followed a list of instructions regarding the all-important business of breakfast and lunch.

I didn't know what to do with myself in that huge apartment. I looked for an interesting book to read, but found only some cooking books and quite a number of fashion, Home and Garden magazines, and an entire set of Encyclopedia Britannica; none of it tempting enough for me to curl up with. I looked out at the lake and remembered I'd never had the time to look at the paintings. It would be like visiting a museum I thought and started by examining a large oil that hung above the living room couch.

It depicted cherubs blowing fountains of water out of their flutes. Looking at their fragile tiny wings, I wondered if it was possible such wings could provide enough lift for the cherubs to fly, and decided it could only happen if the law of gravity had been abolished in Heaven. Then on to the next oil painting: ladies at tea in a garden. The placid scene recalled another such scene, a tapestry that used to hang in our family home. It also depicted a formal garden, but there the similarity ended. The one back home was wrought in fine thread and cloth, while this was oil on canvas. The painting held neither the mystery nor the subtlety of the tapestry I liked as a little girl. The remembered tapestry was more inviting, more real somehow, especially the children. I used to imagine stepping into that garden, as though through a doorway, imagined myself playing with those children round the fountain. I would daydream about the ladies who lived in this lovely garden, and the little children who played there. I would imagine myself among them...

...The sun hangs near the horizon and sends its purple rays to play tag with the children... hand in hand with Hania, we step through the magic door onto the path that leads to the fountain. Its water sprays sparkle and the children run. Hania runs with me to the children, and we play tag, and I can feel the cool drops of the fountain spray...while Madame Butterfly sings her sad song in the next room... on my dad's gramophone. The door is open and I hear her sweet voice...One fine day...he'll come back to me...I

know the words, Dad told me...

But I could not enter this painting. it seemed nothing like that sunny garden of our tapestry. This oil was silent; it could not hold the beauty of the song that Madame Butterfly sings on my daddy's gramophone...her voice was distant now. I wished to hold on to the memory of that song, Hania with me and the children under the fountain spray in the sun...Haniushka, I just missed her so much. I missed the way we were. Our song was silenced... and Nazi marching boots sang out war...

...Four years, and I am nine...we stand on the sidewalk...we're all afraid...yet we all want to look and see...what's coming... monsters? ...Hundreds of boots...each step...a bang. Their jaws are clenched...their jawbones move beneath their skin.

Hania squeezes my hand ...looks up at me...the same question in her eyes as in mine...why?

...Loud shouts...angry voices...I run to the window...look at my Bubby across the yard...she's at her window...looking down...

"Juden, rouse!"

Jawbones move beneath their skin..."Juden, rouse!"

Shouts, growls, barks like dogs..."Juden, rouse!"

Dad and Mom can hear them too.

They sound angry and so loud...I don't understand the ROUSE! "What does it mean?" I ask my dad.

"Out," Daddy says.

"And the word Juden, what does that mean?"

"Jews."

No, I don't understand...

I shook my head to clear what I wanted to forget, but never could. I could not forget the wet slimy venom spewing from their twisted mouths, nor the victims with spittle stain on their faces, having to hear them shout, "JUDEN ROUSE!" They shouted, broke shop windows, shouted "JUDEN ROUSE," a poisonous phrase like hot iron burned into my brain ...branded with Nazi hate.

Even now I could not understand why the mere sight of a Jew could incite men to become monsters bent on inflicting pain and death. What was the cause of this improbable hate and loathing? I could never come up with the answer, but now I began to recognize the full meaning of that phrase. "JUDEN ROUSE!" literally JEWS OUT!

That's what they wanted, shouted us Jews out of our homes, out of our community, out of our lives. "Juden Rouse," was their declaration of murderous intent. Their plan was as incomprehensible as it was simple, to isolate, to imprison, and to exterminate all children, women and men born as Jews, yeah even unto the third generation.

Chapter 22

At breakfast, on the day before my planned departure, Glenda said, "I suppose you may as well stay on with us, attend school here." She sipped her morning coffee, and waited for my response.

Did Glenda really want me to stay? Was she just tossing the suggestion off without having given it much thought? I didn't know, but I figured that if she really wanted me to stay, she would have told me that she'd be glad if I would stay. Despite her words to the contrary, I sensed Glenda couldn't wait for me to go. Her flat remark sounded wrong to me, and though I liked sleeping in the canopied, brass bed, liked waking up to the spectacular view of the lake, enjoyed the elegance of the apartment, I wasn't comfortable there.

I liked Naomi's home more. It wasn't as attractive, but I never had to guess whether or not Naomi wanted me to stay. She made her feelings clear. I had no doubt that she cared for me, and wanted the best for me. We liked each other, but I was often uncomfortable with Glenda. I thanked Glenda for her generous offer, told her how much I appreciated the many gifts and the hundred dollars she had given to me. It was a lovely visit, I told her but Naomi was expecting me back the next day.

Impatient for the train to stop, I began to gather up my three large suitcases. Bob, a student at Wayne State, offered to help. We had made friends while sharing the compartment on the train. With Bob's help, I was ready to get off by the time the train came to a stop. Naomi stood on the platform looking for me. I called out "Naomi, over here," and stepped off the train and into her open arms. I dropped one suitcase on the ground, while Bob set the other two down beside it. Looking at the three cases all lined up, Naomi laughed. "Did the one you left with have twins?"

"Glenda was very generous. This is Bob." I introduced my new friend, expecting him to be on his way. But he just stood around. So Naomi thanked him for helping out. He didn't budge, just stood there with a silly grin on his face. Naomi thanked him again and started to say good-by.

He looked disappointed. "Are you sure? I'd be glad to carry these over to your car."

Naomi said no, and started off, a suitcase in each hand. I hesitated, not wanting to be rude. "Bob attends Wayne University," I said to Naomi.

"So does Bernard," Naomi tossed over her shoulder without breaking her step. Embarrassed, and puzzled by Naomi's rudeness, I picked up my suitcase, whispered, "You've got my number, Bob," then hurried after Naomi.

"I'll call you," Bob called out to me.

I saw Naomi wince. What did she have against him? He was nice, I thought.

Once on the road, she asked about Glenda and the family. I didn't feel like talking, but Naomi would not be put off. She had many questions.

"What's the matter? You tired?"

I blurted out, "Why were you so rude to Bob?"

"Rude? I didn't think so; it was time to be getting on."

"He was very helpful, a pleasant companion on the train, and I could plainly see that he was hurt. What is it exactly you don't like about him?"

Naomi laughed it off, "His blond hair?" After a moment I got the clue. Bernard came from a family of Polish Catholics. He also had blond hair.

"Bob isn't a Jew and neither is Bernard. Is that the trouble?"

"I would think after your experience..."

I interrupted Naomi. "Bernard is not a Nazi, and neither is Bob."

Naomi pulled over and stopped the car. "Are we about to have our first argument, here? You just got home."

What was wrong with me? Why argue with Naomi over a

boy I'd just met on a train? "Sorry, Naomi, I must be tired from the trip." I gave her a hug, and then plunged into a lengthy description of Glenda's family and household, but I omitted the part about Glenda's offer of a permanent home.

All business now, Naomi reminded me to register for my last year of high school.

Attempting to wiggle out, I said, "I quit last year. Remember? They won't let me come back."

As far as Naomi was concerned the subject was not up for discussion. "You need a high school diploma."

I doubted I'd be able to stick it out till the end of the year, but buckled under, registered and went to school. Nobody said I'd have to like it.

School was still a foreign country to me. Frank Sinatra, didn't sent me into a swoon as he did most of the other girls. His type of singing didn't appeal to me. Before the Nazis, my background had been the music from the concert hall and the opera house.

I didn't like the music my schoolmates listened to. The jitterbug they loved to dance seemed jerky and ungraceful to me. Their concerns were different than mine had been for so many years. Most of the girls would rather gaze into a mirror than open a book. I saw them as scatterbrains.

Attending high school in Detroit was for me akin to visiting Mars. The connection between going to school and getting an education didn't work for me there...

...First day of school... I sit in the first row and look at Ms. Bernstein...She picks up the white chalk...touches the blackboard and draws a line. It is straight but it slants up like a ladder someone has put up against the house. I don't know why she's drawing like that, but wait. She draws another line just like the one before, but this one slants down, so now the two lines look like two legs spread apart with a tiny point at the top. Ms. Bernstein moves her chalk a little way down from the top and draws a third line to connect the two she's already drawn.

"What is this," she asks, pointing to her drawing. A triangle with a line in the middle, I think, but before I can say it, another

244

girl beats me to it.

The teacher smiles, "That's what it looks like, but what is it?"

If it's not a triangle, then it must be a picture, but of what?
"A symbol." I'm not sure.

She beams, "It is indeed a symbol. It stands for the first letter of the alphabet. We call this letter an 'A'."

That morning I discover the wonderful game of the alphabet; learn how each letter can be combined with others to make words. I learn that the dark squiggles and lines I see on the pages of the books are letters made into words. Someday, when I learn them all, I will not have to wait till my mom or my dad can read to me. I'll read them myself whenever I want... but then the sirens wake us up and the bombs begin to fall...

Even after the Nazis came, I continued to attend classes, although it was against the law. But then most everything was banned. Verboten, I think that was one of the favorite, most often repeated words in Nazi lexicon. Gradually, every activity, every possession, everything I held dear, family, home, school, books, relatives, all of my life was no longer permitted. The Nazis took away everything I cared about. They sucked me into their Nazi hole-making war machine, where I existed with terror, hunger, and disease. They lost the war. And I survived with nothing but the tattered fabric of my life.

I had drifted until America opened her arms to me, but nothing was familiar here, and nothing reminded me of home.

I had to learn how to live in this strange place. I had to learn a new language, meet and interact with people I had never met before, and attend a school I wasn't prepared for, having missed five years of schooling during the war. I felt lost midst the vast sea of information I didn't have. Placed in the twelfth grade of high school, my mind was set adrift between little understood fragments of knowledge. Chemistry, history, math, all of it may as well have been written in the hieroglyphics of a vanished language.

There was one exception, one subject that got my attention: English. I liked Ms. Plum, our English teacher, and I liked the reading assignments, even if I had to consult my Polish/English

Dictionary every time I came across a word I didn't know. Gradually my collection of English words expanded. I stored them in my brain, as in a treasure house. It became a game, with each new word becoming a winning chip for me. The more words I acquired, the more chips I stored, and so became proficient at the game.

When my stock of English words increased sufficiently, I wrote in English almost every day. With the Polish/English dictionary by my side, I collected yet more words. One day, Ms. Plum wrote big letters on the blackboard, a word I didn't know. The letters spelled, "ESSAY," and while I tried to guess at its meaning Ms. Plum wrote the definition of the word,

"An essay is a type of writing that explores ideas," she explained and invited us to write an essay of our own. She explained that each of us could select a subject for our essay.

"The purpose of this essay is to understand and explain something about your chosen subject. Your thoughts count here. Think of some happy or troubling situation or condition. Think about what makes it so, and then write about it."

Someone asked, "What use is an essay?"

Ms. Plum explained that in order to understand anything we must first be intrigued by it, so we can formulate questions and seek answers. The idea fascinated me. I had many questions but no answers. Perhaps in the process of writing I could come up with at least some of the answers. Here was an opportunity to understand…

…"Bombs," he murmurs. Mom gives him one of her looks, but she can't silence the screams of the bombs… …crash, the bombs shriek down upon us louder…closer… … I jump into the air with each thunderous blast… My eyes tear… dust and smoke fills our throats…hard to breath…we are caught…cannot see across the courtyard…the air grows thick…the sirens scream, bombs whistle/shriek/crash…

I decided to write about the one troubling subject I knew something about. I was so engrossed in my writing I didn't want to stop, not until…

Ms. Plum spoke loudly, "Rutka, Rutka, can't you hear me?"

"What?"

Ms. Plum smiled. "I'd like you to read what you've written."

"Read aloud?" I gasped.

"Please."

I didn't want to. They would laugh at me; they would laugh at my accent. They would not understand. But even as the moisture of cold sweat beaded my forehead, I stood up, feeling compelled to read what I'd written.

"What's the matter?" Ms. Plum asked softly.

Did I look as scared as I felt?

A few quick steps, Ms. Plum placed her hand on my shoulder, and I could smell the sweet aroma of Lilac on her blouse. Ms. Plum took the wrinkled piece of paper from my hand, and scanned the page. I didn't know what to expect. She looked so serious, and even a little sad. She walked back to her desk at the front of the class, and started to read in a somber voice...

...*"Death is inexorable. She takes and gives nothing in return, not even when you beg. She does not hear or care. Just keeps on taking each one that you love, each one you need. She cares for no one. Nothing can stop her. She will not spare a little girl, or a tiny baby boy; will take the children from their mother, take the mother; father too, cares for neither old nor young. They're all the same to her. Death knows no pity."*...

"Inexorable. Who can tell me what that word means?"

Why is Ms. Plum asking this question? I wonder. Have I made a mistake? Did I look up the wrong word? I wanted to disappear, crawl under the desk, anything but look at the vacant expressions on my classmates' faces. The silence seemed to last for hours.

Finally, Ms. Plum looked up from the paper, smiled gently, and asked me to define the word, inexorable.

I had never stuttered before; now I couldn't utter one syllable without repeating it at least once. I opened the dictionary and very slowly, very painfully explained that when I looked in the dictionary for a translation from the Polish, I found the word "inexorable." That is exactly the word I needed. It means that a person cannot be entreated, dissuaded, or begged off.

Whew! That was hard. I sat down, and found Ms. Plum smiling her approval. I could almost feel the warmth of that smile on my cheeks. I felt them grow warm, then red. I was embarrassed.

Chapter 23

The Silverstein family lived in a small rented house in a neighborhood peopled by hard-working folks. Each house looked like the house next door, with the same four or five steps leading up to a small square front porch. There'd be a metal swing sofa at one end, a little table and perhaps a wooden chair on either side of the front door. It was modest like all the other houses on our street. Naomi made it cozy and warm, but I could tell she sometimes wished Irving made more money so they could live in a big house like her married sister Sarah.

Sarah and her husband Yaakov didn't have to rent. They had their own big house in one of the better parts of town. Yaakov, could afford to buy it because he made more money than Irving did on his policeman's salary. Yaakov made more because he owned a flooring business. I was mystified. How could he make so much money from flooring? But there it was, a lovely house with some real nice furniture in it.

I liked Naomi, didn't want to think of her as being envious. But I knew she'd enjoy having a bigger more elegant home than the one she had. After I returned from Chicago and described Glenda's home to Naomi, money, an issue seldom discussed in the household before, now became a more frequent subject of conversations. Naomi would ask me again and again to describe the details of the furniture, sculptures, and paintings in Glenda's home. I grew tired of the subject, and was sorry to see Naomi so interested in mere things.

"Things don't matter," I once told Naomi.

"Everybody likes pretty things. Admit it."

"Yeah, I like them, but it's the people I know and love that really matter to me. I lived in a nice place once, had nice things, and they're gone. One day I'll have other nice things, but Dad and Mom, Hania, they're gone for always. I miss them so very much."

Naomi hugged me. "I care for you, and you know it," she said.

I hugged her right back, glad that she did care for me. But it could never be the same, not the way it was when I was home with my mom, dad, and Haniushka.

People can never be replaced, only things can, I repeated. One thing or another, what did it matter? I entered a kind of vacant time, seemed to be waiting for something else, but didn't know exactly what. I missed Halinka and Marissa, the shared camaraderie, and the teasing and laughter. But they lived in New York now, and I had no friends except for Henrietta. But Henrietta had changed, become an adult with the concerns of a grown-up. With a daughter and a husband to care for, her life was taken up with family matters. Things of greatest interest to Henrietta meant little to me and so I hardly ever saw her anymore.

I knew that Naomi worried about me. She watched me trudge off to school every day then come back to spend the rest of the day with a book. I became lethargic, uninterested in anyone or anything.

"Why don't you go out, have some fun?" Naomi would urge.

"Nowhere to go; nobody to go with, nothing to do and nothing to see," I'd say, wishing Naomi would stop nagging at me. How could I explain my real reasons for becoming a hermit? Naomi would begin to worry in earnest were she to know about the party I went to the last time, and how I had to fight off that obnoxious man who offered me a ride home.

Uneventful days passed in monotony. While my body occupied space in school, my mind was elsewhere. I dreamed of going to New York, seeing my friends again. I was just itching to quit school, and Naomi knew it, but she demanded that I stick it out, get my diploma. Her arguments were hard to dismiss.

"How would you like to live in a rented room, and work a boring job all your life? You must know that's what you'll have to do if you don't finish school," Naomi warned time and time again, and I hung on, one day at a time.

Then one afternoon I found Naomi standing in the living room, reading from an open letter in her hand. Beaming, she glanced up from the letter. "My brother, Ezra is coming to Detroit," she said.

I didn't know she had a brother, had never heard her speak of Ezra. But now I learned that Sarah and Ezra had the same father and mother, but their mother died. Their father remarried and Naomi and Moira had been born to his second wife. That made Naomi half sister to both Sarah and Ezra. Sarah was older than Ezra by several years and after their mother passed away, it was Sarah who took care of her baby brother. Ezra and Sarah would naturally feel closer to one another than to Naomi, a younger sibling and the child of a stepmother. Naomi told me that Sarah wanted to take care of Ezra, who was sick with diabetes. so he was coming to Detroit to live with Sarah and her family.

"Diabetes, what is that?" I asked, never having heard of the disease.

Naomi explained that his body couldn't process sugar, so to control this illness he must get medicine by injection every day. Naomi was very concerned, because as she said, it was most important he get his daily injection of insulin. He risked coma and death if he missed it.

I thought about getting stuck with a needle every day. It would hurt. I wouldn't like it. "Why can't he take it by mouth?" I asked.

"Someday maybe, but right now the only way for him to get this medicine is by injection," Naomi explained.

"Well, why is he coming here? Hasn't he got a wife?" I was curious.

"He lives alone. He's separated from his wife."

The man was all alone and sick; I thought that was sad, and asked, "Has he no children?"

"One son, but he lives upstate, some distance north of the city, where he attends a university."

I was appalled at the thought that Ezra lived alone with no one to give him his daily injection. I told Naomi so. She smiled and said that I was a kind child, but not to worry, "Sarah has volunteered. She'll see to it every day. She's used to it, having taken care of him after their mother died." Ezra was very small at the time. He grew up thinking of Sarah more as a mother, than a sister. Naomi thought Sarah was glad to be able to take care of him again. Besides, both Sarah and her husband Yaakov wanted the opportunity to repay Ezra's kindness. All agreed the best solution for Ezra was to move to Detroit and live with Sarah and her family.

I wondered about Ezra, wanted to know what he had done to earn his family's gratitude. Naomi explained that Ezra's money had made it possible for Sarah and Yaakov to own their home. Naomi and Irving had benefited from no such help. They couldn't afford to buy their own home and had to pay rent every month.

A few days after Ezra arrived in Detroit, we were all invited to visit Sarah and Yaakov's house. I was amused to see Sarah treat Ezra as if he were a prize she'd won at the fair. She fairly glowed with pride at having him there. She told us how awfully she had missed him all the years he was away in New York, and gushed about how happy she was to be reunited with her little brother, all the while holding his hand as if she'd never let it go.

"He should have come here long ago," she said, nodding her head in agreement with her words.

Surely Ezra loved his son and would want to live near him. Although the boy had lived with his mother, Ezra had seen him often as he grew up. Had Sarah forgotten? Here she was speaking as if Ezra had no life except the one they had shared as children.

I looked at Ezra, who through it all just sat there, a small smile playing on his lips. Suddenly he stood up. "I need a walk," he said. "Want to come?" he asked me.

I jumped up eagerly, ran to put on my hat and coat and the two of us went out into the sunny mid-afternoon. It was cold, but we walked quietly together, each lost in our own thoughts. I wondered why he said so little, and why he had left the house so abruptly. Then he began to whistle a melody. I recognized an aria from La Boehme and marveled at how a human being could produce something this beautiful just by breathing it out through his lips. As he walked Ezra continued to whistle seemingly unaware that I was walking beside him. He made his song flow unbound, as if it were a bird imprisoned within the cage of his ribs, and he was letting it go free to sound the deep harmonies of the universe. If I had learned nothing else about Ezra, I would love him only for the song he shared with me that afternoon.

Several weeks later, Ezra's son, Eli, arrived in Detroit to visit his father. Naomi was surprised. She told me that as a university student, he was likely to have little money to spend on the train fare from New York to Detroit.

"He must love his father very much," I suggested.

Naomi nodded her head, yes, but she said that as a student at the university, he was not earning any money.

"How does he pay for food, rent, books, and tuition?" I asked.

Naomi explained about the GI Bill of Rights and how it was designed to pay a stipend to soldiers who had served in the army. I learned that in America, a grateful nation thanked the soldiers for fighting in the war by making it possible for them to obtain higher education degrees. The cost of such an education was high, and normally would have to be paid by the recipient, but the GI Bill of Rights was designed to cover these expenses. Naomi told me that this stipend covered the necessities but no frills.

"Eli had to sacrifice something in order to buy the train ticket," I said.

Naomi agreed. She said that was why she was surprised that he made the trip so soon after his father had come to Detroit. I thought that Eli must love Ezra very much, must be worried about him, and wanted to see for himself that Ezra was being well cared for. I tried to imagine what kind of man this Eli could be. Even before I met him, I figured he was a guy who took his responsibilities very seriously. I was not disappointed when he came to visit us a few days after his arrival.

Not to be outdone by Sarah, Naomi prepared so many delights that there was hardly room for all the food on the table. Eli arrived carrying a small bouquet of flowers, which he handed over to his aunt along with an embarrassed little smile as he stood politely at the open door. Naomi had to take him by the arm and usher him in.

"Let me have a look at you," she said, smiling. "You're so

handsome." She gave him a hug making him blush.

Seymour stood on the side observing the cousin he'd never met. He seemed not to know what to make of this quiet, shy guy. Throughout the visit, Eli spoke only when his opinion or information was called for, and then mostly in monosyllabic words and short sentences. He maintained a quiet, serious demeanor, and despite his 5'10" muscular frame, I sensed something almost soft around his edges.

A curly head of thick black hair framed his round face. His large brown eyes gave an impression of gentleness as he appraised everyone thoughtfully. Eli seldom smiled, unlike the other young men I'd met in Detroit. I wondered why. Though he said nothing about it, it seemed to me that he carried his father's illness about him like a shroud that weighed down any joy in life he may have possessed. Was it only his father's illness, or was it something even worse? I didn't know.

When asked, he told me that he wanted to be an engineer. "Clarkson has a very good engineering department, but I'm hoping to transfer next year to NYU."

"What is this NYU?" I wanted to know.

"New York University," he answered.

"Is it a state school, like Wayne?"

"No, it's a private university, huge with campuses uptown and downtown."

I had never heard of anything big like that, and promised myself to question Seymour about it. This fellow Eli was sure a word pincher, wouldn't part with any words if he could help it. His conversation was stifled, and I was almost glad when his visit was over. Seymour told me later that evening that it takes a lot of money to attend such a big, important university as NYU.

"Does it take more smarts than Wayne U?"

Seymour laughed, shrugged his shoulders and said he didn't know. But in any case, he'd be attending the Yeshiva University, if he could get a scholarship. His mom and dad sure didn't have enough money to send him to college.

"You want to become a Rabbi?" I did not approve.

"So what would be so bad?"

"Then I hope you can." I shrugged figuring it was his life we were talking about.

"Takes money, though," Seymour sighed. His father's salary stretched only far enough to cover their ongoing expenses. I didn't know how Seymour hoped to make his dream come true, and I thought it very sad that he could be prevented from becoming a rabbi for lack of money. Something was very wrong about it.

Before leaving for New York, Eli came to see us again, perhaps to say good-bye. Naomi wanted him to see something of Detroit before he left, so she gave Seymour some spending money and told him to take Eli and me out on the town. "See a movie; go to an ice cream parlor. Have fun," she ordered.

Children of Paradise, was playing in town, and Eli wanted to see it, said it was a classic film that was seldom shown, and he had wanted to see it for some time. I've never heard so many words out of Eli's mouth, and Seymour said, "Okay, tonight is the night."

As it turned out, by the time we arrived at the box office, the show had already started, and all the tickets for the next show had been sold. I had heard about another film playing nearby, but neither Seymour nor Eli wanted to see it, so the three of us sauntered down the street looking in shop windows, and trying to make conversation. When we came upon an ice cream parlor, Seymour suggested we go in.

Unlike the little corner shop where Naomi liked to buy our ice cream, this shop was huge and ornate with its ersatz turn of the century gaslight lamps, and marble floors and tabletops. Behind the long marble counter sat buckets filled with rich brown chocolate, creamy yellow vanilla, all kinds of fruited varieties in pink, green, orange, and even purple ice cream.

"Let's have a sink. We can share it," Seymour suggested.

"A sink?" neither Eli nor I knew what to expect.

Seymour pointed to a white bowl, the size of a bathroom sink.

I was amazed, "How could we eat this much?"

Eli saved us. He pointed to another bowl, half the size of the first one, "Let's order the smaller version."

When the waitress delivered our bowl to the table, I gasped to see so many colored scoops of ice cream. Spoons poised above it, we admired the array of the sweet moist stuff, and then we dived with our spoons straight into the luscious bowl. I went for the dark chocolate. Seymour started with the pale orange, and Eli chose the vanilla. We savored the cold, smooth, sweet orgy of taste, and Eli confessed to having not just one, but thirty-two sweet teeth. I was really happy to see him forget his troubles and enjoy life. The way he brightened up and even laughed, it was like I was seeing him for the first time. I realized that without that constant frown, he looked handsome. That evening turned out to be a magic moment of indulgence, and as we talked and laughed and tasted the fruity delights of ice cream, we became as children, careless and free; we forgot that we had wanted to see *Children of Paradise.*

I saw him one more time before he left for New York. Puzzled about his father and why he came to live with Sarah after all these years, I broached the subject. At first, he responded with silence. He appeared lost in thought, and I noticed that he seemed to carry a heavy burden, something that silenced him; something that allowed no ease. Finally he spoke, letting me understand his sorrow.

Eli had been twenty-years-old, when he learned that Ezra was sick. He told me that Ezra needed a daily injection of insulin to stay alive. But he could not administer it by himself. Eli, a poor student living on GI Bill of Rights, a program that allowed him a small pension while he attended school, had no money to pay for a nurse. When Sarah invited Ezra to come live with her, so she could take care of him, Eli didn't really know her, but wanted to believe her when she made a solemn promise to faithfully inject Ezra with the medicine every day.

Eli would have preferred to take care of his father, but he also wanted to continue at Clarkson College. Located in upstate New York, the school was too far for Eli to commute daily. Besides, he didn't have a car, and could only visit his father by catching a ride with another student. It took over 12 hours to reach Manhattan where his father lived at the time.

Fearful of interrupting his studies, or risk losing his opportunity for a college education, Eli was torn between his need to care for his father and his need to continue at Clarkson. In the end, Eli decided to trust Sarah, his aunt, to trust she would make sure that Ezra received his daily injection. And so he reluctantly returned to school, leaving Ezra in Sarah's care.

The next time I met Eli, Ezra had died and the whole family was sitting Shiva for him. Eli sat on a low stool, head buried in his hands, his thoughts locked in his mind. His grief touched me. I wished there was something I could do or say to comfort him, but no words came. He hardly spoke at all, and only uttered monosyllables when forced to respond to some comment or question.

I understood his silence. He mourned his loss, as I mourned mine. We mourned in silence because no words could replace those who were gone.

His body occupied the stool, but Eli was hardly there. The light conversation around the room, the reminiscence of the way Ezra was, and what he did, just seemed to pass him by. And as I listened, I learned that in his youth, Ezra rode the trains in search of work. I heard them tell about the various people Ezra encountered on the trains. Before leaving, I placed my hand on Eli's shoulder and gave it a little squeeze. He straightened up just long enough to look into my eyes.

"Thank you for coming," he said; then, he returned to the position he'd held before: elbows on knees, face in his hands. One day after he sat Shiva in that house, he went back to New York.

Chapter 24

As the train pulled into Pennsylvania Station, heavy clouds darkened the sky and made the pavement slick with rain. I knew there'd be no one to meet me, pulled on my raincoat, tied a silk scarf around my head, picked up my suitcase, and stepped down to the station platform, where I had to dodge baggage carts, porters, and everyone else crowding towards the exit. Halinka had started a new job so she couldn't take time away from work. Now I stood in the rain, trying to understand her instructions for getting to Brooklyn.

I emerged at the 34th street exit, and then paused, blinking in the glare of the morning sun. I took a deep breath. Cars and trucks belched out their black oily smoke turning the air hazy with pollution. My nose wrinkled involuntarily at the smell, but then I caught another more pleasant whiff of freshly baked pretzels from the cart of a street vendor, who stood not five feet away. Having had no breakfast, I was hungry, sniffed the delicious aroma of hot pretzels, and made my trade with the street vendor, a nickel for a pretzel. Chewing the warm pretzel, I walked down the street looking for the subway entrance. There it was, a half block further on. I knew it by the white painted arrow pointing to a flight of stairs leading down. The legend above spelled, "Downtown." That's where Halinka had told me to go. I descended the steps to the murky interior, and immediately became enveloped in its dank warm air. The train roared into the station, and when it stopped, its doors slid open with a deafening screech. I was about to experience my first subway ride.

The crowd moved as one, and I tried not to stumble as I was herded in along with many other passengers. It all happened so fast. Some of the people were left on the platform, before they had a chance to board, as if sliced off by the closing doors that screeched, cutting them off rudely. The train started to move. It picked up speed, and its grinding noise grew louder as it careened through that dark tunnel with a roar, its brakes screeching at every turn. Sparks flew in the dark, and I feared the train was speeding out of control and was about to crash. I had visions of black smoke and flames engulfing us all. Had I survived the war only to be killed in a subway accident? White-knuckled, I held on to the bench, waiting for the sound of the final crash.

As the train slowed and came to a stop, I couldn't wait to escape and stood ready to disembark as soon as the doors would begin to open. Then I looked about me, and noticed the other passengers behaving as if there was nothing to fear. Indeed, they appeared to be bored and some continued to sit slumped over with their eyes closed. Could they really sleep in this racket? I marveled. But there was no question about it. It became clear to me that only I was panicked. The others behaved as if this mad deafening subway ride was as normal as a walk in the park. That's when I realized that I had behaved like a country bumpkin. In her letter, Halinka indicated it would take a good hour before the train reached Brooklyn, so I sat down calmly, and unfolded Halinka's letter.

"It will be like old times. Marissa lives in Manhattan, so I don't get to see her as much as I'd like, but now that you're coming, the three of us will get together." Her letter was filled with joyful expectations. She looked forward to sharing her room with me, said I was welcome to stay as long as I liked, assuring me that both her aunt and uncle looked forward to meeting and welcoming me to their home.

While grateful, I did not want to impose any longer than absolutely necessary. If it were possible, I planned to look for a room to rent the very next day. Fortunately, I still had the hundred dollars my Chicago cousin had given me at parting. It would keep me till I found a job, which I had plans to start searching for right after finding a room of my own. I hoped Halinka's aunt would be helpful in that respect. She'd lived in the neighborhood for many years and so knew many neighbors. Possibly she could suggest someone with a small room to rent. That's all I'd need to start.

While the train barreled on through the dark tunnel, I thought about Naomi and how very kind and caring she had always been, and how she tried to dissuade me from quitting high school before I obtained my diploma, but I hadn't listened to reason, quit school and looked for work. But without education or skill, all I could find were mundane sales clerking jobs. I wouldn't settle for that.

"You refuse to consider sales girl positions, yet without a high school diploma, what else can you do?" Naomi was hurt and frustrated because I refused to work the jobs I could get, and refused to go back to school.

Naomi begged me to go back, told me I should stick it out. It's only a couple of months more, but I would not budge. "Why are you determined to hurt yourself this way?" Naomi asked.

I had no answer, and stopped trying to justify my actions. Although sorry to cause Naomi unhappiness, I did just that when I told her my plans to leave Detroit without finishing the last school semester.

I had no reason to expect any better opportunity in New York, but reason didn't enter into my calculations. I knew that Naomi's warnings were based on reality, and yet I made my decision based not on reason but on hope. I wanted an interesting job, though I knew that without a high school diploma this would prove difficult. Yet I went to New York looking for a job that I could accept. I could not do otherwise, couldn't go on friendless and alone, despite Naomi's sensible advice and her goodness.

It only took a couple of days before I found a room just blocks from Halinka. The room was small, had a window facing an alley, and offered a view of wash hanging on lines strung between buildings. Not much, but it was all I could afford. I struck a bargain with a woman who lived alone, and who sweetened the deal by telling me the room came with kitchen privileges. That would help me to save money as well. And if I didn't know how to cook, I wasn't worried. How hard could it be? All I'd need was to prepare some quick meals. Cereal, that's what I bought. It became a staple, cold cereal and milk in the morning, and hot cereal and milk for supper. Then I started looking for a job. Halinka offered to inquire if they could let me work at Hudson's where she was employed as a sales girl. I said, no.

Halinka laughed. "What are you going to do? Offer your body to the highest bidder?"

"Not funny. I'll find something," I said, but I worried because the hundred dollars I had wouldn't last long.

I had learned one skill in Detroit. I knew how to type. I found an ad in the paper that called for a clerk-typist. I had to fudge just a little, and wrote, "Benjamin James High School, Detroit, 1948," on the application forms. Well, it was true I did go to that high school in 1948, although I omitted one little fact. I didn't graduate. My prospective employers could draw their own conclusions. I got the job, and was told to report the following Monday morning.

When I reported to my place of employment, New York City's Forty Second Street Library, it took only one look for me to fall in love with the place. I admired the beauty of the two lions guarding the library entrance atop the broad flight of steps. I loved the marble floors, the vaulted ceilings, the circular reference room with its parquet floors, its hushed atmosphere of learning, the small desks, each with its own softly lit brass lamp, an inkwell, and a pen, the card file drawers that lined the walls from floor up to the ceiling all around that vast room. I loved what each card represented, loved every one of those thousands, millions, gazillion cards that held the entire world's knowledge. Such a repository of beauty and learning had to be the very centerpiece of this city's intellectual life, I thought. For a bookworm such as I was, it was home, a place to work and to contribute. No place could be more satisfying.

I was given a desk, a typewriter, and a stack of catalogues containing lists of the latest publications. These were publisher's lists, and it was my job to type purchase orders for each item circled in red. I accepted the pages, more than I could count, with pleasure. Each page contained hundreds of items circled in red, and each item represented a book. Well, what could be better? I didn't mind the work, the long hours of typing out purchase orders. I was a fast typist. I was able to perform the monotonous work automatically, and that left my mind free to imagine how one day I'd become a writer of books whose titles would appear on a publisher's list for other typists to transcribe into purchase orders. Unlike the jobs I had held for short periods in Detroit, I actually liked this work place, liked my co-workers, and for the first time since coming to America, I felt a sense of belonging. Getting this job augured well for me, I thought.

One evening I received a phone call. The man's voice sounded almost apologetic, "Rutka?"

"Who is this?"

"Eli..."

"Eli!" I shouted. "How did you know where to find me?"

"Naomi wrote, gave me your address." His voice was soft, hesitant.

"How are you?" I said brightly, remembering his shyness.

He asked me for a date, "Next weekend, if you're free," he said.

Did he mean free, as in otherwise not occupied? Free, as in not connected to someone? Free as in not restrained by bonds of love, or loyalty, or friendship? Well, I agreed.

Almost a year had passed since I had last seen him, and now he had called me for a date. I told Halinka, "He is coming Sunday"

Halinka was amazed. "No one comes this far just for a date, from Bronx to Brooklyn, are you sure?"

I nodded, "Eli is a gentleman."

"Not too many of those around," she said.

He showed up in a suit and a tie, holding a single red rose. "For you," he said. I brought it up to my face, felt its velvety smoothness, .and. didn't know what to say, forgot that a simple thank you would be fine.

After a moment or two, he smiled, suggested water would keep the rose fresh and would remind me of him after we said goodbye. Modest and thoughtful, unlike anyone else, I liked that about him.

We took a subway to Times Square. I was excited, because I'd heard of this place, but had never seen it. Nothing could prepare me for the real thing, the people, the shops with goods spilling out onto the sidewalks, neon lights blinking advertisements in red, yellow and pink, with colors bouncing off glittering shop windows and the polished cars that sped along the street. Crossroads of the World, there it was, The New York Times Building rising up above us. On top a banner made of lights spelled out the news headlines of the day.

Eli took my elbow and steered me towards a restaurant a couple of blocks away. Tofennetti stood on the corner, its window displaying what looked like a small mountain of potatoes. These potatoes were bigger than any I've ever seen.

"I thought you would like them," Eli said.

I remembered how he had asked me once about my favorite dish. Potato I told him. I liked them baked with lots of butter. He remembered, and I was pleased.

He opened the door for me and we went in. Nice place, I thought, observing the white tablecloths covering each table. Ordering two baked potatoes, he instructed the waiter to bring lots of butter. They were enormous.

"We could have shared one of these," I exclaimed, seeing the size of the potato on my plate. By now three years had passed since the end of war, but I still ate small amounts, and couldn't bear to see food left on the plate. The memory of hunger was too fresh. I didn't want to waste any food.

Thinking that I was worried about expenses, Eli said, "I can afford two of these. They are the biggest bargain in town."

This wasn't something I expected him to say. Talk about money and bargains didn't belong on a first date. Like water and oil, I believed romance and money should never mix. That's no surprise, since what I knew about romance came mostly from the movies, where the crass subject of money never came up in a conversation between a boy and girl out on a date. I was quite certain that talk of bargains was the least fitting subject for a conversation between two romantically inclined people.

I decided to overlook his unfortunate remark, because for the most part he was sweet and considerate. All he needed was a bit of polish. So I started to plan a major make over. First thing, I presented him with a pipe, although he didn't smoke. He liked sports, told me he lifted weights and liked to hike in the woods. Yeah, but I figured some tweeds and a pipe would transform him into one of those cool refined Englishman, stiff upper lip and all. I thought such men were particularly romantic.

I gave him the pipe along with a pouch of tobacco and he smiled gently, thanked me, though not too profusely. He put that pipe away and I never saw it again.

Walks, talks, movies and plays, Eli opened a new world of New York to me. Central Park, Sheep's Meadow, Museum of New York, Museum of Modern Art, Museum of Natural History, and one night, the Davenport Theatre and "Bells."

I had seen opera on stage, but this was my first experience of seeing a play. The theatre was small, seating no more than fifty people. No one paid for tickets as none were offered for sale. During the intermission a hat was passed around for donations. Eli told me this was the longest-running free theatre in the country. It was named after an actor whose name was Davenport. The man was quite old now, but he still performed most nights, acting in a repertory of plays.

The stage was small and dark. Its only illumination was a dim light provided by a small table lamp. The dim stage lighting and the sound of bells created a sense of loss and despair.

"Bells, I hear the bells." These words were repeated throughout the play, and just in case there was one person in the audience who failed to apprehend their significance, the bells chimed throughout the performance. It was a one-man play. Davenport, his hair glowing white, his voice shaking with emotion, fear, or weakness perhaps, kept lamenting "the bells," over and again. I didn't understand the significance of the bells. What was it that haunted that old man so? The actor in his shaky old voice seemed fixated on those "bells, bells," and he kept repeating that same phrase, "I hear the bells…"

Perhaps these bells had augured some awful event? Was it perhaps a ghost story? If so, I couldn't tell what occasioned such a mournful cry. The action and dialogue provided no details of the tragedy, if that is what it was. Mindful that English was not my native tongue, I figured that was the reason I failed to understand it, although I did perceive that some unknown tragically mysterious event powered the performance.

I listened to the sound of the bells ringing on stage, and heard an echo of air raid sirens shrieking in the Warsaw night.

That ghostly sound from the past, that scream of sirens had been both a warning and an announcement of the pending tragedy. Those sirens and the scream of bombs as they fell through the air augured the destruction of our family and our home. They foreshadowed the end of my childhood.

I alone had survived the Nazis. They took all that was dear, tore my life to shreds and left me, with holes where home and family had once been. Haniushka should have grown into a pretty girl who dated boys. She should have married, had a family, but she didn't get to live her life. The Nazis took it from her. Now there was an empty space where Hania's life should have been, an empty space for Mother and for Father too, empty holes in the fabric of my life, for each one I had loved and lost.

Eli was drawn to the sadness I tried to repress, because he'd lost his father and mourned his passing. I, as if by a magnet drawn, felt his unspoken need and answered with my own. When I looked at him, I saw the thoughtfulness and reticence of a shy and hurt young man. When he looked at me, he saw a holocaust survivor. And so we paired our emptiness, our need for someone to love and come home to.

This long walk of mine, this journey made of images, filaments of memories, fragments of a life, and fragile, fleeting ghosts, this long, long walk with all the station stops along the track has brought me home again. Not to my childhood home for that was gone, but to another place, a land I learned to call my own, where our two souls met, Eli's and mine.

About the Author

Ruth Treeson was born in Warsaw, Poland between the two world wars. Nine years old when World War II started, she survived the war and the concentration camps to immigrate to United States in 1947. She taught English at various colleges in New Jersey throughout the 1980's and the early 1990's. She has written both novels and poetry throughout her life. Her poems have been published in various magazines and literary journals. She is currently at work on her fourth novel, An Apartment in the Bronx.

15818261R00156

Made in the USA
San Bernardino, CA
08 October 2014